Sunshine Every Morning
Forever Spring
Hazards of the Heart

From bestselling authors

Dorothy Glenn
Joan Hohl
Dixie Browning

Three men become fathers again

As some very special women
teach them to love…
forever!

ABOUT THE AUTHORS

DOROTHY GLENN

lives in Clear Lake, Iowa. She is a well-known writer of over thirty-four contemporary and historical romances. She's also written as Dorothy Phillips and Johanna Phillips.

JOAN HOHL

was born, raised and still lives in southeastern Pennsylvania. Writing on a personal computer in her third-floor office in the home she has lived in for nearly thirty years, Ms. Hohl has produced some forty-plus novels under both her own name and the pseudonym Amii Lorin. Winner of numerous awards, she is also building a name in mainstream historical romance.

DIXIE BROWNING

has written over sixty books for Silhouette since 1980. She is a charter member of the Romance Writers of America and an award-winning author who has toured extensively for Silhouette Books. She also writes historical romances with her sister under the name Bronwyn Williams.

DOROTHY GLENN
JOAN HOHL
DIXIE BROWNING

A Daddy Again

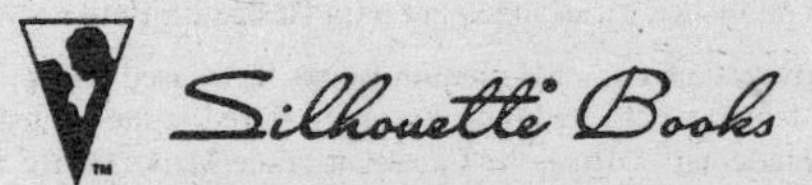

Published by Silhouette Books
America's Publisher of Contemporary Romance

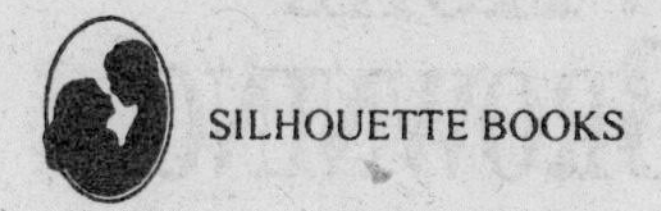

by Request

A DADDY AGAIN

ISBN 0-373-20145-1

This edition published by arrangement with Harlequin Books S.A.

Printed in U.S.A.

CONTENTS

Dear Reader,

I am delighted that Silhouette is reissuing my story *Sunshine Every Morning.* I have had numerous requests for the book, a June 1985 release. The story of Jim Turnbull, the dark mountain of a man with a deep and abiding love for his grandson, parallels the life story of a friend who found himself in a similar situation as he approached forty. My friend did not find the love Jim found with Gaye; however, he was able to maintain a close relationship with his grandson. It gives me a great deal of pleasure to arrange for the characters that I have lived with for several months to find love and happiness.

Do try Gaye's sugar cookie recipe. I've had many letters from readers who tell me it is their family's favorite cookie. And...for one reader the cookies won her a blue ribbon at the state fair.

SUNSHINE EVERY MORNING

Dorothy Glenn

This book is dedicated with love
and gratitude to a special friend,

GLENN HOSTETTER

Chapter One

"You can't mean that!"

"I do mean it, Gaye," Alberta said firmly. "I'm asking you to help me save a life."

"You're callous and heartless to even suggest such a thing! It's...primitive!"

"I'm sorry you feel that way about it. The baby desperately needs your milk, or I wouldn't ask this of you."

"Would you have asked if...?" Gaye was unable to get the rest of the sentence out past the lump in her throat.

"If your baby had lived? Yes. And you may have felt differently, too," Alberta said matter-of-factly, her hands buried in the pockets of her white coat, her fists clenched helplessly. "There was absolutely nothing we could do to save your baby, Gaye. Some infants born with an open spine can be saved. It wasn't possible with yours."

Her voice softened as she looked into her sister's pain-filled eyes.

"I know, Alberta. You told me that, but it's such a kick in the teeth." Slender fingers worked at the edge of the sheet covering her. "It's so unfair—I took good care of myself. I did everything I was supposed to do."

"It wasn't your fault," Alberta said soothingly. "These things happen sometimes, and there are no reasonable explanations."

"I thought something wonderful was going to happen to make up for the miserable time I spent with Dennis." Gaye pushed the heavy brown hair back from her face and looked up at her sister with brown eyes full of misery. "You're strong, Alberta. You've always known that you wanted to be a doctor, and you set about to make it happen. All I ever wanted out of life was a loving husband and children. My husband turned out to be a louse who married me for my inheritance, and my baby couldn't live outside my body."

"It's taken me years to get my life in order after Marshall died. Give yourself time, honey. I'm ten years older than you, and I've learned that healing takes time." Alberta looked affectionately at her younger sister, who looked nearer age eighteen than twenty-eight.

There was little resemblance between the two women. Alberta was tall and broad shouldered, with a sturdy body and large hands and feet. Her square face was framed with dark hair cut bluntly and styled so that it required little care. Gaye, on the other hand, was the epitome of a feminine woman.

"Please think about it, Gaye."

Gaye moved the rich dark brown hair from her neck with a nervous gesture and gazed up at her sister with soft brown eyes. Even now, with their curly gold-tipped lashes tear-glazed, they were beautiful.

"Why can't the mother nurse it?" The skin on her face was matte white and stretched over a perfect oval frame. Her mouth was full, with a natural tilt to its corners. There was nothing flamboyant about Gaye Meiners. She was simply quietly beautiful.

"The mother is a child herself, just a teenager. Her own mother came and took her away less than twelve hours after the child was born."

"They don't want it?"

"They don't want anything to do with it. But it hasn't been abandoned. Its grandfather is very interested in its welfare. It's a long story, and I'd rather not go into it now. I'm not interested in the mother, father, or the grandparents. The baby is my concern. I've got to find a formula that agrees with the child or it'll die."

"Why don't you fly it to the Mayo Clinic?" Gaye blew her nose on a tissue and tossed it in the wastebasket.

"That's what I'll have to do if I can't find a supply of mother's milk that agrees with him. We have a small supply on hand, but there's a desperately ill baby who needs it. This hospital isn't large compared to some, little sister, but we do our best for our patients."

"I know that. I didn't even consider going anywhere else when my baby was due. Oh, Alberta! How long will it take before this heavy lump leaves my heart?"

"It will never leave completely, honey. A part of you is gone forever. It's something that'll stay with you for the rest of your life, and you have to learn to live with it. What I'm asking you to do now is help me save this baby. It's a tiny, helpless little human being that deserves a chance to live."

"Do I have the milk?"

"Yes, but it remains to be seen if it's the right milk for the child. If it isn't, I'll have to risk transporting the baby elsewhere."

"Is it the baby I've heard crying so much?"

"No. This little fellow is too weak to cry very loud. We're feeding him intravenously now." Alberta looked at Gaye. "Shall I bring the baby?" she asked hopefully.

Gaye nodded her head only slightly, and her sister quickly left the room.

What am I doing? Gaye thought wildly. I was going to breast-feed *my* baby. Oh, Mary Ann! I'd have loved you with all my heart and soul! I'd have built my life around you. Tears streamed from her eyes and ran into the hair at her temples. It seemed the well of tears would never run dry. They had run almost constantly during the last twenty-four hours, since Alberta came with the news her child had died. She wiped them on the edge of the sheet covering her and turned on her side so she could watch the doorway.

The small, plump nurse who'd been assigned to her came into the room. "Doctor says I'm to get you ready to nurse. You'll have to wear a mask, too. This little'n has had a bad time ever since he saw the light of day."

"The baby's a boy?" Gaye asked while the nurse fussed over her with disinfectant.

"He's the cutest little black-haired fellow you ever saw. I don't know how that girl could have gone off and left him. I'll swear to goodness. What's the world coming to?"

"Alberta said she's only a child herself."

"Humph!" The old-fashioned snort sounded strange coming from the young nurse. "Child, my foot! She's old enough to know what made the baby in the first place. She should have been forced to take care of her child—at least feed it until the doctor could figure out a formula that'll stay put on his stomach. Between you and me, the mother has less sense than the girl!"

"My milk may not be right for it." It was a strain for Gaye to even talk about it.

"The doctor thinks it's worth a try."

The nurse was bending over her, so Gaye failed to see Alberta come into the room with the tiny bundle in her arms until she was beside the bed. The nurse quickly slipped a gauze mask over Gaye's mouth and nose and stepped back.

"What do I do?" The words came hesitantly. Her heart was beating like a trip-hammer.

"I'll show you." Alberta's voice was muffled behind the mask that covered her mouth. She placed the baby in the crook of Gaye's arm. Gaye tried not to look at it. Instead, she kept her eyes on her sister's face. The small bundle felt warm and cozy against her side. This is the way I'd have held Mary Ann, she thought, and her eyes misted.

"We'll put a bit of milk in his mouth so he can get a taste of it." Alberta's fingers worked at Gaye's breast, and the milk began to flow. "C'mon, little fellow," she urged and shook the small head to awaken him. "C'mon and give it a try."

Gaye could feel the small mouth on her nipple, but there was no movement. He seemed so lifeless. She looked down. His little face was pinched, and small veins throbbed just beneath the delicate skin on his temples. He was so thin! Gaye's arm tightened around the small bundle of life, and it suddenly became the most important thing in the world to her that this tiny mite get sustenance from her breast.

"Let me," she whispered. Instinctively her fingers slid over her breast, and she moved the nipple against the still lips. She rubbed it back and forth desperately until the baby stirred and a frown wrinkled its little face. A tiny tongue came out and licked the drop of milk from its lips. Then its mouth surrounded the nipple, and after several seconds, Gaye felt the sharp tingling pain that lasted for only a short while. "That's the way to do it, little man," she breathed. "Keep going. You're doing fine." She raised shining eyes to her sister. "He's sucking!"

"Thank God! I was afraid he was too weak."

Gaye held the infant close. For the first time since Alberta had come with the news that her own baby had died, she felt an instant of peace. Her sister and the nurse stood smiling down on her as if she had created a minor miracle.

"How old is he?" Gaye watched the baby's face grow pink from the effort to draw the milk.

"Five days. He's lost almost a pound of weight. He didn't have a lot to start with."

"Dr. Wright!" A masculine voice, heavy with concern, resounded down the hall.

"Oh, for heaven's sake!" Alberta turned from the bed. "It's Jim." Heavy footsteps came rapidly down the corridor. "He's like a bull in a china cabinet," she said irritably and moved toward the doorway. It was filled by the body of a big man before she could reach it.

"The crib's empty! Where's the boy?" The voice, loud and deep, filled the room.

"Don't shout, Jim! The boy's being fed." Alberta put her hand on the man's chest and backed him out of the doorway and into the hall. "I had an idea. Let's go have coffee and I'll tell you about it."

In the few seconds the man stood in the doorway, Gaye's eyes took in everything about him, and he frightened her as no other man had ever done. Not only was he big, but his hair was jet black, thick and wild. His brows were as dark as his hair and were drawn together over a large, bony nose. He had high cheekbones, and his flat cheeks were creased in deep grooves on each side of his wide, full-lipped mouth. It was a rough-hewn face with a jaw set at an almost brutal angle. His large, slanting eyes gleamed darkly from between a brush of thick lashes. They darted around the room, passed over her and away. Thank goodness! she thought.

The man had to be a lumberjack, a stevedore, or a steelworker. His jeans were tucked into the tops of calf-high boots, and a faded flannel shirt was tucked into the low waistband of his jeans, the sleeves rolled up to the elbows. Dark hair covered muscular forearms. Gaye could still see him in her mind's eye as her sister's voice retreated down the hallway.

"Who was that?" Gaye spoke softly through the gauze mask, as if she was afraid the man would hear her.

"Jim Trumbull." The nurse giggled. "The name fits the man, doesn't it?" She pulled a chair up to the bed and sat down. "He's a real fistful of man! But nice." She bent over and looked into the baby's face. "We'll let him have a little more and then I'll burp him."

"But who is he?" Gaye asked again.

"The little fellow's grandpa, and he's taking the job seriously. He's here at least three times a day. I think he's sweet, even if he does scare the aides half to death. How he could have got mixed up with the coldhearted woman who breezed in here and whisked their daughter away is beyond me." She stopped abruptly. Color rose in her cheeks. "Oops! Old big-mouth shouldn't have said that. Doctor hates gossip." She threw a towel up and over her shoulder. "Let me have him. Oh, little boy, I hope you don't throw it all up." She held the baby to her shoulder and patted his back gently.

Gaye looked down at her breast with its enlarged wet nipple before she covered it with the sterile cloth. It hadn't been the traumatic experience she'd expected it to be. It had seemed natural to feed this baby that wasn't her own flesh and blood. She watched the nurse handle it confidently, her hands in just the right places on the tiny body to give it support.

"Do you have children?"

"I'm not married. I want a family someday. There...he let out a little air, and not too much came up with it. Just a little more, baby, and you can eat again."

Later that evening, Gaye was sitting in a chair beside the bed when her sister came into the room. Alberta was dressed to leave the hospital.

"Gaye, you've given the Trumbull baby a new lease on life. We'd like to have you feed him every three hours during the night and tomorrow, then we'll see about putting him on a four-hour schedule."

Gaye's brown eyes were full of misery when she looked at her sister, the doctor. "Alberta...can't you pump the milk and feed him with a bottle?"

"We could do that. But we feel the little fellow needs to be held and cuddled. You see, all he'd known was the warm cavern of his mother's body, and now, suddenly, he's been thrust out into the world with nothing to cling to. I've always believed that the secure feeling a mother gives a child while it's nursing is a large part of that child's sense of belonging to a family unit." Alberta sat down on the edge of the bed.

"I'm not his mother! You'll have to find someone else. I'm leaving here tomorrow or the next day. I've got to make burial arrangements for my own baby." Gaye's fingers twisted around each other.

"Arrangements are made, honey. I arranged for a graveside service tomorrow afternoon."

Gaye looked stricken. "Thank you," she murmured. After a hesitation, she said, "I'm going."

"Of course you are. I'll be with you every minute. Then you're coming back here for a few more days."

"There'll be no need for me to come back here. I'll go to your house for a while—that is, if I've not worn out my welcome."

"Don't be foolish. You know you have a home with us for as long as you want. You'd be fine with us. My housekeeper would take good care of you. But I'm asking you to come back here and help me until I can get something worked out for the Trumbull baby."

"He's not my responsibility!"

"I know. He's mine. Stay and help me with him. What's a few days out of your life when it could make all the difference in his?"

"You're not being fair!"

"I know." Alberta's face was set with determination. "When it comes to the life of one of my patients, I'll fight with any means I have. Stay, Gaye. Stay and help me give this infant a start, and I promise you I'll do everything in my power to find a formula he can thrive on."

"Why is mother's milk so important to this baby?"

"I'll try and explain without getting too technical." Alberta paced the room, the heels of her dress shoes making faint clicking sounds on the tile floor. "Several antibiotic properties present in human milk help protect the infant against many infectious and noninfectious disorders. Colostrum contains a large number of leukocytes, which kill bacteria and fungi. Also, there's lactoferrin, an anti-infective protein that helps retard the growth of bacteria by binding available iron." She paused and looked at her sister's wide-eyed, attentive face. "Is this too much for you to absorb all at once?"

"I'm familiar with some of the terms. I got material on the subject from the La Leche League and studied it."

"I know you did." Alberta saw the bleak look come into Gaye's eyes and wondered for the hundredth time if she was doing the right thing in forcing her to care for another infant, even though it was beneficial to both. Professional concern for her two patients took over, and she began to talk. "Breast milk is the correct temperature, and it provides essential nutrients and contains the correct composition of immunological properties that can't be synthesized or added to commercial formulas. But those are only some of the advantages breast-feeding has over formula feeding."

"Enough! You sound as though you're teaching a class. I'll stay a few days, and then you'll have to give me something to dry up my breasts. You know I wouldn't be able to live with myself if I didn't stay and the baby...didn't make it."

"Thanks." Alberta gave a big sigh of relief. "Have you made plans for what you'll do when you're well again?"

"Not really. I'd planned to buy a house near here and devote my life to raising my child. Now I think I'll still buy a house, but I've got to fill my days somehow. I don't want to go back to teaching. My inheritance is still intact, and I can live off the interest if I'm careful. At least I was smart enough not to let Dennis get his hands on that. Why I ever did anything as stupid as to marry that creep is beyond me."

"You were lonely—he was charming. It happens all the time," Alberta said flatly. "You were buried in that little town, first with Mom's illness, then Dad's. You were an easy mark, honey, for an opportunist like Dennis. But that's all water under the bridge. You'll know better next time."

"There won't be a next time!" Gaye said with emphasis. "Any fool that would let herself be wooed and wed in less than a month should be kept in a cage."

"Don't be so hard on yourself. You're a natural mother and homemaker, and your instincts were reaching out. It just happened that Dennis came into your life when you were at your most vulnerable. Give yourself credit for seeing him for what he was and taking the steps to get rid of him."

"I knew within the first month it wouldn't work. Soon after that I knew I was pregnant."

A girl carrying a tray hesitated in the doorway until Alberta motioned her into the room. "I've been invited to dinner with a very interesting, but unusual man," she said after the girl had placed the tray on the bedside table and left the room. Alberta lifted the cover and sniffed. "Hmm...chicken. Looks good and smells better. See that you eat it all. One advantage of a small-town hospital is the home-cooked meals. That and the prices they charge," she added dryly. She bent and placed a kiss on her sister's forehead. "The night nurse knows where to reach me if there's a need. See you in the morning. Okay?"

"Okay." Gaye grabbed her hand. "Thanks for loving me." Moisture filled the big brown eyes. "I don't know what I'd have done without you.'' She smiled through her tears. ''How's that for an old cliché? It may be overused, but in this case, true.''

''It isn't hard to love you, little sister.'' Alberta squeezed the slender hand she held in her large one. Her features softened, and her professional expression dropped from her face like a cloak. ''This is the beginning of a new life for you, honey. From now on it'll be downhill all the way,'' she promised.

Gaye was exhausted when she returned from the graveside service the following afternoon. Gratefully, she crawled into the high hospital bed and stared at the white ceiling. There'd been five people at the service besides the minister: Alberta; her two teenage children, Brett and Joy; and Candy, the nurse from the maternity ward. It was nice of Candy to come, Gaye thought wearily and closed her eyes. The beginning, Alberta said. I suppose if one thing ends, another automatically begins.

The quiet was disrupted by the lusty cries of an infant being carried down the hallway. A nurse came into the room carrying the child.

''My! What a pair of lungs!'' she said with exasperation. ''I'm sure they can hear him down on the main floor.'' She handed the sterile cloth to Gaye so she could wash her breast. ''Here, here, now...'' she crooned to the still-crying infant. ''You'll have your dinner in a minute.''

Blessed quiet prevailed the instant Gaye put the baby to her breast. The little lips pulled with gusto, and a tiny fist pounded against the white globe. The angry redness gradually left his face and was replaced with a glowing pink as he sucked contentedly.

"We can't believe the change in this child. We scarcely heard him cry above a whimper until today."

Gaye ran her fingertips over the fine hair at the baby's temple. If only you were my little boy, she thought. She wiggled her finger into the tiny fist. He grabbed it with surprising strength.

"Don't give him too much before you burp him," the nurse cautioned. She left the room and quietly closed the door.

Gaye's eyes clung to the child's face. Yesterday his skin had a sallow, yellowish tinge. Today it was a healthy pink. If only I could keep him, she thought and instantly chided herself for the ridiculous notion. It was impossible, of course. People didn't give their babies to strangers. Well, some people did, but it was beyond her comprehension that they could do so. What kind of a girl would go away and leave this precious infant? At that moment, dark midnight-blue eyes looked into hers.

"I know you really can't see me, baby. You're too young to focus your eyes," Gaye said softly. "But if you're thanking me for your dinner, you're welcome." She stroked the satin-soft skin of his cheek with her fingertips. "I think you've had enough for now. Let's get some of that air out of your tummy and make room for more."

She placed the infant on her stomach and patted his back. Soon small puffs of air came from the tiny lips, and Gaye smiled her satisfaction. I must tell Alberta to hurry and find a formula for you, she said silently to the baby. Or I may get to liking you too much.

The next few days marched by rapidly.

It was evening. Gaye sat in a chair beside the window and looked down onto the neatly fenced yards that backed up to the hospital grounds. Women were raking and burning leaves and children played kickball in the street, while husbands and fathers stacked the firewood that would cut the heating bills during the long, cold Kentucky winter.

Family. It was a magical word to Gaye. It meant a kinship group, a clan of close-knit, caring creatures. Alberta and her two children were a family, and she, Gaye, lived on the fringe of it, loved as sister and aunt. Shattered was her dream to be loved as a wife and mother, the nucleus around which a family is formed.

She had to get out of there! She needed to get herself back together and get on with her life. Thoughts swirled around in her head, disconnected, half-formed thoughts. She could go back to teaching...join the Peace Corps...open a plant shop...find a place on the cold, rocky coast of Maine and hibernate!

Gaye sat with her back to the door and hugged the blanket-wrapped baby to her. She brought the tiny fist curled about her finger to her lips and kissed it.

"What does the future hold for you, little man? Will you have someone to love you and teach you to love in return?" she murmured. "Will you be a giver or a taker? Will you grow strong in body and mind, or will you—"

There was no sound to alert her to the presence that filled the doorway behind her, but she knew it was there and looked quickly over her shoulder. He leaned lazily against the door casing, looking very much the same as he had the other time he appeared there. He was dressed about the same—jeans, denim shirt, sleeves rolled to the elbows, heavy boots. Gaye stared stupidly. He was a dark, wild-looking man with eyes as black as coals and thick black hair that curled and twisted in complete disarray.

He stared. Gaye felt the hot blood stain her cheeks. She pulled her nipple from the baby's mouth and quickly covered her breast. The child let out a loud yell of protest, and she was forced to turn her attention back to him. The small face knotted with anger, and tiny fists flayed the air.

"Shhhh..."

"What's the matter? What did you do to him?" The man seemed to have leaped across the room.

"Shhh...shhhh..." Gaye bent over the baby and patted his bottom, but the cries continued.

"What's the matter with him?" the voice boomed. He hunkered down beside the chair and leaned over to peer into the baby's face. His head was so close to hers, Gaye felt the brush of his hair against her cheek.

"He's hungry."

"He's what?"

"Hungry." Gaye repeated the word more loudly so he could hear over the baby's loud, angry screams.

"Is that all?" Relief tinged with impatience was in his voice. "Then feed him."

She looked into the dark face only inches from her own. The power and strength of it was obvious. It was the expression in his eyes that grabbed at hers and held them. Although they were piercing, inquiring eyes, they were also filled with great pain. She tore her eyes away, unable to bear the close scrutiny of his.

"Feed him," he said again.

Gaye's eyes swung back to his, wide with surprise. "I will...later."

"Feed him now. For God's sake, woman! I've seen the female breast before."

"I'm sure you have," she snapped. "But not mine!"

"Let the boy eat. I want to talk to you." He reached over and pulled aside the robe covering her breast.

"Stop that!" Instinctively she held the baby to herself in an attempt to hide her breast from his eyes. The small mouth grasped the nipple, and the crying ceased. She tugged the end of the blanket up and over her breast and the baby's contented face. Her own face burned with embarrassment, fired by the deep chuckle that came from the man's throat.

"Why are you so embarrassed? Good Lord! I've seen all shapes and sizes of the female breast—white, black, red, yellow, firm, sagging, small and large. Yours are very nice. In fact, they're beautiful. They're performing the function they were created to do, as well as to arouse male sexual desire."

"Please...get out of here!" Embarrassment was beginning to choke off her breath.

"No," he said flatly. He moved, still hunkered down, and rested his back against the wall. "I want to talk to you. Alberta tells me you're divorced. No strings."

"She had no right to tell you that."

"Sure she did. She's your doctor and your sister. I want you to come home with me and take care of MacDougle."

"MacDougle?"

"Yeah, MacDougle."

"You didn't name him *that.*"

"What's wrong with it? My mother's name is MacDougle."

"That's no reason to burden this child with a horrible name he'll have to live with for the rest of his life," she snapped.

"John MacDougle Trumbull. It's a solid name. It sounds...responsible."

"John? That's better. *MacDougle* would be nothing but a handicap to him. Can you imagine starting school and trying to write it? John or Johnny isn't so bad."

"Not John*ny*. John."

"Johnny is a sweet name for a sweet little boy," Gaye said testily.

"Alberta says MacDougle can go home. I've got everything I think he'll need. Will twelve dozen diapers be enough? I won't have him wearing those paper things."

Gaye gritted her teeth. The nerve of the man! "I haven't applied for the position of nursemaid, and I don't care how many diapers you have, Mr. Trumbull."

"Call me Jim. Now look here, Gaye. The boy needs the best I can get for him. I've watched you walk down to the nursery to look at him, and I've passed this door a few times and looked in to see you holding him. You like him. You like him a lot. Don't try and tell me you haven't become attached to him."

"Of course I like him! I'd have to be out of my mind *not* to like him. And...you had no right to spy on me!"

"Good Lord!"

"Oh..." Gaye suddenly remembered the baby had to be burped. Under cover of the blanket, she pulled the nipple from his mouth and folded the robe over her breast. She lifted him to her shoulder and patted him gently on the back.

"Can I do that? I've yet to hold my grandson." Large hands, with a generous sprinkling of fine black hair on the back, reached for the child. He was so close to her that his chest pressed against her knees. "That battle-ax of a nurse won't let me in the room where they keep him. I have to look at him through the glass, like he was a monkey in a cage at the zoo."

"They can't let just anyone in the nursery."

"I'm not just *anyone*. I'm the boy's grandpa."

"I'm sure you told her that."

"Several times." He was looking at her mouth. His eyes reluctantly moved to the baby lying in her hands. His big hands covered hers beneath the small head and bottom.

"Put one hand to the back of his head and the other one at his back," she warned. "Hold him up against your shoulder and...pat gently."

"Lord! He's so little."

"Not really. As newborn babies go, he's about average size. Pat his back. It'll help him to burp."

"I only have two hands. What'll I pat with?"

"You don't have to hold his head while it rests on your shoulder. Turn his face to the side so he can breathe. He won't break, you know."

"Lord!" he said again. "Are you sure? He's no bigger than the speckled pups I have at home."

Gaye surprised herself by smiling into dark eyes that seemed to swallow hers. This gentleness was completely incompatible with his appearance. She felt a thrill so sharp it pierced her very soul at the sight of the huge man, with the smile of pure pleasure on his craggy face, holding the tiny baby with such loving care.

"He's gained six ounces," she said weakly while her stomach churned with an indefinable emotion.

"You don't say!" He grinned proudly.

"I think he's beginning to focus his eyes."

A small puff of air came from the baby's lips. "Was that it? Is that all there is to it?" He held the baby in his two hands while his eyes searched her face. "Does he have to do that every time he has a meal?"

"He swallows air along with the milk. If he doesn't get rid of it, he'll have a tummyache."

"Is that right? There's so much I don't know, it scares me silly," he confessed. He looked down at the red little face. The baby yawned, and he chuckled softly.

Gaye choked back the lump that rose in her throat and looked away from him. He was so big, so proud and rugged, yet he was so helpless where the baby was concerned.

"Will you take care of him for me?" The words hung between them, and the intimacy there was, bordered on tangibility.

"Mr. Trumbull, I…don't think so. You see, I—" Her large amber-ringed brown eyes looked at him pleadingly, and the tip of her pink tongue came out to lick suddenly dry lips.

"Won't you think about it?"

"Alberta will find someone for you," she said shakily.

"I don't want *someone*. I want you." He placed the baby in her arms. "You and MacDougle seem right for each other. Say you'll do it, Gaye."

"I don't know—" Her voice faltered. She wished he would go away so she could think clearly.

"Then say you'll think about it," he insisted softly.

"All right. I'll…think about it."

"Fair enough." He studied the baby's face and touched his cheek gently with a forefinger. "Raising a child is an awesome responsibility, isn't it?"

Gaye nodded her head and blinked back tears that threatened at the corners of her eyes. She wanted to look at him, but some unknown strong force kept her from doing it.

Finally he stood, and for a long moment he looked

down at them. "See you later," he said quietly and quickly left the room.

Gaye listened to his footsteps going down the corridor. It was a sad and lonesome sound.

Chapter Two

"I am not. I repeat, I am not going to that man's house as a live-in wet nurse!" Gaye jammed a soft billed cap down over her rich brown hair and picked up her jacket.

Alberta walked beside her down the hospital corridor. "You know you're welcome to come and stay with us for as long as you want. I just don't want you to rush out and buy a house because you think you've got no place to go."

"I'm far too practical for that. I told the real estate agent what I wanted and the amount I could afford to pay for it. She said there were several places in town that would fill the bill. She's taking me out to look at them. *If* I find something and settle here, I'll help out with Johnny until Mr. Trumbull can make other arrangements. That's all I can promise."

"Don't get carried away and forget about the noon feeding."

"I won't." Gaye put on the rust-colored jacket and pulled the belt tightly about her waist. It seemed strange, but nice, to have a waistline once again. "Isn't it rather expensive to have me stay here and occupy a room just to feed Johnny?"

"Jim is picking up the bill. He'll pay as long as you stay here. I wish you'd consider staying on for a while. I'm not sure you're up to taking care of an infant twenty-four hours a day."

"I can't believe I've agreed to do this. Frankly, Alberta, I'm wondering if I haven't slipped a cog or two." Gaye's brown eyes were so wide and innocent, yet they seemed to sparkle with mockery.

"It's about time you did something impulsive for a change." Alberta smiled at her and pushed open the glass door.

"Don't mention that word! The only other impulsive thing I've done was to marry Dennis. I can only hope this won't turn out to be as disastrous. Is that the woman I'm waiting for—the one in the station wagon?"

"That's Karen Johnson, the real estate agent. She's a nice person. You'll like her. Good luck. I'll be anxious to hear about what you find."

Gaye waved and walked down the sidewalk. It was as if she were walking into another life. I should be nervous, she thought. Happy? Scared? Angry? Confused? Buying a house is a big step, and I'm acting as if it's an everyday occurrence.

Karen Johnson was a tall, solidly built woman with iron gray hair, but she was so alive you didn't notice her age. From the oversized darkrimmed glasses on her high-cheekboned face to her sturdy brown walking shoes, she oozed confidence. Alberta was right. Gaye liked her at once.

"Fall is a beautiful time of year in Kentucky," Karen said and turned the car onto a street lined with maple trees; the tops had turned a burnished gold, evidence of autumn's frost and the waning strength of the sun.

"Autumn is my favorite season," Gaye agreed. "We had beautiful fall weather in Indiana. The street we lived on had maple trees, and the elms grew so tall that in some places the branches meshed with those across the street."

"Didn't they interfere with the utility wires?"

"Our town was laid out with alleys running the length of the blocks. The utility poles were set behind the houses."

"Sounds like my kind of town," Karen said, smiling.

They'd visited several houses before Karen turned to Gaye and offered to point out the sights. "You were here several weeks before you went into the hospital, and I'm sure Alberta showed you around town, but just in case you missed a few attractions I'll point them out. On the right is our new library—it's really the old library with a new addition. Down the street is the Methodist church, and across from that, the telephone company. These places are all within walking distance of the house I'm going to show you next." Karen gave her a sidelong glance and grinned. "I saved my goody for last."

The three houses Gaye had been shown hadn't really impressed her as places she could call home. Two of them had no yards to speak of, and the third had bedrooms so small they seemed more like closets when compared to the bedrooms back home.

Karen turned the car into a long drive and parked beneath a portico. She turned to watch Gaye's reaction.

"I know I shouldn't say anything negative when showing a property, but in this case I'm going to make an exception. The old Lancaster place may be just too big for you. I want you to see it anyhow. I've fond memories of this place. It was built before World War I. At that time big houses with large rooms and high ceilings were status symbols. It's been in the same family for a number of years. The owner died recently, and the property was inherited by a friend of mine who lives in Florida. Are you interested in seeing the inside?"

"I've lived in a large old house all my life. How many rooms?"

"Four bedrooms and a bath upstairs. A living room, dining room, small glassed-in breakfast room, kitchen and half-bath downstairs. There's a full dry basement under the house and, as you can see from the gabled roof, an attic that's perfect for storage or can be converted into an apartment if you need the extra income."

"No, I wouldn't want that," Gaye said quickly. She opened the car door and got out. "I haven't seen a house with a portico for a long time."

Karen took a ring of keys from her purse and unlocked the side door. "This is a handy entrance and the one most used by the family that lived here."

Gaye was in love with the house from the moment she stepped through the French doors and onto the gleaming hardwood floors. She loved everything about it, from the wide oak woodwork and narrow, deep windows to the solid wood cupboards in the kitchen. She was delighted with the oversized bathroom, its claw-footed bathtub and brass fixtures.

What in the world would she do with all this room? She could make one of the bedrooms into a sewing room, she reasoned, or into a cozy den. The house was only slightly larger than the one in Indiana.

"I'm afraid to ask how much," she said to Karen as they went up the steps to the attic door.

"You may be surprised. Let me show you the attic, and then we'll go back downstairs and talk about it."

The attic was a large, bare room, as Gaye knew it would be. The roof beams and all the studs were exposed, but it was well lit due to the dormer windows.

"A great place for kids to play on a rainy day," Karen remarked and closed the door.

Gaye sat down on the window seat in the living room and looked out onto the broad lawn. The leaves were falling, and pushed by a brisk fall wind, they banked against the row of lilac bushes that lined the drive. She looked back toward the redbrick fireplace and the bookshelves built under the small windows on each end of it. She could visualize her two armchairs sitting there on the braided wool rug she had finished last winter. As she sat there a peaceful coming-home feeling settled over her.

"How much?"

"It's slightly more than the top price you gave me." Karen shuffled the papers in her briefcase and drew out a sheet. "But there are no assessments against the property for street and sewer improvements or other hidden costs. If you're interested, we can make the owner an offer. We'll offer the figure you gave me and see what happens."

"Make the offer. How soon will we know if the owner accepts?"

"I'll call her as soon as I get back to the office."

"My furniture is in storage, but I'll have to buy new appliances. I sold mine with the house." Gaye stood. Now that she had a goal, the world looked brighter. "I may have to borrow or rent a few things until my things arrive."

"No problem. I can lend you some essentials, and I'm sure Alberta can. I'll get Bob, my son-in-law, to haul them for you. He has a plumbing business. He'll check the pipes before the water is turned on, and he'll connect the appliances."

"You talk as though I'll be moving in."

"I don't want to give you false hope, but I'm reasonably sure your offer will be accepted."

Gaye walked around the outside of the house several times. The property took up the whole end of one block. She liked that. She wasn't used to close neighbors. She also liked the shrubs that marked the property line. She got into the car and for the second time that day she said, "I can't believe I'm doing this."

It was straight up noon when she walked into the hospital and took the elevator to the second floor. She saw Jim as soon as she stepped from the elevator. He was standing in the corridor in front of the glass window, looking into the nursery. He looked at her quizzically and came to meet her.

"Where've you been? MacDougle has been crying for ten minutes."

"It won't hurt him to cry a little. It strengthens his lungs. He wasn't due a feeding until now." Gaye waved at the nurse and went on down the hall to her room. She breathed a sigh of relief when Jim didn't follow her. She didn't realize how tired she was until she kicked off her shoes and sank down into the chair beside the window.

John was angry, and he was telling the world about it in the only way he knew. By the time the nurse reached

Gaye's room, he'd worked up a full head of steam and was bawling lustily.

Candy gave Gaye the cloth to wipe her breast and then handed her the baby. The wailing protest was cut off as soon as the hungry little lips found her nipple. Candy went to close the door, but Jim's big frame filled it.

"Excuse me," she murmured and slipped past him and into the hall.

Coward, Gaye thought. She felt as if she'd been deserted and left with the enemy. She pulled the towel up to cover her breast and Johnny's face.

Jim closed the door, came into the room, and sat down on the edge of the bed.

"So you're not coming out to my place to take care of MacDougle." It was a flat statement.

"You're right. I'm not. I've told you that repeatedly."

"Why not? I'll pay you a good wage."

"I want to live in my own house. I made an offer on one this morning."

"Here in Madisonville?"

"Uh-huh. Mrs. Johnson called it the old Lancaster place."

"I know the place. It's big and it's old. What do you want with it?"

"It's none of your business, Mr. Trumbull, but I'll tell you anyway. I sold my home in Indiana and I have to invest the money in another home within the year or pay a huge tax. That's one reason. The other is...well, I like an older house with a lot of yard space."

There was a curious silence as they looked at each other. Gaye slowly absorbed his height, his wide shoulders, the soft dark open-necked shirt tucked into jeans. He certainly wasn't handsome, she decided. He was too rough-hewn for that. She looked at his hands. They were work-roughened, with square-tipped, clean nails. The sleeves of his shirt were rolled up. She wondered if they came from the wash that way. His forearms were covered with fine dark hair. Suddenly it struck her that this vitally alive, masculine man was a grandfather!

"You're a grandfather!" Gaye said the words aloud before she could hold them back. "You must have married young."

"Young and brainless. If it had been today we'd have just lived together."

"You sound bitter."

"I admit it. My teenage daughter came to me when she was pregnant because she didn't want her friends to know she was stupid enough to get *caught.* And because she was too far along for an abortion. I'll never know who MacDougle's father is, but I sure as hell know who his grandfather is. I'll see to it that he's taught to be responsible for his actions."

"It seems to me you should have instilled that in your daughter," Gaye said coolly.

"Before that girl came to me I'd seen her exactly four times since she was three years old. She lives with her mother in France. She doesn't like my life-style and I don't like hers."

"If she's a minor she shouldn't be allowed to choose her life-style."

"Exactly. Her mother has custody. I support her and I furnished a place for her to wait out her pregnancy. Believe me, she hated every minute of it. That's about the extent of my participation in my daughter's life."

"She may have second thoughts and want her baby."

"She'll have to go through hell to get him! She signed him over to me, and I've filed for adoption. Is there anything else you want to know?"

"I'm sorry. I didn't mean to pry." Gaye lifted the towel and peeked down at Johnny. She smiled at the picture he made—sound asleep and the nipple half out of his mouth. She looked up and met dark, piercing eyes.

"You have a beautiful mouth. You should smile more often."

"I haven't had much to smile about lately," she snapped.

"I know, and I'm sorry."

The softly spoken words coming from this bear of a man and the steady gaze of his intense dark eyes caught her off guard. Her heart stumbled on its regular rhythm. Suddenly she felt weepy, thinking of her own tiny baby, but she realized Johnny had helped ease her pain. Under the cover of the towel, she slipped her breast back into the nursing bra and pulled her shirt together.

"Do you want to burp him?" she asked, wanting to share with Jim the gift of his grandson.

The grin softened the hard contours of his face, and amusement glinted in his dark eyes. "Mrs. What's-her-name would have a screaming fit, but let's give it a go. I'll be glad to get MacDougle home so I can pick him up without some old biddy yelling at me."

"What old biddy?" Gaye's brown eyes held a definite shimmer of defiance when she met his glance. All her defenses were raised. "You mean Alberta or Candy," she accused him.

"I mean the night nurse—the skinny one with the dyed blond hair, frog eyes, and the face that looks like a road map. I think they call her Georgette." Jim squatted down beside her and carefully lifted the baby from her lap. Gaye placed the towel on his shoulder and tried not to giggle at his unkind, but accurate, description of the night nurse.

"You can pat him a little harder than that, but don't knock the breath out of him," she cautioned.

"I like holding him. I don't think I ever held Crissy." He rocked back on his heels as if he was afraid to get to his feet.

Gaye watched the expressions flit across his face. His lips were stretched in a smile, and his eyes gleamed with pure pleasure. She choked back the lump that rose in her throat and tuned her eyes away from him, only to have them swing back of their own accord. She was acutely aware of his broad chest and lean body. He radiated more masculinity than any man she'd ever met. And yet he made no attempt to hide his sentimentality. John MacDougle Trumbull would be loved, there was no doubt about it.

"I don't want someone to take care of him who has no interest in him other than as a way to earn money." His words broke into her thoughts.

"You don't need to worry about that. Whoever takes care of him will love Johnny in no time at all." She tried to smile, but her lips felt rubbery. She tried to keep her voice light, but it rasped hoarsely and caught.

His eyes roamed her face. "I'll pay whatever you want." There was a hard edge to his voice that angered her.

"Wages are not the deciding factor, Mr. Trumbull. I'm not what you'd call loaded, but I'm not destitute!"

"Cut the mister, Gaye, and call me Jim." He got to his feet and loomed over her. "What is the deciding factor?" She didn't attempt to look at him. She looked out the window instead. "If it's propriety you're worried about, my aunt lives with me."

"Then let her take care of Johnny."

"She's seventy years old. I wouldn't ask her to take on the responsibility."

"It's your problem, Mr. Trumbull."

The hard-edged line of his jaw and the sudden narrowing of his eyes warned her that he was angry. It stopped her from telling him to butt out of her life and to take his grandson with him. She turned her head deliberately, her hand reaching for the bell to bring the nurse. With a flick of his fingers he moved the cord out of her reach.

"Not yet." The harshness of his voice rasped across her nerves. His next words brought her up and out of her chair. "I made a solemn promise to myself years ago that I'd never marry again. I'll break that promise to get a good mother for MacDougle."

Gaye swallowed hard. She knew her face was aflame. Then pride surfaced. "You think I'm so hard up for a husband that I'd marry to secure a position? Get out of my room. Get out of my life!" She flung the words out desperately. Anger swept through her.

"I'm not insulting you! I find that most women have a price for...everything." His voice was dangerously soft.

Gaye tilted her head defiantly, and her angry eyes raked his face. She wished desperately she was anywhere in the world but here, confronting this arrogant man who held his grandson so tenderly and whose harsh words whipped across her pride.

"I'm not *most* women! In twelve short months I've been married, divorced, given birth to a child who...who lived only a short time. I sold the only home I've ever known, uprooted myself to come here to Kentucky because my sister is here. I'm trying hard to cope with all these changes in my life, and I can't handle anything else." Tears flooded her eyes, and she hated herself for not being able to hold them back.

"You need me and MacDougle as much as we need you." There was no sympathy in his cold, no-nonsense expression.

"You have a lot of nerve saying that! I don't need you or...anyone. I'm buying a house and moving into it. I won't be your live-in wet nurse and that's my final word."

"You're afraid you'll love MacDougle. That's what you can't handle."

Damn him! Could he read her mind? "What in the world is so amazing about that? I admit it. Does that make me a lousy person?"

He bent over her. She could feel his breath on her face, see the stubble on his cheeks, lashes tangled around eyes so black they were mirrors. "Do you think I'd turn my grandson over to a lousy person?"

"Your grandson has upchucked on your shirt. I told you to keep the towel under his face." He was so close to her, she had to sit down to get away from him. "Take him to the nursery."

"And get chewed out for holding him? You'd like that, wouldn't you?" He placed the child in her lap.

"Hand me the towel." She hoped desperately he didn't know how nervous she was. "You've let what he upchucked run down his neck." Her stomach churned with anger and nerves. She shot him a cool look of disapproval.

"Okay. Let's start again." He sat down on the edge of the bed. "I want, more than anything, to have MacDougle with me. I want to watch him grow and get to really know him. But I can wait for that pleasure if I have to. I'd rather know he's being well taken care of by someone who understands and loves him."

"How do you know I love and understand him?" Her retort was quick.

He ignored her question. "I'm willing to let you take him home with you for a while."

"That's big of you!"

"It's a concession I'm willing to make for MacDougle's sake. I've looked forward to having him with me. I've bought furniture and one of those layout things the store recommended."

"The word is *layette.* Perhaps if you'd been as concerned with your own child she'd be here now taking care of hers!" She had wanted to say something to cut him down. Now she regretted the words, but it was too late to recall them. The silence that followed made her more ashamed of those words than any she had uttered in a long while. She couldn't help the wave of apprehension that caused a shiver to travel the length of her spine.

"You don't know a damn thing about it."

She had to apologize. It wasn't her nature to be rude. "You're right, and I apologize."

"Accepted."

He crossed the room to stand before a framed print that hung on the wall. Gaye watched him warily as he slid his hands, palms out, into the back pockets of his jeans. She noticed how the muscles of his back stirred the cloth of his soft flannel shirt. If his size wasn't enough to draw attention to him, certainly that brawny, earthy, untamed look would have been.

He turned. Their eyes caught and held before she lowered hers on the pretext of giving her attention to the baby in her arms. She was aware, however, that his eyes roamed over her—starting at the top of her head and taking in every feature of her face as they moved to her throat and breasts. His eyes lingered there for a long moment before moving back to her face.

"You have the magnificent quality of calmness even when you're angry. You are the personification of motherhood."

Gaye was startled, touched, and then angered by his remark. "Oh, sure!" she quipped. "You'd say that since you want me to be a substitute mother to Johnny."

"MacDougle," he corrected dryly. "Johnny sounds like a prissy sissy."

"Oh, is that right? I suppose you're going to teach him that big boys never cry and that it's sissy to cuddle a doll or a teddy? Do you think playing football or rugby, hunting, trapping and watching Monday Night Football while drinking gallons of beer makes a man?"

"Whoa! What's got you in such a sweat?" He came to stand beside her. She looked up at him. His eyes traveled over her brazenly. "I knew you liked him a lot!" His eyes challenged her to deny it.

"I didn't say I didn't like him," Gaye sputtered. Then, "You...irritate the hell out of me!" She cleared her throat and swallowed hard. "You need a few lessons in diplomacy and child rearing."

"I plan to take a course in child rearing." He grinned at the surprised look on her face. "I admit I'm inadequate in that department."

"That's a beginning," she said dryly.

The phone rang. Jim reached across the bed, lifted the receiver and handed it to her.

"Hello."

"This is Karen and I have good news. Your offer has been accepted."

"I'm so glad! When can I move in?"

"Let's give it until the end of the week. I'll have the house thoroughly cleaned, and Bob will check out the plumbing. The house hasn't been lived in for some time, and something may have gone wrong with the pipes. How long before your furniture arrives?"

"I'll call this afternoon and find out."

"I have a few things you can use, if you're sure you want to move in right away. I'm sure Alberta would like for you to stay with her for a while, but of course, that's up to you."

"I think I need the solitude of my own place."

"Okay, then. If you'll be around this afternoon, I'll come over to the hospital with the papers and we can get the ball rolling."

"I'll be here. And, Karen, thanks an awful lot."

"My pleasure. I'll see you later."

Gaye turned back to the large man at her side. "I've bought a house!"

"You've bought a house," he repeated, taking the phone from her hand and pressing the button for the nurse.

"I knew I wanted it the moment I saw it." Her eyes shone up at him, and she couldn't stop smiling.

He pushed himself away from the edge of the bed. It seemed to her he'd hardly moved at all, but there he was, standing beside her. She had to tilt her head to see his face. He appeared larger, more rugged, almost primitive.

"Are you always so impulsive? You couldn't have spent much time looking over that property."

Gaye's features took on a look of cool hauteur. Her brown eyes lost their softness. They sparkled now from anger. Before she could retort, the door opened and

Candy came into the room, her rubber-soled shoes making little squeaky noises on the polished tile. She skirted Jim's tall figure as if she feared he would reach out and grab her.

"The doctor is waiting to see him," she murmured to Gaye.

"What for? Why is the doctor waiting for him?" Jim's loud voice startled the baby, whose face puckered for an instant.

"Must you be so loud?" Gaye hissed.

"What's wrong with him? Are you keeping something from me?" he demanded in a grating whisper.

"Nothing is the matter with him, Mr. Trumbull. The doctor sees all the babies every afternoon." Candy hurried from the room with the infant, closing the door behind her.

"You keep Candy and the other nurses scared half to death! I'm sure they'll be relieved when Johnny leaves the nursery."

"I don't seem to scare you." There was amusement in his tone.

"You certainly don't," she said with deceptive calm, tucking a long strand of hair behind her ear.

"You're angry again, even if you do act calm and collected."

He was laughing at her, and she refused to answer.

"You're angry because I didn't jump with joy when you announced you made an investment in a property you saw only this morning. It was unwise of you to plunk down your nest egg without making a thorough investigation."

His rational calmness was all the more irritating. It did nothing to douse the blaze of resentment that burned through her, because deep within, she knew he was right.

"You don't know anything about it. Nothing at all! I'll thank you to keep your opinions to yourself." Gaye felt her throat tighten around angry tears.

"Maybe not. But I know quite a bit about you, Gaye Meiners Hutchinson."

"Gaye Meiners. I took my maiden name back."

"Bitter divorce, huh?"

"That, too, doesn't concern you."

He looked at her for a moment, his eyes narrowed, his face thoughtful. He reached out to run a strand of her hair through his fingers. "It's true. I haven't known you long enough to know much about you. But I do know that you're intelligent, loving, and that you were very good at your job. There's nothing flamboyant about you, Gaye. Although you have a capricious personality that shines through...occasionally." His dark eyes lit with mischievous delight when hers became stormy.

"I'm boring! That's what you mean." She tried to push his hand away from her hair.

His long fingers curved around her chin, forcing her to look up at him. "Believe me, you're not boring."

"Don't!" She jerked her chin away from his hand and turned her face toward the window. Nervous hands smoothed the hair back from her face, then welded themselves together in her lap.

"This isn't the time to bring up the subject, not with you sitting there ramrod stiff and...all sour, but I need to make definite plans for MacDougle."

"Then go away and make them."

"I knew you'd say that." There was a lilt to his husky voice.

He was trying to keep from laughing! Part of her wanted to hit him. The other part wanted him to go away so she could fantasize about ways to torture him. She clamped her teeth together and refused to take up the challenge to exchange barbs with him.

"Are you so ticked off at me you'll cut off MacDougle's food supply?"

Her head jerked around as if it were pulled on invisible strings. "You think of me as a...cow!"

"Oh, my God!" He roared with laughter, and Gaye clamped her hands over her ears. She was sure he was being heard in the center of town. "Oh, Gaye, as petite as you are, no one could think of you as a cow! On second thought, maybe a little brown heifer?" His voice teased, but there was unmistakable admiration in his eyes.

"Alberta will have the formula worked out for Johnny in a couple of weeks. After that you're on your own." There was a quiver in her voice in spite of a supreme effort to control it.

"I knew I could count on you." He bent from his great height and placed his lips gently on hers. The pressure of his mouth was warm and firm, and it moved over hers with familiar ease. There was nothing tentative or hesitant about the kiss. He raised his head, his dark eyes searching hers while his fingers held her chin captive. Slowly he winked at her, then gave her chin a shake and walked quickly from the room.

Stunned by his brazen action, Gaye refocused her gaze on the door after he closed it.

"What's the matter with me?" she wailed. "I'm disconnected from my brain! And...I'm talking to myself. That should tell me something!"

Chapter Three

It was the morning after Gaye and Johnny had spent their first night in the Lancaster house, which was now the Meiners house. The doorbell rang and then the doorknob rattled before Gaye could get from the kitchen to the door.

"Cripes!" She could see a dusty black pickup truck parked in the drive beneath the portico.

Jim stood on the steps, his sleeves rolled up even though the ground was white with a heavy frost. The wind was blowing his hair, lifting it off his scowling brow.

"I've been to the hospital. I thought you'd leave MacDougle there until I could bring his bed and set it up."

"There was no need for me to leave him there and make two trips to the hospital in the middle of the night. I borrowed a bassinet."

"You could have stayed at the hospital. You were in an all-fired hurry to move in here," Jim grumbled and walked past her. His boot heels made hollow sounds on the bare floor.

"If you're going to be a grouch, go away," Gaye said to his back.

He stood in the middle of the room and looked around. "What's a bassinet?" he asked, as if it suddenly occurred to him that he didn't know.

"A basket with legs," she said as she passed him. She went through the dining room and into the kitchen, her sneakers enabling her to walk soundlessly. She wore jeans, and a soft blue shirt was tucked neatly into the waistband. "I'm having coffee. Want some?" Without waiting for an answer, she took a plastic foam cup from the package on the counter and poured coffee from the coffee maker. She turned to see him stooping so he could read the thermostat. "Does the temperature suit you?"

"I guess so. Where's MacDougle?"

"Upstairs."

"Alone?"

"No, I left a mad dog up there with him."

He picked up the cup she had left sitting on the counter. "You're very funny this morning, Ms. Meiners."

"I'm glad you think I'm entertaining as well as productive."

He roamed about the huge kitchen, his dark eyes searching out every detail from the light fixture hanging over the island counter to the redbrick wall where at one time a wood-burning cook stove had sat. He walked leisurely out to the glassed-in breakfast room. The sun was shining on the frosted trees and shrubs, turning them into sparkling showpieces. When he turned, he was smiling.

"I'll have to come by here every morning to get my sunshine."

"I don't have a monopoly on sunshine." Jim continued to smile. His eyes glinted into hers, and her gaze wavered beneath his direct stare. A deep inner restlessness flickered to life in the pit of her stomach. How come I've never noticed his beautiful teeth? she wondered.

"I'm not so sure." The words were so softly spoken, she wasn't sure she had heard them correctly or that she understood them. She'd completely lost the drift of the conversation.

"You seem to have a lot of time away from your job. Don't you keep regular hours?"

He shrugged. "I work when the mood strikes me." He sat the empty cup on the counter, and she wondered how he could have drunk the coffee when it was so hot—she was still blowing on hers.

"What's your line of work?"

"I'm a blacksmith."

"A...blacksmith?"

"A welder, too. I like working with metal."

"You're really a blacksmith? Such as in horseshoes?"

"Yeah."

When it became evident he wasn't going to say any more, she said lamely, "I guess this *is* the horse-racing state."

"Are you going to show me the rest of the house?"

"Be my guest. But don't wake Johnny."

"I'll bring his bed in and set it up."

"There's no need. He won't outgrow the bassinet for a month or longer."

"Which room is his?" He stood with his foot on the bottom stair.

"I plan to keep him in my room for the short time he'll be here."

Gaye led the way up the stairs. All her nerve endings tingled under the scrutiny of the dark eyes behind her. Why hadn't she brought Johnny downstairs? She dreaded taking Jim into the intimacy of her bedroom. A shiver of pure physical awareness chased down her spine. She had an incredible urge to turn and run out of the house. They reached the door of her room, and she turned to look into eyes lit with laughter. How, she asked herself, could I have allowed myself to be drawn into this bizarre situation?

His fingers closed over her forearm, and he smiled into her eyes as if it was the norm for the two of them to be standing at her bedroom door. Gaye studied his face, weighing her instinct to trust him against experiences of a past that had almost destroyed her. She waited while he studied her in turn. She didn't really know him, didn't know what to do with him. She wanted him to go, yet she desperately wanted him to stay. A sense of a powerful connection pulsed between them. At the moment it was a quiet, yet profound feeling, but it jolted her into reality. She shrugged his hand from her arm.

"What are you afraid of? I haven't raped a woman for several days."

"Now, you're being funny, Mr. Trumbull." She was shaken and a little out of breath. Where was her painfully acquired self-control?

"Call me Mr. Trumbull again and I'll pinch your cute little tush." He followed her into the room, and his amused eyes went to the king-size bed and back to Gaye.

Her eyes lost themselves in the twinkling depths of his, and the stiffness left her body. She was conscious of nothing except a warmth and completeness that were new to her. She smiled, and her eyes sparkled mischievously as she succumbed to his charm.

"That's better." His voice was surprisingly soft. "You don't have to be on guard with me. If I kiss you again, I'll give you at least a two-second notice. You'll have a chance to slap my face and shout, 'Unhand me, you cad!'" His lips curled in his best imitation of a villainous leer.

"You may be able to carry it off, even without a handlebar mustache and high silk hat." She couldn't hold back the bubble of laughter.

"I carry them as standard gear. Keep 'em in my truck."

Gaye stood back and watched as he bent over the basket that held his grandson. He had powerful shoulders and arms. She could see him as a blacksmith, stripped to the waist, muscular arms and chest glistening with perspiration as he pounded the red-hot iron. "Under the spreading chestnut tree the village smithy stands..." She wondered if Longfellow had such a man as Jim in mind when he wrote the poem. She quietly left the room.

"Come hold the door open for me," Jim said when he came downstairs and found her standing in the bay window. "I'll bring in MacDougle's bed and a few other things I picked up. Seems like all he's got is diapers and things to sleep in. You'll have to help me shop for pants and shirts."

"Pants and shirts?" Gaye followed him to the door. "I don't think you've heard a word I said."

"Yes, I did. You said something about a mustache and a high silk hat." He quirked his brows and grinned.

Oh, God! she thought. His eyes were beautiful, too. "I mean before that." She stood shivering in the open doorway. Jim lifted a box from the truck bed and brought it into the house.

"Something about not having a monopoly on sunshine?"

"Oh, for heaven's sake, Jim! Trying to reason with you is like butting my head against a stone wall. I said Johnny can use the bassinet for as long as he's here."

"Oh, yeah. You did say that." He paused beside her on his way back to the truck. His knuckles caressed her cheek. "He's got a bed. He doesn't have to sleep in a laundry basket. Stop buckin', babe. You don't stand a chance against me and MacDougle."

A few hours later, a bed large enough for a five-year-old stood at one end of the small room next to Gaye's. A blue six-drawer double chest, a different nursery rhyme character painted on each drawer, took up the length of one wall. There were a padded chest full of toys, a rocking horse, a rocking chair, and boxes of clothing and bedding yet to be put away.

"Where shall I put this stuff?" Jim was on his knees, pulling blue blankets out of a box and stacking them on the floor.

"Not on the floor, Jim. Oh, Lordy! Johnny won't be using some of these things for a year. Whatever possessed you to buy them? Three, maybe four blankets is all he'll use. They're not throwaway, you know. I've got a washer and dryer downstairs, and I wash his things every day."

"Okay." He put the blankets back in the box. "I'll stack the boxes in the closet, just in case."

"In case of what, for chrissake? In case we have a blizzard and the furnace goes off, or in case we enter the ice age?"

He stacked the boxes neatly in the back of the closet

and closed the door. He leaned against it and looked about the room. Gaye could almost see thoughts forming in his mind and raised her hand, palm toward him.

"Enough. This is absolutely all he needs."

"The room needs a carpet, a curtain and some pictures on the wall." He spun on his heel. "I'll be right back."

Gaye raced after him and caught him at the door. "Don't you dare buy carpet for my floor!" She grasped his arm. "I won't have it. I hate wall-to-wall carpet."

"But something should be on the floor," he protested.

"Why?"

"Why? Well, because...good God, Gaye! You're not going to let him play on that cold floor?"

"Of course not! You have the craziest ideas. He's just a little baby. He won't be playing on the floor for months."

"How about a thick, fluffy rug?"

"Oh, my aching back!" Gaye flung up her hands. "I give up! Do as you please, but I won't have any nail holes in my hardwood floor."

"Okay." He grinned and went out the door.

Gaye watched until the truck was out of sight, then went slowly up the stairs. She was worn out from pitting her will against the iron will of this wild, forceful man. It was like swimming upstream against a strong current. Johnny began to cry, and she looked at her watch. Noon? Already?

She carried the rocking chair downstairs to the empty breakfast room. She was out of breath and weak by the time she returned to climb the stairs and leaned against the newel post to catch her breath. You're making a mistake, her mind screamed. You're getting in deeper and deeper. Use some common sense and tell him to get the hell out of here and take his grandson before you find yourself tangled in a web you couldn't get out of if you wanted to. All you have to do is stay firm. You did it once with Dennis. Do it again. Later, she told herself. Later, when Johnny is on formula.

She let down the side of the bed and changed the baby's diaper. He looked so tiny in the big bed. She picked him up and snuggled him against her. It was comforting to hold him. Oh, baby, I mustn't love you too much, she thought.

"You poor baby," she crooned. "You've really got your work cut out for you if you're going to live with your grandfather. You won't be able to call your soul your own."

She sat in the sunny breakfast room, nursed the baby and watched the birds gather for their annual trip south. Hundreds of blackbirds swarmed to feed on the grass that had been allowed to go to seed. Johnny went to sleep, and she buttoned her shirt. It was peaceful and satisfying to sit there and hold him. Her fingers smoothed the fine dark hair back from his forehead, and she gently touched his cheeks with her fingertips. She examined his hands. They were broad and blunt, like Jim's, she thought idly.

The birds rose and flew like a dark cloud when the pickup drove up the drive. Gaye heard the motor cut off and the door slam. The side door opened and she heard the unmistakable noise of something being slid across the floor. She automatically closed her eyes. She was afraid to guess what he was bringing in.

Jim made several trips to the room upstairs. The thump of his boot heels on the bare wood echoed throughout the house. I'll have to get a tread on the stairs, Gaye thought, or else insist he take off his boots as a visitation requirement.

She shuddered when she heard a pounding coming from upstairs. I won't be upset, she told herself. I won't be upset.

The tinkling sound of a music box reached her. "Gaye! C'mon up and take a look. Is MacDougle down there?" The voice boomed and echoed in the empty rooms.

Gaye groaned. Where else would he be, for Pete's sake? When she entered the hall he shouted again.

"Gaye!" He stood at the head of the stairs. He saw her—*clunk, clunk, clunk* and he was beside her. "Here, let me take him. You look worn out."

The baby woke. His little face crumpled, and he gave a scream of fright.

"Oh, Jim! Won't you ever learn to be quiet?"

"We'll have to get something on those steps." He took the child from her arms and added, "I'm sorry. But you said it didn't hurt him to cry a little."

"It doesn't hurt him to cry, but he'll be a nervous wreck from being continually startled out of a sound sleep."

"I guess there's a lot I don't know." He held Johnny in his two hands. He had such a happy look on his craggy face it was impossible for Gaye to be angry with him. "Come see what I found at the furniture store."

Gaye stood in the doorway and surveyed the room, now covered with a soft blue rug that extended to within inches of the oak baseboard. A pull-down shade with large, colorful alphabet blocks printed on it hung at the window. A huge gold-framed picture of a clown hung on the wall above the bed, and in the middle of the room, on a metal frame, a cloth swing swung back and forth. Holding the baby to him with one hand, Jim reached with the other and turned a dial on the frame. The soft music of Brahms's Lullaby filled the room. He grinned. He was like a small boy with a new toy.

"Isn't this the damnedest thing you ever saw? We can put MacDougle in the seat, set the timer, wind up the swing and let him go. It's all done automatically. The same mechanism propels the swing and plays the music. Let's put him in it and see how he likes it."

Gaye began to laugh. She couldn't help herself. "You really are the limit!"

"Is that good or bad?"

"I'm not sure. Look at this room. Everything in it is big. Big bed! Big chest! Big pictures! Even the rug is big." The quizzical expression on his face told her he didn't understand what she was talking about. His head, with its scramble of black hair, tilted. His huge hand rested snugly against the baby's back. His eyes played with hers and then began to glow devilishly.

"Forget it," Gaye said. "Just forget it. Put Johnny in the swing. He may not like it and you'll have to take it back."

Alberta came by several evenings later. Somehow she managed to take time from her busy schedule to stop by the house every few days to check on Gaye and Johnny. This evening she stopped on her way home from the hospital.

"The change in that baby is nothing short of a miracle. I won't be surprised if he's gained a half a pound since I weighed him last."

Gaye smiled happily. "Aside from feeding him, keeping him dry and washing clothes, there's not much to do." She sat a tall, frosty drink in front of Alberta and handed her a paper napkin to wrap around it. "When do we start the new formula?"

"In a week or two. At first we'll give it to him once a day and then every other feeding. It will be a gradual changeover."

"I'll be glad when he's settled on the formula. There are times when I feel like a milk cow!" Gaye sat down on a borrowed kitchen chair and waved her sister to the other. "Oh, by the way, thanks for the houseplants."

"It was Brett's idea. He's the one with the green thumb." Alberta took a sip of her drink. "Mmm, good daiquiri. I'd best not drink it all. I'm driving."

"The agent from the transport company called. The moving van will be here next Friday morning."

"It's too bad it's a school day. Joy and Brett would come help you get things settled in the right places."

"There'll be plenty to do on Saturday. I'll take all the help I can get unpacking dishes, books, bric-a-brac, et cetera. I've lived in this bare house almost a month. I'll be glad to have my familiar things," Gaye said wistfully.

Alberta cast Gaye a wary look. "You're not lifting anything heavier than Johnny, are you?"

"No, Doctor." Gaye gave her sister an affectionate smile. "What am I going to do about Jim and Johnny?"

"What do you want to do with them?"

"I want some space. Jim is here every morning. He can't seem to stay away from that baby. He comes by some evenings, too. Sometimes he brings food from the deli, or he brings groceries. My house has become his home away from home." Gaye closed her eyes briefly, then opened them and looked straight at Alberta. "Jim is ruthless when it comes to getting what he wants. He simply disregards any suggestions I make about getting Johnny situated in his home. He acts as if he'll be staying here from now on. Alberta, I'm not going to let that baby wiggle its way into my heart!"

Alberta was a calm woman with an infectious smile and boundless energy. She rinsed her glass at the kitchen sink and sat it in the dish drainer while trying to control the smile she couldn't resist.

"Let him baby-sit," she said when she turned, her face blank of expression. "When he arrives in the morning, be ready to go out. Take that time to shop. Go to the library or to the hairdresser. Jim is perfectly capable of looking after Johnny for a few hours."

"I hadn't thought of that. I do need to shop. I want to order draperies and look for bedroom curtains. I know what I want; it shouldn't take long to find them." Gaye finished her drink. "I wish you'd talk to him, Alberta. He isn't going to look for someone to take care of Johnny unless he's pushed. I need to have a job outside the home, where I can meet people and make new friends."

"He's dead set on you taking care of him. He told me he'd pay you whatever you earned as a teacher."

"Am I supposed to be so grateful for the job that I fall all over myself?" Gaye asked in brittle tones.

Alberta smiled at her unreasonable anger. "We don't want you to do that. Jim was livid when his daughter and her mother were so callously unconcerned about the baby." She leaned back against the kitchen counter and crossed her arms. "The girl came to him when she was almost five months pregnant. He scarcely knows her. She's totally spoiled and mature far beyond her years." She sighed pityingly. "Why wouldn't she be? Her mother lives in the fast lane, and the girl follows in her wake. She's probably been having sexual intercourse since she was fourteen or fifteen."

"That doesn't say much for the father. Why does he allow it?"

"There's nothing he can do. He and Marla were married for only a year or two. Her father is a judge, her two brothers own a prestigious law firm. The family inherited money. I know Jim has grieved for his daughter but wisely stays out of her life. He sees in this boy the family he's always wanted."

"Why would a girl from that background marry a blacksmith?"

Alberta laughed. "You can't deny that he's a ruggedly attractive, earthy man. He's enough to turn the head of any young woman, and some not quite so young, I might add."

"Not mine!" Gaye said staunchly. "I've had a taste of being under the thumb of an arrogant, domineering man. I won't get into that predicament again."

"Dennis Hutchinson was a creep, Gaye. But you're being unfair if you compare all men to him. I've known Jim casually for about ten years. He and my husband were friends. After Marshall died, there wasn't really a reason to see much of Jim. During the past few months I've gotten to know him again, and I like him. I admire him, too, even though some people think him a trifle strange."

"Strange? What do you mean?"

"He's unconventional, to say the least. Jim could care less what anyone thinks of him. He lives the way he wants to live—a simple, uncomplicated life. But don't let that fool you. He has several degrees, plus a master's in mining."

"What a waste. He has all that knowledge and is content being a blacksmith."

Alberta shrugged her shoulders. "You have a master's, and you're not moving any mountains." She smiled to take the edge off her words. "Knowledge is something that stays with you whether you use it or not, Gaye."

"That's true. But I intend to use mine. What do you think about a day-care center for preschoolers?"

"Is that what you want to do?"

"It's something to think about." Gaye walked to the door with her sister. "I don't want to do anything for a while. I need to get settled in here and get to feeling comfortable with myself before starting a new venture."

"Very wise, little sister. I'll try to stop by tomorrow. If not, I'll give you a call."

"I don't think I've ever told you how proud I am of you, Alberta." There was a husky quiver in Gaye's voice. "I want you to know that I love you and I'm so proud of my sister, the doctor. Mom and Dad were, too."

"C'mon...that's nice to hear, but you're going to make me all weepy and I've got to stop by the pharmacy on my way home. Doctors are supposed to be all cold-eyed and businesslike." She kissed Gaye on the cheek. "You're trying to ruin my image," she said accusingly and sniffed dramatically.

It was eight o'clock. Gaye had been up since six. Johnny had been bathed and fed and was asleep in his crib. The dented, dust-covered black truck came up the drive and parked beneath the portico. Gaye stood in the window and watched Jim, bareheaded and coatless as usual, get out of the truck. She opened the door.

"Mornin'."

Jim's dark eyes traveled swiftly over the soft rust-colored slacks and pullover sweater that allowed only a small bit of her white shirt to show at the neck. His eyes lingered on the billed cap in her hand.

"Going out?"

"Yes. I have a few errands to do while you're here. Johnny's asleep."

"I brought doughnuts to go with your coffee." He opened the sack and held it toward her.

"I've had breakfast."

"Chocolate covered. The kind you like."

Gaye avoided his dark probing eyes. Lord, but they were dark and deep. His presence filled the big, bare room with a masculine aura that engulfed her. He raised her chin with his fingers, forcing her to look at the warm skin of his throat, past his smiling mouth and into gleaming eyes that locked with hers. He smelled of clean, sun-dried clothes, aftershave and shampoo. His hair was still wet."

"I've had breakfast," she repeated and was surprised the words came out so easily.

"But not with me. Is the coffee ready?"

"I unplugged the coffee maker. You can make fresh." She moved away from his fingers and picked up her jacket. "I'd better get the show on the road. I've got a thousand and one things to do. Make yourself at home." She slipped out the door.

"Gaye!" Jim called from the steps, and she paused on her way to the carriage house where she kept her car. "What'll I do if he wakes up and cries?"

"Change his diaper and give him a bottle of water. Be sure you warm it."

"When will you be back?"

"I'm not sure. It may be around noon."

"Noon? Can't you take time out for a doughnut before you go?"

"I don't need a doughnut, Jim. I had a bran muffin and cereal. What are you trying to do to me? You've brought hamburgers, pizza, tacos, fried chicken and now doughnuts. In another week I'll be headed for Weight Watchers."

"Good Lord! The world won't come to an end if you gain a pound or two. I suppose you want to look like a string of spaghetti."

"That's better than an...apple dumpling."

Jim was still standing on the steps, the wind whipping his unruly hair back from his forehead, when she drove her five-year-old Buick from the garage. She was intensely aware of the dark, penetrating eyes that met hers briefly as she passed. It was a man-to-woman look, with not even a smile to disguise it. She waved and tried to quell the unexpected rush of feeling by concentrating on getting past the truck without hitting it. She reached the end of the drive and turned onto the street fronting the house. Damn him! Why was she thinking he looked lonely and disappointed standing there on her doorstep?

Gaye drove down to the shopping center, convinced that she had to do something quick about getting her life back on an even keel. She hadn't liked being married. It hadn't been the blissful existence she'd read about in novels. It had been...degrading! She had expected to make adjustments, but she hadn't expected for her lifestyle to be completely rearranged to accommodate Dennis's unorthodox one.

She had been reared gently and had had no recent familiarity with serious economic insecurity. Her parents had believed with old-fashioned fervor that the family should be the axis around which their lives revolved. Their marriage had been protected and preserved to provide a nurturing environment for their children.

Dennis believed in none of the things Gaye had been brought up to believe in. It was only after they were married that she discovered his true character. There would be no children, ever! The most important things in his life were money and sex. He constantly accused her of holding back on both of them.

He'd planned a courtship as romantic as any she had ever read about—dinner, moonlight, flowers, whispered words of love. He had scarcely touched her until the ceremony was over and he was sure his name was on her checking account. Then it was sex, not lovemaking, on his mind. Sex, when the mood struck, regardless of time or place. Gaye shivered. She'd never told anyone of the horrors of her wedding night. Thank God that time in her life was behind her. She turned the car into the parking lot at the shopping mall, determined to forget Dennis and, for the moment, Jim and Johnny.

Shopping, to Gaye, was a reassuring activity in the aftermath of the confrontation with Jim. She searched the department store for curtains and found exactly what she wanted. She ordered drapes from the same store and walked leisurely through the mall. She paused before the colorful window of a children's shop. She was unaware that her eyes slid past the frilly little-girls' dresses and on to the display for little boys. In the back of the window on a boy mannequin were soft blue denim overalls with a red bandanna handkerchief stitched to the back pocket. "You'll have to help me shop for pants and shirts," Jim had said. A smile curled her lips, and her legs moved of their own accord into the shop.

From the mall Gaye went to the supermarket. She'd brought a shopping list and pushed her cart down the aisles, stopping for dishwasher powder, all-purpose cleaner and plastic wrap. Absently she checked items from her list as she filled the cart, her mind still on the size six-months overalls she had bought. They'll be too large for him for some time, she mused. Will the blue stain on his diapers? Why had it been impossible for her to resist them?

She went through the checkout procedure, and the boy followed her to the car, pushing the cart that was loaded to the brim with sacks of groceries. She looked at her watch. It was only eleven o'clock. She had time for an early lunch or a trip to the library. Suddenly nothing was more important to her than to get back home. How easily the word "home" had come to her mind.

The mailman was coming down her drive when she turned into it. She waved, and then all thought of mail fled her mind when she realized the truck was no longer parked in the portico.

"Oh, no! He wouldn't!" she gasped aloud. "He wouldn't leave Johnny alone! Oh, my God—"

She braked the car and hurried to the door. It was locked, and her nervous fingers fumbled with the key. When she finally managed to get the door open, she left it ajar and ran through the empty rooms to the stairs. Her heart was pounding so hard, it caused a pain in her chest and a heavy throb in her throat. The house was deathly quiet. Fear moved her up the stairs. She couldn't seem to move her feet fast enough.

The crib was empty! Thank God he hadn't left him here alone! But...how dare he take that baby out in that rattletrap of a truck! Another thought, one that chased anger from her mind, hit her with the force of a hurricane. Something had happened and Jim had taken him to the hospital! Oh, Lordy! He may have choked, or stopped breathing. What if Jim fell with him coming down the stairs? Don't panic, Gaye. Don't panic.

Chapter Four

Gaye dialed the hospital number with trembling fingers.

"May I speak to Dr. Wright, please? This is her sister, Gaye Meiners."

"Dr. Wright has been delayed at her office. May I have her call you?"

"Yes...no! Can you tell me if you've admitted an...emergency?"

"I'll transfer you to Emergency."

Gaye repeated the question with sobs shaking her voice.

"Not since four a.m.," came the crisp reply.

"Thank you." Gaye leaned against the kitchen counter. Her knees were weak; she was frightened and exhausted. All she wanted in the world was to see Johnny and to know that he was all right. She dialed the number of her sister's office. "This is Gaye Meiners. May I speak to Dr. Wright?"

"Dr. Wright is with a patient, Ms. Meiners. May I have her call you?"

"Has Mr. Trumbull been in with his grandson?" Gaye held her breath while the receptionist asked the question of someone close by.

"No, he hasn't. Is something wrong, Ms. Meiners?"

"No." Relief forced a nervous laugh. "I was out shopping, and when I came home, Mr. Trumbull and the baby were gone. I'm sure they'll be back soon," she added hastily. "Don't bother Dr. Wright. I'm probably just...overreacting."

After she hung up the phone, sobs engulfed her. She had made an utter fool of herself! Johnny wasn't her baby. Jim had every right to take him wherever he wanted. She squeezed her eyes shut, but the tears came through her tight lids in an overwhelming flood, pouring down her cheeks and seeping between fingers she pressed over her face.

The past year had been a nightmare. Everything that could have possibly gone wrong had gone wrong. She had thought she'd marked the year off, sealed it and labeled it over. Each morning since leaving the hospital, she had emerged from her bed, checked her mental condition and assured herself she'd forged a splendid facade of outer serenity. She was pleased with it. She hadn't expected inner serenity. Not yet. That was a gift from heaven. Her security lay in the invincible conviction that God would bestow this gift upon her. Now she wasn't so sure. She feared there was a terrifying darkness deep within her and it would never set her free, never!

Gaye moved through the empty rooms and stood numbly by the window. The house was filled with a thick, eerie silence. Damn Jim Trumbull! He and Alberta had practically forced the baby on her. She sniffed back the tears and prayed the leaden weight in her stomach would dissolve. Maybe she wasn't being quite fair to claim they had *forced* her. She was an adult. She could have said a simple no. But she had assumed the responsibility, knowing that sooner or later it would lead to heartbreak. She hadn't expected it to happen so soon.

She looked at her watch. Ten minutes to twelve. Her breasts were full and aching. She paced and fumed. She'd tell Alberta today that this was *it.* She'd tell Jim to take his grandson and get the hell out of her life. She didn't need this anxiety, heartache and throbbing breasts! Gaye's mind spun in giddy circles and collided head-on with the awful truth.

"I don't want to be alone! I feel so damned lonely!" she wailed. Her distressful cry echoed throughout the empty house.

She leaned her forehead against the windowpane. There were two distinct channels of thought floating around in her mind, fighting for precedence. They zigzagged in and around each other. One was loneliness; the other was the conviction that she had made a dreadful mistake when she consented to take care of a baby temporarily. Now she felt as if everything had stopped but her, and she was whirling around and around in confusion, fear and despair.

The black truck coming up the drive chased all logical thought from her mind. Anger started deep down in the pit of her stomach and surged up. It swelled until she was angrier than she had ever been in her life. Her resentment, prodded by her aching breasts, was very real. At this moment she fervently wished she were uninhibited enough to shout every obscene word she had ever heard.

She hastily wiped the tears from her eyes and wondered vaguely if she looked the way she felt—as though she'd been used to wipe up the street.

Oh, Lordy! she thought. He may not have Johnny with him. He may have taken him somewhere and left him. He could be coming back to tell me he's made other arrangements!

The truck stopped behind the Buick. Gaye flung open the door. She could hear Johnny's muffled cries as soon as Jim got out of the car. He kicked the door shut and hurried up the steps to the door.

"You imbecile! You...fathead! Where in hell have you been with that baby? I've been worried half out of my mind!" Gaye's voice was deep, hoarse, and jerky and didn't at all sound like her own.

Jim came through the door without looking at her. He had a rigid expression on his face, and a muscle jumped nervously in his cheek.

Gaye snatched the baby from his arms, unaware that tears had started again and were running down her cheeks. She went quickly to the kitchen, the only place in the empty downstairs rooms where she could lay the baby down. On the way, she uncovered the red little face, and the baby's gasping, angry screams filled her ears.

"There, there, darling, don't cry. Oh, my goodness! You're wringing wet with sweat. What in the world was he trying to do to you? The idiot has wrapped you in *four* wool blankets! Shhh..." She placed the baby on the island counter and quickly peeled the blankets from him. "Oh, baby...you're soaking wet! Phew! And not only wet! It's no wonder you're so unhappy. It's all up your back!" She glanced over her shoulder. "Don't just stand there," she snapped. "Get me a wet washcloth, a diaper and a dry gown."

"He's hungry."

"I know he's hungry, dammit! But he can't eat in this mess!" She shouted to be sure she was heard over the baby's angry protests. "Shhh...darling. I know you're hot and hungry and wet. You'll be all comfy in a minute." Gaye stood back and peeled off her own sweater. She had forgotten she had it on, and trickles of moisture were sliding down between her breasts.

She had stripped the baby and wiped his little bottom on his wet gown by the time Jim returned. She took the warm wet cloth and finished the sponging, then patted him dry and dressed him, completely ignoring Jim, who stood at her elbow.

"What shall I do with these?" Jim wrapped the soiled diaper and gown in the blankets.

Gaye resisted the temptation to tell him. Instead she said, "Put them on the washer, then go away." Anger was still in her voice. She wrapped Johnny in a light blanket and went to the rocking chair in the breakfast room. With her back to the kitchen, she unbuttoned her shirt and put him to her breast. His cries ceased the instant his hungry little mouth grasped her nipple, and he began to nurse vigorously.

Gaye pulled the edge of the blanket up and over her breast and the baby's face. She was dead tired, both physically and mentally. Her emotions were so strung out she felt like a limp rag, and her shoulders sagged in spite of her efforts to hold them straight.

"Gaye..."

"Go away, Jim. Please give me a few minutes to get myself together." She clenched her jaw as her voice lashed out.

"I'm sorry you were worried."

"Worried? You scared the living hell out of me."

"I took him out to my mother's." He came silently to the side of the chair and hunkered down.

"You could have told me you were going."

"I didn't decide to go until after you left."

"I called the hospital."

"You thought...?"

"And Alberta."

"Oh, God! I'm sorry."

"He was too hot. He could get pneumonia."

"My mother said to wrap him up good and it wouldn't hurt him to take him out."

"Babies have a lot of body heat. Why couldn't your mother come here to see him? He's only seven weeks old, for chrissake."

"He didn't start crying until we were on our way back."

"He was hot, hungry and wet. Didn't you take an extra diaper?"

"I didn't think about it."

Gaye looked into dark, somber eyes, then down to the large brown hand on the arm of the chair. It moved up and down as she rocked, but it grasped the smooth, flat surface tightly, betraying his tension. The deep black eyes never moved from her face. He knelt there, strangely quiet. Gaye felt her pulses warm as she realized their intimate position with the nursing baby between them. He seemed not in the least embarrassed, but the force of her own emotions deepened the color in her cheeks and widened her eyes.

"You have lovely eyes," he murmured.

"Johnny goes on formula in a couple of weeks. We can't go on like this," she blurted. "You've got to find someone to take care of him."

"I thought it was settled that you'd look after him for the time being."

"Can't your mother...?"

"No. That's out of the question. My mother is very ill. That's why I took MacDougle to her."

"I'm sorry. But...surely you have someone. You can hire a nurse from the hospital."

"They wouldn't have the personal interest in him that you have. But if I can't persuade you to keep him, I'll have to do that, or place him in a foster home for the time being, because I'm going away for a while."

"How long will you be gone?"

"I'm not sure—two weeks to a month."

There was a comfortable silence as they shared their concern for the small life between them. Jim continued to gaze at her. His hand lifted, and his fingers lightly stroked the smooth flesh of her forearm almost absently.

"Keep him, Gaye. You know him better than anyone. I won't worry about him as long as he's with you."

Her mind responded to the persuasion of his quiet, seductive voice. The nearness of him was something she hadn't anticipated as being disturbing. She could feel every nerve in her body respond to the pleading in his dark eyes.

"Don't do this to me, Jim." She squeezed her eyes tightly shut as tears welled. Her heart swelled, and she struggled to keep the sobs from breaking loose. "If I keep him much longer, I may not be able to give him up."

"You won't have to give him up. Share him with me. You love him already. Don't you feel, just a little, like he's yours? You've nursed him, made it possible for him to grow strong. He needs your care, needs to feel he's loved and wanted."

"It isn't my responsibility to supply that. How can you ask this of me? In a few weeks, months, years, you may marry again and you'll want him with you. Or his mother may come back. I can give him up much more easily now than I'll be able to later on. I've got to get my head screwed back on right, set some goals for myself, get on with my life."

"What kind of goals?"

What did she want? Gaye's brain pounded with a million thoughts. Somewhere deep inside of her a yearning was screaming to be heard. Just for a moment, she speculated on how it would be if Jim were her husband, Johnny their baby, and he was whispering words of love and meaning them. She'd always had the craving for the kind of love and companionship shared by her parents. She realized that was the reason she had been so susceptible to Dennis. She had believed him because she'd wanted to believe him. She'd allowed him to charm her with promises and bits of flattery. Too much had happened to her to allow a man to work his wiles on her again. Besides, was that what she wanted, to be tied heart and soul to a man for the rest of her life, regardless of his feelings for her? She'd realized on her wedding night that she didn't love Dennis. But what if she had loved him? Could she have walked away from the marriage regardless?

"What am I aiming for?" She repeated Jim's question. "I guess I want to be...happy."

"What would it take to make you happy?"

"I'd have to give it some thought," she said evasively.

"Do you want to marry again and have a family?"

Gaye was shocked by the intensity of his words as well as by his tone. She turned her gaze away from him, miserably conscious of his eyes on her and the fingers that stroked her arm. It seemed to her that the fine hairs on her skin rose to meet his rough touch. All the emotional bruising of the day seemed to melt and flow away through the fingertips of her arm.

"I've no desire to marry again," she said tiredly.

"What did that man do to you, Gaye? Did he mistreat you?"

"He didn't beat me, if that's what you mean." Her thoughts whipped back to her wedding day. She hadn't imagined her life would be anything but beautiful from then on. How quickly she had dropped from that blissful cloud to the hard, cold reality of living with a man who used every opportunity to erode her sense of self-worth and who'd used her as an instrument of his lust.

"What happened to your marriage?" she asked shakily.

"Marla and I weren't suited. Our marriage was a mistake."

"So was mine. It's in the past. I don't want to talk or think about it." His fingers were curled around her forearm. She felt the same connecting warmth she had felt once before when he held her arm.

"The court gave me custody of MacDougle, but I'd have a stronger hold on him if he had a mother."

"He's got a mother."

"Crissy gave birth to him, but as you know, there's more to being a mother than giving birth. I'm thinking of the future. There's always the possibility that Marla and Crissy might decide it would be to their advantage to have custody of him. I want my hold on him to be absolute. That may depend on the type of home I provide for him."

"I can't help you with that."

"You can. You can marry me, and we can make a home for him together." Searing black eyes held hers.

Gaye stared at him, pondering her unease. He was clearly an intelligent man; his eyes absorbed everything they pierced, his mind was quick and alert. He was starkly physical. She couldn't deny that her heart fluttered more quickly in his presence. That's a natural reaction, she reasoned. He is an attractive man, and despite my nightmare of a marriage, I'm not an emotional cripple. Nooo...her pride screamed. I won't jump back into what I just crawled out of!

"I won't do that and you know it," she said with cool indifference.

"You could live here with MacDougle. I wouldn't move in."

"That makes absolutely no difference. I won't do it."

"You could do worse." He grinned with a devastating charm that made his rough features beguiling.

What am I doing here? she thought with a pang of fear. Here I sit, nursing another woman's child, talking to a man I've known less than two months about marriage! If I were smart I'd steer clear of both him and his grandson.

Jim sat down on the floor and leaned back against the wall, his long legs extended and crossed. "You're not very good for my ego." He rubbed his firm chin as if he were in deep contemplation. "I guess I'm getting rusty at this courtin' business."

Gaye smiled, relaxed her guard for a moment, and admitted he was intriguingly attractive. Despite his easy banter, she sensed a tension in him.

"You may be borrowing trouble. Surely the court wouldn't give Mac—give Johnny to your daughter and your wife after they left him in your care."

"Correction. Marla is my *ex-wife*. My God! It's been so long I can't even imagine being married to her," he said bluntly with a grimace. "And I think the appropriate word would be *abandon*, not *leave in my care*. Why would they want him back? Who knows? In the crowd they run with, it may become chic to have an illegitimate child. And there's always the possibility he may inherit. As his guardian, they would have control of the funds until he's of age."

"Will Marla's family try and take him away from you?"

"They may not even know about him. But if they do, I don't think the old man would cause trouble after he knows the facts. I wouldn't trust his sons as far as I could toss a piano."

"Poor little boy. There's no one to love him." Gaye was looking at Jim as she spoke and then realized he might take her words to mean a softening in her refusal to marry him. Her lashes dropped quickly, rich crescents of darkness against her white cheeks. She'd caught something remarkable in the jet black eyes that hadn't been there before. It had been tenderness but a tenderness edged with pain and anxiety.

Under the cover of the blanket, she shifted the sleeping child and buttoned her shirt. Jim got to his feet and stood waiting until she uncovered the baby's face. He reached for him with confident hands and cradled him in his arms.

Gaye watched him leave the room, and then her glance settled on the dusty boots he'd left beside her chair. She foolishly accepted the fact that she had never felt more natural with a man, more comfortable, more female, more excitingly stimulated. Was she falling a little in love with him, or was she just thirsty for all the wonderful raw and masculine enticement he had to offer?

On Friday morning, Jim arrived at the house with the back of his truck loaded with neatly cut wood for the fireplace. He selected a location several yards from the back door, drove two steel posts into the ground and stacked the wood between them. Gaye was in the kitchen when she heard the ring of the hammer against steel. She knew better than to protest this generous gift; he would leave the firewood no matter what she said.

For the past several days their relationship had been a comfortable one. Gaye's intense nervousness had begun to dissipate as she realized she was in complete control of her life and that Jim couldn't demand anything from her that she wasn't willing to give. She felt it inevitable that they would eventually come together with a clash of wills, and she accepted this; the growing relationship between them was taking away the fear that she'd be unable to cope with the clash when it came.

Later, she meditatively watched him as he worked tirelessly arranging the furniture the men brought into the house from the moving van. He had told her with quiet concern she was not to lift or move even the smallest box, but was to sit in a chair beside the door and instruct the men where each piece of furniture was to be placed. Things seemed to fall magically into place under her supervision and the muscles of the dark giant of a man.

In less than four hours, the last of the furniture was placed on the rolled-out carpets, the last box in the kitchen for unpacking. The moving men picked up their packing pads, drew up the ramp and closed the yawning end of the truck. Gaye closed the door as they drove away and leaned her back against it.

"I knew my things would fit into this house perfectly. Oh, Jim! This is going to be a cozy home for all its size." Her eyes caught and held his. Then she looked about the room with smiling appreciation. Her braided rug fit into the space before the fireplace, the platform rocker and the reclining chair on each side. The large winged sofa served as a room divider. "I can hardly wait to build a fire in the fireplace."

"Can you wait until after lunch?"

"I'm too excited to eat."

"MacDougle isn't. He wants his vittles."

"That boy would put a piglet to shame! I swear he's got a built-in clock. He gets formula this noon." Gaye flashed Jim a smile. "Bring him down while I warm it. And, Jim, when you change his diaper, don't drop it on the floor like you did the last time. Put it in the bucket and close the lid."

"Do this, do that," he grumbled. His dark eyes were alight with humor, and they held hers for a long moment.

"And when you pin the diaper, put your fingers between Johnny and the cloth so if you're clumsy, you'll only hurt yourself," she added, her eyes riddled with deviltry. She felt a thrill of excitement race through her in that moment that their eyes met. There was a certain knowledge of each other, a rapport.

"Yes, ma'am," he said meekly. "Bossy dame doesn't think I know anything," he grumbled to himself and took the stairs two at a time.

The excitement stayed with Gaye while they unpacked the boxes and placed dishes and utensils in the cabinets. Jim carried out the packing boxes and returned to find her standing in the middle of the kitchen with a shiny copper teakettle in her hand.

"I can't decide whether to sit this on the end of the snack bar or on the table in the breakfast room."

"How about on the stove?"

"Filled with chrysanthemums?"

"Flowers? I thought it was used to boil water."

"It used to be, but I had it stripped and polished. When I found it at a garage sale it was nickel plated and all black on the bottom. I think I'll put it on the table and fill it with yellow chrysanthemums."

"It's dented, and part of the handle is burned off."

"Of course. Otherwise, how would I know it's old?" She reached into a drawer for a pair of scissors.

He caught her wrist in his hand and gently removed the scissors with his other one. "I'll get them. They're those yellow things alongside the carriage house. Right?" His hand slid down her wrist and engulfed hers.

"I can do it." Her eyes were intent on his straight nose, wide-set eyes and square jaw.

"Sure you can. I've got the feeling you can do anything you set your mind to, Mama Bear."

"Mama Bear!" Her eyes twinkled at him through a forest of thick lashes. "No one's ever called me a bear. A mouse, maybe, but not a bear!" She laughed with languid pleasure. It had been a long time since she'd felt entirely unrestricted, so long since she'd been so completely at ease with a man. She reveled in the happiness the day had given her.

"A *little* mama bear?" he said hopefully. He placed the fist that held the scissors on the top of her head and gently brought it even with his shoulder.

"But I don't have my shoes on, and you have on those darned old boots!" she protested.

"Am I going to have to carry the firewood in my stocking feet?" He gently nudged her chin with the hand holding hers.

"Nooo...I'll put up with the boots as long as you continue to work," she said with false hauteur.

"The woman is a slave driver," he said as if talking to himself. "Small and pretty as a little brown wren, cuddly as a baby bear, but cunning as a fox and as determined as a beaver."

"Thanks a lot, Grandpa Bear!"

"Grandpa? My God! That's right, isn't it? Oh, well, Grandpa is the king of the jungle, you know." His dark eyes held such a teasing, humorous light that his whole face was transformed into a much younger version of the unsmiling man she had first seen standing in the hospital doorway.

"Nooo...I didn't know." Gaye was suddenly breathless. "Then he'd better find his own jungle to roar in."

"He's found it." He bent and kissed her on the nose, as if to punctuate the remark.

Gaye's eyes searched his back as he went to the door. He's excessively tall, she thought. He must be six three or six four. He has extremely broad shoulders for a man with such a trim waistline. I wonder what he does to keep so fit. He's a grandfather! He looks thirty-five, but he's got to be at least forty. Could a man of forty have such a startlingly powerful physique? His movement was so assured, as if he were king of all he surveyed. God help anyone who sought to take something from him!

A spate of nervousness struck Gaye, and she felt almost giddy. She'd acted like a stupid schoolgirl. The thought hit her like a dash of cold water. He had reacted to her teasing as any man would under similar circumstances. She sat the teakettle on the table and hurried up the stairs on the pretext of looking in on Johnny, but—she admitted to herself as she stood before the bathroom mirror—it was really to get her head out of the clouds before she made a fool of herself.

When Gaye came downstairs, Jim was checking the chimney to be sure it was clear of birds' nests and other debris before he built a fire in the fireplace. "I put the flowers in the sink," he said. "Am I invited to stay for dinner?" He lifted a log from the copper boiler. "This thing doesn't hold very much," he muttered.

"No, but you've got to admit it looks nice." Darkness had come swiftly, and Gaye went about the room turning on the lamps. "I like my antiques to be useful. I didn't have a fireplace back home, so I turned the boiler upside down and used it as an end table beside a chair. I think it makes a better wood container. I've got an old bellows and an iron ladle packed away somewhere," she announced proudly. "I'm going to put my coffee grinder in the kitchen, and my little black iron hand pump in the dry sink in the hallway. And...of course you can stay for dinner. I couldn't very well throw you out after all the work you've done."

Jim was replacing the screen after adding another log to the blaze on the grate. "Come here and I'll show you how to work the damper so you won't fill the place with smoke."

Gaye moved over beside him. He stepped behind her, and it seemed to her his large body closed around her. She could feel his chin on the top of her head, stirring her hair, and when he reached around her, her shoulder was firmly pressed against his chest. She prayed he didn't know how breathless she was and how fast her pulse was racing.

"This brass lever controls the amount of air that goes

up the chimney. Turn it to the left and it closes. See how the smoke is coming out into the room? Turn it to the right and the draft takes the smoke up the chimney." His other hand was firmly attached to her upper arm. He loosened it now, and it played up and down her arm from shoulder to elbow. "Are you paying attention?" His lips were close to her ear. Was that his nose burrowing into her hair?

"Of course I'm paying attention." She tried to move away.

"Lesson isn't over." His hand tightened and pulled her back against him. "If you open the damper too wide, all the heat goes up the chimney. The trick is to find a happy medium. Turn the lever all the way to the right, then back just enough so that the smoke goes up and out. Do you get the picture?"

Gaye knew he was looking at her. His hand had stilled on her arm. "Of course I get the picture. I'm no dummy!"

"What's the difference between a dummy and a doll?" he asked softly. His lips were so close to her ear she could feel the warmth of his breath.

"No difference. They both have a head full of sawdust." Her face was so hot it felt scorched. She edged away from him, and he let her go. "You'll have to excuse me. If I'm going to have a guest for dinner, I'd better get with it."

"Who'll be here besides me?" He was standing with his hands in his back pockets. With his shoulders thrown back, the buttons on his shirt strained to hold it together. Once again he looked like the rough, wild man who had demanded, "Where's the boy? He's not in the crib!" Gaye felt the heat of his slanting dark eyes, but it wasn't fear she felt this time. It was an awareness of herself as a woman. She'd never felt it quite so acutely before.

"No one, unless Alberta or Candy come by."

"Good. Let's hope they visit another time. Do you like spaghetti?"

"Love it."

"Okay!" He grinned. "I'll take about an hour. Get yourself upstairs. Take a bath or something. Rest. You've put in a long day. What does MacDougle get tonight?"

Gaye felt another flash of heat on her face. "Ah...not formula."

"Good. That'll keep you out of the kitchen."

"I don't have to be hit over the head to know when I'm not wanted!" She sniffed dramatically.

"How about when you're...wanted?"

There was a flash of pain in her eyes before her lids slipped over them like obedient servants. "Then it may be necessary," she murmured and left the room.

Chapter Five

Gaye took a quick bath. Somehow she couldn't bring herself to linger in the warm suds with Jim in the house. She pulled on a peach-colored velour shirt and pants. It was a well-worn, comfortable outfit. It wouldn't do to wear anything too fancy. Jim might get the idea this was a special occasion. Oh, for goodness' sake! This was a special occasion. It was the first night in her new home with all her familiar things. She brushed her hair with a swift half-angry motion and tried to keep her mind off the big man who had come barnstorming into her life.

She fed the baby and dressed him for bed. This part of her life was very satisfying. She carried him to her bedroom, and laid him on the bed, bouncing him gently, smiling at the cooing noises he made.

"My, my! You are growing," she crooned. "You're going to be as big as your grandpa someday." She ran her fingers over the fine dark hair. The baby spit and cooed and tried to catch her fingers. "Oh, darling! I don't know if I could bear to let you go now." She picked up the chubby infant and held him to her shoulder. "You can come downstairs tonight. You don't have to stay up here all by yourself when you're so wide awake."

It was comforting to hold the small, warm body. Gaye held him to her like a shield and went down the stairs and into the quiet living room. She sat down on the couch and placed Johnny on his back on her thighs. She caught his flaying hands in hers and patted them together while his tiny feet beat a tattoo against her stomach. She tuned the sounds coming from the kitchen out of her mind and gave herself up to the enjoyment of playing with the baby.

"You rascal, you! You're going to outgrow this sleeper before I know it." She stroked his cheek with her finger, and the baby tried to catch it in his mouth. Gaye laughed with delight. "Oh, no, you don't! You've had your dinner. You don't get another ounce of milk until midnight, and in a few weeks you're going to have to sleep through the night. The only reason you're getting extra now is because you got off to a bad start."

"He's growing, isn't he?" Jim had come silently into the room from behind her and bent to place his head close to hers.

"Of course. He's...perfect!"

"Do you think he'll be big, like me?" He reached over the back of the sofa and tickled the baby's stomach with gentle fingers. This seemed to amuse Johnny, and he kicked his feet and waved his arms.

"You'll have to wait until he's two years old to find out how tall he's going to be. He should be half as tall as he'll be full-grown.'' Gaye felt awkward and confused with Jim's cheek so close to hers.

''Is that right? Hmm...that means he'll be six feet tall if he's three feet tall at age two. You've got some growing to do, MacDougle.''

His other arm reached around Gaye, and he caught the tiny kicking feet in his hands. Gaye was painfully aware of being encased within his arms and that his cheek was firmly pressed to hers. A slow, dangerous fire began to seep upward from her toes, and she strove to maintain her quiet composure.

''He's doing the best he can.'' She could feel the movement of her jaw against his.

''With your help.''

He was turning his lips toward her cheek! ''I'd better...take him upstairs.''

''Why can't he stay down here with us?'' His nose was firmly against the hollow of her cheek. ''Am I making you nervous?''

''Nooo...'' She seemed to have two spare hands she didn't know what to do with.

''Well, you're making me nervous—or something. I've got a powerful urge to kiss you. You smell clean and fresh, not all smelly like a cosmetic counter in a department store.''

''I wear unscented cosmetics.'' She said it defensively. She gazed at the large dark hands holding the baby's feet. The backs and the long fingers were covered with fine black hair. They were so close the knuckles grazed her breast.

''You're a rare treasure.'' The whispered words came on a sigh. He nestled his cheek closer to hers, tipped his face and blew down her neck. ''That isn't what I want to do, but it'll have to do—for now.''

"Jim..."

"Don't sputter. I want to enjoy this. You're nice to hold. Soft...well-rounded—"

"Thanks a lot." She tried for flippancy and failed miserably. "It takes time to get back in shape."

"I like your shape. Are you trying to lose weight?"

"Of course! No woman wants to be...soft and well-rounded."

"Why not? What's wrong with soft and well-rounded? I want you to stay the way you are." His hands left the baby's feet, crossed each other and moved to her rib cage. "Why do you want to lose weight? Shall I tell you a secret?" His nose nuzzled the hair back from her ear, and warm lips caressed the lobe. "You look and feel like every sweet dream I've ever had all rolled up in one. No, no...don't struggle. I'm not going to rush the fence." His arms loosened, and his hands came up to cup her head. "You are one sweet little thing," he muttered, half to himself.

Gaye quivered at the singing tension between them. Her heart beat wildly and a shudder rippled under her skin as she tried to retain her composure. She slid her hands under the baby and raised him to her shoulder.

"Let me take him." Jim was in front of her. His large hands moved over hers as he lifted Johnny from her arms. Her gaze lifted involuntarily to his. There was a mesmeric fascination in the soft, sweet smile that curved his lips and was reflected in his eyes. Her own eyes mirrored her confusion. His head tilted slightly. "Don't worry about it. It'll all sort out."

Gaye had never felt less articulate in her life. Jim held Johnny cradled in one arm. He extended a hand to her, and she put one of hers into it. He tugged gently and she was standing beside him. The lamplight shone on the square-jawed, craggy face tilted toward the baby in his arms. He placed a tender kiss on the tiny forehead, and a small light exploded in Gaye's heart. Her gaze slid away, but not before he glimpsed the wretched loneliness in her soft brown eyes.

"Gaye..." His arm went around her, and he pulled her close to his side. "You can have more babies. You and I could give John brothers and sisters."

"Nooo..."

"You could have my baby, Gaye." The softness of his voice turned her to butter.

She broke away from him and walked rapidly to the kitchen. Doubtless Jim would make beautiful, strong children. She was acutely aware that when he touched her, looked at her, her nerves danced along the entire length of her spine. With her natural nurturing instincts, the offer was tempting. She would love to have another baby—Jim's baby—but she wasn't sure she would survive the explosion of more fragmented dreams.

"Shall I put MacDougle in the laundry basket?" The voice in the doorway was friendly, but impersonal.

"Sure. Why not?" Gaye washed her hands at the sink in order to give herself time to get her trembling mouth under control. "I'll get it. It's in the hall. You have to admit it's handy, and it isn't a laundry basket. It's a bassinet." Her voice was calm and disguised her nervousness beautifully. It was a small triumph, and she clung to it.

The meal went smoothly enough despite Gaye's initial doubts. Jim seemed to be superbly at ease, making outrageous remarks about how handsome and smart Johnny was and how, of course, he got it all from his grandpa. It was difficult for Gaye to be casual at first. She felt awkward and ill at ease, but her composure was marble firm, and eventually the meal was over and the dishwasher loaded.

"You're a very good cook," she remarked and hung the towel on the rack after wiping the counter.

"I like to cook. Does that surprise you?"

"Well...yes."

"I have all sorts of hidden talents. I can sew on a button with the best of them."

"Brag, brag, brag!"

His smile changed to a roguish grin. "I don't claim to be humble."

"That, I believe!" She put her hands beneath the sleeping baby and lifted him to her shoulder. "Your grandpa is a braggart, Johnny. Let's hope you didn't inherit the trait."

Laughing, he went to her. "I'll take him to bed." His big, warm hands moved over hers, and he took the child from her arms with gentle sweetness. "C'mon. Let's tuck our boy in for the night."

Gaye took a deep breath to steady the tremor that ran through her. You're ruining my nervous system, she admonished silently as she climbed the stairs beside him.

She waited for him in the doorway and watched as he turned his grandson over on his stomach and covered him with the light blanket that lay at the foot of the bed. His fingers stayed for just an instant on the dark head, and then he glanced around the room.

"This is just the type of home I had in mind for him," he said absently.

Gaye's not-quite-steady fingers found the switch beside the door and dimmed the light.

They went silently down the stairs. At the bottom, Jim looked up at them. "I still think we need a tread on those steps. It'll be safer."

His use of the word "we" almost went unnoticed. Gaye shook herself into alertness. "I plan to have them carpeted."

"When?"

"Soon."

"While I'm gone?"

Gaye lifted her shoulders in a shrug and went into the living room. She sat down on the couch and clasped her hands tightly together. Things were getting out of hand. This was her house! He was taking altogether too much interest in it, and she should say so.

"Jim..."

"I'll be gone for two or three weeks."

The statement made her draw in her breath. He had told her days ago that he would be away for several weeks. At the time, she had thought she would be relieved to have him out from underfoot for a while. When had things changed? Two or three weeks suddenly seemed like a lifetime. Oh, for goodness' sake! What was the matter with her?

Jim seated himself carefully beside her. She sat hunched over, her hands on her knees. He touched the hair resting on her shoulder, then traced a finger down over her rounded back.

"Sit back and relax. I couldn't get into those rape-proof pants of yours with a can opener."

Her head jerked around to see the mischief dancing in his dark eyes. "You like to shock me!" she accused, but she couldn't keep the smile out of her voice.

His hand at her waist tightened and pulled until her shoulder was firmly wedged beneath his arm and her thigh was alongside his. He rested his head on the back of the couch and stretched his long legs out in front of him.

"Ahhh...this is nice." His hand cupped her cheek and forced her head to his shoulder. "Be still," he said when she lifted her head to look at his face. He was watching her from beneath lowered lids, his mouth curved in a satisfied smile. "You're a very restful woman when you let down your guard. Let's just sit here and look at the fire and not borrow trouble. Hummm?"

"You shouldn't...I'm not going to..."

She could feel his laugh against the breast that was pressed to his chest. "You're not going to...what? Let me stay the night?"

"Absolutely not!"

He laughed again. "We're not quite ready for that, but we may be by the time I get back."

"Jim, don't talk like that!" She tried to move away, but his arms closed about her.

"Why not? I want to go to bed with you. I think you want it too."

"You're crude!"

"You said that before. I'm honest. I don't know anything about this courting business, and I'm too old to learn. I don't know anything about hedging and maneuvering and playing games. I want you, and I'll do everything I can to get you. We're comfortable together, we like many of the same things and we have MacDougle."

"You don't know what I like," she said heatedly. "I don't know anything about you at all! I don't know where you live or how you live. I know nothing of your values. You're taking altogether too much for granted."

"Be truthful. Aren't you just a little bit attracted to me?"

Her face turned crimson. "Why...you conceited oaf, you—"

"Don't be embarrassed. Answer my question." His fingers tilted her flushed face up to his. "You better answer or I'll have to kiss you to prove it to you. On second thought..."

His hand slipped to her throat, then moved to the back of her neck. He kissed her without passion on her soft mouth, almost as if comforting a child.

Gaye pulled away in confusion, dismayed by the shafts of pleasure his lips sent along her spine. He pulled her back to him and claimed her lips again. The pressure of his mouth hardened—seeking, demanding, willing her to recognize her own need. His tongue stroked her lips, and she allowed it to enter her mouth. Her breathing became erratic as a fire of feverish longing ignited within her. Her voice was barely audible. "Jim..."

"It's all right, sweetheart..." He was kissing her trembling mouth with incredible gentleness. He kissed her eyes, tracing the outline with sensual, delicate caresses. His kisses moved slowly down her cheek to the corner of her mouth, his tongue moist and probing. Her hand had found its way to the back of his neck, and her fingers buried themselves in the unruly dark hair. She was swimming in a haze, aware only that her body was pressed tightly against his, his mouth warm and tantalizing against her skin.

Gaye's breath caught in a sob and she felt his hand slide up under her velour top and his rough palm caress her naked skin. Shock waves of desire she had thought never to feel again hardened her nipples and twisted her belly. The heavy throb within her caused her to open her eyes and look into his. His eyes drank in every detail of her face, from trembling, kiss-swollen lips to the dilated pupils of her velvet-soft eyes.

"It's all right, sweetheart..." he said again. His voice was a ragged whisper.

She took a shaky breath, her voice very low. "I suppose you'll say, 'I told you so.'" She pressed her face against his shoulder and closed her eyes tightly against the mocking words that were sure to come.

"Why would I say that? I think you turned the tables on me. You've got this old heart beating like a triphammer." His hand began to stroke her hair. "That first night when I saw you sitting in the chair holding MacDougle, it really shook my timber.

"Do you know what I thought? I thought, oh, my God! I've wasted twenty-five years of my life. I could have had a woman like her and MacDougle could be my son, instead of my son once removed. I'd never really thought about motherhood connected with an attractive woman. The women I've known have been sensuous and sexy. You're the softest, sweetest woman I've ever had the privilege to know." He sighed deeply. "Now that I've bared my feelings, are you going to laugh?"

"No! Why would I do that?" She echoed his words and turned her face into the curve of his neck.

He laughed and hugged her so tightly she thought her ribs would crack. "I'm trying to seduce you, you know."

"Maybe I'm trying to seduce you!" Gaye couldn't believe the words had come out of her mouth.

His laugh was a deafening roar in her ear. "Oh, good Lord! Nothing that good could be happening to me!"

He loosened his grip on her and they sat quietly. His fingers moved on her cheek, her ear. Absently, his other hand spread out across her rib cage. It was as if they had both run a hard race and it was time to relax and get their wind back.

"I'll try to get back in a couple of weeks," he said after a long silence.

"Where are you going?"

"I thought you'd never ask. I was afraid you didn't give a damn." He chuckled. "I'm going to Louisville."

"Louisville? That's not so far away. I thought you were leaving the country."

"Will you miss me?"

She hesitated. "What will you be doing up there?"

"Putting shoes on some of the most expensive feet in the world."

"Horseshoes?"

"No, silly girl. Patent leather pumps!"

"How was I to know? I've never known a blacksmith before."

"I'll have to bring you a copy of my book."

"*Your* book?"

"My book. *The Modern Farrier.*"

"You wrote it."

"Sure."

"It has your name on it?"

"Uh-huh."

"I'm impressed! I've never known an author, either."

"You're setting all kinds of records this evening."

She became acutely conscious of his fingertips moving across the skin of her rib cage, his thumb snugly beneath her breast. Exasperated with herself, yet enchanted by him she grasped his wrist in an effort to pull his hand from beneath her top.

"Don't, Jim. You mustn't..."

"Be still. We're doin' nothing immoral."

"Jim...I don't go in for..." she paused, swallowing.

"Casual affairs?" Jim interjected with a grin. "Oh,

honey—one has only to look at you to know that. I bet you were a virgin when you married.''

''What's so funny about that?'' she asked, bristling.

''I'm not laughing. I'm just wishing the hell it had been me. I envy the bastard. Was he gentle with you?'' His last words were an urgent whisper against her cheek.

''It's none of your business!'' She tried to slide away. His arms stopped her.

''Tell me about your marriage.''

''No! I don't want to talk about it.''

''Why did you leave him? You did leave him. No man in his right mind would leave you.''

''I left him because I was pregnant and I was afraid he'd...'' She pushed against him. ''Please let me go.''

''Let me hold you...please.'' His arms fell away from her. ''I'll never use my superior strength to force you. Come to me, Gaye. Let me hold you. It'll be comforting to both of us.''

For a bewildered moment the old pain and agony came boiling back with such power that she felt as though she was back in the house in Indiana and Dennis was hurling insults at her because she refused to go along with one of his outrageous ideas. There was an odd despair in her face. She closed her eyes, and when she opened them Jim was holding out his arms. She hesitated for an instant, then swayed toward him. He folded her to him with gentle urgency.

''Ahhh...babe...''

The tenderness in his voice brought a torrent of tears streaming from her eyes. Something burst within her with a rending force, and she clung to him, inundated by an overriding grief. She hid her face in the curve of his neck. His arms were a band of warmth around her. He didn't speak. His silence was a communication of its own. The loneliness, the awful hurt, the doubts about herself as a woman were washed away as she clung to him and sobbed. It seemed to her she purged herself of the hollow ache that had been a part of her for so long.

After a while she took a shaky breath, her voice very low. "I'm sorry."

"Don't be," he whispered. His fingers gently wiped away her tears. "I'm sorry for making you remember."

His words were fused with such regret and such misery that Gaye raised her head to look at him. His face was filled with tenderness. It wore the same expression it had earlier in the evening when he placed the kiss on Johnny's forehead.

She raised her fingers and stroked his cheek. He shuddered, his arms tightening around her as his mouth moved hungrily against hers. The kiss was long and deep. His tongue teased its way into her mouth with a loving, tender intimacy. He lifted his head, and his dark eyes searched hers quickly. Then he pressed her face to his shoulder and took a long, shaky breath. She could feel the expansion of his chest against her breast.

"Do you want to tell me about it?" he breathed out softly.

"I'd like to." Her fingers trembled as they clutched the front of his shirt.

With the paradoxical innocence of a child she snuggled against him, and words came tumbling out in sometimes long, sometimes short gasped sentences. Anguished, unconnected words that told of disillusionment and broken dreams and finally of fear for her unborn child. She told how her life had become an awful, torturous, never-ending nightmare until she left Indiana and came to Kentucky to be near her sister. She told of her despair when Mary Ann died and her feelings of guilt when she took another child to her breast. Finally she told of finding this house and the feeling of peace that was beginning to come into her life. Her voice trailed away. She was limp and pliable against him, burrowing against his hardness and strength, his presence healing the old wounds like a balm.

The silence that lingered was finally broken by a crude word that escaped Jim's tight lips. "I'd better never meet that sonofabitch!"

Her eyes shot up to his face. It was livid with anger. "Don't make me sorry I told you."

He looked back at her, the anger melting from his face. "I had to come along and complicate matters for you, didn't I?"

"Yes. But I don't know if it was all bad." She leaned her elbows on his chest and looked searchingly into his eyes. "You certainly gave me new things to think about." A wave of worry washed the smile from her face. "I'm beginning to love Johnny so much...I'm afraid. I don't want to go through all that again!"

Jim caught her upper arms and pulled her over onto his lap. He lifted her legs up onto the couch, and she found herself lying against him.

"I don't want you to be afraid of losing John. I want you to marry me. You can be John's legal mother. He needs you and you need him."

"No. I won't marry for those reasons."

"Couldn't you learn to love me?"

A firm hand lifted her face, and Gaye found herself staring up into dark, serious eyes. Oh, yes, her heart cried, but could you learn to love me?

"You don't *learn* to love a person, Jim. You either love them or you don't."

"You're wrong there, sweetheart. You've learned to love John."

"That's different."

"No, it isn't. Back in the olden days most marriages were arranged, and doubtless to say most of the couples loved each other after a while."

"How do you know? Maybe they hated each other, but had to stay together for the sake of the children. That's probably why so many men had mistresses." Her mouth clamped together stubbornly and she glared at him.

"And you wouldn't put up with that."

"Absolutely not!"

He laughed, clamped her tightly to his chest, rolled and stretched out on the couch. She lay on top of him. She struggled to get up. He slid one of his legs over hers.

"Jim!"

"Don't panic." He let her go and held both arms straight up. His leg released hers. "I just want to hold you, feel your weight on me. Relax...I won't hurt you. Damn, but you feel good!"

"We shouldn't..."

"Why not? We're adults."

"That has nothing to do with it. I'm not... We're not..."

"We're not...what?" He chuckled softly. His palm against her head brought her cheek to his chest. She could feel the strong vibrations of his powerful heart. "Have you always been so prim and proper? Don't answer! You have, and I'm glad. I intend to be a strong influence in your life. With me you'll be totally uninhibited." His hand made soothing circles between her shoulder blades. Her limp arm fell over the side of the couch, and a small sigh of pleasure bubbled from her lips.

"Do you like that?"

"Oh, yes!" This was dangerous! Later she'd be sorry. Gaye ignored the warning voice and gave herself up to the intoxicating sensation of being held gently, of not fearing his hands on her body. She felt the tightness of her muscles relax and the strain of long, fearful nights fade into nothingness.

His hand ran up and down her back, slowly stroking, caressing. She turned her face into his shirt, wishing she was brave enough to unbutton the cloth and press her lips to his warm flesh. He shifted his weight; her knees dropped to the couch, and she felt the hard knot of his aroused masculinity. It jarred her out of her lethargy. She put her palms against his chest to push herself away from him.

"Don't let it frighten you," he said softly. "I'm not going to throw you to the floor and have my way with you. Just say you want to leave my arms, and I'll let you go." Her face was so close to his they were almost breathing the same air, so close she couldn't look into his eyes. "I can't help wanting you, I can't help the way my body responds to you, but I can wait. Just don't keep me waiting too long."

It was absolutely unreal to her that she could be here with him like this and he could talk calmly about the hard object pressed to her lower abdomen.

"You can kiss me if you like." His husky voice came to her through the cloud of unreality, and she lifted her head higher to peer down into laughing dark eyes. Suddenly and unexpectedly, laughter burst from her lips. Her hands moved up to his cheeks, scraping across the day's growth of whiskers and into his thick unruly hair. Her fingers closed and pulled.

"Get up and get out of here, Jim Trumbull!" she said between gasps of laughter. "You're strange!"

"Good strange, or bad strange? Never mind. I don't think I want to know. I want my kiss or I'll dump you on the floor."

"I'll take you with me."

"I'll go for that, if you hit the floor first."

"Don't you wish!"

"Yes! Now stop foolin' around and kiss me. I've got four hours of work waiting for me at home."

Unembarrassed and unintimidated, she eased her mouth up to his. Her lips parted softly as they touched his chiseled mouth. She felt the hand on her back slide to her hips and press her down and upward. His mouth opened under hers. Although he made no attempt to control the kiss, she sensed his growing hunger. It was hotly exciting, unfamiliar. The power of it goaded her to kiss him with a fiery hunger of her own. Her tongue darted through his parted lips to taste.

It was so maddeningly good to have her way with him. She was riding the crest of the wildest, sweetest abandonment she had ever known. Her body moved slowly and sensuously against his, her hair fell down and curtained his face. Her kisses became wetly passionate. The need for air forced her to raise her head and press her cheek to his.

"Oh, God! You're sweet!" His voice was a breath in her ear. "I want to beg you not to stop, but I don't know if I can hold on to this control I was bragging about."

Gaye took a deep, trembling breath. "I'm sorry. It's not fair to you."

"Let me worry about that." His hands encased the

sides of her hips, and he lifted them over to rest on his thigh. "It won't always be like this. Sometime soon, I'm going to kiss you everywhere. I'm almost jealous of MacDougle having these." His palms slid up to the sides of her breasts and squeezed gently.

"Jim..." She was suddenly dumbfounded by what she had done.

"Don't be ashamed of wanting me." He lifted her off him and sat up. He smoothed the hair back from her eyes and tilted her chin so she had to look at him. "It's a hell of a time for me to be going away, but I'm already committed. Lady, we've got unfinished business to attend to when I get back. Right now I need a breath of cold air."

He got up and lifted his jacket from the doorknob on the front closet door. Gaye sat on the couch, her hands between her knees. Jim came to her and pulled her to her feet. She walked with him to the door.

"Be careful of that fireplace. Don't build up too big a blaze. And...check the doors—front, back and the basement door—every evening. It'll be a good idea, as long as you're here alone, to keep them locked during the day, too. I'll call you."

He looked at her for a long moment then bent his head and kissed her on the mouth. It was a soft but lingering kiss. When he lifted his head he checked the night lock on the door, then went out and closed it firmly behind him.

Gaye stood in the window and watched the truck lights disappear down the drive. A shudder of longing worked its way down her body. Two weeks seemed a lifetime away.

Chapter Six

The day after Jim left on his trip, Gaye called a local employment agency and asked them to find her a reliable baby-sitter. She was given the name of a woman who lived a block down the street from her. She talked to several of her references. Convinced she was a responsible person, she called and arranged for her to take care of Johnny for a few hours while she shopped for carpeting for the stairs and upper hall.

Lila Nichols was a divorcée in her late thirties. She had two school-age children and a strong desire to supplement her child-support checks by earning money at home. Gaye liked her immediately.

"Do you have time for coffee before you go?" Lila asked after she had deposited Johnny safely in a high crib, far out of reach of the two toddlers that were left in her care daily. "I get hungry for adult conversation."

Her eyes, a bright blue that complemented her dark red hair, were warm and friendly.

"I'd love some." Gaye sat her purse on the dining room table and took off the wool cap that covered her ears. "I wasn't sure I should take Johnny out today. Brrr..."

"Julia, darling, don't bother the lady's purse." Lila gave a two-year-old girl a windup toy to get her attention while she gently took the bag from her hands. "You know what? I think Sesame Street is on. You and Adam watch it while I visit with the lady. Later we'll get out the finger paints."

The kitchen was neat, but looked as well lived-in as the rest of the house. Lila poured coffee in mugs and sat them on the plastic placemats on the kitchen table.

"Everything in this house is geared for toddlers," she said with an apologetic laugh. She reached for a big round jar. "How about a chocolate chip cookie?"

"No, thank you. I'm fighting the battle of the bulge."

"You too?"

"I gained thirty pounds when my baby was born. I have about ten pounds to go to get back to what I weighed before."

"Only ten pounds! Right now I'm looking at thirteen!" Lila grimaced down at her jean-covered legs. "I've got drumstick thighs! I'm convinced that I'd have them if I weighed ninety pounds," she wailed.

"I've never been what you'd call pencil thin myself, but now I'm *too* soft and *too* well-rounded." The instant the words came out of her mouth she wished them back. The image of laughing black eyes beneath thick black brows danced behind lids she narrowed against the flood of memories. Damn you, Jim! Get out of my mind! "I'm determined to get rid of these pounds," she said firmly.

"I've joined an aerobic dance class. The first session is tomorrow night. Want to come?"

"I'd love to! But I'll have to find someone to stay with Johnny."

"Your husband won't do it, huh? Well, mine wouldn't either. He didn't want any of the responsibilities of fatherhood other than providing the kids a roof over their heads and something to eat. His all-consuming interest was climbing the corporate ladder. Oh, well..." She sighed. "It's his loss."

"I'm not married and Johnny isn't my baby."

"Oh, Lord. I put my foot in my mouth! I'm sorry."

"It does sound rather bizarre." Gaye frowned as her mind went back over the events of the past year.

It wasn't until she was in her car on her way to the shopping center that she wondered why she had suddenly confided in Lila. Of course, she hadn't told her the name of Johnny's grandfather or about the relationship that had developed between them. Nor had she told her anything about her own marriage. Only that the marriage hadn't worked out, that she and the man she had married were totally unsuited to each other. Jim was the only person to whom she had ever told the complete story of emotional abuse she had suffered during her marriage. She'd told him things she couldn't even tell Alberta.

Lila had spoken of her former husband with a sadness in her face. They had married young. She'd worked to put him through school. When success came and they could finally afford for her to quit work and have the children she'd always dreamed of having, she discovered he had outgrown her socially and she and the two boys were no longer important to him. He sent the child-support payments regularly, and the boys spent the weekend with him once a month.

Gaye had promised to see if Alberta's daughter, Joy, could baby-sit Johnny on the nights the dance class met. If so, she would call the city recreational department and join the class.

Thursday morning, as promised, the carpet layers came to carpet the stairway and upper hall. By afternoon Gaye wondered how she could have even considered leaving the floor bare. She brought Johnny downstairs, her stockinged feet loving the softness of her stair treads, and put him in the bassinet while she mixed formula, filled the sterilized bottles and stored them in the refrigerator.

"This time next week you'll be on your own, little man," she told the baby and was surprised by the twinge of regret she felt. "It's best for both of us." Johnny cooed and kicked his feet and looked up at her with his dark eyes. "I've got to wean you away from me in case someone else takes over your care. Oh, baby," Gaye moaned. "You're going to be the spitting image of your grandpa."

The doorbell chimed. "Oh, what now? Did the carpet layers leave a tool behind?" Johnny kicked his feet excitedly. "You like that sound? Well, we'd better go see who it is."

It was the postman with a registered letter. Gaye signed for it, then went back to the kitchen, a puzzled frown on her face.

"Who in the world is Simon, Simon and Litchfield?" Her heart fell to her toes when she read, Attorneys: Louisville, Kentucky. "What's Dennis up to now?" She reached for a paring knife and opened the envelope.

She sat for almost a full minute gaping at the check.

Five thousand dollars. She unfolded the paper and scanned the curt, businesslike letter. "Client, James M. Trumbull, has authorized payment for care of his grandson, John MacDougle Trumbull, for the past two months. Hereafter a check for two thousand dollars will be sent on the first of each month. Please present bills for clothing, food, etc., and they will be paid promptly."

Gaye sat staring at the letter and the check for a long while. It was all so impersonal! Jim had put their relationship neatly back into perspective. He was paying for the milk she had supplied from her body, paying for the loving care she had given his grandson. By waving the monthly checks in her face he obviously hoped that she wouldn't be tempted to go out and find a higher-paying job. Tears filled her eyes and rolled down her cheeks. Had he regretted his proposal of marriage and the check was a way to guarantee her services until he could make other arrangements? It was no wonder he hadn't called. He was waiting for her to be impressed by the size of the check!

As the afternoon wore on Gaye was tempted to phone Lila and cancel the dance class. But the more she thought about it, the more determined she was to get out of the house, meet people, and start building the new life she'd promised herself when she came to Kentucky. Johnny and his grandfather had been a detour, she stubbornly told herself, and desperately tried to believe it.

Later she was glad she'd gone to the class. She met two friends of Lila's, both married, childless, and working to make gigantic mortgage payments on their new homes and to pay for the second cars necessary to take them to their jobs. They both confessed they would be bored stiff spending their days with toddlers as Lila did.

The four agreed to meet at a restaurant for coffee before going home.

"What does your husband do?" Kathy, a dental assistant, asked Gaye after they had settled into a booth.

"I'm not married."

"Oh, oh! I guess I asked the wrong question."

Gaye laughed. "No. I'm divorced. I'm...baby-sitting for a friend. That's why I have to get home early—because my sitter is a schoolgirl and tomorrow's a school day."

"Baby-sitting? Oh, God! How awful! How do you stand it?"

"If I was cooped up with a baby every day, I'd go mad and bite myself!" added Lila's other friend.

"Beverly!" Lila exclaimed laughingly. "If I had to get dressed up every morning, five days a week, go to the office and put up with that ding-a-ling you put up with, I'd be so depressed I'd eat myself into a size forty!"

"You two girls need to meet some exciting men." Kathy had long blond hair and was continually throwing it back over her shoulder. "We've got one patient that *I'd* go for if I weren't so in love with Gary. Oh, my God! He's like a caveman, but absolutely gorgeous. I wouldn't mind being thrown over his shoulder and carried off to his cave! He's positively the most physical man I've ever met. He'd be just right for you, Lila. I think he needs a woman who would give it back to him tit for tat."

"I'm not interested unless he's rich and old—got one foot in the grave and the other on a banana peel," Lila said saucily. "My kids are the most important things in the world to me right now. Unless I can find a man who wants to marry all of us, I'll stay single. I've had one man who thought my kids were a bother. I won't ever put them in that position again. Right now they feel loved and wanted. The three of us are a family. That's the way I want to keep it."

Gaye silently applauded Lila. This was a woman with substance.

"Does that mean you won't even date?"

"Date? What's a date? Do you think a man would take me out to dinner and not expect to come back to my place and go to bed with me? Ha! It's happened three times in the last year."

"So? What do you do for sex?" Beverly asked bluntly.

"Without," Lila answered. "My God! The world doesn't revolve around sex. It's a good—no, a wonderful bonus with the right man, but sex for the sake of having sex is a bummer as far as I'm concerned."

"How about you, Gaye?" asked Kathy. "Gary's got a couple of single friends. None of them are anything compared to the hunk I was telling you about. But maybe you don't care for the rugged type."

"I don't mind if he has hair on his chest as long as he has brains in his head," Gaye said lightly.

"Doctor Barker says every female in town from sixteen to sixty has been after this guy for years. He was married once, but that was over a long time ago. I'd say he was fortyish. That's why I thought he'd be just right for Lila."

"Thanks a lot, pal! He'd be too set in his ways for me. Probably hates kids."

"He's got a grandchild. I heard him bragging about him every time the doctor took his hands out of his mouth." Kathy grinned. "Gary knows him. Do either of you want me to play matchmaker?"

Gaye suddenly wanted to be up and out of the booth. She didn't want to stay and hear what Lila had to say. Kathy was talking about Jim, there was no doubt about it! A surge of jealousy swept through her.

"Don't bother on my account," she said when Lila didn't answer. "I'm not ready to be a grandma."

"You might change your mind if you saw him." Kathy raised her brows.

"If he's that great, why not speak for yourself?" Beverly asked.

"I'd never cheat on Gary. But if I did..."

"I've got to be going. I told Joy I'd be back by nine o'clock, and it's almost that now." Gaye gathered up her purse and gloves. She picked up the check. "Treat's on me tonight."

"Okay. I'll treat next time," Beverly said and walked with her to the cashier. "Seriously, if you should want to go out some evening, give me a call. I can always dig up someone for a foursome."

"Thanks. I'll keep it in mind."

Gaye drove Lila to Lila's sister's house. She went inside and returned with two lively boys aged nine and eleven.

"Aunt Betty let us see an R-rated movie," the smaller of the two boys announced as soon as they got into the car.

"She what?" Lila almost shouted.

"You're nothing but a blabbermouth, Kyle," the older boy said with disgust. "It only had violence, Mom. No sex," he continued patiently. "And nothing we haven't seen before. We know the difference between the real thing and make-believe."

"I'm sure you do. But you know the rules and so does

Betty.'' Lila wrapped her arm about Kyle and pulled him close to her.

''Are you mad?''

''Nooo...but you know why we go over the TV schedule and mark off the ones you're not supposed to see. The rule applies at Aunt Betty's house as well.''

Gaye's respect and admiration for Lila were growing by the minute. She pulled into the driveway at Lila's and stopped behind her station wagon. Somehow, to Gaye, Lila seemed to have it all together. This was a woman with her feet flat on the ground. Despite a bad marriage, she'd hung in there and come out of it with all the things that mattered.

''Here's the key, Kurt. You boys go on in and start getting ready for bed. I'll be there in a minute.'' Lila gave her older son the key, and the boys got out of the car. ''I know you're in a hurry to get home, Gaye, but I wanted to say a couple of things. Don't let Kathy and Beverly pressure you into going out with any of their husbands' creepy friends if you really don't want to go. I've been down that road, and believe me, they wouldn't bring anyone around that was worth knowing.''

''Right now meeting a man is my lowest priority,'' Gaye assured her. ''Don't worry. I was burned once. I'm not planning on jumping back into the fire so quickly the next time.''

''My sentiments exactly. Not that I wouldn't like to meet the man of my dreams. But I'm about convinced he exists only in my dreams. This caveman Kathy was talking about is probably meaner than a junkyard dog. They usually are after they reach the far side of forty and are still single. If he'd wanted to share his life with a woman, he'd have found one by now.''

"Is there a chance you'll ever get back with your ex-husband?"

"None. I've already got two kids to raise. I'm not taking on an immature thirty-seven-year-old!" She swore softly under her breath. "I could kill that man for the way he's screwed up our lives. But enough of that, you want to get going. Shall I come by for you on Tuesday night?"

"I'll call you."

Gaye could hardly wait to get home. She wanted to be with Johnny in the quiet safety of her house. She had expected to spend a couple of hours without Jim occupying her every thought, but even during the class he was there—in the back of her mind.

Wouldn't the girls be surprised to know that she had been held in the arms of the "caveman" who was meaner than a junkyard dog! What would have happened if she had agreed to a blind date with the "hunk"? It would never have happened. Jim would never allow himself to be manipulated into that situation. Of that she was sure.

Joy, Alberta's teenage daughter, was firmly entrenched in a TV program and reluctantly got up when Gaye came into the house.

"Hi. Have a good time?" Joy asked.

"I guess so. How's Johnny?"

"I never heard a peep out of him. I went up and looked in on him, like you told me to do. He's sleepin' away."

"I'm sorry I'm later than I expected to be." Gaye took some bills from her purse. "Is this what you're usually paid?"

"More than." Joy was a tall girl. She wore straight-leg jeans and boots with heels. Gaye suspected it was the latest fashion at Roosevelt High. "Thanks! Mom said I wasn't to take anything, but..."

"If you don't take it, I can't ask you again."

"Well, as long as you put it that way." She stuffed the bills down in her jean pocket and reached for her down-filled jacket. "If Mom calls tell her I'm on my way. She can't get used to the idea that I'm sixteen and have my driver's license."

"Thanks, Joy. One of these nights, if I can get a sitter, I'll come to one of your basketball games. Alberta tells me you're the team's top scorer."

"Only for one game. Mom's exaggerating!"

"Moms are like that. I'll leave the porch light on until you get into your car. Night."

After Joy left, Gaye moved about the downstairs, checking the doors and turning off the lights. Her eyes sought the drawer where she had shoved the letter and the check that had arrived today. She was tempted to return the check to Simon, Simon and whatever his name was, but they were only acting on the behalf of their client. How in the world, she thought for the hundredth time since she'd received the check, could Jim afford to pay that kind of money for the care of his grandchild! Blacksmithing couldn't be that lucrative!

She looked in on Johnny. She should absolutely refuse to keep him any longer. She knew she should send him away. And she knew she wasn't going to. This baby had filled spaces in her heart that she hadn't known were empty. Spaces her own baby had not lived long enough to fill. Life would be so bleak without him! What would she have left? Nothing!

She undressed while the bathtub was filling and stared with unfocused eyes at the nude body reflected in the bathroom mirror. Six nights ago she had lain on the couch with Jim. Gooseflesh rippled over her arms and legs as she thought of lying on top of his hard, rugged body, her thighs hugged tightly by his, his masculine hardness pressed to her stomach. During that brief time she'd never been so uninhibited, so uncaring for anything except her pleasure and his. Why had it been so natural and easy for her to assert her female prerogative and kiss him like she did?

The shrill ring of the telephone cut into memories of laughter and gentleness, of lips, warm and sensitive, demanding that she share the kiss. Gaye hurried to the bedroom before the ringing could awaken Johnny. It had to be Alberta telling her Joy had arrived home safely.

"Hello." She stood at the bedside table, thankful for the warm, thick carpet beneath her bare feet.

"So you're home." The voice was oozing controlled patience.

"Jim?" Gaye's heart leaped into high gear and pinpricks traveled the length of her naked body.

"Who else? Why in the hell didn't you return my call? I've been waiting for over an hour."

An irrational anger surged through her. "I didn't know I was supposed to return your call. If I had known, I probably wouldn't have done it anyway."

"What the hell are you so mad about? And what are you doing at a dance class, for chrissake?"

"None of your business, Jim Trumbull, but I'll tell you anyway. I'm taking lessons to become a stripper. I hear there's an opening at Flo's. It won't pay two thousand a month, but I'll have my days free!"

"I don't need any of your smart-ass answers. Didn't the girl tell you I called?"

"No, she didn't."

"I called twice. She said she'd have you call the minute you got home. What are you doing?"

"I'm getting ready to take a bath. Oh, the water is still running!" She dropped the phone and ran down the hall to the bathroom. The water was going out the overflow. She turned off the faucets, grabbed her terry robe from the back of the door and hurried back to the phone. "I'm sorry. I forgot about my bathwater."

"How's MacDougle?"

"He's fine. He'll be completely on formula tomorrow."

"How do you feel about that?"

"Great. It's what I want for him. Which brings up another matter. I got a letter and a check today from your lawyers."

"I thought you'd gotten that weeks ago. Those procrastinating turkeys! Is that the first check you've received?"

"Yes!" she shouted. "And it's the last! Who do you think I am, Jim Trumbull? I volunteered to help you out until you could find a regular nursemaid, and I have no intention of taking that much money for caring for that child. You must think I'm a mercenary bitch!" She paused so she could catch her breath. "If you're so determined to pay that ridiculous salary, I know just the woman for you. She'd be perfect for Johnny. She's got two kids of her own, and she needs the money. As a matter of fact, she just might take you up on the same deal you offered me."

"Are you finished? It's a good thing I'm not there, sweetheart. I'd be tempted to turn you over my knee and pound your butt!"

"Ha! Just what I suspected. When things don't go

your way you get violent. I bet you really are meaner than...a junkyard dog!"

"What are you talking about? Why is your voice trembling? Are you naked and cold?"

"I'm not naked or cold. I'm mad."

"Oh, for God's sake! I'm the one who should be mad. I've been waiting by this phone and haven't had my dinner yet." His soft laugh was like a wind fanning her anger.

"I'm not at your beck and call just because I'm taking care of your grandson!"

"Leave MacDougle out of it. There's something special between you and me, and you know it. You still haven't told me what's got your back up."

"It's the money! Dammit! It's so much, it's...vulgar, insulting! You can't afford to pay that kind of money, and I'm wondering what you think you're going to get for it."

"Okay. Calm down. Look at it like this. How much would it cost for me to hire a cook, a cleaning lady, a nursemaid, practical nurse, chauffeur, teacher? Do you know how much it costs to hire an English nanny?"

"How would I know a thing like that?" She sat down on the edge of the bed because her knees were shaking.

"I didn't know, either, until I called London and asked."

"You what?"

"I called and found out. Let's forget about this for now. We'll talk about it when I get back. You haven't told me about the dance class. Who did you go with?"

"It's a belly-dance class for women who are *soft and well-rounded* and want to compete in the marketplace for eligible males!"

He laughed, and it was as if his breath was stirring

her hair. "You've no intention of letting go of that, have you? Who did you go with?"

"I haven't asked you who you were with this evening."

"Do you want to know? I don't mind telling you. She was a beautiful young thing with long graceful legs, soft brown eyes, a body and a scent that would drive a male wild. She was so busy switching her tail at one male I had a hard time getting on with what I was doing to her." He paused and waited for her to say something. There was silence. "Not funny?"

"Yes, it's funny. It's funny that you're still talking to me when a minute ago you were shouting for your dinner."

"I've missed you...and MacDougle." Silence. "Gaye...say something."

"Mac—Johnny is beginning to sleep through the night. I gave him a bottle at six. I'll wake him at ten and give him another. That should last him until morning."

"I wish he was still nursing. I'd have a tighter hold on you."

Gaye caught her breath sharply. "Alberta says he's doing fine."

"I know. I talked to her today. I wish I was there. Damn!"

"You'd better go eat your dinner."

"Did you put the car in the carriage house?"

"I parked by the drive. I think I'll have a yard light installed."

"Good idea. I'll take care of it when I get back."

"No, Jim..."

"How come you were so late? The girl said you'd be back by eight-thirty."

"I stopped for coffee with some women I met at the class."

"Who?"

"Have you had your teeth worked on lately?"

"Why do you want to know that?"

"I was just wondering. One of the women works for a dentist. She was talking about getting me a date with an interesting man. She could have been talking about you. The description fit."

"Forget it. My God! Are you considering going out with some guy on a blind date? The man's got to be a loser or he'd get his own woman. Now see here, Gaye..."

A bright little devil danced before her eyes. "It would be a foursome. I certainly wouldn't go out with him alone."

"By God! You're not going out with him—period! He's probably a certifiable nut case."

"And you think I'm too stupid and naive to take care of myself? Goodbye!"

"Don't you dare hang up until we get this thing settled!"

"Get what settled? I got along without your advice for almost twenty-nine years, Jim. I'm quite capable of managing my life on my own!"

"I'm not sure about that at all! You picked a bastard the first time around and got yourself in a hell of a mess!"

It was as if he had hit her in the face with a bucket of cold water. "You...how dare you throw something up to me I told you in confidence!" She had to swallow the sobs of disappointment in her throat before she could continue. "I'm sorry I was foolish enough to confide in you. You're the bastard! I want you out of my life. Do you hear! You—and your grandson!'' She was crying. Her voice croaked on the last word.

''Oh, God, babe. I'm sorry. Don't cry. It's only that you make me so damn mad. I don't understand it. Shhh...shhh...I wasn't referring to anything except your judgment of men. You're so...sweet—so vulnerable. That sonofabitch you married charmed his way into your life. Babe...don't cry. Are you still there?''

''Yes, but not for long.'' She forced herself to swallow past the constriction in her throat. ''What you really mean is that I'm stupid and naive. Dennis may have charmed his way into my life, but you're not going to bulldoze your way into it. I mean it when I say start making other arrangements for...for Johnny. He's waking up—I've got to go heat his bottle.''

Gaye broke the connection with her finger and placed the receiver on the table. She stood there trembling for a minute that seemed an hour before Johnny's cries stirred her to move.

Chapter Seven

Dawn finally came.

Gaye had spent the long night hours sorting through every minute she had spent with Jim and through each scrap of conversation that had passed between them. Sleep had come for only a scant hour at a time. She would awaken to lie restless and lonely. Her thoughts were unpleasant company. The sound of his voice and laughing haunted her sleepless hours. "Ah, babe, don't cry." She couldn't remember anyone ever speaking to her so tenderly before—not even her parents, who would have said, "Big girls don't cry."

There were so many things about this man she didn't understand: his wildness, his tenderness. She didn't know anything about his personal life, how he lived, or where he lived. Alberta seemed fond of him, and she was an excellent judge of people.

"Damn you, Jim! Get out of my mind. She got out

of bed, drained the cold bathwater from the tub and refilled it with warm. By the time she dragged herself out of the water, her skin was flushed pink. She dried her hair and brushed it into soft waves. She looked at her pale face and reached for some makeup. With a quick motion she dabbed at her cheeks and her lips, then measured the image in the mirror and frowned with displeasure at what she saw. The sleepless night had taken its toll, but what the heck—there was only Johnny to see her, and all that was on his mind was his formula and a dry diaper.

It was nine o'clock before she remembered to place the receiver back on the hook. Shortly after that the phone rang. She was tempted not to answer it, in case it was Jim. Reason prevailed. It could be Alberta.

"This is Karen Johnson, your friendly real estate agent."

"Hello, Karen." Gaye forced lightness into her voice.

"I've a favor to ask. If it isn't convenient, or if you'd rather not, please say so. There's a gentleman in town who is a relative of the man who built your house. He used to visit there years ago. He's in town for a few days and would love to see the inside of the house once again. I'll understand, Gaye, if you'd rather not give him a guided tour."

"Did you plan to come with him?"

"Certainly."

"What time?"

"Whenever it's convenient for you."

"Give me an hour to tidy up a bit."

"Thanks, love. Bye. See you in a while."

Gaye was almost glad to be wrenched out of her lethargy. She looked around the room, trying to see it with the eyes of a stranger, then moved about quickly, straightening a pillow, stacking magazines and newspapers. She went upstairs, took off the shirt Johnny had burped on, and slipped on a boat-necked knit top. After adding a touch of color to her lips, she ran a brush down over her hair.

Fresh coffee was brewed by the time the doorbell rang, and Gaye put out some sugar cookies she had baked the day before. She'd decided the least she could do for Karen was to be gracious and offer coffee and cookies to the gentleman.

The man with Karen was sixtyish, thin and neat. The black felt hat that sat squarely on top of his white head came off the instant he stepped into the entry.

Karen made the introductions. "Gaye Meiners, Mr. Lambert."

"I appreciate your allowing me into your home." His handshake was firm and his accent definitely Eastern.

"I hope you won't be disappointed in the changes that have taken place over the years."

"I'm sure I won't be. From what I see from here it looks charming." He bent and removed the rubbers from his shiny black shoes.

Gaye hung their coats in the hall closet and led the way through the house. "Would you rather tour on your own, Mr. Lambert? Karen and I can visit in the kitchen."

"I will, thank you." His eyes twinkled. "I remember the house as being much larger. I was just a boy when I was here last. My cousins and I played hide-and-seek from the basement to the attic. Am I invited to have a cup of coffee after a quick look around?"

"Absolutely. I have a young man upstairs who is going to wake up and be very vocal when he discovers his stomach is empty. I'll warm his bottle while you look around."

"Are any of the rooms upstairs off-limits?"

"Make yourself at home." Gaye smiled. "You might peek into the nursery and tell Johnny I'll be up to get him shortly."

"You won't mind? I won't frighten him?"

"Heavens, no! He's a little over two months old, and he'll take all the attention he can get."

Gaye took the bottle from the refrigerator and put it into the microwave. "He reminds me of my father," she said to Karen. "Daddy was meticulous, a refined sort of man. He always put on his coat when he came to the dinner table and stood when a lady came into the room. You don't see many old-fashioned gentlemen anymore."

"Mr. Lambert's that, all right. I really do appreciate this, Gaye."

"I'm enjoying it. I needed something to jar me out of the blahs. But I can't help being puzzled by his wanting to come here. Do you suppose his long-lost love lived here at one time?"

Karen ignored the question and reached for a cookie. "I'd think you'd be so busy taking care of that baby you wouldn't have time for the blahs."

Gaye was thoughtful for a long moment. Is Karen being deliberately evasive about Mr. Lambert? she wondered. Am I imagining it, or is she a little tense this morning? Oh, well, what if the old gentleman does have a deep, dark secret in his past and it's buried in this old house. We all have our secrets and our might-have-beens. She shrugged and smiled.

"What do you know about Jim Trumbull, Karen?"

"Nothing much. Not many people do. The Trumbulls

are very private people. I hear he's spending a lot of time here."

Gaye turned away before Karen saw the tremor pass over her face. "He's fond of Johnny. He calls him MacDougle, but I can't bring myself to call him that." The microwave cut itself off, and Gaye took out the warm bottle. "I'll get the baby and feed him if I can persuade you to pour coffee for Mr. Lambert."

When Gaye walked into the nursery, Mr. Lambert was standing beside the crib. He was gazing at the baby, a half smile on his mouth. He seemed to be unaware of Gaye until she came to the crib, and then the smile broadened when he looked at her.

"It's been a long while since I've seen a baby this small. He's a fine boy, Mrs. Meiners."

Gaye let the "Mrs. Meiners" go by without correcting him, but felt she had to add, "He isn't mine, you know. I wish he was. I'm taking care of him for his grandfather. And he isn't really small for his age. My sister is his doctor, and she tells me he's about average."

Hearing Gaye's voice, Johnny kicked his feet and waved his arms excitedly.

"He's a handsome, strong boy." There was a slight tremor in the old gentleman's voice.

"Yes, he is." Gaye let down the side of the bed. "You *are* a handsome boy, darling. I'll take you downstairs and show you off to Mrs. Johnson." She picked the baby up and cuddled him to her shoulder. When she looked up she found Mr. Lambert watching her with a strangely intense stare. "Look around as much as you like. We'll have coffee and cookies when you finish."

"Thank you."

Gaye had scarcely settled into the rocker with Johnny

snug in the curve of her arm, pulling vigorously on the bottle nipple, when Mr. Lambert came into the kitchen.

"I see you have a fondness for antiques. The rug beater hanging on the wall brought back memories. Who would have thought a rug beater tied with some greens and a ribbon would make such an attractive wall decoration." He sat down at the kitchen table, making himself quite at home, and reached for a cookie. "I haven't had homemade sugar cookies for years."

"I hope you like them. I like to bake, and I also love to restore old things and make them useful." Gaye took the bottle from the baby and held him to her shoulder to burp him. "I enjoy my collection. By the time Johnny is grown up, the treasures will probably be plastic bowls and aluminum pans."

"Do you mind me asking if...ah...caring for children is your profession?" Mr. Lambert asked hesitantly, as if uncertain of giving offence.

"I don't mind you asking," Gaye answered frankly. "I'm a teacher by profession. I lost my own baby a few days after this child was born. My sister is the baby's doctor, and she asked me to take care of him. He needed...a woman's care," she concluded. She was surprised at how open she'd been with a stranger, but she couldn't bring herself to go into details about Johnny's nursing needs.

"You mean the child was left at the hospital for adoption?" Mr. Lambert asked sharply.

"Good heavens, no! Johnny has a grandfather that would fight a bag full of wildcats for him. This baby is wanted and loved, Mr. Lambert."

Gaye hugged the tiny body to her and placed a kiss on the thick black hair. In a small corner of her mind she thought about this polished old gentleman's interest in a tiny baby. He's just being nice, she thought. It's what's called politicking—he probably wants to come back and bring his family on a nostalgic trip through the house. His voice brought her back to the present.

"I can see that he is." His eyes lingered on Gaye and the baby for a long moment. Then, "You'd better move that plate of cookies out of my reach, Mrs. Johnson, if we're going to lunch this afternoon."

Later, Gaye took Johnny to the living room and laid him on the couch. She stood beside the door while Karen and Mr. Lambert put on their coats.

"It's been enjoyable, Mrs. Meiners." Mr. Lambert held out his hand and shook hers warmly. "Thank you for giving me a glimpse into the past and into the future," he added, almost to himself.

"Thanks, Gaye," Karen said. "I'll call you soon. I've found references to this house in the original plat-book that you may want to see."

"Yes, I'd like to see them. Goodbye."

The house seemed very empty when they left. Normally Gaye would have gone to the kitchen and put the coffee cups in the dishwasher, or put a load of diapers in the washer and started the endless chores connected with caring for an infant. But nothing was normal today. She wasn't even interested in rummaging around in the boxes of antiques Jim had carried to the basement.

Johnny went to sleep on the couch, and she let him lie there. She sat down in the big recliner, picked up a magazine and thumbed through it idly. She saw nothing to catch her interest. Her thoughts were unpleasant company, and the afternoon dragged slowly by.

Late in the afternoon the paperboy came by to collect. When Gaye went to the front door, she noticed Mr. Lambert had left his rubbers sitting beside the door. She tried to call Karen, but the line was busy. Johnny woke fretting because his diaper was wet, and Gaye forgot about calling again.

By ten o'clock she was exhausted, tired both in mind and body. She soaked in a hot tub to ease her tense muscles and crawled beneath the covers on her bed. Her pulse pounded in her temples as she tried to crowd all thought from her reeling mind. Her head was splitting from the pressure, and she pressed her fingers to her temples. Oh, dear Lord in heaven. When would she ever have peace of mind?

Gaye stirred contentedly. A warm, sweet lethargy covered her like a cozy blanket. Sleepily she wondered about the gentle touch on her cheek and the soft buzzing sound in her ear. She didn't want to wake up. Yet she drifted pleasantly out of a deep exhaustion-induced sleep. Her mind slowly became aware of warm, gentle lips traveling across her cheek and settling on hers. Hers opened invitingly. She tried to lift her arms to hold on to the wonderful dream. It was all so sweet—so deeply real.

She awakened suddenly out of the sweet ecstasy and pulled back in alarm. Panic seized her, and she struggled wildly against the arms holding her. Whimpering, frightened sounds bubbled up out of her throat. Her heart felt like a humming bird gone mad inside her chest.

"Shhhh...babe. It's me...Jim. I didn't mean to frighten you."

The sound of his voice penetrated her mind. She was flooded with relief so intense it was almost beyond bearing, and the panic drained out of her. She sank back onto the pillow.

"What are you doing here? How did you get in?"

"I'm here because I couldn't stay away, and I let myself in with the key I took the day I brought MacDougle out to my mother's."

"You scared the fool out of me!"

"I hope so. Because you've worried the fool out of me." He chuckled. His face was so close to hers she had only to turn her head slightly and their lips would touch. "Are you usually such a heavy sleeper? I kissed you half a dozen times before you woke up."

"I was tired. I didn't get much sleep last night." She moved her head back, trying to see him in the dim light made by the digital clock on the bedside table. His hair was tumbled as usual. It occurred to her then that he was kneeling beside the bed. "You shouldn't be here," she protested in a ragged whisper.

"Why not?" His arm slid beneath her shoulders, and he pulled her to him. "Right here is where I want to be. It's been a week since I held you and kissed you—"

His mouth touched hers softly, gently, and moved against it. There was nothing hurried or demanding about the kiss or the way he held her. She could have backed away and he would have let her go. A sigh trembled through her, and her own lips moved against his, blindly seeking comfort. He lifted his head and rained tender kisses on her eyes, cheek, throat. His hand moved to brush the tangled hair from her brow.

"I want to hold you for the few hours I'll be here," he whispered. "Let me...I'll just hold you, if that's what you want." His fingers moved into her hair. He was leaning over her, his lips a breath away. "I *need* to hold you, sweetheart."

A sudden flood of tenderness overwhelmed her. She longed to kiss his lips with sweet, lingering softness, to comfort and hold him, to soothe his brow with her fingertips. She tilted her chin until her lips came in contact with his. The wonder of it, the thought that this big, rugged maverick of a man needed *her,* filled her with pleasure. A fierce feeling of protectiveness came over her. She hugged his shaggy head to her.

He covered her face with kisses. "I was afraid you wouldn't be here. I thought you might have decided to go out with some creep who would've...pawed at you, scared you."

"No."

"I'll take you wherever you want to go."

"I'm not real fond of nightlife."

"I'm glad. I'd rather spend evenings here with you." His lips nuzzled her breast before seeking her mouth. His was sweet, his breath warm and smelling faintly of mint. His cheeks were pleasantly rough against her face. His arms were the only arms in the world, his lips the only lips. Something deep within her was stirring. She moved restlessly, a hunger gnawing at her relentlessly.

"Jim..."

He pulled away from her and waited. Now is the time to tell him to go, a small voice in her head whispered. There'll be no turning back! In one more minute it'll be too late. She didn't listen. She tugged on the hand holding hers.

Minutes later he lifted the covers, and she moved to make room for him. The bed curved to accommodate his weight when he lay down beside her. His arms reached for her, gathering her close.

His body was hard and warm and big. He cradled her to him with a gentleness that brought tears to her eyes. Gaye felt the tension in her muscles loosen. Reality was fading. The inner qualms were slipping away. He captured one of her hands and pressed her palm to his chest.

They lay that way for a long moment, their mouths softly touching.

His hand roamed up and down her back, over her hips, moving the thin cotton cloth of her nightgown. Her fingertips roamed over his chest and smooth shoulders to his neck, lightly fingered his ear and plunged into his wild thick hair.

"You smell good, feel good," he whispered huskily.

"So do you." In a wonder of discovery, her hand caressed his body, finding the corded muscles of his shoulders, the nipple buried in the fur on his chest, the flat abdomen that trembled beneath her touch. Her fingers paused at the top of his jockey shorts and feathered upward.

"Don't stop!"

"Your skin is so...smooth."

"Yours is like satin."

"Even the hair on your chest is soft."

"Not as soft as...this." His hand slipped beneath her gown. His fingertips lightly combed.

"We sound like kids."

"But we're not. I'm a grandfather and you're...sweet beyond my wildest dreams. It's as if I've never touched a woman's body before. Everything is new and different."

"For me too. Why did you come back?"

"Ah...babe. I've had a hell of a day. I hurt you, and I couldn't stand it till I made it right. Can you forgive me for lashing out like a jealous fool?"

"I overreacted. I've never told anyone except you how it really was with Dennis. And then when I got the check, I felt firmly put in place. When my baby died I was desolate. I don't know now what I'd have done without Johnny. I think Alberta brought us together as much for my sake as for his. I'm beginning to love him very much."

"How about his grandpa."

"Oh, Jim! This *wanting* may not be love."

"It's a damn good start. Don't think about it. I don't want anything to spoil the next couple of hours." His lips tingled across her mouth with feathery kisses. His legs moved apart and braided with hers. "Sweet and soft. I haven't quite figured out what it is about you that draws me to you. I only know I want to be with you all the time. I'm jealous as hell of everything that touches you. Even this." He pulled at the gown and spoke with his lips against her mouth. "I like the way you taste, the way you look, the way you are with me."

"Like now?"

"Especially like now. When you kissed me the other night, I thought for sure my control would snap and I would crush you. I wanted to be....inside you so bad."

The arms holding her tightened. She wondered if it was his heart or hers pounding so wildly against her breast. She wrapped her arms around his naked torso. Her ragged breath was trapped inside her mouth by his lips. He rolled so his hand could move up under her gown to her breast. It filled his palm. His strong fingers stroked and fondled as carefully as if he were holding a precious life in his hand. His lips left hers and he gulped for air.

"You were made to be loved and cherished," he whispered urgently. "I'll never hurt you. I'll take care of you always, if you'll let me."

She couldn't speak. Her palms slid over muscle and tight flesh as if she had to know every inch of him. His sex was large, firm, and throbbing against the thigh pinned between his. Strange. She didn't feel threatened by it. She was awed that this giant of a man trembled beneath her touch and yet demanded nothing she was not willing to give.

"Darling..." The word came from her lips like a sigh.

He turned her on her back. His bare leg swung over hers and held her softness pinned to the yielding mattress. His masculine scent filled her nostrils. He lowered his head, and she felt the wetness of his tongue through the thin cloth of her gown as he held it to the bud on her breast.

"You mean it? Am I your darling?" He nuzzled the soft mound with his lips.

"Yes! Oh, yes... Do you want me, darling?" Her hands slid down over taut hips and pressed his hardness to her thigh.

"More than anything. You?" His hand moved over her body, and suddenly it was there at the mysterious moistness.

"I...could get pregnant." She breathed the words in his ear.

"You...might not."

"I'm probably fertile as the Nile," she moaned.

"Then you'd have to marry me. Would that be so bad?"

She gave a small, strangled cry. Tremors shot through her in rocketing waves. She grabbed the thick wrist of the hand resting on her belly and pulled the exploring fingers from between her legs.

"I want..." It was a quivering whisper.

"Say it, sweetheart! Oh, God! Say it!"

"Yes, yes! Oh, yes!"

A low moan came from him. He supported himself on his forearms, cupped her head in his hands and rained tender, soft kisses on her face.

"Let's get rid of the gown, sweetheart. I want to feel your breasts against my chest, your heart beating against mine."

Her hands moved over his back and down under his shorts. She rubbed her palms over his hips. "If you'll get rid of these..."

He claimed her mouth again. She clung to him, her hands stroking his shoulders and back. She was drowning in desire, an emotion she thought never to feel again. He moved away from her as they shifted their weight. In an instant they were back together, naked and straining to feel every inch of each other.

"Even with your arms tight around me, I feel so free."

"I'll never hold you with strength. I'll hold you with love."

"Don't say that!" she whispered urgently. "It's too soon."

"Okay, sweetheart. Okay."

His lips, sweet and firm and knowing, moved over hers. She felt the rough drag of his cheeks, the caressing touch of his wild hair against her forehead. She'd dreamed about being kissed like this, kissed with gentleness and caring. The strength and the taste of him filled her senses. His hand roamed over her back to her buttocks, caressing her into surrender.

"I may be making the biggest mistake of my life, but I don't care," she whispered. "Show me how it could be if we truly loved."

He lifted his mouth and started to say something, then groaned deep in his throat and rolled her onto her back. She gave herself up to his kiss with an abandon that made hunger leap deep inside of him. His hands and his mouth moved down over her body with a velvet touch.

His lips captured her nipple, and the rough drag of his tongue was so painfully exquisite, she drew a gasping breath.

"I've wanted to do that from the very first. I'd feel myself growing and I'd breathe deeply and say, Oh, God, don't let me embarrass myself and scare the hell out of this sweet woman. I wanted to take off your clothes and taste every bit of you until you were hot and wet and wanting me. But it's more than that. I want you willingly, wanting me—only me."

"I can't believe I didn't dream you..." She wrapped her arms around him, spread her legs so his thighs could sink between hers, and pulled his weight down on her. Cradled together, they rocked from side to side.

He took her mouth in a hard, swift kiss, but the kiss wasn't enough. Only by blending together could they even begin to appease the hunger they had for each other. He lifted his hips. Her hand urgently moved between them to guide him into her.

"Jim..." She arched against him in sensual pleasure.

"I'm not hurting you sweetheart?" His cheek was pressed to hers, his words coming in an agonized whisper.

"No! Darling, no..." Even now he demanded nothing, gave everything. His concern brought tears that rolled down her face. He turned his head and caught them with the tip of his tongue, then found her mouth and kissed her with lips wet with her tears.

The spasms of pleasure that followed were like a gorgeous dance throughout her body. At times it was like an enormous wave crashing over her. At other times it was like a gentle wind caressing her wet, naked body. The whole world was the man joined to her. His mouth and her mouth were as one. He was at home in her, moving gently, caressing, loving—she arched her hips hungrily and he wildly took what she offered.

It's so wonderful! She thought. The tip of him touches my very soul. I feel so...beautiful! She had never known such an exquisite feeling. It was an ecstasy too beautiful for words.

She wasn't really aware of when it ended. When she returned to reality Jim was leaning over her, his weight on his forearms.

"You all right, babe?"

The sweet, familiar smell of his breath, the light touch of his lips at the corner of her mouth, brought a small inarticulate sound from her. She tightened her arms around him, holding him inside her warmth, and hungrily turned her mouth to his. Her hands moved to his tumbled thick hair and fondled his neck and the strong line of his shoulders and back, then came up to stroke his cheeks and caress his ears.

"You're all right?" he asked again when he finally lifted his head.

She laughed softly, caught his lower lip between her teeth and bit gently.

"Yes! Oh, yes." She sighed, then struggled for words to express her feelings. "You've brought me something new. I feel like we've done something wonderful...together. I feel filled with you—I think I'll always feel empty without you there." Her breath caught and she couldn't say anything more.

"Sweet, my sweet. You've brought something new to me, too." His lips rubbed hers in sensual assault. "I want you to feel empty if I'm not there." Their passion swelled, rocked them, enveloped them in a swirling, translucent world where nothing existed but the two of them and the ecstasy they shared.

Afterward, lying side by side, they held each other while their bodies adjusted to the aftermath of passion. Her head rested on his arm; her arm was curled about his chest, her palm flat against his back.

"I wasn't too rough with you, was I? I tried to keep control, but it slipped away and I lost myself in you."

She smiled against his mouth. "You were wonderfully gentle. Thank you. I have never fully...participated before. I never imagined it would be so all-consuming."

He gave a deep male sound and his arms tightened. "I could kill that guy!"

"Shhhh...no. Now I know how wonderful you are. I'm falling in love with you, Jim. Don't break my heart." Her voice ended in a sob.

He tilted her face up, kissed her deeply. "You're mine, sweetheart. You and MacDougle belong to me."

She believed him. She stretched lazily, her thighs sliding through his hair-roughened ones. "I feel so good. I feel contented and happy. I feel...wonderful!" She giggled against his chin and nipped it.

"You are. Believe me, you are!"

Chapter Eight

"I hate to leave you, but I knew when I came I could stay only a few hours."

Jim sat on the edge of the bed and pulled on his boots. The light from the lamp shone on his hair, and for the first time Gaye noticed silver threads among the coal black. He'd dressed in tan cord trousers, and a soft blue Western-cut shirt with pearl snaps was tucked neatly into the waistband. His boots were polished cowhide, and even her inexperienced eye could see that they were custom-made. He looked different. She'd never seen him in anything except jeans, denim shirt, and scuffed boots.

He turned and looked down at her. His eyes possessed a mysterious magnetic force, and she couldn't look away. He smiled, and she felt immersed in a sumptuously delicious joy. She felt as if she were floating several inches above the bed. He bent and kissed her mouth with a demanding pressure.

"This next week will seem like a month." He stood. "I'll use the bathroom and be right back." He paused in the doorway and looked back across the room. Their eyes met, held, and he winked at her.

As soon as she heard the bathroom door close, she sprang out of bed and snatched up her gown. She slipped it over her head and hurried to the closet for a robe. She'd never felt so carefree with another human being, but she shied from the thought of his seeing her naked. She only had time to run the brush through her hair before he returned. He came up behind her, wrapped his arms about her waist and rested his chin on the top of her head. The breath caught in Gaye's throat. She felt her insides warm with pleasure as she looked at their reflection in the mirror. She had never before experienced this melting, letting-go sensation that invaded her innermost being.

"Don't look at me like that, or I won't be able to leave you." He bent his head and pressed his face into the curve of her neck.

She turned in his arms and slipped hers about him. Her warm, moist lips traced the line of his jaw and moved upward to settle very gently on his mouth, where they moved with sweet provocation. Love and tenderness welled within her. A lovely feeling unfolded and traveled slowly throughout her body. They stood quietly, as if to absorb the feel of each other.

"You must go." Her voice was weakened by the depth of her emotion. "Shall we look in on Johnny?"

They went to the baby's room. Jim's arm was around her, his hand resting intimately on her hipbone. The baby was sleeping soundly. They stood beside the crib. Gaye looked up at Jim with a mischievous sparkle in her eyes.

"You're not like any grandfather I've ever known."

"You're not like any grandma I've known," he teased.

"Will Johnny call you Grandpa?"

"I hope he'll call me whatever *our* children call me—Dad, Pa, old man, hey you—"

Her heart leaped at the thought. "They'll have more respect than that! I'll see to it."

"Yes, ma'am."

Downstairs, Gaye watched him shrug into a shearling coat. He seemed as big as a bear.

"Did you drive down from Louisville?"

"I flew down and got a taxi. I told him to come back about now." Jim looked out the front window. "Here he comes. Come kiss me, sweetheart."

"Will you fly back?"

"Uh-huh." He opened the coat, pulled her against him and lifted her off her feet. He kissed her long and hard. "I'll call you tonight."

"Will you be able to catch a flight at this time in the morning?"

"Don't worry about it. There's a charter waiting for me."

"A charter?" He set her on her feet, and she moved back so she could look up at him. "I really don't know much about you, do I?"

He turned with his hand on the doorknob. "We'll take care of that when I get back. I like to think of you and MacDougle waiting here for me." As he turned, his glance fell on the rubbers beside the door. He gave them a little kick with his booted foot. "Where did they come from? Who's been here?" His words dropped like a bomb. His glittering dark eyes were fixed on her. Hers were fixed on his stern mouth.

"A friend of Mrs. Johnson's left them here. She

brought him to see the house.'' The censorious look in his eyes was so reminiscent of the way Dennis used to look at her when she had displeased him, it cut through her like a knife.

''You let a strange man in the house on that woman's say-so? You don't know anything about her. Why did she bring him here?''

''He wanted to see the house again. He used to visit here when he was a boy. He was a nice man and he liked Johnny, too. Why are you acting as if I've committed a crime?''

''I worry about you and MacDougle here alone.'' He grasped her shoulders with his two hands. ''Trust me, Gaye. Please be careful about who you let in the house. I wouldn't put it past my former in-laws to kidnap MacDougle.''

''They wouldn't send an old man to do it,'' she said crossly.

''How do you know? You've no idea of what means they'll go to to get what they want.''

She stared at him and felt her heart slide to the tip of her toes. ''Let's not quarrel,'' she whispered and tried not to cry.

''I'm sorry, sweetheart.'' He came to her and hugged her tightly to him. ''I want to keep you safe. I've been happier here with you and MacDougle than I've ever been in my life. I want it to last.''

''The only thing you have to worry about is stray blacksmiths who have a key to my door,'' she said and smiled through sudden tears.

The cabdriver sounded the horn. ''Oh, hell! Bye, sweetheart.'' He kissed her as if he wanted to draw her into his body. He whispered something through the kiss that sounded vaguely like, ''You belong to me now.''

His hands were bruisingly tight on her shoulders when he set her away from him. "Bolt the door after me. Sleep in this morning if MacDougle'll let you. You didn't get much sleep tonight." His grin was so endearing her heart almost melted.

Gaye moved to the window to watch the lights of the cab move down the drive. The house was quiet. The only thing to break the silence was the ticking of the mantle clock. She sat down on the couch and tucked her feet beneath the robe. He was gone, and what had happened between them seemed like a dream. Never had she felt so adored, so cherished. Was it possible for him to be such a considerate lover without loving her?

What did she know about Jim other than that he was sweet and gentle, and she had shared the most wonderful experience of her life with him? He expected her to marry him, and she didn't even know where or how he lived. Have I had my head in the clouds? she asked herself. I really don't know him. How can I let him talk about our having children together? Our life-styles may be so totally incompatible that I won't be able to live with him...no matter how much I love him. I don't want to be miserable for the rest of my life!

Long before daylight she had convinced herself that before she allowed herself to be immersed in Jim's life, she had to know more about it.

She was feeding Johnny his morning formula when the doorbell sounded. Holding him cradled in one arm, she went to the door. A shiny black car was parked beneath the portico. Mr. Lambert stood on the step, his hat in his hand. Gaye smiled a greeting, slipped the latch on the storm door and backed away to protect the baby from the cold gust of air that came in when he opened the door.

"Good morning."

"Good morning. Hello there, young man. Are you having breakfast?"

"What stays in him counts for breakfast," Gaye said, laughing.

"I'm on my way to the airport and stopped by to pick up my rubbers. I hear it's snowing in New York."

His friendly smile prompted Gaye to say, "I thought my sugar cookies had brought you back." He laughed, and it flashed through Gaye's mind that he didn't laugh often. "I have some left, and fresh coffee, if you have time."

"I'll take time...if you're sure you don't mind the interruption." He took off his overcoat and laid it over the back of a chair.

"Johnny and I are glad for the company." She led the way to the kitchen. "The cups are in the cupboard on the right and the cookies in the jar on the counter. It isn't often I have to ask a guest to wait on himself, but Johnny needs to finish his breakfast and take his morning nap."

"It's the least I can do. Please carry on."

Gaye heard the clink of the cup in the saucer and the rattle of the lid on the cookie jar as she fed the baby.

"You little...stinker! Don't you dare blow! Oh, Johnny, now you're laughing. I think you like to be all messy."

"That's typical of a boy," Mr. Lambert said as he pulled at the creases in his trousers after sitting down at the table.

"He's very alert for his age. Did you notice how his eyes searched for you when he heard your voice? You're a smart boy, aren't you, darling?" Gaye cooed at Johnny and maneuvered the bottle into his mouth again.

"You must love children. First a teacher and now a nursemaid. Do you plan to marry and have a family of your own?"

Gaye looked up to find the sharp eyes fixed on her. If he wasn't such a nice old gentleman she would almost think he was asking these questions for some reason of his own.

"I'm thinking about it," she said slowly, still trying to understand why he wanted to know.

"It'll be a lucky boy who comes home from school to a cookie jar full of these." He took a deep bite of a large, round cookie. A dusting of sugar sprinkled his dark suit, but he didn't seem to notice.

"Do you have children and grandchildren, Mr. Lambert?"

"Yes, I have children, Mrs. Meiners. And I doubt if a one of them can bake sugar cookies." He added the last dryly. Then, as if to change the subject, he said, "I wonder if you would be kind enough to let me jot down the recipe?"

"I'll be happy to share it with you. My mother passed it down to me. I'll take Johnny up to bed and be right back."

When she returned, Mr. Lambert was helping himself to a second cup of coffee. "Can I pour a cup for you, Mrs. Meiners?"

"Yes, please." She brought her recipe book to the table. "This makes a large batch of cookies. Are you sure you want it?" She smiled up at him. He seems so out of place in the kitchen, but perfectly happy to be here, she thought.

"Absolutely. You should start a franchise and go nationwide."

"Now, that's a thought!" she said with a happy grin.

"I can see it now—Gaye's Cookies on the grocers' shelves."

"Don't laugh, young woman. A Kentucky colonel did it with fried chicken." Smile lines deepened the wrinkles in his face. Gaye could tell he was enjoying himself immensely, and the seed of apprehension Jim planted in her mind was pushed to the far corner and forgotten.

"I'll write down the ingredients. Almost any cook will know how to put them together. I always chill the dough before I roll it out and then dip the top of each cookie lightly in sugar and spices before I bake them."

She wrote swiftly and passed the paper across the table. The hand that reached for it wore a large diamond ring. Gold cuff links were visible on the sleeves of his white shirt. The ridiculousness of the situation hit her, and Gaye laughed into his eyes.

His lips twitched into a smile. He reached into his pocket for dark-rimmed glasses and perched them on his nose, then read the recipe. "I should be able to handle that," he said confidently. "I haven't thought of buttermilk in years. We used to have it at home when I was a boy."

"If I don't have buttermilk, I sour a little milk by adding a small amount of vinegar."

"I'll stop on my way from the airport and get buttermilk."

"Don't tell me you can cook!" she teased.

"I can scramble an egg with the best of them," he said with a broad smile. "But my coffee will float a rock." He folded the paper and placed it carefully in his inside coat pocket. "I've taken up enough of your time. Thank you for inviting me to stay."

"I've enjoyed it. When you come back to town, stop by and bring me your recipe for scrambled eggs. Mine are like rubber. Oh, excuse me, I hear Johnny, and he sounds as if he's terribly unhappy about something."

"May I come along and say goodbye to the young man?"

"Of course."

Mr. Lambert followed her up the stairs. The baby's face was red, and he was protesting being left alone in the only way he knew.

"Now, now. My goodness, what's the matter? You're getting spoiled, young man." Gaye picked him up, and the loud wails of indignation ceased immediately. "You rascal, you!" she chided.

"May I hold him? It's been years—"

"If you're sure. He may slobber on you."

"I don't mind." He reached for the baby and held him cradled gently in the crook of his arm, turning from side to side. The look on his face was one of gentle regret. His eyes clung to Johnny's face, and Gaye could see that his jaws were tightly clenched.

He's probably remembering when his own children were babies, she thought, and for a moment she felt a stab of pain in her heart, remembering her own child.

"Thank you," he said simply when he handed the baby back to her.

Gaye laid him in the crib. "Go to sleep now," she suggested softly.

In the living room she held Mr. Lambert's overcoat. He slipped into it. "Thank you," he said and picked up his rubbers. "It's been a pleasure, Mrs. Meiners."

"For me too. Goodbye, Mr. Lambert."

Gaye closed the door behind him and then moved the curtain aside so she could look out. A uniformed man was holding the car door open. A chauffeur had been waiting in the car all this time! For goodness' sake! Gaye shrugged and dismissed it from her mind. She was behind in her work; Johnny's washing had to be done.

Candy, the nurse from the hospital, came by in the evening. Gaye was waiting for Jim's call. She was relieved when her friend stayed only a few minutes, saying she was meeting her sister at the shopping mall.

It was ten o'clock when the phone rang. By that time Gaye was as nervous as if she were waiting for her first date. She laid down the novel she had been trying to read and let the phone ring for the third time while she took deep breaths to steady her nerves, then picked up the receiver.

"Hi, sweetheart. Were you in the bathtub?"

"Ah...no."

"I know it's late, but I couldn't get away sooner. Have you missed me today?"

"Of course. Ah...Johnny's fine. He seems to be taking to the formula well." She really didn't know what she was saying.

"That's good...I've thought about you all day." There was a long pause, and she heard him make an exclamation of annoyance. "I'm trying to tie up some loose ends here. I'll have to go to New York before I come home, but that'll take only a couple of days."

"New York sounds a million miles away from Madisonville."

"It's only a few hours by plane. Talk to me. What did you do today? Did anyone come over?"

"Candy came over for a short while, and...Mrs. Johnson's friend came by on his way to the airport and picked up his rubbers. Nothing exciting. Jim...I'm confused. We've got to talk when you get back."

"Confused about what, sweetheart?"

"You...and me. Last night I was happy, but today

I'm wondering what it all means. Maybe what we feel for each other is just a physical thing."

"Physical attraction is the beginning of most relationships, Gaye. I'd hate for you to love my mind, but hate my body. This doesn't happen to me overnight. I was attracted to you from the start. I wish I didn't have to be away from you right now, but this thing in Louisville has been planned for a while. I'm winding up some affairs here." He turned away from the phone and spoke to someone. "Good Lord! All the people do here is party. I wish I was there with you. Are you upstairs in the bedroom?"

"Yes. I've been reading."

"I have to go. I'll call you tomorrow night. What nights do you go to that exercise class?"

"Tuesday and Thursday."

"I'd rather you'd skip that while I'm gone."

"But why, Jim? Joy is a reliable baby-sitter."

"I'm sure she is. It's just that...I don't exactly like the idea of MacDougle being there alone with a teenage girl."

"I've already made plans. My friend is picking me up." The sound of the music and the laughter in the background prodded her to ignore the worried tone in his voice. The deep-sated ache in the center of her body, a jealous ache she recognized with reluctant dismay, stirred her to anger. "I'm here during the day. If you can spare a moment you can call then."

"You're ticked off and I don't blame you. But do this for me, sweetheart. Stick close to the house until I get back. You know I wouldn't ask you to do it if I didn't think it a necessary precaution."

The long tense silence was broken by a feminine voice: "Jim, darlin', c'mon."

Anger and resentment came boiling up. "I'm not at your back and call, Jim. I think I told you that once before. Don't ask me to structure my days and nights to suit your whims. I won't do it. I'm not a child to be told do this, do that. I think you'd better get back to your friends. The party may poop out without you."

Another long pause. "They're not my friends. They're acquaintances. There's a world of difference between the two," he said quietly. Then, "All right. Take care of our boy. I'll call sometime tomorrow. Bye, sweetheart."

"Bye." Gaye hung up the phone and burst into tears.

The weekend passed. Jim called every day. Sometimes the calls came early in the morning and at other times in the afternoon. The conversations were brief and impersonal. She didn't mention the fact that Mr. Lambert had liked her cookies so well he'd wanted the recipe or that he'd sent her a lovely houseplant. They talked mostly about the baby and the weather. He called Tuesday morning while she was feeding Johnny.

"How're you doin'?"

"Fine."

"MacDougle all right?"

"He's fine, too."

"Anything new and exciting?"

"Not unless you think scattered garbage is exciting. Dogs got into it last night."

"Did it snow much there?"

"Several inches. I'm glad I had snow tires put on my car."

"Are you thinking of taking MacDougle out in this weather?"

"Why not? He isn't a hothouse plant. He's got a car seat. He'll be safe enough."

"I was thinking of you, too, sweetheart. I wish you wouldn't go out unless it's absolutely necessary. The roads are slick."

"It snows in Indiana, too, you know. I've been driving on it since I was sixteen." Gaye found her temper rising. What's the matter with him? she fumed. "Don't plan my days for me, Jim. I'm a big girl, I can take care of myself."

"I'm not so sure about that." There was a hard, impatient edge to his voice. "I'm merely telling you driving conditions are bad all over the state. Anyone with any brains at all stays off the roads unless it's absolutely necessary to be on them!"

The quiet hung heavily after he spoke, and Gaye had the inescapable feeling that if he were here he'd be tempted to shake her. She had the mad impulse to feed his anger.

"Evidently I've been functioning without brains for nearly twenty-nine years. That's quite a feat! I've got to go, Jim. You're interrupting our breakfast."

"That's too damn bad! You hang on there and listen to me! No damn exercise class is worth getting your neck broken!"

"Johnny is your concern, not me!"

"Johnny?"

"Your grandson—little person—tiny hands, small feet! He's blowing formula all over himself. I've got to clean him up. Bye. Call again when you can spare the time."

She hung up the phone. The satisfaction she felt lasted for only a moment. She knew he was right about the roads, and she also knew she had been unreasonable.

In the late afternoon Lila called to tell her the exercise class had been canceled due to the weather. She said her boys had planned on an evening at her sister's and were disappointed. Did she mind if they came over for an hour after dinner?

The prospects of a long, lonely evening had not been pleasant, and Gaye welcomed the opportunity for company.

She checked the cookie jar and decided to make a fresh batch of sugar cookies. When she opened the notebook to find the recipe, she thought of the dapper Mr. Lambert. She wondered if the refined old man intended to make the cookies himself. Impossible! He probably had a housekeeper or a cook. Gaye thought about the look of regret on his face when he held Johnny. What had he been thinking at that moment? He had children, so he probably had grandchildren, perhaps even great-grandchildren, yet he seemed sad.... She shrugged the thoughts away and uncovered the mixer.

It had stopped snowing by the time Lila and her boys arrived. They stood in the entry and removed boots and coats.

"It isn't bad driving now. But if the wind comes up, look out!" Lila placed her wet boots on the mat and instructed her boys to do the same.

"I hope the wind comes up." Kyle gave his brother a playful push. "No school."

"Pray, Gaye. Please pray the wind doesn't come up!" Lila pleaded and rumpled the hair of her oldest son. "I've always wanted to see the inside of this house. Oh, it's beautiful!"

"Thank you. I baked fresh cookies, boys." Gaye led the way to the kitchen.

"Eat in here," Lila said when her youngest son started back to the living room. "You'll get crumbs all over."

"Rats! We wanted to watch the fire."

"Let's all go in and sit beside the fireplace. Don't worry about the crumbs, Lila. They'll sweep up."

Later, Gaye found a deck of cards and got the boys started on a game of crazy eights.

"Have you lived here long, Lila?"

"Five years this spring."

"Do you know...Jim Trumbull?"

"I don't know him. I've never even seen him, but I've heard of him." She lifted her brows and her eyes teased. "I've heard he stops here quite often."

"It's his grandson I'm baby-sitting."

"I thought so," Lila said with a grin. "But I didn't want to ask."

"Is there anything that goes unnoticed in a small town?"

"Not much. And especially if it concerns Jim Trumbull."

"What do you know about him?"

"Not much," Lila said again. "He lives about five miles out on the county road. He has a gate across the lane leading to his house. It sets back in the timber, and you can't see it from the road. His mother and his aunt live with him. But I guess you know about that. What exactly is the matter with his mother? I've heard a nurse goes out there every day."

"I wouldn't know. He's very closemouthed about anything to do with his personal life." Gaye tried to keep the quiver out of her voice.

"It set the gossips to work when his daughter went into the hospital to have her baby. Up until that time people had forgotten he even had one. I guess he's been divorced for a long time. When his ex-wife came in a chartered plane and took a limo to the hospital to get their daughter, their tongues worked overtime. I've never heard anything *bad* about him, Gaye. He's probably just a nice person who values his privacy. That's as much as I know about him except that I heard he isn't exactly poor. You can't blame him for that."

"He can't be rich. He's a blacksmith. He wrote a book about it."

"A blacksmith? I've never heard that. I heard he has some weird iron sculptures out at his place and an assortment of animals, including some very fine horses, but I haven't heard of him being a blacksmith."

"Oh, well, it doesn't matter," Gaye said tiredly.

The phone rang. She excused herself and went to the kitchen to answer it.

"I'm at the airport in New York. I just got in." Jim's voice. Somehow she felt unreasonably irked that he should call while they were discussing him.

"I'm having coffee with a friend."

"Who?"

"The dance class was canceled so my friend from the class came over," she said irritably. "Did you think I was entertaining someone from the Mafia?"

"No I didn't think that. I'm interested, that's all."

"She's perfectly respectable. Her two sons are with her."

"I'm glad you have someone to keep you company this evening. Gaye, about this morning..." The placating note in his voice irked her even more.

"You acted as if I'd take Johnny out in a blizzard and risk his life on unsafe roads. I'm surprised you think I'm even capable of taking care of him." The anger she was feeling echoed in her voice. Oh, good heavens! she thought. I'm acting like a shrew and I can't stop!

"I ask you to exercise a little caution. Is that too much to ask? Did you have a bad day?"

She wanted to say, Hell, yes! Every day you're away is a bad day. Instead she said, "It was all right." Her throat felt as if it had a rock in it.

"I've missed you."

"Oh, sure."

"Dammit, Gaye!" he bellowed. She moved the phone from her ear and let it rest on her shoulder. His patience snapped. His anger and frustration seemed to surge up and boil out. She caught snatches of angry words. "If I was...smart-ass answers...damn mad...what the hell are you trying...unreasonable! By God...give you a damn good... Now you listen to me....I've had about all...enough on my plate without you.... Are you...to...or not?" There was a kind of desperation in the jerky way he spoke. "Answer me, damn you!" he shouted, and his tone savaged her, sending shivers of anxiety down her spine.

"How can I answer when you keep shouting? You must be making quite a spectacle of yourself at the public phone booths."

"To hell with the spectacle I'm making of myself. Who the devil cares? It's you and MacDougle that concern me."

"If all you're going to do is shout at me when you call, then don't!" She heard a muffled curse and scraped up enough courage to say, "I refuse to be dominated by you or anyone else, Jim. I won't be told when to breathe and when not to. Even Alberta gives me space, and I'm a lot closer to her than I am to you."

"There is no one in the world closer to you than I am," he said, and his voice was surprisingly calm. "No one has a greater right to look after you than I do. Oh, hell! I'll call tomorrow. Goodbye."

Gaye stood for a moment after the connection was broken. What she really wanted to do was crawl in bed and cry; instead she put a half smile on her face and went back into the living room.

Thursday night she went to the dance class, but declined the invitation for coffee at a local restaurant later. When she returned home Joy didn't mention having received a telephone call, so she asked her as she was leaving.

"Were there any calls?"

"No. Were you expecting one?"

"Not really. By the way, congratulations on making the honor society."

"Thanks. Will you be needing me next Tuesday?"

"Sure, unless you have something planned?"

"I've got something planned all right. I want to go to France next summer with a group of French students. I need to earn money."

"You can count on steady employment here."

"Thanks, Aunt Gaye. See ya soon."

Gaye closed and locked the door. Two days had gone by without a call from Jim.

Chapter Nine

A week went by. The wet, dirty snow was covered with a clean blanket of white. Thanksgiving came and went. Christmas lights began to appear. *Twelve days without a word from Jim.*

Lila called on Tuesday morning. "Will you drive tonight? I know it's my turn, but my old bucket of bolts is being stubborn again."

"Sure. I'll pick you up at the regular time. Johnny and I went to my sister's for Thanksgiving, and I tried to eat 'the whole thing.' I feel lumpy and pudgy, but I enjoyed every calorie."

"Christmas is coming on," Lila moaned. "I'll be big as a house by New Year's Eve."

Gaye forced a laugh. "I doubt that."

"Oh, say, the captain of the neighborhood watch program called last night. There's been a strange blue car in the area for the past week. He asked me to pass the word along. It's nothing to be alarmed about. I don't get too excited about these reports. Someone probably has out-of-town relatives visiting for the holidays."

"You're probably right, but I'll pass it along to the sitter. See you tonight."

Gaye had spent the long days refinishing the primitives she had brought from Indiana. She carried them up from the basement a few at a time and worked on them in the kitchen so she could be near Johnny. At night, if sleep wouldn't come, she would read or turn on the television and watch the all-night movie channel.

When each dawn came she would ask herself the same question. Why had she fallen in love with Jim Trumbull? Why had her body responded to his and longed for him, as it did even now? Why did the sound of his whispered words haunt her sleepless hours, and why couldn't she forget the pleasure that had flowed between them?

Each night she asked herself, why is he staying away? Will he call tomorrow? She also had begun to question her own stability. In a year's time she had fallen desperately in love with two different men who were as unlike each other as day and night.

She didn't know what she would do without Lila's friendship. They talked to each other at least once a day on the telephone. Being confined to the house with children, Lila was forever needing something from the supermarket that Gaye dropped off after she finished her own shopping.

Gaye spoke to Alberta daily, but her sister was a busy woman and Gaye tried not to take up time Alberta could spend with her teenage children.

Johnny was developing a personality of his own. It hadn't taken long for him to learn that the more noise he made, the more attention he received. Gaye dressed him in the denim overalls she had bought for him and took him to the photographer. He proved to be a regular ham—loving the lights and the noise—and she was sure the pictures would be adorable.

Gripped by her need to clear her mind of thoughts of Jim, Gaye threw herself into the exercise routine with vigor. She let the music envelop her, let her ears hear only the voice of the instructor.

"Two, three, four...higher, higher. Pull those muscles, girls. One, two, three, stretch. Keep the legs straight, Lila. Two, three, four, touch the floor, Kathy." Gaye felt her heartbeat accelerate, felt the muscles pull, felt the power of the music forcing her to keep pace with it, felt the sweat trickle down between her breasts.

"On the floor, girls. We'll level off with something slower. You've lost weight, Gaye. I'll have to use you as an advertisement for my class. Here we go. One, two, three, four, stretch and hold..."

Gaye scarcely heard the instructor call her name. The song, "Bridge Over Troubled Water," flowed out of the speaker. It was one of her all-time favorites. I won't cry, she told herself sternly. I won't. Dear Lord, she prayed, let me get over him. Please...let me not care.

After the class she peeled off her sweat-soaked leotard, showered and dressed. While she was waiting for Lila, Barbara, the instructor, called to her.

"You're looking great, Gaye. You've really lost weight."

"I hadn't noticed. I haven't weighed myself lately."

"Not weighed yourself lately?" Lila came out of the dressing room and echoed her words. "If I pass up a doughnut, I run to weigh myself to see if it's made a difference. It isn't fair!"

"When they passed out fat, I got a double helping, too," Barbara said, laughing.

Gaye wondered where in the world the tiny instructor had put the extra helping of fat.

"Kathy and Beverly want to stop for a drink. Is that okay with you, Gaye?" Lila looked hopeful, and Gaye shrugged indifferently. "Would you like to come along, Barb?"

"No, thanks. I've got a husband and two boys at home. They've probably got the house torn apart by now. I'll see you next week."

Gaye would rather have gone home, but she didn't want to disappoint Lila. They followed the women in the other car to a nightclub. The outside of the building looked like a warehouse; the inside looked like an exclusive restaurant and bar, which it was.

They paused in the entry to allow their eyes to become adjusted to the dim light, then Kathy led the way to the bar. They sat at a round table in padded barrel-back chairs. Gaye reminded herself to be pleasant, to smile, to not act as if she'd rather be anyplace else in the world but here. She ordered rum and Coke.

"I love it here. They serve the most fabulous lobster." Kathy was definitely in her element. "What do you say we treat ourselves to a night out when we finish the class."

"What? And put all that weight back on? I wonder if they have a salad bar?" Lila giggled.

"If they did, it would cost an arm and a leg. You might as well go for the lobster."

"Speaking of 'go for'—isn't that your caveman coming out of the dining room with the tall blonde?" Beverly stretched her neck to get a better look.

"Dammed if it isn't! Look, Lila. Isn't he gorgeous?"

Gaye knew who they were talking about even before her eyes landed on the big man in the dark suit. Her heart dropped to the pit of her stomach, and she felt the blood drain from her face. She glanced quickly at Lila and found her staring at her. She shook her head in a silent plea, and her friend nodded. Gaye sat stone still, as if the slightest movement would cause him to look her way, and thanked God that they were sitting in the darkest corner of the bar.

"I wonder who that is with him. I haven't seen her around here before. I'd remember the clothes, if not the woman."

"She's no sweet young thing. She looks more like a member of the Four Hundred Club. God, he's handsome! Mature! Rugged! How'd you like to go to bed with a hunk like that? I bet he's like a leashed stallion!"

"You can talk, Kathy, but if he made a pass at you it would scare you to death." Lila reached for a cocktail napkin and wrapped it around her glass.

Gaye couldn't take her eyes off the couple across the room. He'd had a haircut. His hair had been *styled.* These thoughts came to her among others: the white shirt makes his skin look darker, and the suit is tailor-made to fit his broad shoulders. The woman with him acts as if they've known each other forever and that he belongs to her. Oh, God! Why did I come here tonight? Gaye, you fool. This hurt reaches into your very soul. It was never like this with Dennis.

Jim helped the woman into a long fur coat and took her arm, and they passed out of Gaye's sight. She sat numbly, grateful for Lila's chatter. The other two girls launched into their plans for a Christmas skiing holiday. Gaye pretended to listen, nodded occasionally, and when she finished her drink refused to order another.

"No more for me, either," Lila said. "I'd just as soon head 'em up and move 'em out toward home. I don't know, Gaye, if we should leave these two lambs here for the wolves or not."

"I think they're capable of handling most anything that comes along," Gaye said lightly. "Have fun, you two."

Lila didn't speak until they were in the car and on their way to her house.

"What gives, honey? I saw your face when you saw Jim Trumbull. That was Jim Trumbull wasn't it?"

"Yes, it was him. I thought he was out of town. I haven't heard from him for a while, that's all. I guess I was just surprised to see him dressed up." She laughed and prayed it didn't sound too forced. "He didn't look like the same guy."

"Are you going to continue taking care of his grandson?"

"That's a decision I have to make before long. If I want to teach in this school district next year, I should be putting in my application." Gaye turned the car into Lila's driveway. "How come the boys didn't go to Betty's tonight?" she said, desperate to change the subject.

"Kurt thinks he's old enough to baby-sit Kyle. Tonight is a trial run. I see the house is still standing, so maybe he is old enough. Talk to you tomorrow." Lila got out of the car with a wave of her hand.

Gaye drove slowly down the block. Her shoulders slumped, her lips trembled on muttered words. "Jim, you monster! Why didn't you tell me you were coming back? And why did I have to see you with that woman! I could have handled it without that!"

She passed Joy's little car in the driveway and drove

around to the carriage house. The new yard light lit up the area, and she was no longer afraid of the walk to the side door. One more hurdle to cross, she thought as she closed the garage door. Get Joy out of the house and I can sit and think about what I am going to do.

Joy left immediately after stuffing the bills in her pocket. "I never heard a peep out of Johnny, Aunt Gaye," she said at the door. "See you next week."

Gaye stood in the middle of the room and listened to Joy rev up the motor and shoot off down the drive. Then she removed the fire screen and put another log on the fire. She padded through the house in her stocking feet and turned out all the lights except the small one in the hall, then slumped down in the recliner.

She didn't know how long she had been sitting there listening to the crackling fire eat up the log. She thought about taking some aspirin or a bath, but she did neither. She sat quietly, scarcely moving a muscle. There was a numbness inside her, a disappointment so great Gaye couldn't put a name to her emotion. The doorbell chimed, and she lifted her feet off the ottoman with regret. Joy had, more than likely, forgotten her schoolbooks.

Gaye switched on the lamp beside her chair and reluctantly went to the door. She flipped on the outside light, unlocked the door, and opened it.

Jim stood on the steps, his hand attached to the elbow of a tall blond woman in a hooded fur coat. He wore his shearling coat and his head was bare. His hair was no longer neatly combed, but wildly windblown. She stared at them blankly as she wrestled with the conflicting emotions that stormed through her. Resentment, anger...love; they were all there, beating against the wall of her heart. Her first impulse was to slam the door. How could he do this to her? The deceitful, conniving jerk! Jealousy ripped through her with biting pain. Then pride took over and gave her courage a needed boost.

"Good evening, Mr. Trumbull." Her calm voice and placid expression masked the wrenching ache that tore at her heart.

"Hello, Gaye. I know it's late, but we came by earlier and saw that the baby-sitter's car was here. We drove around awhile and—"

"And you want to see your grandson. I understand. Come in." Gaye stepped back and swung open the door.

The first thing she noticed about the woman was the perfume; the second thing was how tall she was.

"Gaye, this is Jean Wisner. I've talked so much about MacDougle, she thinks he's unreal and wants to see him for herself."

"He's definitely real," Gaye said carefully and was proud her voice was steadier than her stomach. "May I have your coat?"

"Thank you, but we won't be staying that long," Jean announced as if she were speaking to a butler or a maid.

Jim frowned and shrugged out of his coat in what seemed to Gaye a deliberate contradiction of his lady friend's words. She threw him an impatient glance.

His presence filled the room. Gaye moved quickly to the other side of the couch. She hadn't looked at him since her startled eyes had met his when she opened the door. She could feel them on her now. She felt warm, almost suffocated. Her throat hurt, and she swallowed before she spoke again.

"I'll take you up to see Johnny," she said and moved toward the stairway. She'd be damned if she'd let them wander about in *her* house alone! "He sleeps through the night. He's one of the rare babies who never gets his days and nights mixed.'' She knew the woman was directly behind her when she started up the stairs. The perfume! Phew! She hated strong, sweet scents—it was the reason she used unscented cosmetics.

''Johnny? I thought his name was MacDougle,'' Jean corrected her.

''Mr. Trumbull calls him that, but his name is John MacDougle. While he's in my care I like to think of him as Johnny.'' Gaye was proud of the fact that she was able to respond coolly to Jean's thinly disguised thrusts.

Gaye stepped inside Johnny's room and turned the round switch beside the door, making the dim light brighter. Jean went immediately toward the crib. Jim paused in the doorway. Gaye tilted her head and looked up at him. The heady bliss she had shared with him was being destroyed bit by bit. She felt as if the licorice black eyes beneath the thick, straight brows were reading her innermost thoughts, attacking the barrier she had erected to protect her pride.

They exchanged a charged look before Jim's eyes released hers and he moved toward the crib. Her eyes, filled with the awful hurt she refused to allow him to see, followed him. He bent over and lifted Johnny, swinging him up into the crook of his arm.

''The little devil is awake, Gaye.'' He looked back over his shoulder. His face was beaming with pride. She prayed the wretchedness she was feeling wasn't reflected in hers.

''He's beautiful! Adorable!'' Jean held out her arms, and Jim let her take the baby. ''You're a darling,'' she cooed.

Johnny's face puckered, and he let out an earsplitting cry of terror.

''He's frightened!'' Gaye moved almost without being

aware of it and snatched the baby from the fur-clad arms. She turned her back on the two startled people beside the crib and cuddled him to her. "It's all right, darling. Sshhh...don't cry. No one is going to hurt you. Sshhh..." she whispered reassuringly. Johnny gasped a few times, and then his crying ceased as abruptly as it started. "There, there...you're all right."

"It's my fault. I shouldn't have tried to hold him." Jean moved over beside Gaye and looked anxiously at the baby.

"He isn't used to strangers," Gaye said, more sharply than she knew.

"I can see that. I'm sorry I frightened him." She took hold of a tiny fist and Johnny spotted the large, sparkling diamond on her finger. He grabbed for it, a grin splitting his toothless mouth. "I think he's decided he likes me. Do you think he'll let me hold him now?" Gaye released the warm little body reluctantly. The instant Johnny felt himself being transferred from Gaye's arms he let out a cry of rage. Jean shoved him back at Gaye and stepped back. "I'm afraid you're going to have a mama's boy, Jim," she said impatiently.

"What's so bad about that? MacDougle feels safe with Gaye. She's his security."

"You shouldn't allow him to be so dependent on one person. Each time you change sitters, he'll have to adjust. He needs to know that any number of people will look after him."

Gaye went pale. Her eyes quickly sought Jim's face. He looks tired, she thought. The hard bones of his jaws were clenched, and there were shadows under his eyes like bruises. The lines on each side of his mouth were lines of fatigue. Her breath caught in the back of her throat. He was watching her through half-closed lids.

"MacDougle needs to get back to sleep. C'mere, laddie. You're not afraid of me."

Jim came close to Gaye. His hand moved caressingly down her arm to cover hers as it cupped the small bottom. She felt the pressure of his fingers squeeze gently before he lifted his grandson to his shoulder. Johnny grabbed a handful of Jim's hair and held on. His other hand flayed at Jim's face.

"Hey...there! You learned a few tricks while I was gone." He bounced the baby in his arms, and the infant giggled.

"He knows you, all right. You must spend a lot of time with him." Jean's face swung toward Gaye, her gray eyes appraising. Gaye could feel the intensity of envy within them.

"I spend as much time with him as I can." Jim deftly put his grandson in the crib.

"I see you've done this before." Jean moved to the doorway and turned to look about the room. "He'll need more space than this before long."

A sudden knifelike anger stabbed through Gaye. "Mr. Trumbull will be making other arrangements for him soon, Mrs. Wisner. Perhaps you'd like to take on the job. It pays well." The patronizing tone in her voice fit perfectly with the tilt of her chin.

Jean looked down at her coolly from her superior height. "I could handle it. I have a big house and reliable household help. That's an idea, Jim. Bring him out to Bowling Green and I'll look after him for you."

Jim's dark eyes were on Gaye when he spoke. "Thanks for the offer, Jean, but the boy stays here...with me." There was a finality to his statement, and Jean flounced from the room.

Gaye turned down the light and followed them down

the stairs. At the bottom she paused on the last step and found herself looking into a ruggedly handsome, amused face. The twinkle in his eyes infuriated her and frightened her. Her heart gave a sickening leap. The big jackass knew she was jealous!

"I like the stair carpet, Gaye."

"I'm glad, because you paid for it," she replied with an indifferent composure she was far from feeling.

"It's rather warm in here. If we're not going, I'll have to take off my coat." Jean's impatient voice cut between them.

"We're going," Jim said softly, still looking at Gaye.

Her head was pounding. She was unable to get her thoughts together. She was tired and confused and wanted them to get the hell out of her house before the plastic expression on her face cracked and crumbled. She felt limp and as drab as a pile of wet laundry beside this willowy, perfectly groomed, confident woman. Her only defense was to force her thoughts inward. Play the game, Gaye. Be perfectly polite. If you break down, he'll know he's gotten to you. She stepped around Jim and went to the door.

"Are you all right, Gaye? You look tired."

"I'm fine, Mr. Trumbull. You?"

"Fine."

"You're dead tired, darling." Jean pulled the hood of her coat up and arranged it carefully over her perfectly coiffured head. "I know for a fact you haven't had much sleep since we left Europe. Not even you, darling, can go three days with a couple hours' sleep."

Gaye pulled open the door. "Good night."

"I'll be back," Jim said as he passed her.

She resisted the impulse to slam the door behind them and immediately switched off the outside light. "I hope you fall down the steps and break your fool neck!" she muttered. "You'll be back, all right! Damn right, you will!" A wave of self-pity washed over her. Why did it have to hurt so damn much?

Gaye drew a warm bath and tried to soak away the feeling of hurt and disappointment inside her. She was nervous and jumpy and on leaving the tub slipped into her gown and went into the baby's room. He was sleeping soundly. Her fingers gently stroked his head and the tears finally came. A deep, shuddering sigh convulsed her body as the questions throbbed in her brain. To give Johnny up now would be like giving up her own baby all over again. How could she bear it? Would Jim come for him in the morning?

Jim. She didn't want to remember how tenderly he had made love to her. The hellish nights she'd spent with Dennis were like a black cloud, and the time she'd spent in Jim's arms was the silver lining. She stood beside the crib and weighed the pros and cons. She could continue to take care of Johnny if she wanted to. In spite of everything, she was certain that Jim wanted what was best for his grandson. But could she do it? No, she decided. It would be better to make a clean break. Better for her and better for Johnny.

She went to her room, crawled wearily into bed and pulled the coverlet up over her ears. She drifted into a sort of trance. Sleep eluded her for what seemed hours. Finally a deadly lassitude crept over her and she slept.

She awakened suddenly. The telephone was ringing. Frightened, she sat up and reached for the light switch. The light sprang on, and she squinted against its harshness, searching for the phone with sleep-drugged eyes. Just as her hand found it she realized it wasn't the phone, but the doorbell. Good Lord! It must be Jim—he said he'd be back.

Gaye sat on the edge of the bed, fully awake. She wouldn't let him in. He could come back in the morning. But...maybe it wasn't Jim. It could be an emergency—Alberta! She grabbed up her robe and crept down the stairs. A long dark car was parked beneath the portico. *Bang!* The door rattled beneath the heavy pounding.

"Open the door, Gaye. I know you're there. I saw the light go on in your bedroom."

It *was* Jim! No! she screamed silently. I can't face you tonight. She stood slumped against the wall, her heart galloping in her breast while a thousand tiny hammers pounded her head.

"Let me in. I want to talk to you."

A sharp rap caused her to jump back. Had he lost his mind? He was making enough noise to wake up the whole neighborhood.

"Open the door! Dammit! I'd be in there if it wasn't for that goddamn bolt!"

"Go away, Jim. We can talk in the morning."

"We'll talk now!" he shouted. The pounding that followed jarred the windows.

"You're waking the whole neighborhood."

"I know how to really wake them up. I'll get in the car and sit on the horn. That ought to do it."

Should she let him in and get it over with? While she was trying to decide what to do, automobile lights flashed in the room. A car came swiftly up the drive and screeched to a halt.

"Hold it right there!" an authoritative voice commanded. "Hands up. Turn around."

The police? Oh, dear heavens! Gaye leaned weakly

against the door. She'd forgotten about the neighborhood watch program. She turned on the outside light and opened the door.

"Who are you and what're you doin' here?" Two uniformed policemen confronted Jim.

"Jim Trumbull, Officer Callaway."

"Jim? What the hell are you doin'?" We've had at least five calls reporting everything from a break-in to disturbing the peace."

"My lady friend is a heavy sleeper!" Gaye gasped at the implication of his words. Jim turned. "There you are, darlin'. Were you going to make me sleep in the car tonight? I'd much rather sleep with you."

"You...jackass!" Gaye felt sick, filled with humiliation and self-contempt for what she had allowed to happen, which gave credence to what he was saying. She stepped back and tried to slam the door. Jim moved quickly and stuck out his booted foot.

"Oh, no, you don't. Calm down, sweetheart. I know you're mad at me, but I'll make it up to you. As you can see, I've got my work cut out for me tonight," he called laughingly over his shoulder to the officers.

"Okay, Jim. See you, 'round."

"I don't want you here," Gaye protested, but Jim pushed her aside, came in and closed the door.

"Hush up and turn on the light."

Gaye numbly moved through the gloom to the lamp beside the chair, switched on the light, then headed for the stairs. Jim's roar halted her.

"Gaye! I'm almost dead on my feet and my temper's on a short fuse. We'll talk here or upstairs; it's up to you."

Gaye turned and looked at him. A kind of brittle calmness possessed her. He was taking off his coat. He still wore the dark suit, but the tie was loosened and hanging askew. He looked tired and haggard, but she refused to soften toward him.

"I made a mistake the other night when I allowed you to stay. I've no intention of making that mistake again. So if that's what you're here for, you might as well leave."

She knew her biting words affected him. His lips tightened, and his brows drew together in an ominous scowl.

"Make some coffee. This is going to be a long night."

"We can talk in the morning."

He ignored her words. She watched him take off his suit coat and toss it carelessly aside, take off his boots and place them beside the chair. He went to the fireplace, and carefully and methodically, he began to arrange shredded paper and kindling to build a fire.

"Jim..."

"Dammit, Gaye! Can't you do this one thing for me without arguing?" The scowl on his face made him look older and more fierce.

He was very angry! Feeling more panic-stricken than she ever had in her life, Gaye almost ran to the kitchen.

Chapter Ten

"I saw you at the bar tonight. Do you make a habit of stopping there?" He was sprawled in the recliner, his feet on the ottoman.

The attack hit Gaye like a dash of cold water the instant she came into the room. She paused at the end of the couch, then set the coffeepot and mug on the table beside his chair. She answered him with a question of her own.

"Does that make me unfit to care for your grandson?" She sat on the end of the couch and curled her feet up under her robe.

"You saw me there with Jean. Why don't you say it?" He was staring at her. Her eyes flew to him, then just as quickly darted back to her tightly clasped hands in her lap.

"Yes, I saw you there. How was Europe?"

There was a long pause, and she thought that either

he hadn't heard her or he planned to ignore her. Finally he said, "I didn't notice. I was there on business." Then, with his dark eyes fixed firmly on her face, he asked, "What were you doing at the bar?"

"What does one usually do at bars?" she said flippantly, unaware of the stricken look on her face. The silence between them was heavy and deep. Her eyes moved from him to the floor. For a moment she was incapable of speaking. Then anger stiffened her spine. "Can you think of a better place for a single woman to make friends?"

"If I thought that was true, I'd—" he snarled.

"You'd what?" Gaye jumped to her feet. Her face paled. "I think this has gone far enough, Jim. I don't have to sit here and be insulted in my own house. I want you to leave." His glittering dark eyes blazed into hers. She gazed at him blindly, waiting, her own eyes fixed on his hard, sensual mouth.

Suddenly the anger left him. "I'm sorry," he said wearily. "Sit down and talk to me. I've been worried sick. The last ten days have been pure hell." He held her eyes with his. Now he could see the ravages in her face, ravages no cosmetics could disguise. Her cheeks were hollow, her skin so pale it seemed transparent, her brown eyes, usually so soft and shining, bruised and sullen. "You've lost weight."

"Don't change the subject!"

"Okay. I've got a million things to tell you, and I don't know where to start. I went to Europe to see Marla, got stuck with Jean—oh, hell! I can't lose you and MacDougle!" he blurted. In the silence that followed he rested his head against the back of the chair and closed his eyes.

Gaye's body tensed as she tried to stop trembling. She

sank back down on the couch, her eyes fastened on his face. He confused her, excited her, angered her. Wisps of dark hair lay on his forehead, matching eyebrows that were as thick and straight as if they had been put there by the stroke of a paintbrush. There was a tension and vibrancy about his body that made her think of a coiled spring. The tightness in her stomach worsened; her eyes misted, blurring her vision. The tension had made her lightheaded.

"I've known Jean for ten years. We were involved in a business venture together. That's over now," Jim said quietly.

He'd been so still and quiet she had thought he'd gone to sleep. Now she realized he'd been watching her through shuttered lids. Somewhere in a quiet little corner of her heart she felt a stab of pity for him—he seemed so weary.

"She doesn't want it to be over," Gaye said with a weary sigh of her own. "She's in love with you."

"She only thinks she is." Jim spoke completely without vanity. "Jean would be bored with me in no time at all. She only wants what she can't have. We'd never hitch together. She'd make a lousy mother for MacDougle, for one thing. The other, and the most important reason I'd never marry her is that I'm head over heels in love with someone else."

"If you mean me, Jim, I'm not buying it." There was a slight tremor in her voice when she spoke, but her eyes met his unwaveringly.

"I do mean you, Gaye. And I'm going to do everything I can to see that you buy it. We should have had this talk the night I came back, but I didn't want to worry you. Besides, I had other things on my mind that night." The change in his face was magical. A soft, loving light shone from his dark eyes. His words and the sound of his deep voice touched something in her memory, making her heart jump. His eyes caressed her flushed face.

"We could have talked on the phone. But all you did was shout at me." Her lower lip quivered as she remembered.

"I know, and I'm sorry about losing my temper. My only excuse is that I was worried. I guess I can also blame it on the fact that I haven't had anyone to share my anxieties with for so long, I find it hard to do." After a pause, he said quietly, "Marla and Crissy are going to try and take MacDougle away from me. It would be their way to snatch him and work out the legal tangles later."

"No!" She stared at him in alarm. "Why? Why do they want him now? They didn't want him when he was so little, and so...weak and needed his mother's milk so desperately!"

"Money and status are the important things to them. Marla's family never approved of me. I got along with the old man all right, but his sons think I'm crude, uncultured—a barbarian!" he said with an amused laugh.

"If you didn't want me to leave Johnny here alone with a sitter and go to the dance class, why didn't you say so? What if someone had come while I was gone? Joy would have been frightened to death!"

"I didn't tell you because I knew you'd be worried. I put a round-the-clock watch on the house. You were followed even when you went to the grocery store, and I called the agency every day. I was reasonably sure you and MacDougle were safe for the time being, or I'd have been back. I wanted to get some business matters and this thing with Marla cleared up so when I came home I wouldn't have to leave again."

"I can't believe this! Why do they want him now

when they didn't want him a few months ago? What are you going to do? Can they take him away from us?" Gaye was so upset she didn't realize she had used the word "us."

"They're going to try, sweetheart. I met with Marla's brothers in New York. Someone has shown up who claims to be MacDougle's father, someone whose family hasn't produced an heir for a good long while. It's very important to some of the European families that their lineage continue. It seems there's a chance for a good marriage for Crissy—money and title not excluded," he added bitterly. "I went to France to talk to Marla and reason with her, but she and Crissy were off skiing in the Alps, and knowing I'd be madder than hell, they made sure I couldn't find them."

"Was that the reason you went to Europe?" She hoped that it was. She didn't want to think he had taken a holiday with Jean.

"Yes and...no. I sold six head of registered Appaloosa horses that Jean and I owned together to a breeder in Southern France. A part of the deal—and this wasn't sprung on me until later—was that I'd fit them with a special type of shoe for that terrain. Another thing that was sprung on me at the last minute was the fact Jean was going along. I'm also selling a farm I have near Bowling Green that joins one Jean owns. I don't plan to retire. I'll still have my fingers in a few things, but I want to spend most of my time here with you and MacDougle."

"Why did you let me think you were a blacksmith?" The bitterness she had felt for so many days seemed to dissolve in one shuddering sigh. All that remained was a tiredness and a doubt that she and this man could ever be totally compatible.

"I *am* a blacksmith, sweetheart. I love the work. I'm mapping out a course to teach at the college trade school this spring. It's a craft that helped to build America to what it is today. The West would never have been settled without the blacksmith. I'm also a mining engineer, investor, welder, writer, teacher, grandfather and I'm Irish to boot." He grinned.

"Be serious. I'm worried about Mac—about Johnny. To know he's with people who don't really love him, who're just using him for their own selfish reasons, would be more than I could endure!" She knew she was about to lose control. She clenched her jaws against the sobs that almost choked her.

"They're not going to take him away from you, Gaye. I told Marla's big-shot lawyer brothers that they'd get MacDougle over my dead body." A mischievous sparkle lighted his eyes. "They seemed to think that was a pretty good idea, especially after I slammed one of them into the wall."

"You didn't! They could have had you arrested, and how would that have looked at a trial!" She couldn't help but smile as the mental picture flashed through her mind.

"I need you, sweetheart. I need your calming influence. C'mere and let me hold you." He was stretched out on the recliner, his feet on the ottoman, his arms open.

It was tempting, but Gaye shook her head vigorously. There were too many unanswered questions. He seemed to read her mind.

"Tomorrow I'll take you and MacDougle out to my place. I want you to meet my mother and my aunt. I want you to know all there is to know about me. You already know that I'd rather be here with you than anywhere else in the world. I want you and need you like I never believed I'd want and need a woman. I'm not a young man, Gaye, but I'm financially secure if that's important to you. It's taken me a long time to find the woman I want to spend the rest of my life with. I'm not going to let you get away from me." He spoke so softly and so sincerely she could almost believe him. But there was still the hurt inside her.

"If what you say is true, why did you bring Jean here?" She looked at him in angry bewilderment.

He looked back at her calmly, and for a long while he didn't speak. Then, he said, "Anything I say will sound like a half-ass excuse. The truth is, and I didn't even know it at the time, I was crazy jealous when I saw you at the bar. You looked right through me, and my imagination soared, especially when I saw who you were with. Two of those women have quite a reputation around town. It hit me with the force of a freight train that you'd decided you wanted to play the field."

"But—"

He lifted a hand. "Let me tell you. I want you to know everything about me, and that includes my weaknesses. Jean is a beautiful woman, and when she insisted on seeing MacDougle, I brought her here. I was stroking my own ego. I wanted you to see that another woman thought I was desirable. It sounds like high-school stuff, doesn't it?" He raked his fingers through his hair. "Love makes people do stupid, unpredictable things. You'd think that a man my age would know better."

"I'm sorry you had so little faith in me." The words came out over the lump in her throat. "You could have called me and let me know you were in town."

"Jean met me at the airport. She'd taken an earlier flight from New York. She told me she had spoken to one of Marla's brothers and he'd revealed some new developments in Marla's plans to regain custody of MacDougle. Jean said she had made reservations and would tell me about it over dinner. I shouldn't have believed her, but I did. Her information didn't amount to a hill of beans!"

"I thought she lived in Bowling Green."

"She does. Her folks live here. Jean married into money, but ever since her husband died her main goal in life has been to marry me. Jean enjoys the chase. I got her interested in the horses, hoping she would find someone else. She's a snob at heart. But for some reason she thought she could polish me up and make me presentable." He laughed, a low chuckling sound. "I learned a long while ago, my darling, that I can be no less than what I am. I will bend if I honestly can, but I'll never change myself to someone else's specifications."

Gaye closed her eyes. She had to think! She had to sort out her emotions, untangle the confused motivations and decide what she really wanted out of life. The endearment, the low, persuasive voice were wreaking havoc with her logic. She opened her eyes to see Jim leaving the chair. He bent and placed another log on the fire, replaced the screen. He straightened up, his eyes focused on her with an intense expression—loving, possessive, hungry and...wary.

"Marry me, Gaye. Marry me and we'll fight for MacDougle together." He sat down beside her. She held out her hand, palm up, as if to hold him away from her. He took it in his and moved it to his chest. She felt his heart leaping under it. The rest of him was still; a peculiar, silent waiting was between them.

"Can you possibly be thinking that I want you because of MacDougle? If you're thinking that, you're wrong. You underestimate yourself, sweetheart. I meant it when I told you that you're every sweet dream I've ever had rolled into one."

"Jim...don't be so nice to me. I can handle it much better when you...bellow and roar." Sudden tears ached behind her eyes.

"And I will again, sweetheart. I'm not a patient man. But...I've got a heart full of love for you."

Very softly she said, "Oh, Jim. I've been so miserable."

His eyes, soft with love, drank in her face. Then, with a deep sigh, he took her in his arms and held her close, her head resting on his shoulder, while he gently stroked her hair. They sat quietly, hugging each other, for a long while. Then he lifted her chin.

"I love you, babe. I love you. I never thought I'd ever say that." His voice was husky and quivered with emotion. Her words melted on her lips when she tried to speak, swept away by his kisses. "Hold me. I need you, my love." There was an anguish in his voice that pierced her heart.

"I...love you. Jim, I do love you!"

"Ahhhh...that's what I wanted to hear." He kissed her long and hard, his mouth taking savage possession of hers, parting her lips and invading them in a wild, sweet, wonderful way. His hands began to stroke her, moving everywhere, touching her hungrily from her thighs to her breasts. He leaned back and stretched out on the couch, taking her to lie on top of him. He positioned her thighs between his, pulled her up to lie on his chest and pressed her head to his shoulder. Her face found refuge against his neck. She felt his hands on her buttocks, pulling her tightly against him.

"Ahhhh..." he sighed. "This is the way it was the night before I left. I'm home. I'm really home."

He fell asleep almost immediately with his arms wrapped around her. She lay relaxed and contented on top of him. This moment was hers, and nothing could take this away from her. She listened to his steady breathing and watched the vein pulse in his throat. She burrowed her lips into the opening of his shirt, her nose into the fine black hair. He smelled male, with a faint overtone of soap and deodorant. She was suddenly conscious of the soft, vulnerable, male part of him nestled snugly against her upper thighs. A feeling of protectiveness for this big, rugged, lonely man washed over her, and she wanted to hold him to her breast and comfort him.

Feeling wonderfully happy and relaxed, Gaye closed her eyes, thinking she would wait until he was sleeping soundly before she got up and went up to bed.

Then she, too, fell into a dreamless slumber.

Gaye became half awake and realized she was lying in bed and Jim's head lay on her breast. Fleeting memories of being carried up the stairs, of having her robe removed and being tucked into bed, flitted across her mind. She'd been so tired. She had opened her eyes one time and had seen Jim's face; then, feeing so loved and cared for, she had drifted back to sleep.

A sound penetrated her consciousness, and she came instantly awake. Johnny was crying. She glanced at the clock on the table. It's no wonder he's crying, she thought guiltily. It's almost an hour past his regular feeding time.

The weight of Jim's head on her breast was achingly sweet. Her arms curved about him tenderly. She had never felt so completely a woman as she hugged the shaggy head and pressed her lips to his forehead. This big, rough, self-assured man needed her!

She eased him out of her arms and tried to move away so she could get out of bed. His arms reached for her and pulled her snugly against him. He curled around her like a contented kitten.

"Don't go," he whispered against the top of her head.

"I've got to. Johnny's crying for his bottle."

"He's had you all to himself for weeks. It's my turn," he grumbled sleepily.

Gaye laughed softly against his hairy chest. "You big baby. You've got to learn to share."

"Well...all right. But kiss me first and...come right back." His words were husky and love-slurred.

She lifted her lips, his mouth taking hers in a kiss that engaged her soul. His lips hardened, and her own parted under them, admitting him, submitting. She touched the tip of her tongue delicately against his mouth and felt him tremble, felt his body stir against her stomach. His hands moved to her buttocks to press her against him.

"Jim...we can't...." Her muttered words were barely coherent.

He loosened his arms and she rolled away. "Bring him in here." His voice reached her at the door.

Johnny was wet, hungry and angry. Gaye changed his diaper, put him in a dry sleeper and carried him downstairs. He was somewhat happier by the time the bottle came from the microwave, and sucked on it lustily as she carried him back up the stairs to her bedroom.

Jim lifted the covers, and she lay down beside him holding the infant in her arms. Her head rested on Jim's arm, and he pulled her tightly into the curve of his body. He lifted his head and his lips nuzzled her cheek. His hand cupped his grandson's bottom and he shook him gently. The baby smiled around the nipple in his mouth.

"You little imp! You're not playing fair." He placed kisses along Gaye's jawline and whispered in her ear. "You went downstairs without your slippers. Your feet are like ice cubes. No...don't move them away." He lifted a warm bare leg over hers and pressed her feet to him with the bottom of his. "Your feet wouldn't be this cold if you were still breast-feeding him," he murmured.

"Oh, Jim. Do you think they'll take him away from us?" She turned her head so she could whisper against his mouth.

"We'll do everything we can to see that he stays right here where he belongs."

"Your daughter signed away her rights to him. She doesn't deserve to have him."

"My lawyer says they'll probably say she signed under duress, that I pressured her into signing him over to me. But don't worry about it now, sweetheart."

"I can't help worrying. He's ours!" Her arms tightened about the infant.

"We'll build the best case we can to keep him legally without digging up dirt. But if we think there's a chance we'll lose him, I'll pull out all the stops. I know things about Marla and my daughter that the *National Enquirer* would love to know, and I'll spill everything before I'll give him up to them."

Gaye was shocked at the viciousness in his voice. "Good heavens! Do you think it'll come to that?"

"It could. Marla sees a chance to get a titled husband for Crissy. We're going to have to get our house in order, sweetheart. And that means getting married right away. I'd planned to wait and give you a chance to get adjusted to the idea. It isn't a quick decision on my part.

I hope you know that. I've wanted you since that first day when I came into the hospital room and saw you nursing MacDougle,'' he said huskily, and his hand burrowed between her and the baby to cup around her breast. ''Are you going to nurse all our kids?''

''I suppose so.'' Her lips desperately sought his. After the long, deep kiss, she whispered, ''Oh, Jim! It's like a wonderful dream with a nightmare hovering over it.''

''MacDougle's asleep, sweetheart. I'll put him back in the crib so I can have you all to myself.'' Jim kissed the bare warm curve of her neck, following it to her ear and back to the hollow in her shoulder, covering her skin with light, tantalizing kisses.

''Turn him over on his tummy and cover him.'' She ran the tip of her tongue around the velvety inside of her lips as his had done, and her heart leaped in anticipation.

Jim lifted the infant from her arms and held him against his bare chest. His dark eyes moved from his grandson to Gaye's face. His smile was beautiful.

''I'm a fool to be so happy. But I'd given up on meeting a woman like you and having a family of my own.''

''No more of a fool than I am.'' She was thrilled by the deep, velvety look absorbing her and held out her arms. ''Put the baby down, love, and come back to me. The next hour or so is mine.''

When he returned Gaye had time for only one thought: He's handsome with his clothes on, but naked he's magnificent! Jim slipped into bed beside her and without any hesitancy claimed her lips in a fierce kiss. She opened her mouth and honored his ownership. Her heart beat with pure joy. He was forging chains that were binding him to her forever.

''Sweetheart, you're so beautiful. How have I survived this long without you? I love the feel of your breasts and the taste of your mouth. You're so soft, so feminine, so incredibly sweet!'' His words were groaned thickly into her ear.

The deeply buried heat in her body flared out of control, and she sought his mouth hungrily. Her hands moved to his back, digging into the smooth muscles. He stroked her, whispering words, their meaning muffled as he kissed her soft, rounded breasts, nibbled with his teeth, nuzzled with his lips. He was totally absorbed in giving her pleasure and at the same time pleasing himself.

''Jim...''

''Hmm?''

''Jim, darling—''

His hands cupped her hips and lifted her to him. ''Do you really want to talk, love?'' he asked an instant before his mouth settled over hers and the tip of his tongue found welcome inside her lips.

She couldn't have talked then if she had wanted to. Besides, she had forgotten what she was going to say.

Gaye cooked breakfast while Jim showered. He came down to the kitchen carrying his grandson in the crook of his arm. His black hair was wet and glistening. It seemed strange to Gaye to see him in her kitchen wearing the trousers to his dark suit and his wrinkled white shirt, opened at the neck and the sleeves rolled up to his elbows.

''I changed his pants. Phew! How long until he uses the bathroom like civilized folk?''

Gaye laughed happily. ''A couple of years, at least.'' She lifted bacon out to drain on a paper towel. ''How many eggs?''

"Three or four...and toast. I'm hungry as a bear."

"And you look like one, too." She let her fingertips drag across the stubble on his cheek. He grabbed her hand and brought it to his lips.

"I'll have to start shaving morning and night." He flashed her a wide, happy smile. "I don't want my whiskers to scratch your soft skin." He cupped the back of her head with one hand and kissed her soundly.

Gaye's arms went around him. The infant squirmed between them. This was more than she'd ever hoped to have. She leaned into his kiss, and when he released her she looked up at him with eyes shining with love.

"I'll gladly have my face scratched for that," she whispered.

While they were eating breakfast, Jim told her about his mother.

"She's the fourth generation to live on the farm. She and her sister have lived there together since my father was killed in the Pacific during the war. I went to school on my father's insurance money, roamed around a bit, married and decided the fast lane wasn't the life for me. I came back to the farm and have been there ever since, except for occasional business trips."

"Will we live there?" It was the first time the question of where they would live had crossed her mind.

"We'll live wherever you want to live. If you want to live here in your house, it's okay by me. If you want to live out at the farm, I'll build you a house. My mother is in the advanced stage of diabetes. She's very frail and almost blind. After my mother is gone, my aunt will stay in the home place for as long as she lives."

"Are you an only child?" Gaye asked quietly.

"Yes. I was born after my father went to war. It was lonely being raised without a father or brothers and sisters. We'll see that it doesn't happen to MacDougle." His eyes held hers, and her heart thudded painfully at the tenderness she saw there.

"Did Crissy stay with your mother while she was here?"

"No. I wouldn't subject my mother and aunt to her rudeness. I had a mobile home moved in for her to live in." His voice was quiet and solid as steel, and Gaye wished she hadn't asked the question.

"Is that where Johnny and I would have lived if I'd come out to the farm to take care of him?"

"Yes. I thought you'd rather have a place of your own. But since you didn't come, I had it hauled out."

"I'm sorry about your mother's illness."

"All I can do for her now is see to it that she's as comfortable as possible and that she stays in her home. That's what she wants to do. I wanted to take you out to see her before I left, but I wasn't sure how you'd react. It's not a glamorous place by any means, but it's my home and I love it and I hope you'll love it too," he said tersely, his face dark and taut with feeling, his eyes the smoldering black she knew so well.

She covered the back of his hand with her palm, and his turned to clasp tightly about her fingers.

"How could I not love something you love so much? It doesn't matter to me where we live as long as I'm with you."

"Thanks, sweetheart. You like this house. You feel at home here and so do I. We can live here until we decide what we want to do. We may want to build a new house on the farm, or remodel the old one for our large family." The endearing grin that made him look years younger spread over his face. "Shall we stay here today and start work on that project? I'm not getting any younger, you know."

"We worked on that this morning, Mr. Trumbull." Gaye got up from the table and gave a strand of his hair a little jerk when she passed him. He grabbed her arm and pulled her around and down on his lap. His lips nuzzled her neck.

"You tease! You make me want you so, I can't keep my hands off you."

Gaye wound her arms about his neck and hugged him fiercely. Her hands moved across the muscles of his back and up to grasp his hair, pulling the tip of his nose against hers. "Our boy needs his food," she said in a loud whisper.

Jim looked over her shoulder at the infant. "Young man," he said sternly, "we're going to have to come to an understanding about this woman. I'll share her during the day, but at night she's all mine."

Chapter Eleven

Gaye sat beside Jim in the big sedan. He had removed the padded car seat from the Buick and installed it in the back seat of his car for his grandson. The morning had flown by almost as fast as the landscape was flying past now.

"What will your mother think about all this? Will she be surprised?"

"She'll be pleased. I've told her about you." His long fingers burrowed down between her thighs and pulled the one next to his tightly against him. "But even if she wasn't, she wouldn't say anything. She taught me to be my own person, just as she is."

Gaye sat back in the seat and drew a deep breath. Tomorrow she would be married to this man. She hadn't even had the chance to tell Alberta and Lila yet about the marriage ceremony that would take place at the Methodist church.

Twenty-four hours ago she had been miserable and had thought she would never be happy again. Now her life had taken on a new radiance. It seemed so right to be sitting here beside Jim with Johnny strapped safely in the seat behind them.

She started when she heard Jim's voice. "What's the matter, sweetheart? Are you worried about meeting my mother and aunt and seeing my home?"

"No. I'm not worried about anything. That's what bothers me. Everything seems so right for me. It's as if this had been planned out in advance. The only thing that keeps me from being supremely happy is the threat of losing Johnny."

"Don't worry about that now. Let's take things one step at a time. Marla asked me to give him back to them; I said no. The next step is up to them. My former in-laws are very mercenary, yet very proud. They would hate to have this dragged through a court of law and all the dirty linen aired. That's a big plus in our favor."

Jim braked sharply as they rounded a curve and waited patiently for the rural-mail carrier to pull off the road. The grass that filled the ditches on each side of the road and grew along the fence line was now dried by the frosts. They passed through a heavily wooded area, the leafless branches of the trees stark against the sky, and came to the flat farm country. Occasionally they passed a farm where the huge barn dwarfed the house, a one-lane track connecting it to the road. The pastures were marked off with a network of white board fence, a small number of horses in each enclosure. At one farm a beautiful black horse, its lead rope attached to the circular exercise machine, trotted majestically with his head and his tail high.

They talked off and on, but impersonally, about the

land, wild animals and birds. Jim was a conservationist, and part of his land was a game preserve. He was vehemently opposed to indiscriminate hunters. He was especially vocal about hunting with a bow and arrow.

"I've found several deer that had crawled off to die with an arrow stuck in them. About a month ago I came on a horned owl that had been killed. I sent it to the state conservation commission, where it'll be preserved and shown to schoolchildren. Sad as it is, someday that may be the only way they'll see one."

He told her about the horse farm he had over near Paducah and the breeding program for his registered Appaloosa horses. He explained his reason for selling the farm at Bowling Green.

"The offer was just too good to turn down," he said with a grin.

The road bent to the left, Jim turned abruptly to the right and onto a narrow drive. A metal gate barred their way, and he got out to open it. The drive was smooth and covered with fine gravel. Evergreen trees crowded the lane as it wound back into the hills. As the trees began to thin, Gaye caught a glimpse of the farmhouse. From a distance it looked small. As they drew near she could see it was made of native stone. The front part of the house was two storied, the back part a single story with a side porch attached. A long board porch with a single step and a sloping roof ran across the front of the house, with two front doors opening onto it, and continued along the side. There were several barns and sheds and a newer building that sat off to the side in a grove of trees.

Jim stopped the car in front of another gate. A picket fence enclosed the home area. Gaye immediately thought of the song "Old MacDonald had a Farm." A big shepherd dog barked a greeting; ducks and geese waddled about the yard. Big fluffy chickens, both red and white, cackled and strutted. Two sheep looked them over indifferently and went on eating grass. Just when Gaye thought she had seen it all, her startled eyes found a billy goat perched on top of a pile of neatly cut wood.

After Jim closed the gate behind them, he got into the car and sat looking at her. Finally he spoke. "I have to put the car in the garage." He jerked his head toward the woodpile. "Ralph will lose no time climbing on top of it if I leave it out. He can cut up a vinyl top in no time at all." He searched her face. "You're so quiet. Does it overwhelm you?"

"I was just thinking of what a wonderful place this would be to bring a second-grade class. Some of the children I've taught have never been on a farm or seen animals outside a zoo."

Jim laughed. "What you see is only the tip of the iceberg. I've got cows, horses, a raccoon running around that refuses to leave, a couple of burros and a donkey named Hortense. About the only thing you won't find here is pigs. Someone gave me a runt to raise when I was a boy. We couldn't butcher it after I became attached to it. It grew to be about seven hundred pounds and died of old age. He'd probably eaten seven hundred dollars worth of corn during his lifetime."

Gaye watched his face. He seemed to be relieved. Was he afraid I'd be disappointed? she wondered. She had to admit it was a little more than she'd expected. But now that she saw him in these surroundings she could see why he'd never be happy with a woman like Jean Wisner.

They drove to a garage behind the barn. The door raised as they approached the building. Jim drove inside and the door came down. He pulled in alongside his black pickup truck.

"This garage is the only building on the place that's animal- and bird-proof. I don't care much about driving to town and finding I've brought along a chicken or a cat." He turned off the motor, swung an arm up over her head and gripped her shoulder, pulling her to him. "I want to kiss you. I've been thinking about it all the way from town." His voice lowered huskily as his lips came close to hers.

"Then get on with it, love. I've been waiting, too." Her eyes danced lovingly over his face, and her hand inched up to curl about his neck.

The kiss was long and deep and full of promised passion that flared whenever they touched. His fingers moved up into her hair, their touch strong and possessive. She took his kiss thirstily. She wanted to stay there forever. His lips pulled away, but he drew her closely to him.

"I love you," he said quietly.

"I love you, too. I want to be with you forever."

"You shall be. My life has been empty up to now. You fill it completely." He kissed her again. Her lips were clinging moistly to his. His hand slipped inside her coat and up under her sweater. His eyes held hers while his fingers cupped about the flesh held in the lacy cup. Her nipple hardened, and drops of milk moistened her bra. "You still have milk," he whispered huskily.

"A little."

His lips fell hungrily to hers. They were demanding, yet tender. His tongue deeply invaded the mouth that parted so eagerly and grazed over pearl white teeth.

"We'd better stop this or I won't be able to go into the house for a while."

She laughed and pulled away from him. "We're like a couple of teenagers making out in a parked car. C'mon. Your mother and aunt will wonder what we're doing."

Jim carried the baby and Gaye walked beside him. Ducks and chickens were waiting when they came out of the building. Jim threw out a handful of grain he took from the barrel inside the garage door. A big white duck pecked at the shiny end of Gaye's shoelace, and she jumped back.

"You have to watch out for Kathryn," Jim said. "She gets pretty aggressive and can hurt you. She'll make a grab for anything that looks good to eat." Kathryn quacked, fluffed her feathers and strutted ahead of them.

"Do they all have names?"

"Most of them. We have two pet crows, so don't be frightened if one of them swoops down and lands on your shoulder. They like shiny, pretty things, too." He smiled down at her. "I took off my watch one day, and the minute I laid it down one of them grabbed it and flew up in a tree and hid it. I had a heck of a time shimmying up that tree to get it. Sometimes they'll meet the truck at the end of the lane and fly beside me all the way to the house."

"This is a wonderful place for children. It's no wonder you wanted your grandson with you."

They went up onto the porch that ran along the side of the house. The door opened as if someone had been watching and waiting. Jim stood back so she could enter.

Her first impression was that she had stepped back fifty years. The kitchen was warm, cozy and neat as a pin. A big black cookstove and an upright kitchen cabinet sat side by side. Shelves curtained with checked gingham lined the walls. In the middle of the room a round oak table and high-backed chairs sat on an oval braided rug. A potted African violet sat in the center of the cloth-covered table.

The woman who stood beside the door was elderly. She was small and neat and held herself erect. Her dress came within six inches of the floor and was covered with a bibbed apron. Soft gray hair was smoothed back and twisted in a bun at the nape of her neck. Her eyes were dark and met Gaye's warily. Gaye was thankful for Jim's big bulk that crowded into the doorway behind her.

"Hello, Aunt Minnie. This is Gaye."

"Hello." Gaye held out her hand. The woman hesitated and then took it for an instant in hers. Her eyes swung to Jim's, then down to the infant in his arms, and a smile faintly lifted the corners of her mouth.

"Hold him, Aunt Minnie, while I help Gaye with her coat." Jim placed Johnny in her arms. She held him carefully and moved away. "I forgot to tell you that Aunt Minnie doesn't speak," he whispered in her ear. He took her coat, hung it on a wooden peg beside the door and hung his beside it.

"We should take him out of the bunting bag," Gaye said gently. The woman lifted her gaze from the baby to Gaye. Gaye smiled and reached for the strings to untie the hood, then pulled down the zipper. "So you decided to wake up, did you?" she said to the wide-eyed child and lifted him out of the bag. She waited for the silent woman to place it on the back of a chair and handed Johnny back to her, praying he wouldn't cry as he had done the night Jean took him. He didn't. Gaye gave a sigh of relief and looked about.

Now she could see some modern equipment tucked away out of sight—an electric stove, a refrigerator-freezer, a washer-dryer. She caught a glimpse of a dishwasher adorned with a crocheted scarf and another potted African violet. I'll bet it's never used, she thought with a smile.

"We'd better take them in to see Mama, Aunt Minnie. She'll accuse us of plotting against her," Jim said teasingly and put his arm across the thin shoulders and gave her a hug. "Aunt Minnie has been a big part of my life," he said to Gaye. "I can't remember a time when she wasn't here for me to come to."

It was clear to Gaye, Jim's aunt adored him. She looked like a tiny sparrow standing next to him. She smiled up into his face, her eyes flashing a message only the two of them understood.

Jim enfolded Gaye's hand in his, and they followed the slim, erect figure through a dining room and into a living room, where a narrow stairway divided the front rooms and led to the rooms above. She led them into a large room. Jim's mother lay in a high hospital bed beside a large plate-glass window. She appeared to be a fleshier version of her sister.

"Hello, Mama. I brought Gaye and MacDougle to see you."

"Good. Bring her over so I can get a look at her."

Jim pulled Gaye toward the bed. Gaye remembered him telling her his mother was almost blind, and she wondered how much she could see.

"Hello, Mrs. Trumbull."

"Hello, lass. Sit down so I can see your face. Jim says you're not silly pretty." Gaye sat down and leaned forward. The gray head lifted, the clouded dark eyes narrowed and strained. "You'll do." She let her head fall back. "I like her face, son. Does she have any gumption to go with it?"

Gaye's startled eyes sought Jim's—his were twinkling. He towered above them, and she had to tilt her head far back to see his face. At this moment he reminded her of the Jolly Green Giant. His hand gripped her shoulder, and she returned his smile.

"Yes, Mama. She's not only got horse sense, she's got good teeth. Show her, honey." Gaye pinched him on the leg. He squeezed her shoulder in retaliation. "We're going to be married tomorrow. She knows a good thing when she sees one."

"I figured she was the one you wanted. It's time you took a wife. This'n got to be an improvement over the other'n." There was a touch of humor in her voice.

Jim's laugh was loud and boisterous. "She is. I waited a long time to find her. She's a lot like you, Mama. She's sassy and independent, but smart as a whip and has all the mating instincts. I'll be able to manage her if I keep her pregnant."

Mrs. Trumbull chuckled and Gaye's jaw dropped in amazement.

"I'd like to see that, son. You'll just have to tell me about it. Are you going to say anything, girl?"

"How can I?" Gaye sputtered. "You two seem to have things figured out."

"You've got grit, lass. You'll need it with my Jim."

"It seems I'll need a strong back, too."

Mrs. Trumbull laughed again, and Gaye wondered how she could be so cheerful. She got up from the chair when Jim urged his aunt toward the bed.

"MacDougle is growing by leaps and bounds, Mama."

"Lay him here beside me, son. Oh, my! You had hair like this when you were a baby. Didn't he, Minnie?"

Gaye stood back and watched. There seemed to be no lack of communication between the sisters. Johnny kicked, blew spit and enjoyed the attention he was getting. Jim hovered over them for a moment, then backed away to stand beside Gaye. His arm came around her and she looked up. The sad expression on his face touched her deeply, and her eyes misted over.

"Aunt Minnie, do you suppose you and mama can manage MacDougle for a little while? I want to take Gaye out to my workshop."

The gray head nodded eagerly, and Jim urged Gaye to the door with his hand in the small of her back.

The minute they stepped out the door, the big white duck ran to greet them, fluffing her feathers and quacking.

"Nothing this time, Kathryn. Run along, you're getting too fat. You'll find yourself in someone's pot if you're not careful." Jim spoke in a conversational tone, as if the duck understood every word he said, which she must have done because she turned and walked haughtily away. "Begone with you, too, Ralph," he said to the goat that walked up behind them and tried to get in between them. "You'll have to wait until Gaye gets acquainted with you before you get familiar."

"Oh, Jim," Gaye said and laughed, her eyes shining as she looked up into his. "This is a wonderful place."

"I'm glad you think so, sweetheart," he said, and his arm hugged her to him. "I want to show you my iron sculptures."

He led her down a dirt path toward a low building set among the trees. Nestled among the grasses along the path and backed against bushes and trees were an assortment of animal figures made of iron and painted in dull earthy colors. A deer, its head held in an alert position, stood partially hidden among the lilac bushes. In the grasses were rabbits, and attached to a tree trunk was a saucy squirrel. There was a skunk trailed by little ones, a fox, a turkey with its tail feathers spread, lambs, cows, goats, all life-size.

"I can't believe this." Gaye's laugh rang on the crisp, cool air. "I love the way you've placed them in their natural surroundings. They're *good,* Jim."

"I don't know how good they are, but it's something that gives me pleasure to do." His dark eyes ravished her face, bright with happiness.

"People should see them," she said enthusiastically. "You should share your talent. Have you sold any of them?"

"One or two." He shrugged. "C'mon. I want to show you what I'm working on now." With his arm about her he led her into the building. A half-finished figure of a horse stood braced against a framework. Jim handed her a glossy picture. "This is Falcon Grey, the stallion that started me in the breeding business. Someday he'll stand beside the gate to the farm."

"He's beautiful," Gaye murmured, but her mind was saying, How could I have fallen in love with a man I knew so little about? She looked into his craggy face and her eyes mirrored the love in her heart. "So are you," she whispered.

"If you look at me like that, sweetheart, I'll—"

She moved close to him, delighting him by snuggling in his arms. "You'll what?" she murmured and held her lips up for his kiss.

He kissed her quickly. "I'll forget that it's cold in here, and that MacDougle may be squalling by now, and ravish you."

"I'm tempted," she said against his lips before she pulled away from him. "Is this where you do the horse-shoeing?"

"Sometimes. But I have a mobile unit in the truck, too."

"You're a man of many facets, Mr. Trumbull."

"Sure I am." His eyes teased her. "I'm sweet, adorable, kind, overly intelligent, and patient."

"All true except for the last one, and I suspect your grandson doesn't have much either. We'd better get back to the house."

Later, when they were in the car going back to town, she asked him why his mother wasn't in a hospital or a nursing home.

"It's her choice," he said simply. "She wants to be home even if it means she won't live as long. A nurse comes each morning, and the doctor visits once a week."

"But in case of an emergency what would they do? Your aunt couldn't call for help."

"They don't feel Aunt Minnie has a handicap at all. She's been that way since birth. I've made a tape recording. All she has to do is dial the number and turn on the machine. They're not out there alone. I have a man who lives on the place and looks after the animals. Even when I'm there I spend most of my time in the shop."

"We should come here more often. I feel so selfish now about not wanting to come out to the farm to take care of Johnny. All the time you've spent with me, you should've spent with them."

"I don't crowd them, sweetheart. They would resent it if I hovered over them. They're both proud and independent women. They live the way they want to live."

"Like you, darling. Oh, Jim! I love you so much."

* * *

Large, fluffy snowflakes fell on Gaye's wedding day, covering the ground like a blanket and making everything sparkling white and clean. Lila and the two preschool children she took care of during the day came to stay with Johnny while they went to the church for the ceremony. Alberta and her two teenagers and Candy, the nurse from the hospital, had been invited to the ceremony and would come to the house later in the evening for a small wedding reception. Lila and her children were also invited. As long as it was impossible for Jim's mother and aunt to attend the wedding, Jim arranged to have the ceremony filmed and recorded to play back for them later.

Gaye wore a soft blue cashmere suit she had worn only a few times before. She wore her snow boots and carried slender high-heeled pumps in her hand.

"Is this your only coat?" Jim asked as he helped her into a hooded parka.

"It's the only one suitable for this kind of weather."

"We'll remedy that," he promised and slipped into a dark overcoat. He had made a trip to the farm and returned with several boxes and suitcases of his personal things.

On the way to the church he stopped at the florist for a bouquet of white roses for Gaye and a boutonniere for himself. Jim had said he would take care of everything and he had. He even ordered a wedding cake to be delivered to the house while they were away.

In the church foyer Jim dusted the snow flakes from his dark, shaggy head and hung their coats on the hooks in the alcove provided. They stood for a moment in the back of the almost-empty church, Gaye's trembling hand clasped firmly in his. Alberta, Brett and Joy sat in the first pew and Candy sat behind them. The minister came out to stand at the end of the aisle, and the guests stood and faced the back of the church.

Slowly and solemnly, their fingers entwined in a knot of love, Jim and Gaye came forward and took their places to say their vows. The ceremony itself was simple. The minister, a portly man with wisps of gray hair combed over his almost-bald head, spoke his words in a hushed, reverent tone.

It was not a fairy-tale wedding. There was no music and there were no banks of flowers for them to stand before. Gaye was not a virgin Cinderella. Jim was no Prince Charming. It was basic and *real.* Today she was joining her life to that of a rugged, earthy man who would love, cherish and protect her and their children. They would live out the days of their lives together, grow old together. She wouldn't wake up again to a day of loneliness stretching out before her.

"Do you, James, take this woman...in sickness and in health...to love and to cherish...?"

The voice brought her back to the present, and her eyes went quickly to Jim's and found that he was looking down at her.

"I do." He spoke only to her.

"Do you, Gaye, take this man...?"

At the proper time Jim slipped a narrow gold band on her finger. She was scarcely aware of it. His dark, serious eyes held hers until the ceremony was over. He bent down and brushed her trembling lips with his, and interlaced his fingers with hers.

"Congratulations, Jim. Welcome to the family." Alberta kissed his cheek. Joy and Brett shook his hand while Alberta folded her sister in her arms. "I'm so happy for you, Gaye," she whispered, her eyes bright with tears. "You and Jim will have a good life together."

"Oh, Aunt Gaye, I thought it a shame there weren't going to be many people here, but it was so private, so special. This is just the kind of wedding I want." Joy looked up at Jim. "Do I call you 'uncle' now?"

"Of course," Jim said, and everyone laughed.

After the guests left the foyer, Jim and Gaye followed the minister to his office and signed their names to the marriage certificate. Jim put his name beneath hers with bold strokes of the pen. He took some bills from his wallet. The minister shook his head.

"A donation for the Sunday school," Jim insisted. "You can expect a horde of new students in a few years."

The minister glanced at Gaye's suddenly flushed face and accepted the bills. "Well, in that case—thank you."

Alone in the church foyer, Jim took her in his arms and kissed her tenderly and reverently.

"Hello, there, Mrs. James M. Trumbull," he whispered between kisses."

"What's the M. for?"

"Guess."

"MacDougle?"

"What else?" He chuckled, and she could feel the movement against her breasts.

"It was a beautiful ceremony," Gaye said, her eyes moist.

"You're a beautiful bride."

"I *do* love you."

"Keep saying it, sweetheart. It makes me want to move mountains for you."

"I don't want you to do anything as dramatic as that. I just want you with me for the rest of my life."

"I wish we'd met when we were younger. We've wasted so much time."

"Don't waste time wishing for what might have been. We may not have been suited for each other then."

"I doubt that," he said strongly, his dark eyes glowing warmly. "But let's go home and argue about it...in bed."

Gaye felt a sudden, delicious rush of joy. She was utterly in love with this man, the real man behind the rough exterior. She laughed aloud at the thought of what Kathy, the woman from the dance class, would say about her marrying the caveman. Caveman? With her he was a gentle pussycat. She suspected she saw a side of him he never showed to anyone else.

"What are you laughing about?" Jim helped her into her coat.

"I was wondering if you were going to throw me over your shoulder and carry me off to your cave?"

"Why would you be wondering a thing like that?"

"Never mind. I'll tell you tonight...in bed."

Gaye sat close beside him in the car, her hand curled possessively beneath his inner thigh. The warm light in his eyes and the smile on his face told her more than any words that this was a special day in his life. He stopped at the liquor store for a bottle of champagne, and she waited patiently, her eyes glued to the door where he would come out. Full realization had not yet soaked in that he was hers, exclusively hers.

Jim returned to the car and they kissed. Gaye touched the smile creases near his mouth and fingered the thick dark brows. They lingered in the snow-covered car. She wanted to touch him everywhere. The intimacy they shared was heady. Her hand moved along his thigh until he captured it in his.

"You sure put a strain on this old man's control," he said huskily. "We'd better go home."

They drove slowly. It began to snow in earnest. Huge, fluffy flakes splattered against the windshield. Gaye rested her cheek against the side of his arm and looked up at him with laughing eyes.

"I'm sure Lila won't stay long," she murmured.

"If she stays a minute, it'll be too long," he said and leered at her lustily. "I'm going to attack you the instant she's out the door."

"Cross your heart and hope to die?" she said in a singsong voice.

"Poke a needle in my eye." He mimicked her tone.

Their laughter rang deep and joyous.

Jim pulled into the drive and braked behind Lila's station wagon. Gaye gathered up her roses and got out of the car. Lila was standing just outside the door. From the expression on her face, Gaye knew immediately something was terribly wrong. Her heartbeat paused, then began a mad gallop.

"What is it? Lila! What's wrong?"

"Two men and a woman came. They took the baby!"

Her shocking words knocked Gaye right off her cloud. The magic had ended.

Chapter Twelve

"Sonofabitch!" Jim pushed Gaye ahead of him through the open door. "Did you call the police? Why in the hell didn't you," he roared when Lila shook her head.

"They had papers, a court order. One of the men said you had taken Gaye away so the parting wouldn't be so painful. The woman went upstairs and got Johnny."

"When? What did they look like? What kind of car were they driving?" Jim fired questions at Lila. His facial muscles were stretched taut with a terrible tension.

"Right after you left." Lila twisted her hands together in anguish. "I think they came in a cream-colored car with a brown top."

"What did they say?"

"They said they had a court order. They showed me the papers. I don't know about such things, but they looked official. The man was so self-assured. He..."

"Was the woman tall? Did she have black hair?"

"Yes. She had black hair and thin eyebrows. She was wearing a fur coat and high-heeled boots. One of the men was thin and had black hair with gray on the sides. The other man was heavyset and didn't say anything. I'm sorry, Gaye. Oh, God, I'm so sorry. I opened the door, and before I knew it they had pushed their way in. I didn't know what to do!"

"Marla and those damn brothers of hers!" Jim's angry voice filled every corner of the house.

If Gaye hadn't been so numb she would have trembled at his rage. Instead she stood motionless. She had a strange emptiness inside. The feeling was familiar, and after a moment she identified it. She'd felt this way after her baby died. No wonder she felt the same, because there'd been another sudden death. The death of happiness. She wondered vaguely when the numbness would wear off, and grief tear at her.

Lila's young charges sat quietly on the couch—two small bewildered creatures watching the big angry man.

"Did they take his formula?" Gaye spoke in a calm voice, as if they were discussing the weather.

"No. The woman came down with Johnny wrapped in a blanket and they left. They didn't take anything, or ask for his bottles."

"They don't know what to feed him. He'll be sick!" The sense of a waking nightmare dropped from Gaye. This was real!

"They had someone watching the house," Jim snarled. "They knew we'd left MacDougle here. Damn!" He shrugged out of his overcoat and went to the telephone. He talked to someone at the airport. "I want to know every charter that has come in and gone out in the last three or four hours. Yes, some bastards have snatched my grandson. I know who it is! To hell with the police! I've got to stop them before they take him out of the country. Thanks, Tom. I'll be out there as soon as I can."

Jim called another number and talked to his attorney. When he finished he took the stairs two at a time and minutes later came back down the same way. He was wearing jeans, a sweater and boots. His hair was wild, his slanting eyes gleamed darkly, his jaw set at a brutal angle. He was in a dangerous mood.

"C'mon, Gaye. We're going to get our son back and crack a few heads while we're doing it." Gaye's eyes were full of misery when they looked up at him. He put his hands on her shoulders and gave her a gentle shake. "Now isn't the time to lose confidence in your old man. We'll get him back if we have to go all the way to France." He opened the closet door and snatched a stocking cap from the shelf, put it on her head and pulled it down over her ears. He turned to Lila. "I'm sorry I was so abrupt. You couldn't have stopped them." He took Gaye's hand and pulled her to the door.

"Wait!" She broke away, ran up the stairs to the baby's room and threw some things in the diaper bag. Downstairs, she added a couple of bottles of formula from the refrigerator and returned to Jim. "He'll be wet and hungry."

"Good thinking."

"I'll lock the house and go on home. Shall I call your sister?" Lila's face was still pale and her voice quivered nervously.

"Yes, please." Gaye went to her and hugged her briefly. "We don't blame you, Lila. Please don't feel bad."

"You'll call me?" Lila asked tearfully.

"As soon as we can."

Jim had cleaned the snow from the windshield by the time Gaye came out. He swung the car in a sharp turn and they were out the drive and on the street.

"I'm depending on this snow to keep the planes grounded," he said and turned on the defroster as the inside windows began to steam up.

"How do you know they'll go by plane?"

"That's the only way they know to travel. When I called the airport they said a small Learjet came in about noon and that the pilot was in there now trying to file a flight plan, but they doubted if the plane could take off because of the snow."

"It may not be them."

"They arrived in that plane, and they may try to leave in it. But they may have a larger plane coming in that could fly in this weather." He swore viciously. "If she weren't a woman I'd break her neck!" he snarled and rolled down the window to rid it of clinging snow so he could see before he crossed an intersection.

"How far is the...airport?" A sob tore from her throat and Gaye closed her eyes against the thought of not ever seeing Johnny again.

"Don't fall apart on me, honey." Jim's hand worked its way beneath her skirt to cup the inside of her nylon-clad knee. "You should have worn slacks. You're trembling."

"I'm not cold. I'm scared." Her chin quivered slightly and her voice was trembly.

"It was stupid of me not to think they'd have someone here keeping an eye on us, sweetheart. Someone probably followed me to the florist last night and heard me say we were going to be married today. They notified Marla and she flew in this morning to wait her chance.

When we catch up to them, I'm going to slap a kidnapping charge on them. I'm surprised those stupid brothers of hers took a chance like this. There must be a lot of money at stake."

"Will you really do that?" She had to keep talking or she would cry.

"You're damn right! They've screwed around with me long enough!"

She could hear the menace behind his angry words. He was like a combustible furnace ready to explode. I've got to be calm, she thought. The wrong word from me could be the spark that ignited the blaze in him. He's so angry he could kill someone!

They turned up the one-way drive leading to the low, flat terminal building. It was flanked on each side by steel hangars. There was a charter service and a flying school in the complex. The one commercial airliner that had stopped here, Jim explained, had canceled its run, and now the airport was serviced by two commuter-plane companies.

Jim stopped the car at the main entrance, opened the door and got out. Gaye jumped out of the car and trailed him into the terminal lobby. His long legs ate up the distance from the door to the front desk. He threw back a folding counter and went into an office. He turned at the door.

"Stay here." He threw the words back over his shoulder, and Gaye halted in her tracks. She stood there, suddenly realizing that there was nothing she could do to calm him. It would be like pouring a cup of water on a roaring blaze.

Gaye remembered the diaper bag and ran back to the car to get it. It was getting dark. The wind pulled at her, whipping her face with snow and tugging at her skirt.

There was no activity on the road or in the sparsely occupied parking lot. All around her there was only the approaching darkness and the curtain of driving snow.

Jim was coming out of the office when she returned to the lobby. He had another man with him, and the man was trying to reason with him.

"I know you're mad, Jim. I don't blame you. But don't do anything they could use against you. They're not going anywhere. The pilot is too smart to take off in this. We won't give him clearance. If he takes off without it and something happens to his plane, his insurance isn't worth a damn."

Gaye trailed behind them. They stopped at large double glass doors used by incoming passengers and peered through the glass at a small, slick plane parked at the gate.

"They're in there, huh?" Jim pushed on the door.

"No, Jim! Please wait." Gaye caught his arm.

"Wait for what, for God's sake?"

"Wait for the police, Jim. Please..."

"They won't let you in the plane. Come on upstairs and we'll talk to them on the radio. The lady's right. Call the police." Gaye was grateful for the man's support.

"The minute they see the police they'll take off. That pilot can't afford to be a part of a kidnapping, and Marla and her brothers can't afford the publicity. The old man would kill them."

"Then let's try and talk them into giving up."

"It makes sense, Jim," Gaye pleaded.

"All right, sweetheart. This is my wife, Tom. We were married today. It's a hell of a way to spend a wedding night."

"Congratulations, Jim. Best wishes, Mrs. Trumbull."

He extended a hand to her, and Gaye put hers into it. "You're going to need all the help you can get to keep up with this fellow." He shot Jim a smiling glance. "How can an ugly old boy like you be so lucky?"

Jim ignored his friend's attempt at lightheartedness and was already headed up the stairs. "We'll give it a try, but if they're not out of there in ten minutes, I'll turn the damn plane over!"

Tom opened the door to the glass-enclosed radio room. A man wearing a headset swiveled around on his chair.

"People are crazy. There's a damn fool coming in. I told him the airport was about to close down. He's coming in anyway."

"Where's he coming from?" Jim asked tersely.

"From the East. Hold on." He turned back to the radio, and Jim started for the door.

"Wait," Tom said. "Wait and talk. This guy will be in, in a few minutes, and then we'll radio the plane. They're not going to be able to stay out there all night. It's a blizzard, man."

"They could've sent for another plane. I'm not waiting."

Gaye and Tom followed Jim down the stairs again. At the double doors Tom said, "Wait until this plane lands and I'll help you roll out a boarding stair. Wait here, I'll be right back."

Jim paused. "All right. But I'm getting in that plane and getting my grandson if I have to take a crowbar and force open the door." He turned to Gaye and put his arm around her. "How are you doing, love?"

"I'm all right. I think we should call the police and let them handle it. You might get so mad you'll hurt someone, darling."

His arms tightened around her, and his lips smoothed the hair from her temple. "Don't worry. I won't do anything foolish, but they won't leave here with that boy, I promise you that!" She could feel the leashed anger and shuddered to think of that anger being directed at her. They stood quietly, holding on to each other, giving comfort by touching.

Tom returned. "The plane's down. As soon as they disembark and we get them out of the way, we'll go out."

Jim and Gaye turned to watch the plane turn slowly, pull into position guided by a man with a flashing amber light, and stop. The door was flung open almost immediately, and the stairway rolled down. Two people came down the stairway holding to the rail. The powerful gusts of snow-filled wind buffeted them.

Gaye turned her head away from them and buried her face against the smooth leather of Jim's coat. She was afraid for Jim, afraid for Johnny. If Jim tried to break into the plane they might shoot him! Oh, God! She couldn't bear it if anything happened to him. She clutched at his arms and felt him stiffen and draw away from her.

"What the hell!"

Gaye lifted her head, and her startled eyes saw a man in a black felt hat and an overcoat coming in through the double doors. Jim's hands seized her arms and lifted her away from him as if she were a small child. She saw Tom reach out and take hold of his arm, trying to restrain him.

"You're not going to have my grandson!" Jim shouted. "I'll fight to keep him and I'll fight dirty." The threatening words exploded from him in an angry torrent that carried into every corner of the building. He was shaking with rage.

Gaye took a step forward. "Mr. Lambert? Is that you?" she asked, bewilderment making her doubt her eyes.

"Yes, it's me, Mrs. Meiners. How are you?" The neat old gentleman carefully removed his hat and flicked the snow from it with is gloved hands.

"How the hell do you think she is?" Jim roared. "What's going on here? Do you know him?" he demanded roughly and grabbed Gaye's arm and spun her around.

"Yes! He came to the house with Mrs. Johnson. Jim...?" Her pulse leaped with fear when she looked into his blazing eyes. "What is it? Do *you* know him?"

"You're damn right I know him!" he gritted through twisted lips. "He's my former father-in-law. The father of those damn fools who're trying to take MacDougle away from us. He's the kingpin of the family and just as rotten as the rest of them!"

"Oh, no!" Gaye sagged against him. She was sure she would faint. Her rubbery legs could scarcely hold her. What had she done? Why didn't she believe Jim when he cautioned her about strangers? The eyes she focused on the old gentleman standing calmly by were icy and accusing. "Mr. Lambert, why didn't you tell me who you were? You used me and you used Mrs. Johnson to get in the house. It was rotten of you!" The words came out through the lump of pain in her throat.

"Mr. Lambert-Moyer, you mean," Jim spit out caustically. "*The* Lambert-Moyer! Law! Stockmarket! Banking! Politics! And now, kidnapping!"

"Can we sit down and discuss this calmly?" Mr.

Lambert spoke in a quiet voice. "You may find out that I'm not quite as rotten as you think."

"No, by God!" Jim shouted. "I'm going to get that boy!" Gaye could hear the anguish in his voice.

"Mr. Lambert, they've got Johnny out there." Gaye forced her tongue to make the necessary movements. "They came and took him while Jim and I were at the church. They didn't take his formula, and if they try to give him something else he'll be sick. Make them give him back!" Her eyes pleaded. "Please..."

"Don't beg, Gaye!" Jim's sharp command came from above her.

Gaye turned on him like a spitting kitten. "I'll beg, plead, get down on my knees and kiss his feet, if that's what it takes to get Johnny. Take your pride, Jim! Take your pride and shove it!" she shouted. She was so frightened and so steeped in misery she had to lash out at someone. She wasn't aware of the look of surprise that came over Jim's face or the way his nostrils flared with pride when he recognized her fighting spirit.

"She doesn't have to beg, Jim. I came out here a few weeks ago to find out what sort of person was in charge of my great-grandson. I visited in her home and returned when she wasn't expecting me. I came away well satisfied that she was far more capable of shaping a young life than Marla and Crissy. I told Marla and my sons to back off and be satisfied that the boy has a good home. I found out this morning what they're up to. I apologize for the grief they've caused you, Mrs. Meiners."

"Jim and I were married this morning, Mr. Lambert. Our hearts are full of love for Johnny." Gaye broke away from Jim. "Can you make them give him back to us? At least let us take care of him until all this is decided."

"It's decided, Gaye," Jim exclaimed angrily.

Gaye ignored him and spoke directly to Mr. Lambert. "They're out there in the plane waiting for permission to take off. If they take him out of the country we'll never see him again." The words came with a sob. "Jim's going out there. Someone will be hurt...."

"There's no need for Jim to do anything. They know that I'm here. They heard my pilot talking to the tower and knew I was coming in. I've instructed my pilot to tell them that I'm coming aboard." Mr. Lambert's voice was low-pitched and even-tenored, as if nothing could move him to anger.

"Let me go with you. What will they do? Will they let you have Johnny?" Gaye struggled to keep from crying.

"They'll let me have him. I still control the family purse strings; therefore, I still control the family." He said it rather sadly. "Try to keep this...wild man calm until I get back." He glanced at Jim and then set his hat carefully on his head.

Gaye watched him go back out into the blizzard. In the wavering light from the terminal she saw the man who'd come with him take his arm as they braced themselves against the wind. She watched until they went up the hastily rolled-out boarding stair, then turned back hopefully to Jim.

"Oh, darling! It's going to be all right. I can't believe that Mr. Lambert is Johnny's great-grandfather."

"Well, he is. I always rather liked the old boy, even if he did do a lousy job raising his kids." Jim put his arm around her and pulled her close to him. "He's always stood by them even when they were wrong, and I'll be surprised if he doesn't this time. We'll wait and see. Something had better happen soon. I'm about at the end of my tether."

They stood with their faces pressed to the glass doors, straining to see through the blowing snow. Gaye held tightly to Jim's hand. The minutes seemed like hours.

"He was nice, Jim. I liked him. He sat at the kitchen table and ate sugar cookies while I fed Johnny. We talked about...different things. I even gave him the recipe for my mother's sugar cookies." She talked to keep from thinking about what was going on in the plane.

"You what?" Jim asked in a brittle tone of surprise.

"He wanted my sugar-cookie recipe. They *are* good, Jim. You've downed an entire batch all by yourself. I copied it off for him. He was going to make them, he said. I can't help it if he's Marla's father. I like him." She chattered nervously, completely unaware that her nails were digging into Jim's hand.

"Evidently he likes you," Jim said slowly, and his warm breath made a mist on the cold glass of the door. "I can't fault him for that."

When the plane door opened, Gaye heard Jim suck air deeply into his lungs. She squeezed his hand and kept her eyes riveted on the door. Oh, God! she prayed. Let it be all right. This man I love has such strong feelings, is so...violent when he hates! But when he loves, he loves—

One shadowy figure came down the steps first, helping the one that followed. They reached the snow-packed concrete of the runway, and Gaye could see that Mr. Lambert was carrying a bundle. Her breath stopped and held, then let out in a gush when the door opened and she heard Johnny's angry muffled cries. She rushed forward, her eyes brimming with tears.

The elderly man lifted the blanket from the baby's

red, tear-wet face and placed him in her arms. Jim was beside her. She was conscious of the relief in his big body as his arms enfolded them and he hugged her and the infant to him.

"Thank you, Mr. Lambert. Oh, thank you..." she whispered tearfully. Then, "Jim...get his bottle—he's so hungry!"

"Is he all right?"

"Yes, yes. Sshhh...darling," she crooned. "It's all right. We've got you now.... Sshhh...you'll have your bottle and then we'll go home. Hurry, Jim—"

Jim's fingers were shaking, but he managed to get the nipple on the bottle turned in the right direction and in the baby's mouth. The cries ceased immediately, and there was only an occasional sob as Johnny sucked vigorously on the nipple. Jim led Gaye to a chair. He knelt down beside them and held the bottle while she peeled back the blankets.

"He's so wet!" she whispered to Jim. "We've got to change him before we take him home."

"Let him eat first," he whispered back. "Then I'll hold him while you change him. I'll get Tom to follow us in his four-wheel drive. I'm afraid the roads will be closed soon."

Gaye's eyes were wet and shining. Johnny's small hand curved contentedly about her finger. She blinked rapidly to hold back the tears.

"Oh, Jim. I couldn't bear to lose him." She leaned over the baby and rested her forehead against Jim's cheek.

When Jim stood he towered over Mr. Lambert-Moyer. He extended his hand. "Thank you, sir."

"You won't have any more trouble, Jim. I'll see to it." The old gentleman's eyes kept returning to Gaye and the baby. "You may have got a lemon the first time, Jim. But you hit the jackpot the second time around. I hope you appreciate her."

"I do. Believe me, I do. She's a good mother for our grandson." His throat clogged and he cleared it noisily.

"Mr. Lambert..." Gaye held up her free hand to grasp his. "Please keep in touch. You'll always be welcome in our home. Come and see us. Johnny should know his great-grandfather."

"I'd like that." Mr. Lambert gripped her hand tightly. "He may like my sugar cookies even better than yours." Gaye noticed he was blinking his eyes rather rapidly.

"Did you really make them?" she asked lightly.

"Of course. I find they brown on the bottom much better if you use a stainless-steel cookie sheet."

"Really? I'll have to get one. Goodbye, Mr. Lambert. I'll never be able to thank you enough."

"Goodbye, Mrs. Trumbull. And thanks are not necessary. It was my duty to do the best I could for my great-grandson. Goodbye, John," he said softly and touched the baby's cheek briefly with his fingertips, then extended his hand to Jim. "Goodbye, Jim."

They watched him until he reached the door, where he paused and set his black felt hat carefully on his head before he went out into the blizzard.

Jim, wearing only his pajama bottoms, lay sprawled on the couch in front of the fireplace. His head rested on the arm at one end, his bare feet on the other. A plate with a half-eaten piece of wedding cake was on the floor beside the couch. The rest of the cake sat on the dining room table, with several pink sugar roses missing and deep grooves where small fingers had scooped up icing. An apologetic note from Lila lay beside it.

Gaye came down the stairs, spotted the dish on the floor and came to pick it up. Jim grabbed her arm, causing her to lose her balance. She came crashing down on top of him. She heard a whoosh as the air exploded from his lungs when she landed on his stomach.

"Ha! Serves you right for being so rough. All you had to do was ask me."

"Ask you what?"

"Well...you know. To come and lie down on top of you so you can..."

"Can what?"

"Put your hands up under my nightgown?" she whispered and stretched out full-length on him.

"And?"

"You're impossible! Did you call to see if your mother and your aunt were all right?"

"Of course I did. Don't change the subject. What did you think I wanted to do to you?"

"I don't know," she said innocently and worked her palm between his hard-muscled stomach and her soft one. "The same thing you did to me as soon as we got Johnny to bed? Is this what we're talking about?" She felt his body jolt from her touch and laughed against his cheek.

His hands slid under her nightgown and cupped her bare buttocks, holding her tightly against him, capturing her hand between them.

"Are you about at the end of your tether, love?" she whispered teasingly. "You were marvelously patient while I was getting Johnny settled."

"*MacDougle* is going to have to learn to share!"

"*Johnny* is just a baby. He's too young to learn anything."

"*MacDougle* is old enough to know all he has to do is cry and you come running."

"That's because he's been through a traumatic experience, as we have."

"When we get our baker's dozen am I going to get just one-thirteenth of your time?"

"Thirteen? That means I'll be pregnant for almost ten years!"

"You'll be cute pregnant."

"I'll be fat! I'll have to go to the exercise class three times a week."

"Oh, no! I'll give you all the exercise you need." He moved her rhythmically against the part of him that had sprung to rigid hardness. "It'll be a lot more fun," he whispered against her mouth.

She placed her lips firmly against his and kissed him deeply, thrilled that he responded, yet let her have her way with him. She felt a warm desire burn from deep within and spread through her. She answered the gentle thrusts of his hips with a pressure of her own. Her clinging lips lifted a fraction from his, her forehead rested against him, their eyelashes tangled.

"I love you, my caveman, my gentle giant." She filled her two hands with his wild dark hair.

"I love you, too."

She had never hoped to see such love in a man's eyes when they looked at her. She felt truly loved and cherished.

"I like to feel the weight of you on me." He slid his palms over her buttocks and thighs.

"Is that what makes your heart pound?"

"Is that my heart? I thought it was yours."

"How about throwing me over your shoulder and carrying me off to your cave?" she asked in a seductive whisper.

"Arrrr...aw!" He snapped his teeth together. His reaction was so quick it almost startled her. He rolled, got to his feet with her in his arms, flung her over his shoulder, gave her bottom a swat and took the stairs two at a time.

* * * * *

Dear Reader,

Hi!

Here I am—once again—so pleased to be able to bring you another reissue of one of my stories. This one, *Forever Spring,* is the seventh and final installment in what had originally been intended as a three-book series… the so-called Metal Trilogy.

Thing was, I began to have problems from book one, *Texas Gold,* when a subcharacter, known as "One Tough Hombre," began sniping at the back of my mind, nagging for his own story. Annoyed with him, I told him, "Pick a number, hombre, and get in line."

He did.

Fortunately, I got through the second book, *California Copper,* without any like demands from other persistent subcharacters.

I was on a roll!

Naw.

For then, as luck would have it, I was happily writing away on the third book, *Nevada Silver,* when along came another character, whispering *Falcon's Flight* into my by now somewhat rattled mind. I mean, really, friends, a trilogy is three books…is it not?

The characters standing in line inside my head didn't care, so it just grew and grew. *Lady Ice* evolved from *One Tough Hombre,* and from *Lady Ice* came *Forever Spring.*

Are you confused? So was I. Still, I enjoyed writing my seven-book trilogy, and I promise, *Forever Spring* is the last of the lot. I hope you enjoy the story.

Happy reading,

Joan Hohl

FOREVER SPRING

Joan Hohl

Chapter One

"What a helluva time to start over."

"I beg your pardon?"

Paul Vanzant glanced around sharply at the sound of the soft inquiry. "What?" He frowned at the woman staring up at him. She was seated in a protected niche in the rocks, her arms clasped around her drawn-up knees.

"I said, I beg your pardon," the woman repeated, watching him as he plodded through the sand to her. "Since I'm the only other person on the beach," she said, flicking one hand to indicate the deserted shoreline, "I assumed you were speaking to me."

"I'm sorry." A rueful smile curved Paul's lips. "I hadn't realized I was speaking aloud." He came to a halt a few feet before her and lifted his shoulders in a resigned shrug. "I find myself doing that a lot lately."

"Understandable." The woman's smile was faint.

"It is?" Paul's tone was mildly questioning; his glance was intent, comprehensive. Even though she was seated, he could tell the woman was rather tall. Her figure was full, rounded, not overblown but not svelte, either. She was not beautiful in the accepted sense; her features were too strong, too well-defined. But she was attractive, and her hair was a thick, gorgeous mass of chestnut waves, now blowing freely in the brisk breeze. "Why is it understandable?" he asked, smiling easily.

"I do it myself," she responded, returning his smile and leaving him breathless. "Ever since the season ended I've caught myself muttering my thoughts aloud." Releasing her grip on her knees, she raised one arm. "Would you give me a hand up?"

"Certainly." Intrigued, Paul grasped her hand and drew her to her feet, which were, he noted, encased in expensive but battered-looking running shoes. "Why since the season ended?" he asked when she was standing beside him.

"I've been pretty much alone since then," she explained absently, brushing the sand from the seat of her faded jeans.

"I see," Paul murmured. Then he frowned. "No, I don't see."

The woman laughed, and her face softened into real beauty. "No, I don't suppose you do. My name's Karen Mitchell," she said, extending her hand. "I own a bed-and-breakfast, and since the end of summer there haven't been many tourists in search of either."

Paul clasped her hand. "Paul Vanzant. And, coincidentally, I was on my way to your place."

The woman slanted a questioning look at him. "On the beach?" she asked in a skeptical tone.

"No. Of course not." Paul's lips twitched into a

smile. "I was driving along, watching for your sign, and couldn't resist the lure of this stretch of shoreline." He lifted his shoulders again in that self-deprecating shrug. "I parked the car and started walking." He shifted his gaze toward the road and frowned. "My car's along there somewhere."

"Not in much of a hurry, are you?" Karen grinned.

"I gave up rushing for Lent."

"This is October." Her grin widened.

"I enjoyed it so much I extended it." Paul grinned back at her. "So, will you rent me a room?"

"But how did you know about my place?" Karen asked, playing for time while trying to decide if she should trust herself alone in the house with him.

Paul smiled in understanding and approval of her caution. "The taciturn proprietor of that picturesque general store in town recommended your place to me." He frowned, remembering. "Come to think of it, he said he'd give you a call and tell you to expect me."

His dry description of Calvin Muthard, owner of the one and only general store in the small nearby town, was so accurate that Karen didn't doubt for an instant that Paul had spoken to him. "When was that?"

Paul shrugged. "Thirty minutes or so."

"That explains it, then." Karen matched his shrug. "I've been out here on the beach for some time. If Calvin said he would call, then he called."

"You could give him a call," Paul suggested.

Karen's smile was wry. "Knowing Calvin, he'll keep ringing until he reaches me."

"So, will you rent me a room?"

"Why not?" Karen laughed. "I've got plenty of them, all empty."

"Good." Paul turned away. "I'll get my car and..."

His voice trailed away and he turned to her, a smile on his lips. "Where *is* the house?"

Karen's ordinary brown eyes grew bright with amusement and were suddenly not at all ordinary. Tiny gold flecks sparked light in their dark depths, mesmerizing Paul for an electric instant. The odd moment was broken when she pointed to a building beyond the rocks and dunes.

"It's that monstrosity right there." She smiled at him over her shoulder. "You can't miss it, even if you want to."

The house was large and solid-looking. Victorian in design, it appeared to have weathered every storm nature had flung at it. Its dignified form appealed to Paul

"It's beautiful," he murmured, studying the structure. "I can't imagine how I missed it."

"I can." Karen's soft laugh caused an unusual tingling reaction at Paul's nape. "You were walking with your head down. The few times you did glance up, you stared out to sea."

"You were watching me?" Pondering the strange sensation at the back of his neck, Paul made a show of examining the veranda encircling the house.

"I'd tired of watching the gulls and talking to myself." Karen's voice retained a hint of laughter. "You were a diversion."

"You live in that house alone?" One eyebrow peaked as he shifted his gaze to her face.

Karen nodded. "For now."

Intrigued but unwilling to pry, Paul suppressed the questions that sprang to his tongue. "I'll get the car and meet you at the house." Pivoting, he headed for the road.

"I'll start a pot of coffee," she called after him.

"Great, I could use a cup," Paul shouted back, suddenly aware of the sharpness of the wind and the inadequacy of his poplin jacket.

The car was farther along the road than he had thought, and by the time he slid behind the wheel his fingers were numb with cold. Blowing warm breath into his cupped hands, Paul stared at the stretch of deserted road and frowned. Accustomed as he was to the noise and pace of city life, Paul could appreciate the solitude afforded by this empty section of the Maine coast. He himself had recently vacated a similar section. And yet for a woman to be on her own and living in a house that size... Paul's frown deepened. Was she safe here? A prickling of alarm startled him out of his introspection. It was none of his business, he thought impatiently, shoving the key into the ignition. How and where Karen Mitchell chose to live was no concern of his. Besides, he mused, driving the car off the soft shoulder and onto the road, she was no longer alone. He was here now.

The house was even more fascinating on closer inspection. Though definitely weathered-looking, it had none of the brooding quality one might expect of a large, isolated house surrounded by sand dunes and facing an ocean. Pulling the car onto the sandy drive at the side of the house, Paul killed the engine, then sat gazing at the building while attempting to identify its attraction.

Welcome. Haven. Security. Paul went still as the words rushed into his mind. He had been wandering aimlessly for months. Winter would soon eclipse fall. Was he subconsciously seeking a secure, welcoming haven? Had he also secretly hoped to find the warmth of a woman as well as the warmth of a solid shelter?

Ridiculous! Paul's aristocratic features set into forbidding lines. He owned two perfectly adequate homes, both equal in size to Karen's. And when he was ready he would go back, at least to his primary house in Philadelphia. As for hoping to find the warmth of a woman? Paul winced. He had not experienced even the slightest urge for a woman's company in a very long time. He had existed without that particular physical urge by necessity. He needed lodging, nothing more.

Yet there was a lure to this particular section of the coast, an attraction Paul had not felt during the weeks he'd spent in his son's cottage farther up the coast. That inexplicable lure was the reason he had pulled the car off the road to walk the deserted beach.

But the beach hadn't been deserted, Paul mused, narrowing his eyes as he stared at the large house. Was it Karen's magnetism that had been tugging at him? Paul blinked in surprise at the fanciful thought.

What utter nonsense! Paul shook his head to clear his mind. He was long past the age of believing in fateful attraction, if in fact he had ever been of an age to believe in it. The only lure here was the call of nature and a house reminiscent of another, gentler age, and it was a summons Paul didn't have the time to indulge. He had drifted, rudderless, for too long. It was time to get back to working—and living.

Staring at Karen Mitchell's house without really seeing it, Paul's thoughts wandered back to a time when he had enjoyed life, years before the death of his wife, an event that had occurred six months previously. Learning of his wife's infidelities had robbed his personal and business life of all the joy he'd derived from it. And yet Paul had continued, living a lie at home and at the office until the day his wife had driven her classic Corvette into a bridge abutment. At that point, he had literally dropped out. Within weeks he had formally retired from the banking work he loved and had closed the house in which he had laughed and loved and raised his two children. He had been wandering ever since.

Grimacing, Paul deliberately drew his gaze from the house. Peter was expecting to hear from him; and what his son was expecting to hear was that Paul was coming home, this time for good. He'd stay the night, then be on his way.

His dark eyes coolly remote, Paul swung the car door open and slid his tall body from the expensive vehicle. Striding purposefully to the back of the car, he removed only one of his cases from the trunk.

Karen swung the heavy door open as Paul mounted the veranda steps on the seaward side of the house. As he crossed the threshold the aroma of rich coffee, combined with the scent of an exciting female, assailed his senses. Against his will, Paul found himself inhaling both seductive fragrances.

"Are you hungry?" Karen asked as she closed the door, shutting out the rising wind.

"Yes." Paul smiled at the realization that he'd been unaware of his empty stomach until that minute. "As a matter of fact, I'm famished." His smile turned wry. "I believe I forgot to eat lunch."

"Well, then, just drop your bag here in the hall," she said briskly, indicating the spacious hallway connecting the identical doors. "Dinner won't be ready for several hours," she continued, turning away from the wide central staircase and walking toward an open doorway to her left. "But I can warm up some croissants for you to have with your coffee, if you'd like?" She paused in the doorway, eyebrows raised.

"I'd like that very much, thank you," Paul answered with stiff formality. He noted her speculative frown as he bent to set his suitcase at the foot of the stairs. Chiding himself for his coldness, he attempted a lighter tone. "Is there somewhere I can wash up?"

Karen's expression eased as she nodded. "There's the powder room." She motioned to a door to the right behind the staircase. A smile teased her lips. "Be careful, though. You're rather large and the room's rather small. You could bump into yourself by merely turning around."

Paul found the room every bit as small as she had warned it would be. A hint of a smile touched his lips as he washed his hands at the tiny sink. The powder room was an afterthought, he guessed, and had more than likely been a closet originally. The room wasn't much larger than a rest room on a commercial jet plane. Paul imagined Karen in the cramped space, and his smile broadened to reveal strong white teeth. Sharing the room with her would be interesting, he reflected, if not downright adventurous.

A shocking stab of sensual awareness sobered him. Staring at his reflection in the mirror above the sink, Paul was amazed at the color tingeing the taut skin over his high cheekbones. His appetite was suddenly sharp, but not for warm croissants. He wanted a woman. Paul frowned at his dark-eyed image. No, he wanted a particular woman! The sensual awareness tightened inside him, tensing every sinew and muscle in his body.

Incredible. Paul closed his eyes and savored the painfully pleasant sensation of arousal coursing through him. He had been convinced his wife had dealt a death blow to his natural sex drive long before her own demise. And now to discover his mind and body reactivated and humming with anticipation because of an errant thought about a full-figured woman in a minuscule powder room was more than incredible, it was astonishing and damned funny!

So why aren't you laughing? Paul silently demanded of his somber reflection. It couldn't be that after all this time you've forgotten how to approach a woman with the intention of seduction, could it? Drawing a deep breath, Paul stared into the mirror and watched his features lock and his lips twist derisively. No, he hadn't forgotten, but seduction was for young, eager men, and he was no longer either.

Paul shrugged his shoulders and turned away from the mirror, bumping his lean hip on the edge of the sink as he moved. Laughing softly, he eased his tall frame from the room. The exciting inner tension was gone; Paul couldn't help but wonder if it would return.

It slammed into his midsection like a body blow the instant he stepped into the kitchen to find Karen bending to remove a tray from the oven. The faded jeans hugged her firm, rounded bottom. His breathing suddenly shallow, Paul fought an urge to cross the room and stroke his palms over that enticing curve. Fortunately, Karen decided the inner battle by straightening before he could make a move.

"Take off your jacket and sit down," she said, sliding a small tray of steaming croissants onto the stovetop. "And help yourself to the coffee," she added, inclining her head toward the glass coffeepot and cups on the table.

Aroused again and relieved at the opportunity to sit down, Paul still managed to remember his manners. "Can I help you there?" he asked, inching toward the table.

"No, thank you." Karen shot a quick smile over her shoulder as she transferred the hot pastries from the tray to a napkin-lined basket. "But you can pour a cup of coffee for me, please."

"Of course." Shrugging out of the jacket, Paul draped it over the back of a chair as he slid onto the seat. To his amazement, he found his hands steady as he poured coffee into the two cups. Applying mind over matter, he had his responsive body under control by the time she sat down opposite him.

"Smells delicious," he murmured, inhaling the aroma of the hot croissants.

"Help yourself," she invited. "There's butter and preserves." She indicated the containers with a flick of her hand as she reached for her cup.

"Not joining me?" Paul asked, breaking one of the crescent-shaped rolls.

"No." Karen shook her head. "I'm on a perpetual diet, and midafternoon croissants are not a part of it." Lifting her cup, she sipped at the steaming black coffee.

"Diet?" Paul paused in the act of slathering wild-strawberry preserves onto a piece of the roll. His frowning gaze made a brief survey of the upper half of her body; his memory retained a clear vision of the lower half. "You don't need to diet." The sincerity of his tone was proof that he was not merely being gallant.

"Oh, but I do." Karen's smile held an odd, bitter slant. "I love to cook and I love to eat," she said in a flat voice. "I pay for my indulgence in pounds...usually around my hips."

Personally, Paul considered her rounded hips uncomfortably alluring. Prudently he kept his thoughts to himself. "My problem's the direct opposite," he said for the sake of conversation. "I often forget to eat, and I have to remind myself to do so to keep from losing weight.'' He popped the bite of roll into his mouth and chewed with relish.

Her expression mocking, Karen cradled her cup in her palms and leaned back in her chair. ''I should have such a problem,'' she drawled, tilting her cup in a silent salute. Her gaze boldly noted the breadth of his shoulders and chest and the evidence of well-developed muscles beneath his bulky knit sweater. ''For all the lack of nourishment, you appear to be in great shape.''

Paul's smile was wry. ''For my age, you mean?''

''For any age,'' she retorted. ''How old are you?'' There was a hint of challenge in her voice.

''I'll never see fifty again.'' Paul smiled at her look of genuine astonishment and tossed her challenge back at her. ''How old are you?''

''I'll never see thirty again,'' she said in a dry tone. ''As a matter of fact, I celebrated my thirty-seventh birthday last Tuesday.''

Something, some infinitesimal inflection in her voice, alerted Paul. ''Alone?'' he guessed.

Karen hesitated, then sighed. ''Yes.''

''You have no family?'' Paul probed gently, not sure exactly why he was bothering.

''I have two sons,'' she said brightly—too brightly. ''They're away at school. I...received lovely birthday cards from them.'' Her smile was as bright as her tone, and as suspect. ''Do you have children?'' she asked swiftly, allowing him no time to question her further.

''Yes, two also,'' Paul answered. ''I have a son and a daughter, both grown and married.'' Memory softened his expression.

''Grandchildren?'' Karen guessed.

Paul's smile was gentle. ''Yes, a six-week-old grandson from my son and daughter-in-law, and my daughter is currently a lady-in-waiting. The child is due at Christmas, on or about their first wedding anniversary."

"That's nice," she murmured, blinking as she glanced away. "I love babies."

Once again, Paul became alert to an odd tone in her voice. For a moment she looked so lost, so unhappy, that he had to squash the urge to go to her and draw her into his arms. "Your husband?" he asked very softly.

"I'm divorced." She turned to look at him as she stood up. The vulnerability was gone; an invisible curtain had been drawn, concealing her feelings. "If you've finished, I'll show you to your room." Her voice was steady, free of inflection.

Paul had the strange sensation of having been shoved outside, into the deepening dusk and frigid wind. The sensation disturbed him more than a little. Why it should bother him was baffling. He had grown used to being in the cold and the dark with the opposite sex. His wife Carolyn had kept him there for years. Feeling a chill, Paul tossed down the last of his coffee and stood up. "Ready when you are," he said in an even tone, plucking his jacket from the back of the chair.

Following Karen up the wide staircase proved to be a test of endurance for Paul. She had a lovely, graceful stride, shoulders back without being stiff, spine straight without being rigid, and her hips had a gentle, unpracticed sway that profoundly affected every one of his senses. Sweetly erotic images flashed through his mind as he trailed her down the hall, his darkened gaze fixed on the movement of her hips. His mind smoky from the heat of his thoughts, Paul was only vaguely aware of the room she ushered him into. The inflectionless sound of her voice pierced the sensuous fog.

"Of course, if this room doesn't suit you, you may

choose any of the other six guest rooms,'' she was saying, moving to the long windows to pull the drapes open. ''I thought this would be best since it has its own bathroom and looks out over the beach and the ocean.'' She swept her arm toward the view as if offering him a gift.

''This will be fine.'' Paul glanced around the room without really seeing it as he dutifully walked to stand beside her at the window. Darkness cloaked the land, and low-hanging clouds obscured the moon and stars. Paul could see very little except for outlines and the curling white of cresting waves. But standing this close to her he could smell her distinct scent, and his body tightened in response to it. Relief shivered through him when she moved away.

''Well, then,'' Karen said briskly. ''I'll get bed linens and towels. It'll only take a minute to make up the bed.'' She was walking from the room before she'd finished speaking.

Keeping his back squarely to the room, Paul stared into the night, his thoughts just as black. What was wrong with him? he wondered bleakly, clenching his fists as he heard her reenter the room. He was reacting to Karen like a teenager with a hormonal explosion. He wanted to grab her, touch her—everywhere. He wanted to kiss her, bite her, thrust his tongue into her sweet mouth! Oh, God, how he wanted! Paul was shuddering inside when the snapping sound of a sheet being shaken dispelled the erotic thoughts teasing his senses.

''Is there something I can help you with?'' Paul closed his eyes, despairing of the hoarse sound in his voice.

''No, thank you, I'm just about finished.'' Karen's tone had an edge that tugged at his attention, an edge that held a hint of—what? Trepidation? Outright fear?

Raising his eyelids fractionally, Paul turned slowly to face her. Moving swiftly, economically, her hands smoothed a candlewick bedspread over two plump pillows. On closer inspection, he thought he detected a slight tremor in her competent hands. Was Karen afraid of him? Paul mused, watching as she carried a stack of towels into the adjoining bathroom. Had she sensed his reaction to her, and was she now regretting renting him the room?

Avoiding his eyes, Karen walked into the room and directly to the door to the hallway, by her manner convincing Paul his speculations were correct.

"I'll leave you to get settled in," she said, reminding him of a wary doe as she hesitated in the doorway. "Dinner will be ready at 7:30." Turning abruptly, she strode from the room.

"Thank you." A grimace twisted Paul's mouth as he realized he was speaking to thin air; Karen had fled. A sick despair sank heavily to the pit of his stomach. She was afraid of him, he thought, raking a hand through his hair in frustration. Dammit! The last thing he'd wanted was to frighten her. Sighing, Paul turned to stare into the unwelcoming darkness of a cold night.

Karen was also staring into the night. Directly across the hall, in a room that was a twin to his, she stood at the window, her trembling fingers clutching the old-fashioned carved wood frame. Her breathing was ragged and uneven; her stomach felt queasy.

What had come over her? The silent cry battered her mind. Her senses were jangling; her emotions were freaking out! And all because of a man who was almost twenty years her senior!

But, oh, glory, what a man! Shutting her eyes tightly,

Karen shivered deliciously in response to the image of him that consumed her mind. Aristocratic. Patrician. Handsome. Cultured. Endearingly preoccupied. The adjectives crashed into each other as they rushed forward. At fifty-whatever, Paul Vanzant was the most compelling man Karen had ever met.

And he probably thinks you're an absolute idiot! A sigh whispered through her lips as Karen accepted the mental rebuke. She was thirty-seven years old and the mother of two teenage sons. She had experienced the satisfaction of a successful career and—though briefly—the love of a dynamic man on the way up. She was well educated and well traveled. And she had conducted herself with all the aplomb of a wide-eyed, tongue-tied, backward young girl being presented at court.

But Lord, the man was *fantastic*! Feeling as if she were melting inside, Karen tightened her grip on the windowframe and leaned forward to press her forehead against the cold pane. She longed to stroke the white wings highlighting his black hair at his temples— No! She longed to stroke the entire length of his tall, muscular body. Sensual awareness flared to life, and she quivered in response to the mere thought of touching Paul.

Was she losing her mind? Or had she simply been too long alone? It had been five years since Karen had been with a man, five years since the separation and subsequent divorce that had shredded the fabric of her marriage and life. Embittered, she had embraced celibacy, not grown frustrated because of it. Karen hadn't wanted anything to do with a man, and she certainly hadn't wanted to share intimacy with one.

Intimacy. Karen moaned softly as the word echoed

inside her whirling mind. Male-female intimacy meant silken touches and deep, hungry kisses and an even deeper, all-consuming possession.

Suddenly weak and shaking, Karen turned her head to press her flushed cheek to the cool window. With her mind's eye she could see Paul, naked and beautiful, his dark eyes shadowed by passion, a sensuous smile on his sculpted masculine lips.

"Yes, yes."

The jagged, breathless sound of her own voice startled Karen into awareness. Breathing deeply, she glanced around in confusion. What in the world was she doing? Her face grew hot and then cold at the answer. Her movements jerky and uncoordinated, she walked to the low double dresser and picked up her hairbrush. Drawing the brush through her wind-tossed curls, she frowned at the slumbrous glow in the brown eyes reflected in the mirror. Was this the same self-contained woman who had turned her back on her career and all her activities in the city to return to her childhood home? Karen wondered tiredly. Could the woman in the mirror possibly be the same person who had determinedly removed herself physically and mentally from the pleasures of the flesh?

Karen shook her head and dropped the brush onto the dresser. This would not do. Paul was, for whatever reason, obviously in transit. He would stay a while, and then he would go. And unless she was very careful, he could take a part of her with him. Karen knew she could not let that happen.

She was vulnerable to him. Why she was vulnerable to this particular man was unimportant—at least for the moment. She had to get herself firmly under control. Paul Vanzant was the stuff dreams were made of, she decided sadly. And dreams of that sort were for the young and innocent, not the wise and embittered.

Drawing a deep breath, Karen squared her shoulders and smiled at her reflected image. "He's in his fifties," she said in a soft but bracing tone. "He has grown children, and he's a grandfather. Children and grandchildren presuppose a mother and grandmother. Where is she?" A spasm of pain flicked across Karen's face. "He's on the move, you fool!" she chided her image. "His wife is more than likely at home, playing the doting grandma." She shut her eyes against the sting of tears and closed her mind to the bittersweet yearning to fill the emptiness of her body and arms with a tiny new life. Denying the image of a child with Paul's aristocratic features in miniature, she opened her eyes again, wide. "He's too old for a serious new commitment. He's too old to be running around while his wife sits waiting at home. And he's too old for you."

Feeling like the idiot she'd accused herself of being, Karen spun away from the dresser, unwilling to face the sad-eyed woman reflected in the mirror above it. She had work to do. There was laundry in the dryer to be folded, and a wet load waiting to be transferred to it from the washer. She had to scrub potatoes for baking and clean and chop vegetables for a salad. She had to make a batch of biscuits. She didn't have time to indulge in fantasies about a man she had met less than two hours before and knew absolutely nothing about. She had to get her house and head together.

Acting on the thought, Karen rushed from her bedroom and down the wide staircase. She flicked on the radio in the kitchen on her way through to the laundry room. Throughout the following hours, coherent thought was held at bay by the blaring racket and agonizing screams commonly referred to as "heavy metal."

Karen had a blasting headache, but her chores—and the potatoes—were done. She had showered and dressed in a silky overblouse and a flattering, if practical, denim skirt. Her hair was brushed into soft gleaming waves; a minimum of makeup enhanced her clear, naturally pale face. The table was set in the small dining alcove and the scallops were simmering in an aromatic sauterne butter sauce under the broiler. The noise issuing from the radio ceased abruptly. Spinning around, Karen glared at the tall, too-attractive cause of her feverish activity.

"Why did you do that?" she demanded aggressively, quickly gliding a glance over the appeal of his body, which was clad in casual but obviously expensive pants and a white sweater.

"Why?" Paul repeated in disbelief. "To prevent both deafness and madness," he answered in a scathing tone. "I was beginning to think I'd walked into bedlam."

"The music keeps me company," she retorted.

"It'll turn your brain to mush," he snapped. "I thought you were an intelligent, sensible woman. You can't possibly enjoy that...that..."

"Noise?" Karen supplied the applicable word, sighing inwardly at her erratic behavior. "No, actually I hate it."

"But then why play it?" Paul slowly crossed the room to her.

Karen held her ground but withdrew inwardly. "Because I was dissatisfied with my own thoughts," she admitted. "And the noise blanked them out."

Compassion softened his tight features. "You were thinking about your children?" he asked softly.

Feeling not an ounce of shame, Karen clutched at the

excuse. "Yes, I was missing my children." There was a grain of truth to her assertion, she assured herself, meeting his compassionate gaze boldly. For had her boys been in the house that afternoon, she probably wouldn't have been sitting on the beach and so would not have met him and thus would not have found herself wildly attracted to him in the first place. The rationale was unpalatable to Karen, but it was the best she could come up with on the spur of the moment.

Chapter Two

"You do a mean scallop scampi."

"Thank you." Karen glanced up at Paul, an uncertain smile hovering at the corners of her lips. The compliment, coming so unexpectedly after his near-total silence during the meal, both pleased and confused her. "I'm glad you enjoyed it."

"I did," he said, pausing a moment before continuing, "I enjoyed it very much, even though I realize I wasn't very good company throughout the consumption of it."

Karen lifted her shoulders in a half shrug. "Conversation is not a guest requirement."

Paul smiled. "Perhaps it should be."

"Perhaps." Karen frowned and shrugged again. "But if a guest is preoccupied..."

"This particular guest is preoccupied by speculation about his hostess."

"Me!" she exclaimed, experiencing an odd thrill of excitement.

"Yes, you." Refilling his coffee cup from the carafe she'd placed on the table, Paul leaned back in his chair and gazed at her intently.

"But what about me?" Karen shook her head impatiently. "I mean, what were you speculating about?"

"The fact that you're living alone in this large house, for one thing," Paul answered, indicating the entire building with a flick of his hand.

Karen followed his hand motion with her eyes. "I was born in this house," she murmured.

"Which explains absolutely nothing."

"I wasn't aware of owing—" she began, her voice strained.

Paul interrupted her. "Of course you don't owe me a thing, especially explanations, but that doesn't preclude my curiosity about you." He shrugged and smiled; the smile got to her.

"Okay, I'll indulge your curiosity." Karen inclined her head in thanks as he filled her coffee cup. Cradling the warmed china in her palms, she sat back and smiled. "Fire away."

Paul's lips curved with wry amusement and a hint of suggestiveness. "On any subject?"

"I won't guarantee an answer," Karen drawled, "but you can give it your best shot."

His laughter was slow in starting but rapidly grew into an attractive rumble that filled the small dining alcove, and Karen, with warmth. The room absorbed the sound, and so did Karen. A delicious tremor shivered through her as he raised his cup in a salute.

"Now I'm intimidated." Paul sounded anything but intimidated. He chuckled at the look she gave him. "I don't know if this is my best shot, but to begin, why are you all alone in this large leftover from another era?"

That one was easy, and Karen responded immediately. "Actually, I've only been alone for a few weeks. I employ three people, two women and one man, during the season." She smiled dryly. "In fact, the house is, or was, in effect closed until spring."

"But the proprietor of that store said—"

Karen cut in to ask gently, "Exactly what did Calvin say?"

Paul frowned in concentration. "He said, well, just maybe you'd be willing to rent me a room for a night or two." Paul mimicked Calvin's Yankee twang.

Karen laughed in appreciation of his effort. "Precisely. Calvin knows full well that I close the place at the end of September, and he admitted as much."

"You spoke to him?"

Karen nodded. "While I was finishing dinner. I did tell you he'd persist until he reached me."

"Yes, you did," Paul confirmed, beginning to frown. "So, what's your verdict?" His dark eyebrows peaked. "Are you planning to toss me out on my, er...ear the minute I step away from this table, or have you decided to let me stay the night?"

"You may stay—" she paused to grin "—as long as you like. It appears that you made quite a good impression on Calvin."

"Indeed?" Paul managed not to laugh.

"Oh, yes, indeed." Karen didn't manage it; she laughed softly. "And, as Calvin is generally an excellent judge of character, I'll accept his recommendation."

"I knew there was something I liked about that dour-faced, hard-nosed Yankee," Paul commented drolly.

Swallowing her laughter at his deadly accurate description of Calvin, Karen pushed back her chair and stood up. "Question period over?" she murmured hopefully, beginning to gather the dishes together.

"Over!" Paul exclaimed, rising quickly to help clear the table. "I've only asked one question."

"Well, then," she sighed loudly, "can we put it on hold until after cleaning up? I detest clutter." She frowned at the littered table.

"Certainly." Paul nodded. "I'll even assist." His gaze trailed hers to the table, and his mouth curved into a grimace. "I can't abide clutter, either."

Oddly, knowing they shared one small trait made Karen feel closer to Paul. And, though she told herself she was being silly, the feeling eased the reluctance she was experiencing about being questioned further by him.

Two pairs of competent hands dealt swiftly with the dinner debris, freeing them of the chore within minutes. With the dishwasher swishing in the background, Paul opened the bottle of white wine Karen produced, while she retrieved two stemmed glasses from the lovingly cared-for hundred-year-old hutch in the formal dining room. Carrying the bottle casually by its long neck, Paul strolled into the spacious living room; Karen followed after giving the kitchen one last critical appraisal.

Ensconced in a wide-armed, deeply cushioned easy chair, Paul offered Karen a wry smile as she settled into the corner of the matching sofa. As he poured out the wine, he put her own thoughts into words.

"It would appear that we have at least one thing in common," he said. "We are both apparently overly tidy people."

Karen's smile matched his in wryness. "Why do I get

the sneaky feeling that you've also been accused of being a fussbudget?"

The bottle went still, poised over the glass. The stream of clear liquid ceased flowing. Paul slowly raised his gaze to meet hers. The light of impish humor glowed in the dark depths of his eyes.

"You, too, huh?" When Karen nodded, he grinned. "My daughter Nicole once told me that though I wasn't exactly clean-crazy, I most definitely was straighten-up-nuts."

Karen's laugh of delight rippled through the room, adding a dimension of comfort unrelated to the bright down-home decor. "I think I'd like your Nicole," she said when the amusement subsided. "She sounds like fun."

"She is now, because she's happy." Paul's expression was somber. "But there was a period, a very long period, when she seemed barely alive, never mind fun."

There was no way Karen could let his statement pass. Reaching to accept the glass he held out to her, she voiced her interest. "There was a time when your daughter was unhappy?" For some inexplicable reason, she couldn't imagine a child of Paul's being unhappy—which was really silly, Karen knew. Most children suffered periods of unhappiness for one reason or another.

Paul's hesitation was brief but telling. He obviously didn't want to discuss his daughter. "Nicole was involved in an auto accident some years ago," he said finally. "She withdrew from life, from her family, while she worked out the aftereffects of the damage." The minute emphasis he placed on the words *her family* spoke volumes about his own worry and anxiety during that period.

"She was handicapped?" Karen asked softly, even as she told herself to let it go.

"She was a model," Paul said slowly. "A rather famous model. The crash left her face, neck and shoulder scarred." His tone, or rather the complete lack of it, revealed much about the anguish he'd felt at the time.

Still, Karen couldn't let the subject drop; she had to ask. "But she's all right now?"

Paul's lips curved into a gentle, contented smile. "Yes, she's more than all right. Nicole's not only happy, she is deeply in love with her husband." Parental love and pride glowed from his softened dark eyes.

"I'm glad," Karen said, simply but with utter sincerity. "And your son?" She was completely aware that the roles of questioner and questionee had been neatly reversed; she hoped to keep it that way. A small smile teased her lips as the glow brightened in his eyes. It was obvious to Karen that Paul unconditionally adored his son. Being in the same emotional condition concerning her own boys, she could appreciate the pride shining from his eyes.

"My son Peter is—special." Paul went still as his eyes widened fractionally. "Good Lord!" he muttered.

"What?" Even though his voice had been low, the tone of it affected Karen like a shout. "What is it?" she asked, glancing around as if she expected to see a visible cause for his distress.

Paul gave a sharp shake of his head. "I told Peter I'd call him this evening." He sighed. "And now I've very likely got both Peter and his wife Patricia worried."

Not quite understanding his agitation, Karen motioned toward the hallway. "There's a phone less than ten feet away from you in the hall. Be my guest."

Paul's expression changed instantly. A teasing gleam

sprang into his eyes to banish the shadow of concern. "It's a long-distance call. My son lives in Philadelphia."

Karen sipped her wine daintily before responding in a dry tone. "I'm in an expansive mood." She indicated the foyer with a negligent wave. "Better take advantage of it. It doesn't happen often."

"You're a bit austere with the purse strings?"

"Nooo..." Karen drew the word out slowly. "I'm a true product of my New England upbringing and *very* austere with the purse strings." Her soft lips tightened. "It was one of the biggest bones of contention between me and Charles."

"Charles?" That one softly spoken word from Paul reversed the roles again.

Karen sighed into her delicate glass and took a deep, fortifying swallow. "Charles Mitchell."

"Your former husband?"

She nodded once, then attempted to deflect the question she could see hovering on his lips. "Aren't you going to make that call?"

Paul's slow smile sent Karen's hopes crashing down in flames. "It'll keep until morning. So will Peter. I'll catch him at the office."

She gave it one last shot. "But you said they'll worry."

"They're used to it." His drawl was heavy. "They've been angsting over me for nearly six months. Another night won't make much difference either way."

His enigmatic statement sank a solid hook into Karen's already aroused interest in him. She wanted to know everything, anything, about him. Paul didn't allow her the seconds needed to sort her queries into a semblance of order.

"You were telling me about Charles," he said, scattering her thoughts.

"I was?" She gulped at her wine and suddenly the glass was empty. Frowning at it, she held it out for refilling.

"Well, no," Paul admitted, tipping the bottle over her glass. "But I was hoping you would." Topping off his own glass, he lounged in the roomy chair and offered her a bland, innocent look.

Karen wasn't fooled for an instant; but she did feel inordinately thirsty. After several more deep swallows of the wine, her tongue loosened considerably. "What exactly did you hope to find out?" She didn't hear the fuzzy sound of her voice, but Paul did. He fought the urge to smile.

"Would it be terribly crass of me to admit to hoping to hear the entire story?"

"Terribly," Karen muttered into her glass before taking another gulp. "But as I said, I'm in a strange, expansive mood tonight."

Not to mention slightly into your cups. Paul decided Karen was both cute and attractive with her Yankee edges blurred, but prudently kept his thoughts to himself. "Then I'll be crass and ask for the story, from the beginning."

Karen worked at an affronted expression and failed miserably. To salve her feelings, she took another sip of wine. "I met Charles Mitchell while in my junior year of college in Boston." Her lips twisted self-mockingly. "I was in love, married and two months pregnant before the start of my senior year. Needless to say, I never did graduate."

Pondering the twinge of emotion he felt stab at his

midsection, Paul kept his tone free of inflection. "Go on."

"Life was wonderful for ten years—love, marriage, the two sons resulting from it and even the career I embarked on when Rand, my oldest, and Mark, my baby, were seven and five respectively." Her sigh was revealing and hurt Paul in a way he didn't understand. "At least I believed it was wonderful."

"Charles didn't?" he probed softly.

Karen shook her head. She certainly was excessively dry. She allowed herself another sip of the wine. "You must understand, Charles worked very hard. He was always dynamic, ambitious. It was part of his charm. Everyone knew he was going places." She suddenly needed another, deeper swallow of wine. "The problem was, Charles was going places with several different women."

"What? You tolerated that?"

Karen's body jerked in reaction to the sharpness of Paul's voice.

"Tolerated?" Karen stared at him blankly, beginning to really feel the effects of her unaccustomed self-indulgence. Then his question registered. "I didn't know!" she cried in self-defense. "I was so...so stupidly happy, I never dreamed..." Her voice gave way to tense silence as she noticed the uncanny stillness gripping Paul. What had she said to induce that stark expression on his handsome face? She closed her eyes and shook her head. When she opened her eyes, his expression was bland, free of strain. Had she imagined his look of near agony? Paul didn't allow her the time to work it out in her cloudy mind.

"Don't tell me, let me guess," he drawled sarcastically. "A close friend dropped the hint that set you thinking and doubting and finally confirming. Right?"

There was something in his tone, a tip-off to what he was thinking, but...Karen shook her head. Her senses were too fogged to permit in-depth thought. Instead, she sighed and answered his query. "No. If they knew, and I feel certain they did, my friends were too full of concern about hurting me." Her smile was tired. "Charles told me."

"The bastard." Though Paul's voice was little more than a murmured snarl, Karen heard it.

"Yeah." The twang was thick and uncontrived. Her shoulders lifted, then dropped. The action said reams more than mere words would have. She tipped the glass to her trembling lips while a voice within her silently asked how in the hell she'd gotten into this discussion and, more importantly, why?

"Karen?" The edge of concern in his voice was obvious. "Are you all right?"

"Dandy," Karen quipped, swallowing an unladylike hiccup. "I think I may be slightly smashed, but I'm just dandy."

Paul's smile was gentle with compassion. "You don't drink much as a rule, do you?"

"Much?" Karen giggled. "I rarely drink at all. I keep the wine in stock for the paying guests." She gazed at him with cloudy-eyed intent. "It has a tendency to unhinge the mind and loosen the tongue, doesn't it?"

"Hmm," Paul murmured. "But not to worry, you're safe."

Deeper and deeper. Karen narrowed her eyes. What was he telling her—without telling her? Was she safe because he simply wasn't interested? But that didn't equate, she told herself, remembering the strength of the vibrations his body had transmitted to hers almost from the moment they'd met. Or had the attraction all been from one side—hers? The thought was almost sobering...almost. And at the moment the thoughts were all just too much effort.

"I want to sleep." Her childlike request bounced off rock.

"No, you don't." There wasn't an ounce of give in Paul's voice.

"Yes, I do." Karen sniffed and blinked owlishly. "I'm so sleepy." Moving very carefully, she set her glass aside and stumbled to her feet. "If you'll excuse me, I think I'll go on up." She started toward the hall, the mere fact of her forgotten glass saying more than words about her condition.

"Stay right where you are." The tone of authority in Paul's voice halted her abruptly at the base of the wide stairway. Not even in her tipsy state could Karen consider disobeying his arresting command.

"Paul, please." Turning her head slowly, carefully, for the room had suddenly begun to sway, Karen gave him a weary look. "I must lie down."

Paul rose as he set his own glass aside. "No, Karen." He shook his head gently as he walked to her. "Chances are that if you sleep now you'll wake up sick. What you need is some exercise in the fresh air."

"Exercise!" Karen moaned. "Fresh air! You mean—like outside?"

"Yes." Paul was not altogether successful in masking his amusement.

"But it's cold outside!"

"You forgot 'baby.'"

"What?" Karen glowered at him.

"Forget it." His lips twitched. "You'll need a coat, a warm one. Where would it be?"

Still glowering, Karen motioned distractedly at the closet inside the front door. "There's a navy peacoat in there somewhere."

Eyeing her narrowly, Paul reached for the closet door. "If you bolt for the stairs, I'll catch you," he warned, reading her intentions correctly. When her shoulders slumped in defeat, he turned to rummage inside the closet. He found the jacket on a hook near the back of the closet and a navy-blue knit cap on a shelf above the row of hooks.

Tired, fuzzy and thoroughly cowed, Karen stood docilely while Paul buttoned her into the jacket and tugged the hat onto her head and over her ears. When he turned to steer her along the hall to the side door that led to the beach, she tilted her head to run a misty-eyed glance over his sweater. It was warm, but not warm enough.

"What about you?" she muttered, stepping by him onto the veranda and immediately gasping at the chill wind that stole her breath. "Where's your coat?"

"Close at hand." Grasping her upper arm, Paul descended the veranda steps and walked to the side of his car parked in the sandy driveway. Pulling the back door open, he withdrew a down-filled nylon ski jacket. "I tossed this onto the back seat when it warmed up today about noon."

"I see." She didn't, of course. Karen didn't see or understand anything. A frown tugging her delicate eyebrows together, she watched as he shrugged into the brown-and-white jacket. She began to move automatically when he started walking toward the beach. "Where were you coming from today?" she gasped, quick-stepping to keep up with his long stride. "And please slow down!"

Paul shortened his gait at once and slanted an apologetic smile at her. "I'm sorry. What was your question?" His innocent tone didn't fool her for a second. Karen was slightly tipsy—she wasn't unconscious.

"You heard."

His laughter was low, and too darned attractive. "I was coming from farther up the coast." He hesitated, as if in silent debate about continuing. Then he shrugged. "I'd spent the past couple of weeks in the small place my son owns up there. I closed it for the winter this morning."

Paul released his hold on her and draped his arm around her shoulders as they approached a high sand dune. Plowing through the loose sand, they moved as one around the dune and down onto the more solidly packed sand on the beach.

"And you're heading for Philadelphia?" she asked, breathing a little easier as they attained firmer ground.

"Yes." He paused, bringing her to a stop as he stared out at the white-tipped, inky sea. "It's time I went back to work."

"What kind of work do you do?" Following his lead, she turned when he did, feeling her low shoes sink into the moist sand as they strolled along, inches from the lapping wavelets.

"I was a banker."

Karen was not surprised; Paul looked like a banker. "Was?" she prompted, growing less fuzzy as the brisk breeze dispersed the aftereffects of the wine.

"We can talk about that later," Paul said, a trifle imperiously. "I want to hear about your ex-husband."

"Oh, Paul," she sighed.

"You started it, now finish." His tone was unrelenting. "What did you mean when you said he told you about the other women?"

"Exactly that." Karen's shoulders moved in an uncomfortable shrug. "After over ten years of marriage, Charles came to me requesting—no, demanding—a more modern, civilized relationship." Her voice betrayed her tightening throat. Even after five years, the memory had the power to infuriate her.

"Continue."

Paul's terse tone pierced the haze of anger in Karen's mind. She exhaled sharply. "I didn't, truly didn't, understand what he was talking about. Charles was happy to enlighten me." A shudder rippled through her body, and Karen felt grateful for the weight of Paul's arm around her shoulder, tightening to steady her. "He said that a modern, civilized marriage should never include the restrictive bonds of fidelity."

Paul was quiet, too quiet. Karen could feel the tension tautening his muscles, but before she could question him he again nudged her into speech.

"Finish. Get it out of your system."

"There isn't much more. He suggested we stay together, as a family, but that we both—" her voice went flat and hard "—share the wealth, as it were."

At any other time, the viciousness of Paul's curse might have shocked Karen, but on a dark beach, in a darker frame of mind, she endorsed the expletive.

"Since you're here, alone, I'm assuming you told him no."

"I told him to go to hell."

"Bravo."

Paul's one word of approval and praise warmed Karen throughout the hour they trudged through the sand in companionable silence. She didn't know why his commendation warmed her; she only knew that it did.

"And your sons?" Paul broke the unstrained silence as they were shrugging out of their jackets. "How did they react?"

Karen blamed her shiver on the chilly wind and managed a faint smile. "Who ever knows with children? There are moments I tell myself that they are handling it all very well." She lost the smile. "And then there are other times I feel positive they are blaming me because I left their father." Feeling the sting of incipient tears, she swung away, heading for the kitchen. "How about a cup of hot chocolate?"

The subject was closed; Paul accepted her decision. "I'd prefer tea," he said easily, strolling into the room behind her. "Less calories, you know." His teasing ploy worked, drawing a genuine smile from her.

"Tea it is." Karen started for the stove, then paused to glance at him over her shoulder. "And, Paul, thanks for insisting on the walk. It helped."

"Feeling better? Less disoriented?"

"Yes." She actually laughed. "If a little foolish."

"Not necessary." He crossed the brick-tiled floor, coming to a stop mere inches away from her. "We're all allowed our weak moments."

Karen lowered her eyes. "But perhaps we should have them when we're alone."

"I'll never tell." He raised her chin with the tip of one finger. His smile was heartwarmingly tender. "How about that tea?"

Karen felt amazingly good the next morning. Humming to herself as she prepared breakfast, she reiterated her last thought before sleep had caught up to her the previous night: *Paul Vanzant was a very nice man...and darned sexy, too!*

Smiling, she turned away from the stove, intending to dash up the stairs and knock on his bedroom door to tell him that breakfast was almost ready. Paul strode through the back door before she could take the first step.

"Something smells good." He smiled and inhaled deeply. "No, everything smells good."

Karen laughed. "I thought you were still asleep. I was just going to rouse you."

"I've been up for hours," he said, shrugging out of his jacket as he went toward the hall closet. *And I've been aroused ever since I got here!* Paul kept the thought to himself, savoring the sensation like a warm fire on a bitter day. He was feeling good. Wrong! He was feeling great. His mood was infectious. He had Karen laughing easily moments after returning to the kitchen.

"How 'bout a walk?" he asked the minute they'd finished eating.

"I have work to do!" Karen protested, though not too strongly.

"Like what?"

She held up one hand, ticking off fingers as she listed the day's chores. "Dusting. Laundry. Bed-making."

Paul gave her a considering look, then nodded once. "Okay. I'll help. We'll cut the chores in half."

"But you're a guest!"

"Big deal." He grinned; she melted. "I'll help you clean these breakfast things away. Then I'll do the beds while you start the laundry. And then..." He grinned again at her bemused expression. "I'll call Peter while you do the dusting." He snapped his fingers. "Nothing to it."

* * *

"Are you always this organized?" Karen scuffed the toe of her running shoe in the sand, just to break the smooth surface, and slanted a questioning glance at the tall man pacing beside her. It was their second walk of that day. Long rays of afternoon sunlight bounced a glitter off the undulating sea that almost stung the eye. Working together, she and Paul had wiped out her chore list for the entire week, except for the trip to the supermarket in town.

"It's atavistic." Paul laughed down at her. "I come from a long line of fussily neat, well-organized Dutch folk."

"Oh, brother!" Karen rolled her eyes.

"Hey, don't complain." His laughter deepened. "The work's done, isn't it?"

"All except dinner, which won't get done unless I get back to the house pretty quick," she retorted with her innate New England practicality.

"I give up." Paul pivoted on his heel. "Let's go make dinner." He walked so fast that Karen could barely breathe, let alone protest his intent. But she dug in her heels the instant they walked into the house.

"I'll cook dinner," she declared, planting her hands on her hips. "You go take a shower or read the paper or, better yet, try your son once more."

Paul appeared about to argue until she made the last suggestion. Having made two failed attempts to contact his son, he was feeling a trifle concerned. "Right." He nodded. "I'll try Peter again." He swung away, but paused in the doorway. "It's been a good day, Karen. Hasn't it?"

Karen's smile was soft, as was her voice. "A very good day, Paul. Thank you for it."

"No thanks necessary. The day was free. Ours to

take.'' He grew still, a frown drawing his dark brows together. Then he smiled. ''As all the days are, by damn!'' Striding back to her, he grasped her upper arms, drew her to him and kissed her gently on the mouth. When he raised his head, a smile curved his lips. ''That was even better than the walk.'' Releasing her abruptly, he strode from the room.

Startled, delighted, Karen stared at the empty doorway, a bemused look on her kiss-softened face. Lifting her hand, she touched the tip of her fingers to her tingling lips.

''By damn!'' she murmured in a tone of wonder.

Chapter Three

"You are an excellent cook." Lifting his wineglass, Paul tilted it in a silent salute before drinking the last pale drops. "The broiled scrod was every bit as delicious as last night's scampi."

"Thank you." Pleasure warmed Karen's cheeks and glowed from her brown eyes. Flattered out of proportion to the simple compliment, she lowered her gaze to her plate. The meal had been good, she supposed, although she wasn't as positive as he—she'd been too aware of his presence at the table to really taste any of it. Appalled by the tremor in her fingertips, Karen raised her glass and gulped the last of her wine. Obviously remembering the night before, Paul arched his brows as he hefted the wine bottle. She smiled and nodded. He refilled her glass the instant she set it on the table again.

"We may as well finish it," he said, pouring the last of the chardonnay into his glass. Cradling the glass, Paul leaned back in his chair. He sat bolt upright again as a gust of wind rattled the panes in the long windows in the bowed alcove. The wind made a low, moaning sound as it whipped around the house. Paul frowned. "Storm brewing?"

Karen nodded. "I heard a weather report while I was finishing dinner. There's a storm moving up the coast. It could be messy."

"Messy?" Paul glanced at the windows as another blast of wind slammed into them. "In what way?"

"Thunder, lightning, rain, the possibility of sleet and/or snow. Gale warnings have been posted and high tides predicted," Karen said, repeating the forecast she'd heard earlier. "Surely you felt the temperature dropping while we were on the beach?"

Paul's eyes narrowed as he nodded. At his back, the wind turned into a low roar. "The house is secured?" he asked sharply.

Karen smiled. "Reasonably. There are a few things that need doing, but..." She lifted her shoulders in a helpless shrug.

"What things?" Leaning forward, Paul set his wine on the table.

"A couple of shutters on the second floor are loose," she said, annoyed. "And the storm doors must be hung."

"Why haven't these things been done?"

His imperious tone changed her annoyance to anger, and she bristled inwardly. Who did he think he was, anyway? And why was he ruining the easy camaraderie between them? Strangely hurt, but trying to control her temper, Karen replied evenly. "I called the man who does the work for me, but he has a long waiting list. I must wait my turn." A mocking smile shadowed her soft lips. "The house has withstood over a hundred years of storms. It won't blow away, I assure you."

"I didn't think it would," he retorted. Lifting his glass, he leaned back again, his attitude one of supreme indifference to the racket outside. "But I don't like leaving things unfinished." Raising his glass, Paul sipped the wine appreciatively, looking for all the world like an indolent, refined aristocrat. "I'll fix the shutters and hang the doors as soon as the storm wears itself out."

Karen stared at him in openmouthed amazement, stunned by the contrast between his appearance and his blandly voiced statement. Not even his efforts of that day had prepared her to hear him calmly offer to do the job of a handyman. "You?" she blurted out, unaware of the implied insult.

A dry smile curved his lips. "Why not?" he inquired politely. "I believe my capabilities run to a hammer and a screwdriver as well as bed-making and kitchen duty."

Karen suddenly, inexplicably, felt every bit as rattled as the windows behind him. Paul had given her a gentle but unmistakable verbal smack. She felt both ashamed and embarrassed by her rudeness. She had leaped to conclusions based only on appearances, an error she rarely made. Her fingers plucked nervously at the woven place mat beneath her plate. "I'm sorry," she murmured, glancing down and issuing a silent command to her fingers to be still. Paul's reflexes were quicker than hers. Leaning forward, he stilled her fingers by covering them with his own.

"Why are you suddenly shying away from me, Karen?" he asked, his voice so soft it felt like a caress.

Her head jerked up. "I'm not!" she said, much too forcefully, her lips burning with the memory of his brief kiss.

Paul's dark eyes met her gaze. "Yes, you are," he said. "And I know why."

She was suddenly hot, and cold, and breathless. Wanting to jump and run, but unable to move, Karen moved her head slowly back and forth, silently negating the known but unstated. She bit her lip to keep from crying out when his hand tightened around hers.

"You know why, too."

"No." Her voice was raspy, whispery, fearful. She didn't want to hear it, didn't want her feelings, her *needs*, put into words.

"Karen."

The low, aching sound of his voice shuddered through her receptive body. Her head moved again, sharply. This couldn't be happening, not to her! Not with this man! A gasped "Oh" burst from her slightly parted lips, as retaining his grip on her hand, Paul set his glass aside and got up to circle the table to her.

"Paul, don't." The whisper was nothing more than a token protest. Karen knew it, and Paul knew it, too.

"I must." Grasping her arms, he drew her up and into an embrace. "I wanted more this afternoon, Karen," he said in a tone growing harsh with passion. "I don't understand it any more than you do. But I need to taste your mouth again. I *must* have your mouth." A wildness darkened his eyes as his gaze fell on her trembling lips.

"Paul, this is crazy!" Karen's weak tone was unconvincing. "We don't know—" Her voice was lost inside his mouth.

Unlike his earlier, gentle touch, his kiss was at once hard and demanding, and his body was, too. His arms tightened, crushing her soft breasts against the muscled strength of his chest. Frightened by the intensity of the sensations searing through her, Karen struggled against his hold. She went still as his tongue entered her mouth. Her senses reeling, she felt his hands move on her back, one up to her head, fingers tangling in her hair, the other to the base of her spine, fingers splaying over her buttocks. She felt him change position. One leg eased between her thighs and was immediately followed by the other. The pressure stretched the denim material of her skirt, molding it to the most feminine part of her. Cupping his hand, he drew her up and into the shocking heat of his body.

"Paul!" she gasped, tearing her mouth from his. "You must stop!" Karen could feel his heart thumping against her chest, could hear the erratic sound of his harsh breath, could smell the dizzying mixture of sharp after-shave and aroused male. He frightened her; he excited her. She felt as if her insides were melting.

"I know," he said unsteadily. Drawing deep gulps of air into his lungs, he rested his forehead against hers, but his hand continued to press her body to his. "I feel you trembling," he said on a roughly expelled breath that teased her lips. "I don't want to frighten you, Karen. Please believe that."

"I...I do." Karen was telling the truth; she did believe him. The strain in his voice convinced her that he was as confused as she was by the intensity of the attraction flaring between them. Held rigidly at her sides, her hands ached with the need to touch him, caress him, hold him. She clenched her fingers in desperation. "Please, let me go." Karen's throat felt tight and achy. "I must clear the table." She was half hoping he'd refuse, and she sighed softly when he complied.

Paul reluctantly slid his hands from her body, then stepped back, a wry smile slanting his lips. "Do you want me to leave?"

"Now, tonight?" Karen exclaimed, her jangled senses clamoring a protest. "There's a storm building out there!" As if to reinforce her statement, a gust of wind slammed against the house. "Where would you go?" Glancing away from the passion still smoldering in his eyes, Karen stared into the darkness beyond the windows. She didn't want him to leave, and it required all her control to keep from clutching him to her. She started when his hand caught her chin, turning her to face him.

"You didn't answer my question, Karen," he said tightly. "Do you *want* me to go?"

Unconscious of the implied sensuousness of her act, Karen moistened her dry lips with the tip of her tongue, shivering at the naked hunger revealed in his eyes as he watched her. Thrown off balance by the intensity of her response to him, she jerked around and began clattering dishes and utensils as she gathered them together.

"Answer me!"

The sharpness of his tone lashed at her, and with a muffled sob, Karen whipped around to look at him. "No!" she shouted. "No, I don't want you to go!" Gripping the dishes in her hands, she spun on her heel and dashed into the kitchen, wincing at the harsh sound of his voice as Paul cursed fluently.

Dammit! Dammit! Dammit! Feeling about to explode, Paul stormed into the living room. A fire leaped merrily in the fireplace, sending forth a rosy light to enhance the welcoming comfort of the room. Paul wasn't soothed by the warmth of the fire or the appeal of the deeply cushioned chintz-covered chairs and sofa, the brightly colored braided oval rug or the glow from the softly burnished copper lamps set on the solid wood tables. If anything, the tranquil ambience of the room merely added irritation to his already abraded sensibilities. Flinging his body into a chair, he stared broodingly into the crackling flames.

Why had it happened, here and now? Paul asked himself agitatedly. More to the point, *how* had it happened? A burst of dry, humorless laughter eased the tension in his throat. Had he genuinely believed that his sex life was a thing of the past? Yes, he had convinced himself that the drive was gone forever.

"Fool!"

The ridicule wrapped up in the sound of his own voice brought a self-mocking smile to Paul's lips. Impotence. Merely allowing the word to form instilled a sense of sick dread in him. But he had believed it to be true. For six years, Paul had lived with the feeling of dread. Six long years. Sighing softly, tiredly, he rested his head against the back of the chair and closed his eyes.

More than six years earlier, in the classic last-to-know fashion, he had learned of his wife's infidelities and her proclivity for younger men—compliments of a well-meaning friend. At the time, something had seemed to die inside Paul. His body had not responded to either his wife or any other member of the opposite sex since then. At first, his lack of response had terrified him, yet pride had kept him from seeking medical advice. Then, as time passed and his interest waned, Paul had resigned himself to never again experiencing the sensual thrill of his blood running hot and wild and his body tautening in anticipation. And now, after six years, to have his body awaken to urgent, pulsating life, not once but repeatedly within a matter of some twenty-four hours, was stupefying, to say the least.

Not repeatedly, incessantly, Paul thought wryly, feeling his muscles tense and the sweet flame of desire sear his loins as a vision of Karen came into his mind.

What was it about her? Shaking his head, Paul dismissed the question as unimportant. The why of it didn't matter—not now. What did matter was the life and passion quickening his body and teasing his mind. He wanted her. His desire was strong and hot, and he wanted her so much it actually caused him pain. God, it was wonderful!

"Where is your wife?"

His sensual reverie shattered by Karen's quiet voice, Paul shot up in the chair. His mind still clouded by a haze of passion, he stared at her uncomprehendingly.

"My wife?" he repeated blankly.

Karen's lips tightened. "Yes," she said distinctly. "Your wife." Her steps light, her walk graceful, she crossed the room to stand before him. Her gaze was cool and direct. "Where is she now?"

A flash of understanding removed the frown creasing Paul's brow. He had told her he was both a father and a grandfather, but that was all he'd told her. And after the trauma of her revelations the night before, they had both carefully avoided any subject even bordering on the personal all day. They had talked of many things, all of them impersonal. But now, Paul realized that Karen needed answers—she believed him married and looking for some extramarital action. And considering her own experience with Charles, she was probably somewhat militant, and rightfully so. A slight smile teased Paul's lips. No wonder she was looking at him in that insulted, accusatory way.

"My wife is dead, Karen," he said, rising to stand in front of her. "She's been dead for almost seven months."

"I'm sorry." Her lashes swept down to conceal her eyes, but not quite fast enough to hide the flash of relief that they revealed.

Reaching out, he caught her hand with his. "You needn't be," he murmured, feeling heat shoot up his arm as he stroked his thumb over the back of her hand. "She had been on a course of self-destruction for years."

Karen started, and her lashes swept up again. "You mean she committed suicide?" she breathed.

"No." Paul shook his head sharply. "At least not consciously. It's a long, unsavory story, and..." His voice faded. He couldn't simply say "...and I'd rather make love to you than talk about her now."

"I'm sorry," she repeated.

"Don't be." Paul was hurting again and enjoying every nuance of physical pain. Lifting her hand, he brought it to his lips. His tongue tested the tips of her fingers and found them delicious. "She was driven by demons no one understood. She's at peace now." As he finished speaking, he drew one finger into his mouth to suck gently on the tip. Satisfaction shimmered through him when Karen gasped, then shivered.

"Paul." Her voice was low, quivery. "What are you doing?"

"Tasting you." A slow smile curved his lips. "You taste like lemon-fresh dish detergent."

"I...I had to wash the broiler. It doesn't fit in the dishwasher."

Paul's smile deepened. Karen's tone was revealing in its uncertainty. "I find I'm developing a taste for the tartness of lemons," he said, deserting the finger and drawing her hand to his shoulder. "But I still prefer the sweetness of your mouth." His objective stated, Paul slowly lowered his head, allowing her time to retreat if she wanted to. She didn't.

Desire surged through Paul's body as Karen lifted her head, silently offering her mouth to him. He groaned and covered her mouth with his parted lips.

This time his kiss was different; the difference destroyed the last of Karen's resistance. Though his lips were as hard as before, his mouth was gentle on hers, coaxing a response from her. Murmuring words she couldn't hear but understood nonetheless, he played a sensual game with her lips, nipping at them and sucking on them in turn, then lightly skimming his tongue over her sensitized skin.

When Paul finally slid his tongue into her mouth, Karen had been reduced to a whimpering, shivering mass of receptive readiness. Her muffled moan of pleasure electrified him. Gentleness gave way to spiraling hunger. The kiss became an almost violent clash of greedy mouths, each seemingly intent on devouring the other.

Circling her hips with one arm, Paul pulled her into intimate contact with his body. His right hand captured one breast, fingers teasing the crest into tight, aching arousal. Karen shuddered in reaction to the pleasure splintering throughout her body. Her mind whirled. Her senses exploded. Her empty body throbbed a demand for fulfillment. A low moan of protest burst from her throat when he deserted her mouth to seek her ear with his lips.

"Come to bed with me." Paul's voice was harsh with strain, his breath hot, his body rigid.

It was sheer madness, and Karen eagerly divorced sanity. Arching her body into his, she closed her eyes and let her head fall back, exposing the vulnerable cords in her neck to his voracious mouth.

"Karen. Karen." Paul wrenched a moan from her as he drew the moist tip of his tongue down her throat to her fluttering pulse. "Come to bed with me." The touch of his tongue whipped her pulse beat into thunder. The noise created by nature outside paled by comparison.

Consumed by an intensity of passion she had never before experienced, Karen was oblivious to any and all outside influences. The force of the worsening storm battering the house went unheard by her, as did the spit and crackle of the dying fire in the grate. She herself was a living flame contained within a raging storm; the blaze was beautiful.

"Karen?" Paul brought his hands up to grasp her head, making her look at him as he stared at her with eyes lit from within by the desire running rampant through his body. "We need each other tonight." His raw voice revealed the fine edge he was teetering on. "Say yes."

"Yes."

Paul went absolutely still for an instant, not even seeming to breathe. Then a fine tremor rippled through his body. His voice was little more than an aching whisper.

"Where?"

The time for hesitation was long past. Having accepted the idea of going to bed with him, Karen moved swiftly to consummate her commitment.

"My room," she said, grasping his hand as she whirled away, heading for the stairs.

They ran. Hands clasped, they dashed up the stairs, along the hall and into Karen's bedroom. The door stood wide open behind them; in their haste, neither Karen nor Paul noticed.

Between quick, hard kisses and brief, eager touches, they literally tore the clothes from one another's backs. Paul dragged Karen into a crushing embrace the instant they were free of the confining material. The mat of hair on his chest scraped her breasts into tingling arousal. Her soft curves yielded to his tightly bunched muscles. His mouth was hot; her lips were parted and ready for his.

Denied the food of love for such a long time, their bodies were starving, his to fill, hers to be filled. Their hands moved restlessly in unison, stroking, kneading, caressing. Their bodies strained as if to absorb and be absorbed, one into the other.

"Not enough, it's not enough," Paul groaned into her mouth, moving her inexorably toward the bed. "I want more. I want everything."

"Yes. Yes." Karen's senses swam as he bore her back onto the bed. "Now, please," she sobbed, grasping his hips as he moved between her thighs.

He could not hold back, and she didn't want him to. Communicating her desire by pressing her fingers into his taut buttocks, she raised her hips as he thrust his forward. A cry of exquisite pleasure was torn from her arched throat as his body surged into hers, making them one.

Karen did not hold back—she could not, not even the small, inhibited portion of herself that she had never been able to allow her husband to own. Feeling stronger, more vital, more alive than she'd ever felt in her life, Karen abandoned herself to the sensual fury of Paul's driving possession. He had demanded everything; her body granted his demand.

"Yes, like that," he groaned as she curled her legs

around him in a lover's embrace. "Hold me close, tighter, tighter."

"Oh, Paul, yes!" she cried, arching her back as he drew her breast into his mouth.

"Lord! I want more and more," he gasped, grasping her hips to lift her up and into his cadence. "I can't get enough of you!"

"Paul. Paul!" Karen gave a low-pitched scream as his momentum drove her over the edge of reason and into the realm of shattering, pulsating release.

"Oh, God! Karen!" Paul's harsh cry of triumph echoed through the silent room a moment later.

Karen awoke to the chill sound of sleet being flung against the windows by a wind howling in rage and the warm feeling of a broad palm stroking her thigh. Reacting to both sound and sensation, she murmured appreciatively and moved toward the source of the warmth. Paul's skin was heated, his body aroused.

"I want you again," he whispered, brushing his lips along her jawline to her ear, then over her cheek to the corner of her mouth.

"I know." Turning her head, Karen returned the caress by gliding her lips over the taut skin on his face.

"For purely scientific reasons, you understand." Amusement underlined his serious tone.

"Indeed?" Karen's lips quirked into a smile. "Name one."

"Well, there's the obvious, of course."

"And that is?" Her smile deepened.

"Sweet lady, I'm over fifty, remember?" Paul's tone held a suspicious hint of self-satisfaction. "It'll be worth the experiment just to find out if I *can*."

As she could feel the strength pressing against her

thigh that assured her he *could*, Karen laughed softly. "Name another," she insisted, catching his lower lip carefully between her teeth.

"I have a scientist's curiosity to find out if you're really as good as I thought you were or if I was just that anxious."

Amused and challenged at the same time, Karen pulled away from him and sat up. "You thought I was good?" Reaching across the bed, she switched on the small lamp on the nightstand, wanting to see his expression when he answered. He quickly hid a twitching smile when she turned back to him.

"Well, yes, as I said, I *thought* you were good." Paul's tone was suspiciously bland. "But, as I also admitted, I *was* anxious and therefore not very objective."

"I see." Actually, Karen saw more than was good for her equilibrium. Paul was lying flat on his back, his torso bathed by the soft golden lamplight. Silver glinted in the dark hair at his temples and in the curly mat on his chest. Fascinated by the silver strands, Karen wondered if they grew in the line of darkness that ran from his chest across his midriff and under the sheet draping his concave abdomen.

"What do you...see?" Paul's tone tightened perceptibly as he watched her eyes widen slightly as her gaze settled on the sheet.

"Uh...um...what?" Karen jerked around to look at him. The sudden movement set her bare breasts swaying, making her aware of her nudity for the first time since she'd sat up. Dismayed by her impulse to cross her arms over her chest, she straightened her spine and looked at him with hard-won composure.

Her effort was wasted on Paul; he was too engrossed in staring at her breasts to notice. Warmth suffused

Karen's body as he slowly lifted his hand from the bed to gently, tentatively touch one quivering tip with one finger.

"Beautiful," he whispered, lightly stroking the crest to aching attention.

"Is, uh..." Karen was finding it extremely difficult to sit still. "Is this part of the experiment?" she asked, swallowing to ease the sudden dryness in her throat. Paul smiled as his stroking finger wrenched an involuntary gasp from her lips.

"This *is* the experiment," he said, raising his shadowed eyes to hers. "Although I readily admit to being overanxious," he murmured, transferring his finger to give equal consideration to her other breast. "I've reached the conclusion you are an exceptionally good bed partner."

A sexist remark if Karen had ever heard one, yet instead of feeling insulted or annoyed by it, she felt ridiculously complimented and pleased. She also felt an urge to lean forward to grasp his hand and bring it to her. Her breasts hurt and felt heavy. She silently willed him to cradle their weight in his palms. The pad of his finger continued its maddening stroke.

"Paul?" His name barely whispered from her tight throat.

"Yes?" His voice was low and raw. His finger flicked, igniting a blast of sensation that Karen felt in the depths of her femininity.

"You're driving me crazy!" she gasped, shuddering.

"What are you gonna do about it?"

Karen gazed at him in astonishment. Taunting challenge gleamed in his dark eyes. Indecision held her motionless for a long moment. Claiming exclusive rights to the role of conqueror, Karen's former husband had never allowed her to play the aggressor. Paul was not allowing it, either; he was demanding it. An unfurling flame of excitement consumed her last lingering shred of inhibition. Accepting his challenge, she coiled her fingers around his wrists and drew his palms to her breasts. A satisfied smile tilted the corners of Paul's lips. Moving slowly, she pressed her body against his hands as she lowered her head to his chest. Paul's smile fled, and he inhaled sharply as she curled her tongue around one tight bud nestled in the silver-and-black mat on his chest.

Paul's fingers flexed in reaction to her caress. "More, please," he groaned, gently kneading her soft flesh. "I love the feel of your mouth and hands on my body." To reinforce his claim, he moved one hand to the back of her head and speared his fingers through her hair.

As she nuzzled into the salt-and-pepper curls, Karen's senses were assailed by the heady scent of soap and musk. Her tongue tingled with the slightly salty taste of his skin. Feeling free, unfettered, she explored his chest leisurely before gliding her lips down the slight incline from his rib cage to his navel. Paul's fingers gripped her hair spasmodically as she dipped her tongue into the shallow indentation. His body jerked when her moist lips continued to follow the dark, downy trail.

"Karen!" Paul grasped her shoulders, halting her lips mere inches from their destination. "I can't take any more. I want to be inside you."

Karen gave him a dry look.

"I appreciate the thought, and I'll probably beg you for it some other time." His smile was rakish with promise as he pulled her on top of him.

Karen gasped; the unique position held appeal, exciting appeal. Straightening, she stared into his eyes, thrilling to the taut expectancy that flashed in their depths as she carefully straddled his hard thighs. His hands grasped her hips. Their gazes dropped to watch as she lowered her body, sheathing him deep inside her silken warmth.

"That's good," he groaned, arching up into her. "So good."

"Yes," Karen sighed, quivering as his hands sought her breasts. "I never knew anything could feel this good." Her breath lodged in her throat as he thrust upward again. She began to move responsively.

"Slowly, slowly," Paul crooned in a hoarse tone. "I want to savor every minute of it."

Releasing her breasts, Paul reached up to cup her face with his palms and draw her mouth to his. While she rocked against him, his tongue reflected the slow thrust-and-retreat motion of his body. His hands slid down her neck to her shoulders. Stroking, caressing, he glided his palms down her body to where their séparate beings were joined into one.

Karen's breathing was shallow and then deep by turns. Inside she felt like a time bomb about to run out of seconds. She was trying to maintain the slow pace Paul wanted, but it was becoming more and more difficult to hold herself in check. White lightning zigzagged through her when she felt him work his fingers between their fused bodies.

"Now, Karen," he cried, suddenly increasing his thrusting cadence. "Now!"

She was moving wildly, gasping his name, when the last second ticked and her inner bomb exploded, flinging her into a whirlpool of ecstatic exhaustion.

Chapter Four

A persistent rapping sound finally succeeded in piercing to the depths of the most restful slumber Karen had enjoyed in years. Prying her eyes to half-mast, she lay listening to the regular beat, eyebrows meeting in a frown as she tried to identify the cause and location of the disturbance. The noise ceased and her expression eased, only to tighten again when the rapping resumed.

"What the—" muttering, Karen tossed back the tangled covers and swung her legs over the side of the bed to sit up. A twinge of complaint in her thighs brought memories of the night before rushing into her mind. Blinking once, she scooted around to stare at the empty bed. Heat flooded her face as vivid images of the nocturnal activity played out upon the rumpled sheets flashed through her suddenly cleared brain.

Where was Paul?

Thinking his name brought his image to her mind and

a deeper flush to her cheeks. Had she really caressed him, kissed him and then— Moaning softly, Karen fell back onto the mattress, at once embarrassed by her actions and hopeful of an opportunity to repeat them.

Heat suffusing her body, Karen curled into a tight ball. Her throat felt thick and clogged. Her body felt heavy and overly warm. Her emotions felt battered and her mind was sluggish. Separate threads, one of shame, the other of anticipation, tangled inside her, tying her entire nervous system into knots.

Like pulsating impulses, individual and distinct scenes flashed in her memory, making her hot and cold by turns. Moaning softly, Karen buried her face in the pillow. A half sigh, half sob rose to choke her as she inhaled the scent that her mind would forever connect exclusively with Paul.

As her mind formed his name, her throat expelled the choking sob.

What had come over her? Karen asked herself, her thoughts scattering as her mind sought reasons—or excuses—for her uncharacteristic behavior. Never, not even with the man she had married and believed herself deeply in love with, had she so abandoned herself while in the throes of lovemaking. It simply wasn't like her. And since her divorce she had not experienced the slightest desire for a man, any man. Yet she had responded wildly to Paul.

What must he be thinking about her now, in the light of morning? Karen wondered, blanching at the thought. If upon awakening Paul had labeled her a wanton woman, she had given him ample reason to do so. She had behaved wantonly!

But then, Paul had behaved like the male equivalent of a wanton, whatever that might be.

The realization that she and Paul had in fact been perfectly matched in bed resolved the emotional upheaval. The sense of shame subsided, overcome by a sense of anticipation. Uncurling slowly, Karen raised her arms and stretched languorously.

There was a stirring deep inside Karen's body, a tingling response to her memories and thoughts of Paul. She wanted him again; it was as simple and basic as that. With realization came resolution. She had never allowed herself personal indulgence. Raised to work hard and apply herself conscientiously, she had always done the "right" thing. She had been a virgin when she married; she had known no other man but her husband. She was no longer an idealistic, wide-eyed young girl; she no longer expected the world or her own niche in it to be perfect. She was getting uncomfortably close to forty and lately had begun to feel vaguely that life was slipping through her fingers, not unlike the sands in an hourglass. Surely every individual was to be allowed one step off the straight and narrow? Karen asked herself. Her lips twisted in bitter remembrance.

Her former husband had spent more time dancing off the straight and narrow than walking on it. *He* had not paid the price of loneliness and uncertainty about encroaching middle age! Why then should she? Karen demanded silently. She was her own person, a free adult, fully capable of making her own decisions. Should she feel shame and remorse because her senses had rejoiced in the act of giving her body in sweetly satisfying abandonment?

No! The cry of denial rang inside Karen's head. Paul had not taken her, nor had he used her. Rather, Paul had shared with her the beauty of exquisite pleasure given and received. And, though she and Paul were strangers, they were also lovers. Karen had no idea how long her lover would stay with her. But then, did anyone ever know what the future held? The question darkened Karen's eyes with remembered pain. In the final analysis, she had been forced to acknowledge that the man she had loved, married and created children with was a stranger to her. And she had given that man everything of herself. She had only given her body to Paul. As the mist of pain cleared from her eyes, Karen decided she could live with the knowledge of her gift to him.

She had behaved wantonly—and she had loved every second of it! A slow smile curving her lips, Karen stretched again, sinuously. She felt wonderful—no, she felt much, much more than merely wonderful. She felt beautiful, and she had never before felt beautiful. She felt bone-deep satisfaction, and she had never before experienced that feeling, either. But most of all she felt as though she had not been expertly loved but exquisitely cherished, and that feeling warmed her inside and out. And the perpetrator of every one of her delicious feelings was not only a man she barely knew but a fantastic, excitingly virile man who, in his own words, would never see fifty again!

Where was Paul, anyway? Frowning again, Karen absently smoothed her hands over the spot where he had lain and sank into the memory of Paul's fiercely gentle possession. She felt quite certain she could happily laze the day away in dreamy expectation of the coming night—if it weren't for that annoying rapping noise, which had resumed after a long pause of blessed quiet.

The sound intruded, breaking the spell. Sighing, Karen left the bed, deciding she might as well get dressed and investigate. If she had any luck at all, the racket was being caused by Gil Rawlins, the handyman she'd called to prepare the house for winter.

Some twenty-odd minutes later, showered and dressed in her usual workday attire of faded jeans and a sweat-shirt, Karen was stripping the sheets from the bed when the hammering, which had ceased once more while she was in the bathroom, commenced outside her bedroom window. Tossing the linens to the floor, she walked to the window and opened it. A welcoming smile on her lips, she stuck her head through the opening to call a greeting to Gil.

The man poised on the ladder, busily hammering nails into the shutter hinges, in no way resembled the short, stocky Gil Rawlins. This man was lean and muscular, and the physical work he was engaged in was at odds with his elegant appearance.

"Paul?" Incredulity lent a hollow note to Karen's voice. "What in the world do you think you're doing?"

The hammer paused in midswing. Paul slanted a smile at her before following through. "Good morning to you, too." The hammer made contact with a resounding bang. Paul relaxed against the ladder with negligent ease. "And I don't *think* I'm doing anything—I *am* fixing the shutters." His smile widened. "In fact," he continued, indicating his work with a motion of his head, "this is the last of the lot. I'll be finished shortly."

"Finished?" Karen frowned. "How long have you been at it?"

"Since first light." He grinned at her look of astonishment. "I'm a creature of habit, and I always wake at dawn." His grin grew decidedly suggestive. "Regardless of how, ah, active my night happened to be."

Karen felt a sting of color on her cheeks that had absolutely nothing to do with the sharpness of the tangy sea breeze. Feeling unequal to the rakish gleam brightening his dark eyes, she lowered her glance.

"Did you, er—" she paused to clear her suddenly dry throat "—have you eaten anything?" Karen glanced up to catch a tender smile curving his lips.

"No." He shook his head and arched one dark eyebrow. "Are you offering to cook me breakfast?"

"Well, the sign out by the road does advertise bed *and* breakfast."

"I seem to recall dinner, as well." Paul's tone was low, shaded sensuously by the memory of the bed that had followed rather than preceded the meal.

The warmth in Karen's cheeks intensified. Her voice was low and tinged with uncertainty. "Since you're the only guest, I—I decided to include lunch and dinner in the reduced fall room rate."

"I'll try to earn my meals." Though Paul's tone was somber, his eyes gleamed with devilry.

He had certainly earned his breakfast!

Karen's face flamed as the thought flashed into her head. As if he could actually read her mind, Paul burst out laughing and nearly lost his precarious perch on the ladder. With a muffled exclamation, he grabbed for the windowsill and caught Karen's hand. His position once again reasonably secure, Paul grinned into her frightened eyes.

"Unless you want a severely injured guest on your hands," he said, still grinning, "I suggest you withdraw from this window and let me get on with the work." Moving carefully, he shifted his hand to the sill alongside hers.

"Are you sure you'll be all right?" Karen frowned with concern.

"I was doing fine until you popped your head out and

distracted me." As he stared into her anxious eyes, Paul's grin slowly faded. "Karen," he said in a low, chiding voice, "I am not the complete dilettante. I assure you I will be fine." He paused an instant, then continued even as she began to protest, "Unless, of course, I starve to death first."

"Paul—"

"Go," he ordered, hefting the hammer. "I'll be finished in a few minutes."

Wanting to argue but deciding she'd better not, Karen withdrew her head and closed the window. Gathering up the bundle of laundry, she left the bedroom and went downstairs, half expecting to hear a cry followed by a crash.

His expression pensive, Paul ignored the cold sea wind biting at every inch of exposed skin on his body and stared at the windowpane that reflected the sparkling sunlight.

Had he come on too strong? he mused. His lips curved in self-derision. Yes, of course he'd come on too strong; he had been coming on to Karen much too strongly from the beginning. He was, in fact, behaving like a wild-eyed pubescent boy subservient to his hormones.

But damn, Karen did have the strangest effect on him! Paul's smile acquired a sensuous tilt. Gripping the hammer in his right hand, he slammed a nail into the shutter hinge with commendable accuracy. The similarity between the act and his performance the night before was not lost on Paul. Without warning, his body tightened and the muscles in his thighs quivered with taut readiness. Laughing aloud from the sheer joy of the almost painful arousal, Paul hammered another nail home.

Okay, he had come on too strong, and much too soon,

Paul admitted to himself. But Karen had responded so warmly, so sweetly, and it had been so long, so very long since he'd felt even the most minute twinge of need for a woman's warmth and sweetness, that he could not dredge up a hint of regret for his impetuosity.

Paul let his arm drop to his side. The hammer and the shutter, indeed even his precarious position on the ladder, were momentarily forgotten. Closing his eyes, he savored the revived heat of passion rushing through his body.

Lord, it felt good to experience the life quickening his body after nearly six years of feeling dead sensually. Relishing the tightness in his loins, Paul opened his eyes, tossed back his head and laughed into the chill autumn breeze. He felt young and strong and equal to anything life had to offer. He wanted to make love to Karen all day and then all night.

But first... Paul laughed again. First he had to finish repairing the shutters. The hammer struck the nail with a resounding bang.

Although she strained to hear the slightest sound as she loaded the washer before hurrying into the kitchen to start breakfast, Karen's fears for Paul went unrealized.

Tension coiled within her as she automatically prepared the meal. Paul should be making an appearance in the kitchen at any moment. What could she say to him? Karen swallowed around a tight knot forming in her throat. Feeling awkward and inept, she overbeat the eggs and clattered the cutlery as she set the table. The eggs she'd scrambled were ready to be served when Paul sauntered into the kitchen. Coming to a stop near the sink, he struck an elegant pose and held his arms out.

"There, you see? I'm still in one piece."

"I'm sorry."

"That I'm still in one piece?"

"No, of course not!" Karen frowned at his teasing smile. "I'm sorry about insulting your capabilities."

Paul's smile turned wry. "It wasn't so much my capabilities that were insulted as much as my intelligence," he informed her in a dry tone. He didn't notice her deepening frown as he turned to the sink to wash his dusty hands.

Karen mulled over his words as she filled two plates with the steaming food and carried them to the table. "Will you bring the toast?" she asked, indicating the breadbasket on the countertop with a distracted motion of her head.

"Certainly." Eyeing her narrowly, Paul picked up the linen-covered basket and strolled to the table. "What's the problem?" He raised one brow as he sat down opposite her.

"I'm not sure I understand," she confessed, frowning at the stream of coffee she was pouring into his cup.

"Understand what?" Paul asked, his knife poised over the sausage nestled next to the home-fried potatoes on his plate.

Karen finished filling her own cup with the aromatic coffee before glancing up at him. "I'm not sure I understand exactly how I've insulted your intelligence."

"Oh." Enlightenment brought a tiny smile to his lips. "It's quite basic, really." Paul's shoulders moved in a half shrug. "Any person with a modicum of intelligence can perform almost any task. All that's required is a willingness to do the work and application of common sense." He smiled. "And although I'll readily admit that my life's work was not of the physical variety, I do consider myself a reasonably intelligent person, and fastening shutter hinges hardly requires all that much brain- or muscle-power.'' He smiled slightly. ''Now do you understand?''

''Oh, yes, I understand now.'' Karen didn't return his smile. Inside she was simmering. What a condescending son of a— Fortunately, Paul interrupted her thoughts before she blurted them aloud.

''Since I was only teasing to begin with, it's really unimportant, anyway.''

Karen blinked. ''You were teasing?''

''Yes, of course.'' Paul smiled wryly. ''Karen, I face myself in a mirror every day. I know exactly how I look.''

''Look?'' she repeated blankly, so confused she forgot her feeling of awkwardness. ''I'm afraid you've lost me.''

''I'm a banker, and I look it,'' he said, his voice flat with self-knowledge. He raised one hand for her inspection; it was not the hand of a day laborer. The fingernails were short, blunt and clean, as was the entire hand. Karen couldn't detect a hint of callus on his palm. ''Hardly the hand of a man accustomed to hard physical work, is it?''

''No.'' Karen frowned. ''So what?'' She had never been enthralled by dirty fingernails and rough calluses.

''So I fully understood your skepticism concerning my capabilities with a hammer, let alone a ladder.'' Paul's gentle smile contradicted the savage knife thrust he made into the innocent sausage.

''It bothers you!'' she exclaimed, astounded by the realization.

''It never did before, but lately, yes, it bothers me.''

''Why?'' Karen stared at him, her breakfast forgotten. Her eyes revealing the confusion she felt, she slowly lowered her gaze to the upper half of his body. Though slender, Paul was by no stretch of the imagination spare. His chest and shoulders were not those of a professional athlete but were broad enough to draw admiring glances. He was muscular without appearing overdeveloped. Mr. America he wasn't, and thank heaven for that, Karen thought, smiling as she lifted her gaze to his slightly narrowed eyes. "There's nothing wrong with the way you look," she declared in a tone of utter conviction.

"Thank you." A flush tinted the taut skin over Paul's high cheekbones. "But if that's true, why were you so amazed to discover me repairing the shutters?" His dark eyes gleamed challengingly.

"You didn't answer my question about why the way you look bothers you," Karen said evasively.

Paul slanted an arch look at her. "Ladies first," he insisted in a teasing tone.

Suddenly impatient with the discussion, Karen swept his torso with a cool, calculating glance. "Okay, I'll confess," she said, meeting his gaze. "You have the appearance of a born-with-the-silver-spoon aristocrat. There's an aura of breeding and elegance about you that conflicts with the idea of any kind of physical labor. Not that you look incapable of labor—it's just that you've never had to perform it. And that's why I was surprised to find you repairing the shutters."

"I see." His breakfast forgotten, Paul stared at her for a few tense moments. Then a smile twitched his sculpted male lips. "An aura of elegance, hmm?" He arched one dark eyebrow very effectively. Karen gave way to a grin.

"Yes. A definite aura of elegance."

"You find this, er...*aura* attractive?"

Karen's grin curved into a wry smile. "I always believed that actions speak louder than words," she murmured, obliquely referring to her eager response to him the night before.

"You were satisfied with my nocturnal labor?"

A warm flush began at the base of Karen's throat and crept upward to her cheeks. Yet, even flustered, she caught the hint of uncertainty in Paul's tone. Could he possibly harbor doubts about his own prowess? she wondered, examining him more closely.

Paul's expression could only be described as austere, but there was a tenseness about him, as if...Karen searched her mind for a fitting phrase that would define the emotion she sensed emanating from him. Then it hit her. It was as if he was waiting for a life-or-death verdict to be handed down!

Forgetting her embarrassment, Karen obeyed an impulse to reach across the table and slide her hand over his. "Yes, Paul, I was satisfied, deeply satisfied," she admitted in a soft, steady voice.

The slow movement of Paul's chest revealed the soundless sigh he expelled. "So was I," he said, turning his hand to glide his palm against hers. "I was deeply satisfied in more ways than you can imagine."

Karen was both intrigued and confused by his cryptic statement. Satisfied in more ways? she repeated to herself. What— The forming question was washed from her mind by a flood of sensations activated by the feel of his fingers lacing with hers. Biting back an exclamation of pleasure, she raised her gaze to his darkening eyes.

"Paul?"

"I want very much to experience the satisfaction again." His voice was low and warm and fantastically sexy. Excitement warring with trepidation inside her, Karen blurted out the first thought that jumped into her mind.

"But we haven't even finished breakfast!"

"Karen..." Paul's voice dropped to a crooning, heated whisper. "The hunger clawing at me cannot be appeased by food." Lifting her hand, he bent to brush his lips across her fingers, and Karen felt the heat from his mouth in every nerve ending in her body.

"It's...it's morning!" Karen's voice was reedy, her breathing uneven.

"Yes." Paul's lips explored her knuckles.

"The sun's shining!"

"Yes." His tongue slid provocatively between her fingers.

"Paul." His name sighed through her slightly parted lips.

"I want to be with you, a part of you, now, in the morning, and here, in the sunshine."

Karen surrendered, simply because she wanted to. "Yes."

Retaining his hold on her hand, Paul stood and moved around the table to her. Smiling into her widened eyes, he dropped to his knees. With a gentle tug, he drew her down next to him. Moving carefully, as if she were constructed of the most delicate spun glass, he lowered her to the carpet. Looming over her, he captured her gaze with his dark eyes and the hem of her sweatshirt with his fingers. Swiftly, smoothly, he drew the shirt from her body, exposing her unfettered breasts to his heated gaze. A shiver rocketed the length of her spine as he lowered his head to her breasts.

"Paul. Oh, Paul!" Karen cried his name huskily, twisting and arching her back in response to the pleasure he created by flicking his tongue over one tingling crest. As his lips closed around the aroused peak, his hands slid to the snap on her jeans.

"Help me." Paul's voice held an enchanting mixture of plea and command as he released the zipper and tugged on her jeans.

Helpless against the sensuous excitement rushing through her body, Karen kicked the loafers from her feet and lifted her hips from the carpet. In the next instant she was naked and vulnerable to Paul's eyes and touch. But within moments she was not alone in her vulnerability. Pushing upright, Paul literally tore the clothes from his body. Noticing her smoky-eyed gaze, he stood over her, quivering as she examined him.

Karen stared at his tall form with fascinated curiosity. In the unforgiving light of day, Paul's body was even more appealing than when cloaked by darkness. His well-muscled shoulders and chest tapered to a flat abdomen and narrow hips. His lightly haired legs were long and well formed. And, in full arousal, he presented a breathtaking image of the primal male. And the primal male excited the primitive female inside Karen. Obeying a life drive as old as time, she opened her arms in silent invitation.

"Karen." Paul groaned as he dropped to his knees between her thighs. "You don't know," he murmured tightly, grasping her hips to lift her to him. "You can't possibly know..." His words were drowned by the harsh breath he inhaled as he joined his body with hers.

For an instant, Karen was confused, wondering what he had started to say. Then it no longer mattered; nothing mattered but the spiraling tension luring her toward the edge of reason.

Paul's chest felt constricted from lack of air. His entire body felt tightly wired, and he held on to the last of his control with grim determination. Beneath him, Karen twisted and arched and whimpered his name; her panting voice was the sweetest sound he had ever heard. Never had a woman, any woman, responded to him so freely or given herself to him so completely. In these few moments of possession, Karen was his in an incomprehensible way that transcended the merely physical. In an effort to maintain that exquisite if inexplicable sense of ownership, Paul fought to contain the fire of desire consuming his mind and body. He would pleasure Karen before he sought his own ecstatic release.

Paul was hovering on the brink of sensual discovery, gritting his teeth, when Karen gave herself to soaring completion. Buried deeply in her warmth, holding her tightly to him, Paul shuddered, then followed her over the edge of reason.

He didn't want to move. As his breathing returned to normal, Paul decided he could happily spend the rest of his life as he was at that moment: his body still joined with Karen's, his head pillowed on her soft breasts.

It was not be be. The phone rang.

"I must answer it," Karen said softly.

"Why?"

"It's one of my quirks," she confessed, pushing against his chest. "I can't stand not answering a ringing phone."

Paul sighed but moved to untangle their bodies, stretching out on the carpet beside her. The instant she was free, Karen scrambled to her feet.

"Aren't you going to dress?" she asked, scooping her clothing from the floor before heading toward the kitchen and the shrilling wall phone.

"Eventually," Paul murmured, stretching.

Clutching her rumpled garments to her chest with one hand, Karen reached for the receiver with her other hand

and turned to glance back at Paul. His long body lay sprawled in a patch of bright morning sunlight. His eyes were closed. A tiny smile of satisfaction curved his lips. At that moment, Karen wanted nothing more than to ignore the persistently ringing phone and run into the dining alcove to cuddle next to him on the floor.

Indecision held her hand motionless in midair for a moment. Then, sighing softly, she grasped the receiver and brought it to her ear.

"Hello?" she said with barely concealed impatience.

"Karen?"

Karen frowned as she identified the anxious strain in the voice of her former mother-in-law. "Yes. Judith?" Her frown deepened. "Is something wrong?" Immediately after asking, she thought of her boys, who were in prep school in Vermont. Panic tightened her throat at the muffled sound of a sob at the other end of the line. "Judith, what is it?"

"Karen, it's Charles. He's had a heart attack!"

Charles? Karen's mind went blank for a moment. Charles was not yet forty years old! "When?" She had to push the word past her frozen lips.

"Late last night. I've been with him since he was admitted to the hospital." Judith paused for breath. "Karen, he's asking for you and the boys. Will you come?"

Karen's gaze flew to the man basking naked in the morning sunlight. *Paul.* Pain streaked through her mind and her heart. While she and Paul had been together, Charles had been fighting for his life. Shame and defeat decided the issue.

"Yes, Judith, of course I'll come. I'll be there as soon as possible."

Raising her eyes, Karen found her gaze captured and held by Paul's steady regard.

Chapter Five

Staring into Paul's eyes, Karen heard herself respond distantly to Judith Mitchell. Her lips moved, forming words of agreement.

"Yes, I'll leave as soon as possible."

Paul rolled onto his stomach to relieve the unnatural twist of his neck. His eyes narrowed at the sound of her voice, and the content of her words.

"Yes, I'll drive down and collect the boys on the way."

Judith's anxious voice rattled in Karen's ear. Enmeshed by a pair of eyes shading to black, Karen heard without hearing.

"I don't know." Impatience clawed at her nerves, her mind, her emotions. "Judith, I simply can't give you a definite time!" Karen could hear her own building anxiety and took a quick, settling breath. "I promise you, I will have the boys there as soon as possible."

The panicky voice at the end of the line rattled again; Paul began to move. Karen's control snapped.

"I have a lot to do, Judith! And unless I get off this phone, I'll never get there! Yes. Goodbye." Without turning to look, Karen moved her arm to replace the receiver. Plastic clattered against plastic before the receiver nestled into the cradle. Paul was moving; Karen stopped breathing.

Paul came up off the floor with the liquid agility of a man half his age, his muscles tensed, as if ready to spring into whatever action proved necessary.

Karen's voice had been so low, so anxious, that he had heard only bits and pieces of her end of the conversation. But from her tone, Paul knew something was wrong, very wrong. Her face, moments before flushed with the soft glow of pleasurable satisfaction, was devoid of all color. Her eyes, recently slumbrous with repletion, were now wide and cloudy. Her mouth, seconds before full and moist from the caress of his lips, was now pinched and bracketed with lines of strain.

Her mouth.

The muscles lacing Paul's stomach clenched. Alarm billowed to encompass his tightening chest.

Karen's mouth was lost to him; he knew it. Despair invaded his mind and coiled deep down in his gut. He didn't go to her—he couldn't move, couldn't think. In that instant, not understanding why or how, Paul knew that when Karen's trembling white lips finally moved he would once again find himself outside in the cold, looking in, longing for warmth.

He wanted to curse. He wanted to scream a denial of the rejection not yet voiced. Paul stood motionless, unconscious of his nakedness, his narrowed gaze riveted to the stark expression on her face. Time froze for an endless instant. Encapsulated within that moment Paul felt the converging rush of anguished emotions and burgeoning, paralyzing fear. Supreme effort was required to form one word, a word that was like a death knell. "Karen?"

It was not unlike coming out of a trance. Karen blinked, and the timeless instant was over—everything was over. Pleasure and contentment were of a realm not intended for thirty-seven-year-old divorcées with teenage sons. Reality was shame, and self-disgust and pain. The pain she was feeling was streaking through her body now—the pain Charles had suffered while she had been taking her pleasure.

Karen shivered. The spell was broken. The harsh light of morning poured through the windows of the alcove, gilding Paul's tense body with spangles of gold. His nakedness was beautiful and so very natural, and yet it was an affront, an insult to her senses and shame.

"I must go." Her voice lacked substance; her eyes lacked life.

"Go? Go where?" Caution curled around the edges of his carefully controlled tone. "What has happened?"

"To New Hampshire to collect my boys, and then to Boston," she responded woodenly, her manner relaying unspoken words that pierced his heart with tiny poison darts. "Charles has had a heart attack, and he has been asking for me and his sons." Her throat worked, indicating more than the need to merely swallow. "I must go at once."

"Yes, of course you must go, but—"

Karen shook her head sharply, cutting off his words, cutting off his breath.

"There are no buts, Paul!" Her arms moved aimlessly. "I must leave at once!" As she moved, her bare sole made contact with a section of floor tile that had not been warmed by her flesh. A frown drew her eyebrows together as the sensation of chill enveloped her foot. Reluctantly, as if fearing what she'd see, Karen lowered her gaze.

Her glance skimmed, shied away, then came back to slowly examine her own unadorned body. She swayed from the strength of the shudder that tore through her. Memory flashed, too clear, too sharp, too damning. Vividly, as if rolled across a movie screen, a picture formed in her mind, a picture of two people, two *middle-aged* people, washed by sunlight, consumed by each other while in the throes of making love on the floor—no!—indulging their physical hungers!

The mental reenactment was demeaning, and it was demoralizing. What had seemed beautiful at the time took on shadings of ugliness. Karen swallowed against a rising tide of bitterness.

He had to stop her!

The silent inner command unlocked Paul's frozen muscles. Not even certain exactly what he had to stop Karen from doing or thinking, he knew he had to put a stop to it at once. Three long strides were all that were required to propel him from the dining alcove and across to where she stood, still hovering near the wall phone. Paul extended his hand as he took the third step. Karen flinched and shrank back.

Her act caused the second toll of the death knell sounding inside his head.

"Don't touch me, Paul, please." Karen knew she couldn't let him touch her. She couldn't bear to have him touch her—she'd collapse, fall apart, and she didn't have time to fall apart.

"Karen, what in hell is going on inside your head?" Paul's voice held more plea than demand.

"I'm naked!" Karen shouted. "You're naked!"

"So what?" he shouted back, frustration heavy in his voice. "What do clothes have to do with anything?"

Karen's head moved awkwardly as she glanced around, seeing nothing, feeling everything. "I've got to bathe and dress." Her breath lodged in her chest. "I've got to pack. *I've got to go for my boys!*"

Paul's hand flashed out to grasp her wrist as she spun away from him. "Hold it." His fingers tightened when she tried to yank free. "I said hold it, dammit!" His harsh tone stopped her frantic bid for release, but she refused to look at him. Paul's chest heaved with a soundless sigh. "That's better. I want you to tell me who you were speaking to on the phone and exactly what that person said to you to cause this hysterical reaction."

He wanted? *He* wanted? *Hysterical?* Anger ripped through Karen with the devastating force of a flash fire. She could look at him now; she could glare at him.

"Who do you think you are?" Karen's tone was scathing. God! She hurt, in her mind, in her heart and, worse, deep down in her soul—her so recently blackened soul. Her slicing tone cut into another soul, leaving it wounded and bleeding. "Just who in the hell do you think you are to question me?"

"Your lover."

Anger receded. Senses ceased rioting. Karen's brain switched to stun. It was an irrefutable fact: Paul Vanzant, wanderer, vagrant, whatever, was her lover. Conflict ascended. She was torn between two separate needs. Her arms ached to curl around his trim waist; her palm itched to slap his aristocratic face. She did neither. In a tone that was free of expression, Karen related the phone conversation to him—at least what she could remember of it. Paul's features settled into austere lines as she spoke.

"It's a flagrant imposition on ties that no longer bind." Breeding, culture and sheer male arrogance were expressed by Paul's tone.

"He's their father!" Karen protested, beginning to tremble. "Suppose it were you lying there in that hospital bed. Wouldn't you want your son, your daughter?"

Paul conceded the point with a slight inclination of his head. "Yes, of course. And I understand your willingness to take his sons to him." His lips flattened. "What I don't understand is your intense reaction to the news of his attack." He paused, as if hesitant to voice his suspicions. Then he squared his shoulders. "Are you still in love with him, Karen?"

"No." Simple truth rang in her voice. She shook her head. "No, Paul," she said more strongly, "I am not still in love with Charles. He very effectively killed the love I felt for him by confessing—or, more accurately, bragging—about his other women."

Paul's shoulders didn't slump with relief, though the urge was great. "All right. Then why all this panic?"

"My boys—" she began, her tone heating again.

"I understand that," he interrupted, slashing his hand through the air. "What I don't understand is your withdrawal." She opened her mouth; his hand slashed the air once more. "And you are, already have, withdrawn from me. I want to know why."

Why? Karen gaped at him. Didn't he know? Didn't he feel the slightest twinge of remorse? Couldn't he see exactly how that phone call had exposed their behavior?

They were strangers—strangers! And yet, while her sons had gone innocently about their business and her sons' father had fought the pain of a heart attack, two strangers to one another had gone at each other like alley cats at mating time!

Didn't Paul see or understand that?

Karen's breath trembled from her quivering body on a sigh. No, of course Paul couldn't see or understand. He was a man, after all. And men viewed these things differently than women. Hadn't she had proof enough of exactly how men viewed the male-female relationship?

Her response was too long in coming. Paul's fingers tightened around her wrist.

"It was a mistake."

His fingers flexed, and Karen flinched.

"I'm sorry." The pressure was immediately eased. "What was a mistake?"

He knew. Karen was positive that though he had asked, Paul knew what her answer would be. She didn't hesitate.

"Us," she said, repressing a shudder. "The entire situation." Her gaze crept to the sunlit spot on the alcove carpet, then skittered away again. "Our, our—" She couldn't force the words past her lips.

"Our lovemaking, dammit!" Paul barked.

"It was all an enormous, dreadful mistake," Karen went on, as if his harsh definition had never reached her ears.

Paul's perfectly defined features grew taut with impatience. "Why?" he demanded harshly. "In what way was it a dreadful mistake?"

Though Karen trembled visibly, she met his drilling stare without flinching. "It all happened too soon. We don't know one another." Her trembling increased. "In simple terms, we were both motivated by lust, sex for sex's sake alone." Her trembling gave way to a violent shudder. "I—I feel as though I've not only betrayed myself but the trust of my children, as well," she said in a stark, shaken tone.

"And now you're drowning in guilt and shame and God knows what else." Paul's fingers loosened, releasing her imprisoned wrist. "You're wrong, you know." His voice held little hope of her hearing, or of her believing him if she did register his words.

Karen shook her head, confirming his lack of hope. She felt his sigh to the depths of her being—felt it, but could offer no solace to him, or to herself.

"I must go." Clutching the clothing to her now-chilled body, she turned away.

"Wait."

As had happened before, Karen found herself unable to disobey his commanding tone. She stopped but refused to look at him. "Paul, I must..."

"You must think about what you're doing," he finished for her. "You can't simply toss on some clothing, pack a bag and run out the door."

Since that was precisely what she'd been prepared to do, Karen glanced over her shoulder to frown at him. "Why can't I?"

"Has the house been secured?" he asked, oddly detached.

"No, but—"

"Do you have any idea of how long you'll be gone?"

"Well, no, but—"

"Have you notified the authorities at the boys' school to expect you?"

"You know I haven't!" Karen snapped, impatient with him and with herself. "But—"

"But what?" Paul's tone, his eyes, his attitude, were cool. He had accepted her decision; he had little choice at that emotional moment, but he couldn't accept hasty disorganization.

"I—" Karen's hands lifted, then fell. "I don't know."

"I do."

Her mind a whirling mass of feelings and confusion, Karen stared at him with dulled eyes. "Okay," she finally said. "If you know, tell me."

"I intend to." Paul swept a cool glance over her, then shifted his gaze to his own body. His lips twitched into a smile that was completely without humor. "The first thing we're going to do is dress. After that we're going to make fresh coffee, sit down and discuss what has to be done."

Karen launched into an argument. "But—"

"Karen," Paul snapped impatiently, "the only way to get started is to get started. Now please stop arguing and go get dressed."

Karen went, quickly, if not exactly at a dead run. By the time she was once more clothed and protected by the concealing garments of respectability, she felt more like herself. She was ready and able to cope with the situation—but she wouldn't allow herself to consider *which* situation.

As she rushed downstairs and into the kitchen, the realization hit her that Paul, on the other hand, was supremely ready to cope with any and all situations.

He was dressed in a knit pullover and faded jeans, jeans that should have looked odd on his elegant body but somehow looked perfect—perfectly fitting, perfectly appealing, perfectly sexy. And as if his attire wasn't demoralizing enough, he had cleared away their uneaten breakfast, loaded the dishwasher, brewed a fresh pot of coffee and warmed the blueberry muffins she'd planned to serve at lunchtime. Karen's renewed sense of confidence ebbed considerably.

"You didn't shower," she accused peevishly, trying to bolster her flagging ego.

"Of course I did." Paul spared her a chiding look as he carried the glass coffeepot to the table. "Sit down, have some coffee, and we'll plan the day." It wasn't an invitation, it was a direct order. "And bring the basket of muffins with you." He didn't bother glancing back to see if she'd comply; he obviously took it for granted that she would.

Karen bristled while she toyed with the idea of telling him precisely what he could do with the muffins, but on reflection decided it wasn't worth the effort. She had more important things to do than start a yelling match with a man she was unlikely to ever see again after they left the house and parted company.

Unlikely to ever see again. The echoing phrase induced a weakness that conflicted with the nervous energy urging her into constructive action. Wanting to run, possibly in several different directions at once, Karen snatched up the basket and followed him to the table.

Silence prevailed for long moments; tearing silence, brittle silence, an "I'll scream if it doesn't end" silence. Yet, when Paul quietly broke the silence, Karen started as though he'd shouted.

"You are taking the car?"

"What?" she asked blankly.

Paul regarded her with infinite patience. "The car, Karen. I assume the compact I saw in the garage earlier is yours."

"Oh! Yes. It is mine, and I am taking it."

"Where in New Hampshire is this prep school?"

The school. Her boys. Karen fought back a resurgence of shame and guilt.

"Karen?" His patience was not quite as infinite.

"Ah...halfway," she replied vaguely.

"Hmm." Paul murmured into his cup before very casually placing it on the matching saucer. "Halfway from where to where?" His lowering tone and brow finally got through to her.

"I'm sorry!" She flushed. "The school is approximately midway between here and Boston." Her shoulders tilted in a helpless shrug. "The location of the school was a symbolic concession under the terms of the divorce." Her smile didn't quite make it. "An indication that, symbolically at least, Charles and I are still sharing the children."

"I wouldn't touch that statement with a forked stick," Paul commented, knowing full well his derisive tone said it all.

"I know." Karen sighed her weariness. "Could we get on with the plans, please?" Arching her brows, she reached for a muffin she really didn't want.

Paul continued. Succinctly, concisely, he outlined exactly what he considered had to be done; naturally, he was absolutely right on every point. While he spoke, Karen nodded, agreeing with every suggestion, and crumbled the muffin onto her plate.

"Fodder for the gulls?"

Karen trailed his gaze to the tiny pile of crumbs on her plate. "I'm not hungry," she said defensively.

Paul's lips curved into a small smile lightly tinged with tenderness. "A dead giveaway to your emotional condition," he observed, referring to her earlier admission regarding her love of food.

"I suppose." Karen tossed the agreement out carelessly, making it clear she was not about to allow him to reopen that particular topic. Paul got the message.

"You have friends in Boston?" he asked with a fine display of restraint. "People you can spend time with while you're there?"

"Oh, yes." She offered him her first genuine smile since answering the phone. "I also have my business there."

"Business?" Paul sat up straight. "What sort of business?"

"I own a specialty shop...fine gifts, china, bric-a-brac and such. It's called Garnishes." She grimaced. "Of course, being way up here in Maine, I no longer manage it myself. Charles has been overseeing it for me." At the thought and mention of her former husband's name, Karen wet her suddenly dry lips. "I'll need to make other arrangements."

"A modern, civilized divorce," he muttered, harking back to the confidences she'd made in a wine-induced haze. "And yet another statement I wouldn't touch with—"

"All right!" Karen snapped, pushing her chair away from the table. "Shouldn't we get on with what must be done?" As she was already crossing the kitchen floor to the sink, he had little choice.

The full October harvest moon blessed the landscape with shimmering silvery light and danced in a glittering path on the cresting sea.

Huddled inside her robe, cold even in the warmth of her bedroom, Karen stood at the window, staring into the brightness of the night and the darkness of her thoughts.

A few feet behind her, her small bedside clock rhythmically ticked away the minutes of the night. The alarm on the clock was set for six. All was in readiness. Due entirely to Paul's penchant for detail, the house was secure, made safe in the event Karen's stay in Boston should turn out to be an extended one. Except for the windows she stared out of and the two in Paul's room across the hall, all the windows in the house were covered by sturdy, locked shutters. The solid wood storm doors were in place at the front and back of the house. Her nearest neighbor had been contacted and informed that Karen would be away; the taciturn neighbor had said he'd check on the property every day. A large suitcase and a garment bag had been packed and were now in the corner by the door. She had talked to her sons' guidance counselor; he had assured her he would break the news about their father gently to the boys and have them ready to leave when she arrived at the school. Her car had been checked out and the gas tank filled at the service station in the small town. Karen planned to leave the house by 6:30.

Every contingency that could have been thought of had been thought of by Paul. The single thing left for Karen to do was to get some much-needed sleep, but for her, sleep was elusive. At 10:20 on a sparkling autumn night, Karen was wakeful with thoughts of her lover.

What was he doing now, this very moment, as she stared into a sea reflecting the restlessness she was feeling. Was he asleep? Karen's chest heaved in a deep sigh. Confused, torn by emotional conflict, she had deliberately distanced herself from him. Throughout that long, busy day, while tension had crackled between them, the atmosphere had been cool.

But the distancing was of her own choosing; the coolness was what she preferred, wasn't it? Despair sank like a weight in her stomach. Denying the sensation, Karen squared her shoulders and raised her chin. Yes, of course she preferred the cool distance. She'd had her moment of self-indulgence; it was now time to pay the price.

The cost was high, in terms of self-esteem, in terms of mental anguish, in terms of self-respect. Karen bit her lip as her mind cried a protest.

She was not a loose woman easily used!

A soft, choking sob challenged the silence of the night. She wanted the distance between them, yes. But couldn't he have fought against her decision, just a little? Had Paul had to accept it without the least resistance?

The previous night's storm had moved out to sea, leaving behind tranquillity. Outside, the night was calm. Inside Paul, a storm raged fiercely, creating havoc and disruption.

He wanted to be fair. He was trying to be understanding. But he was fighting a losing battle within himself, because most of all he simply wanted. Denying that want, Paul paced the large, comfortable room, fingers raking through his silver-kissed dark hair at regular intervals.

He hurt in all the ways there were to hurt—in body, mind and emotions. And although he readily admitted that he had absolutely no right to interfere with Karen's decisions, admitting that didn't make the hurt easier to bear.

Paul's narrowed gaze sliced to the closed bedroom door; his mind's eye sliced through it and the door directly across the wide hallway. Was Karen sleeping? His inner vision created images of her that drew a muffled curse from him.

Of all the inopportune times for that bastard to—Paul cut the thought short, surprised by its vehemence. Even in his burning hell of wanting, Paul could not accuse Charles Mitchell of deliberately suffering a heart attack simply to interfere with his ex-wife's love affair.

Halting at the window, Paul stared bleakly into the night. Besides, he reasoned, exhaling a sigh, even without the call about her former husband, Karen probably would have discovered another reason to withdraw from him, even if she'd had to manufacture one. The call might have precipitated the withdrawal, but he felt positive that it would have come anyway before too long. Paul was even positive he knew why she would have withdrawn.

To a man of Paul's intelligence and experience, reading Karen's character was not at all difficult. Although certainly not without its complexities, Karen's personality was as clear as the cloudless fall sky spread out before him. She was genuinely a good, moral person. She very obviously believed in right and wrong and lived her life accordingly. She worked hard and stood firm on matters of principle, and since that damned call, her principles were giving her hell about sleeping with a man she barely knew. Paul accepted her decision—at least he was trying to.

Heaven knew it wasn't easy. But the fact that he'd found Karen after years of believing he'd lost the ability to cherish a woman like her made acceptance more difficult. What they had shared, the sheer beauty of that sharing, had left a mark, a greedy hunger in every cell in Paul's body. And he believed Karen was special—how else could he explain her seemingly effortless power to arouse him, to awaken the sensuality in him? Oh, yes, Karen was definitely special to him. She was the kind of woman a man wanted by his side—in good times, in bad times, in his home, in his bed.

Merely thinking the word "bed" tightened every muscle in Paul's body. *Karen.* He needed her. But therein lay the cause of his dilemma. Because he had needed her too soon and had given in to that need too soon, he had shaken her, forced her to question herself as a person. He was now paying for his hasty actions and, he felt sure, would continue to pay.

The piper has presented his bill.

Paul grimaced as the thought crept into his mind. Instinctively he knew he would be facing a long, cold winter. He also knew that he would survive; he had already survived more than six years of endless winter. This autumn had been a reprieve, a tantalizing breath of spring, a zephyr of renewal on the barren plain of his frozen soul.

Eyes shut, Paul endured a violent shiver. He didn't want to go back to being dead in spirit. He had been captivated by the heady waltz of life. Opening his eyes, he turned to look at the closed bedroom door.

The piper has presented his bill.

As he took his first stride toward the door, a grim smile tilted the corners of Paul's lips. He would pay the bill without complaint. But nothing—not heaven, not hell and not Karen Mitchell—would stop him that night. Paul's jaw firmed as he pulled the door open.

He would pay the bill—but he would have one last dance.

Chapter Six

Paul didn't knock. Grasping the doorknob, he turned it and pushed the door open. He didn't wait for an invitation to enter the room, either. His expression determined, he walked into the room.

"Paul?" Karen's startled whisper was nearly drowned by the sound of the door banging against the wall. Her body stiffened visibly; her eyes widened with apprehension and, Paul thought, hopefully, a tiny spark of suppressed excitement. "What—what do you want?"

Talk about obvious questions! Paul might have laughed, and he was tempted to smile, but he couldn't manage either expression. Hell, he realized with a jolt of shock, he could barely breathe!

The slant to his raised eyebrow was rakish; the slant on his lips was pure enticement. Paul had no way of knowing the toe-curling effect his appearance had on his quarry. Moving slowly, he crossed the room to where she stood, framed by the window at her back.

He was barefoot, and the pads of his feet made soundless contact with the soft carpet. *Stalking!* The word flashed into his mind and shivered the length of his spine. He suddenly felt slightly light-headed, and his pace nearly faltered. *Stalking.* It was a heady thought, conjuring up images of strong, silent predators closing in on the desired prey.

Paul savored the feeling, liking it, relishing the vision of himself as the hunter—he, Vanzant, the man who was more king of the carpeted boardroom than of the broad savannas. He tingled with all kinds of anticipatory thrills.

"Paul?"

Her voice was hoarse, reedy with emotion. Paul absorbed the sound of it into his expanding fantasy. She was his, if not forever, at least for this last night. All he had to do was stalk...and take. The realization dissolved the last lingering thread of hesitation and doubt. He had spent his life giving. He had surrendered his manhood giving. For this one night, he was finished with giving. He would take anything, everything he wanted. His stride firm, Paul advanced on the woman he could taste with every one of his clamoring senses.

She knew what to expect. With heightened tension, Paul could see understanding flare deep in her eyes. Flecks of gold excitement sparked within the brown depths. She was fighting a battle with self-denial. Paul could actually see the inner war being waged. The visible proof of her struggle against herself increased his own tension to an unbearable heat. And he could see the instant need for surrender weakened her resistance.

As he came to a stop inches from her, Paul threw back

his head and laughed; the sound was not unlike the victory roar of the deadly jungle beast.

Karen was his!

His laughter thrilled and frightened her at one and the same time. There was something different about Paul this night; he was not the same man who had drawn her with such care and tenderness onto the floor of the dining alcove that morning. The man she now faced revealed not a trace of tenderness. Sheer male animal gleamed from his narrowed dark eyes, a feral male animal on the scent of his mate. His appearance terrified her with excitement.

Wanting him, and afraid of the intensity of her own sudden wild, inexplicable needs, Karen stopped breathing and slid one foot back, edging away from him. The smile that curved his lips halted her shifting foot. Karen froze for an instant that was an eternity. Then, gasping, she spun away.

Her movement came too late. Paul's arm whipped out, and his fingers wrapped around her wrist. With the most negligent of tugs, he whirled her around. Her chest collided with his, igniting fires in places in her body that were already warm and willing. Before she could draw a full breath, he was swinging her up into his arms. With three long strides, Paul was by the side of the bed. He grunted, and the sound was one of deep pleasure. Then he lifted her up, high, and tossed her onto the bed.

"Paul!" The cry exploded from Karen, a one-word protest that lacked conviction. "What do you think you're doing?"

Paul paused in the sublimely casual act of removing his robe to glide a calculating glance at the enticing length of her body. She was clad in a sheer nightgown. One dark eyebrow peaked tauntingly.

"I'm going to give you a memory to take with you to Boston."

Tension coiled over her shoulders to converge in a knot at the back of her neck. Applying conscious effort, Karen eased the white-knuckled grip she had on the steering wheel. The road undulated in front of her like an unwinding ribbon, moving her toward a reunion with her sons and uncertainty about their father. Behind her, the road of ribbon whipped back, and contained a long expensive car.

Karen flicked a glance into the rearview mirror and felt the knot in her neck contract. The midnight-blue vehicle gleaming in the pure sunlight of a perfect Indian-summer day trailed her small compact at a safe distance of three hundred feet. But before too long, the road behind her would be empty, regardless of how many vehicles replaced it on the highway. The first leg of her journey lay a little more than an hour away; Paul would be going in another direction after they parted company near the town where the small, exclusive prep school was located.

The edges of the road blurred as a film of tears misted her eyes. Lifting one hand from the wheel, she brushed her fingertips impatiently over her eyelids. The midnight-blue car shot past her as her vision cleared. Startled, Karen sniffed and frowned as the right rear turn signal on the blue car began to pulse. Without conscious thought, she followed the larger vehicle off the road and into the parking lot of a small, rustic-looking restaurant.

Paul stepped out of his car as she parked alongside

his vehicle. "Time for a break," he said, opening her door for her.

Gathering the remnants of her emotional control, Karen nodded and suppressed a sigh. It was not time for a break; it was time for them to go their separate ways. They were within an hour of the school and her boys. And, she realized, taking note of their location, they were minutes from the interstate exchange. Paul would change direction at the interstate. She would go on to—Karen blinked rapidly, fighting a fresh surge of tears.

She had spent the morning deliberately not thinking of the night before, and she couldn't afford to think about it now. Raising her chin, Karen stared off into the distance and felt a sharp pang in the center of her chest. Farther north, in Maine, the terrain lay barren and ready for winter. But here, a little farther south in New Hampshire, autumn clung to the landscape with a fading glory. Even muted, the colors were beautiful and an affront to her senses. Karen wasn't aware that she had come to a stop to stare resentfully at nature's display until Paul voiced a quiet observation.

"The blaze must have been fantastic a short time ago."

His low-pitched voice jolted through her, leaving a hollow sensation in the pit of her being. He was referring to the colors of the panoramic landscape, but Karen applied his comment to the scene they had acted out the night before. And the blaze had indeed been fantastic. Glancing up at him, she suddenly felt as empty and barren as the Maine coast.

"I'm hungry." Her voice was rough, but Karen didn't care. She hurt. Dragging her gaze from his somber face and avoiding the insult of the surrounding color, she rammed her hands into the side pockets of her soft wool slacks and strode toward the entrance of the restaurant. She told herself that she didn't care whether or not Paul followed her. She almost believed it, but then she was becoming adept at lying to herself.

"Karen?"

Paul was at her heels—like a well-trained pet, Karen thought, fighting the insidious spread of pain. But she knew this man was no pet, no sleek, well-schooled tabby. Not Paul. No, hidden behind this man's facade of elegance and sophistication a tiger crouched, ready to spring and devour when aroused. Karen's soul bore the scars of his teeth and claws.

Her silent analogy induced a shiver deep inside her that threatened to release scrupulously buried memories. Terrified she'd drown should the flow escape, Karen yanked open the door and entered the restaurant. The smile she offered the hostess was much too bright and hurt like fury.

"Two?" The hostess was middle-aged and had a pleasant face; her smile was practiced yet attractive.

"Yes, please."

"At a window," Paul inserted in an authoritative tone. "We want to enjoy what's left of the foliage." The smile he offered the hostess transformed the older woman's from plastic to the genuine article.

Watching the woman bloom beneath the warmth of Paul's exceptional good looks and charm, Karen experienced a thrill of vindication; she *wasn't* the only woman to feel an immediate attraction to him. Small consolation perhaps, but when one was desperate, one clung to even tiny shreds of pride.

The table was placed directly before a wide, undraped window that afforded a spectacular view of the gently rolling countryside. Red, orange, rust and splashes of green dazzled the eyes of any and all beholders. Karen lowered her gaze to the linen-covered tabletop.

"We must talk."

Karen's fingers clenched on the small luncheon menu the hostess had placed in front of her. Paul had said exactly the same words to her that morning as they'd stood drinking a cup of coffee at the kitchen counter. He had repeated the words as they'd stood at the rear of her car after loading her luggage into the small trunk. Now, as she had earlier, Karen shook her head.

"There's nothing to talk about." Absently moving her left hand, she stroked one finger the length of the tines of her fork. "You're going home. I'm going to Boston. End of story."

"No, dammit! That's not the—Karen!" His tone, which had been sharp with annoyance, softened with concern at her involuntary gasp. Karen had pierced the tip of her finger with the tine.

Karen dismissed his concern with a shrug as she stared dispassionately at a tiny drop of blood. "It's nothing." Her right hand was groping for a napkin when Paul grasped her left hand and drew the injured finger to his lips. The touch of his lips against her skin was excruciating; the flick of his tongue against the tiny puncture was devastating and threatened to undo Karen's precious store of composure.

"Paul, please don't," she protested in a strangled tone, tugging her hand back. His hold on her tightened.

"God, Karen, don't look at me like that." His breath misted her flesh, and the agonized sound of his voice misted her thoughts.

"Like—like what?" Karen could barely speak for the thickness in her throat.

"Like..." Paul lowered his eyes as he turned her hand, exposing her palm to his lips. "Like you've been dealt a killing blow." He reverently touched his mouth to her palm.

Karen felt his kiss like a stiletto thrust to her heart. She tugged reflexively against his grip. Paul began to raise his eyes at her action. His eyes flickered and widened as his gaze noted a crescent-shaped bruise on the inside of her wrist. His curse was all the more shocking for the very softness of it.

"I've marked you." His gaze seared the bruise. "And I've hurt you—" his breath shuddered from his body "—in so many ways." His lips bestowed a quivering blessing on the mark. "I'm sorry, Karen. I never meant to hurt you in any way."

"I know." Karen had to pause to swallow, to breathe, to absorb the tremors racing up her arm from her wrist.

While she hesitated, Paul glanced up. His night-black eyes betrayed regret, resignation. "I don't want to leave you here like this." His grip on her wrist tightened as a shiver moved through her body. "Karen, let me follow you into Boston." His voice was rough with strain.

"No!" Karen shook her head and pulled her hand from his grasp. A vision rose to torment her mind, an image of herself attempting to explain Paul's presence to her sons. Mark, her baby, was still young enough at thirteen to accept as fact whatever his mother told him. But her eldest had developed into a very savvy fifteen-year-old. Rand would immediately identify and disdain the relationship between his mother and a man other than his father. "No," she repeated, drowning in a fresh flood of guilt and shame. "It's impossible."

"It's not impossible. Nothing—" He stopped speaking as a young waitress approached the table to take their order. Paul cursed under his breath and snatched up the menu.

Karen lowered her gaze to the cardboard that was quivering suspiciously in her hand. But her reprieve was short-lived. Paul resumed the argument the instant the waitress moved on to another table. Karen had already forgotten what she'd ordered.

"Karen, I can wait in a hotel. You can't be expected to spend every waking hour with your sons or cooling your heels in a hospital." Lines of tension scored his face, revealing his frustration and, for the first time since she'd met him, his age.

"No, Paul." Karen rushed the refusal, too tempted to give in to his suggestion. "I'd have to explain..." The expression in the eyes she raised to his was stark, reflecting her inner conflict. She took a breath before continuing. "I'd have to explain to my boys, Charles, his parents. How could I make them understand something I don't understand myself, about myself?"

"You're a mature woman, Karen!" Paul exclaimed softly. "Except for the possibility of your children, you don't owe explanations to anyone." His voice lowered dangerously. "Least of all to that—"

"Paul!" Karen's shocked voice cut across his low snarl. She glanced around quickly to see if he'd been overheard. Their nearest neighbors, a middle-aged foursome, were busily discussing the merits of the menu, quite oblivious to the drama close at hand. "Name-calling solves nothing! Don't you understand? I *can't* continue. It's impossible."

Paul's eyes gleamed with a mounting anger that masked a sense of desperation. "And I'm telling you nothing's impossible, not if you want it badly enough."

His tone hardened. "And I want it badly, Karen. You'll probably never know how very badly I want it."

Want. The single word hammered inside Karen's mind while the waitress served the meal. *Want.* The echo of it mocked her throughout the ordeal of making believe she was eating the sandwich she couldn't remember ordering and didn't taste even as she consumed it. *Want.* Dammit! It was the wanting that had placed her in this untenable hell of guilt in the first place.

He had wanted. She had wanted. And because they had appeased their wants with one another, she was now suffering the pain of self-doubt and shame.

"Karen, we need to talk," Paul said urgently as she placed her empty coffee cup on its delicate saucer. "Let me follow you. Meet with me in Boston. I'll give you my word that I won't touch you. I'll give you all the time you need to sort out your feelings. But let's at least talk it out. I want to explain..."

Karen had had it with the word "want." Pushing her chair back, she surged to her feet and hurried from the restaurant. She wanted nothing more at that moment than to never hear the word *want* again for as long as she lived.

Paul caught up to her as she was fumbling to unlock her car. He didn't try to restrain her. At least, not physically. The soft urgency of his tone was restraint in itself.

"You're going to throw it away, aren't you?"

At the end of her patience, pulled off balance by conflicting needs and emotions, Karen turned on him, lashing out.

"Throw all *what* away?" she demanded, angry and scared. "We don't know each other. We don't even know if we like one another! We felt an attraction, a highly combustible chemical attraction, and we both responded to it." Her shoulders drooped. "But now it's time for reality." Karen forced herself to look at him. "You have a family, a life in Philadelphia. And I have two boys who may be facing the possibility of losing their father. I think someone once said that when reality walks in the door, sensuality flies out the window. The window is open, Paul. The time for flight is now."

"It's not true." Paul smiled faintly as she began to frown. "I do know that I like you. You are very easy to like."

For one fleeting instant, Karen's smile rivaled the brilliance of the sun-sparkled day. Then it was gone, as was the light of hope that had sprung to life in Paul's eyes. Obeying an impulse, she reached out to touch him. Then, just as quickly, she withdrew her hand.

"I like you, too." Her smile had the power to break a cynic's heart. "You're bossy as hell, but I like you, Paul Vanzant."

"Karen." He moved toward her, but she was faster, opening the door and slipping behind the wheel.

"I must go," she said, her voice edged with desperation. "They're expecting me." She bit her lip, then looked up at him. "I'll never forget you. Goodbye, Paul." She pulled the door closed between them.

"Karen!"

The sound of the engine roaring to life muffled his cry of protest. Throwing the car into reverse, she backed the vehicle away from him. Again she hesitated, staring at him as if unable to tear her eyes away. Then she spun the wheel. Tires screeched, and the car shot forward. Karen heard Paul's angry voice through the closed window.

"Damn you, Karen!"

* * *

"Will Dad be all right, Mom?"

Stifling a sigh, Karen managed a patient smile instead. It was at least the dozenth time her youngest son had asked that same question.

"I don't know, honey," Karen answered honestly. "Grandma didn't know when I spoke to her. It was too soon after the attack. But hopefully by the time we reach Boston the doctors will have more information for us."

"I don't want Dad to die, Mom." Fear reduced Mark's voice to that of a very young child's.

"Oh, honey." Karen reached across the seat to grasp the boy's hand. "I know. I know." Understanding and compassion clenched at her chest. "Try not to think about it." Karen hated being reduced to trite, inane motherly platitudes, but as a mother, what option did she have? "Just hope, and pray, and—"

"Dad's not going to die, ya nerd." The jeer of disgust came from the half boy, half man sprawled on the back seat.

"Rand," Karen murmured warningly, capturing his reflection in the rearview mirror.

"Well, does he hafta whine and talk so dumb?" Rand argued defensively.

"But I'm scared!" Mark sniffled. "What will we do if he—"

"Will ya stuff it?" Rand's voice rose, then cracked.

"Randolf!"

"Aw, Mom!" The boy glared into the mirror at her for a moment, then quickly lowered his gaze. Rand was not quick enough to hide the sheen of tears in his eyes.

Karen's fingers contracted around the abused steering wheel. Rand was every bit as frightened as Mark was; his belligerence was a ruse to conceal his fear and uncertainty. Karen longed to comfort both boys, reassure them, soothe them as she had when they had been small and had run to her with scrapes and bruises. If only she could hug them and kiss them and make it better, she thought, feeling suddenly inadequate and unequal to the task before her.

Without conscious direction, Karen's gaze sought the mirror, not to seek the wounded eyes of her son but to study the highway unwinding behind her. There were all types of vehicles jockeying for position on the multilane highway, but not one of them was painted a midnight blue.

A man is never there when you really need him, she told herself, her throat working to ease a growing tightness.

With her youngest son weeping softly on the seat beside her and her eldest alternately yelling at him, then pleading with him to "bag it," Karen was much too upset and distracted to consider the incongruity of her blanket condemnation of men, most particularly the man she had refused to have there when she needed him. She was hurting on more levels than she'd ever realized there were. She was tired. She felt alone, really alone, for the first time in her adult life. She felt too close to the edge of defeat. She was beginning to get frightened, and beginning to question her ability to cope with the traumatic effect on her sons in the event Charles succumbed to the heart attack.

He can't die! The protest rang inside her head, accompanied by one boy's sobs and another boy's muttered imprecations. Damn you, Charles Mitchell, don't you dare die!

Karen's glance flicked to the mirror.

Oh, God, Paul, where are you?

* * *

Where was she now? Nearing Boston? In Boston? Perhaps already at the hospital—with Charles?

Paul grunted in self-disgust and sliced a resentful glance at his wristwatch. He had promised himself he would not think about her. He had warned himself he could not afford to think about her. He had failed miserably to keep his promise.

How had her sons reacted to the news about their father? Paul sighed. Karen's boys were another subject he had vowed not to consider. But dammit! he said to himself, he was a parent, too! He had raised a son through the difficult teenage years. He knew firsthand how very deeply children felt about all kinds of things, important and mundane. They would be a handful for her, Paul decided, his tight lips smoothing into a gentle smile of reminiscence. Hell, children were usually a handful, even on the best of days!

She should have support.

The tightness was back, flattening his lips. He should be with her. He had wanted to be with her. He still wanted to be there for her.

Where *was* she now?

With favorable driving conditions, Karen could be in the city and at the hospital by now. Was the bas—Paul cut his thought short. Had Charles Mitchell's condition improved at all? Paul sincerely hoped so. He hoped so for the boys' sake. He hoped so for Karen's sake. And, not even sure why, he hoped so for his own sake.

He missed her. It had been only a matter of hours since she'd left him breathing in the exhaust fumes from her car as she'd roared out of the parking lot, and yet he missed her like hell on fire. Paul exhaled heavily. With his control on his mental responses undermined, memories of the previous night rushed to the fore to tease his senses and torment his body.

Lord! Had he really behaved like that, all macho and masterful? The mere concept boggled his mind. Never, never before in his life, had Paul displayed such aroused heat or such vigor! And damn him if he hadn't reveled in every second of the display.

Paul's thigh muscles grew taut; he shifted on the leather seat. How, he wondered, was Karen feeling about her own responses and participation in the previous night's activities? She'd refused to discuss it that morning, had in fact shied away from even looking directly at him until they had stopped for lunch. Paul grimaced. Had he succeeded in adding more self-doubt and guilt to her overscrupulous conscience? He fervently hoped not, yet feared he had.

Paul's spirit flagged. He had an empty feeling that warned him he'd be missing Karen Mitchell for a long time to come.

Karen greeted the usual tangle of midafternoon traffic in Boston with a heartfelt sigh of relief. Her spirit felt battered from having to constantly comfort her sons.

She had a pounding headache from the increasing pressure of the tension at the back of her neck. Her eyes were gritty from incipient tears and the lack of sleep the night before. And her mind felt abused from fighting the memories of why she hadn't slept the night before. In comparison, the need to maneuver the crazy-quilt mess of one-way traffic in the historic city was a piece of cake.

"Are we going to Grandma's first?" Mark asked.

Karen stole a glance from the street to offer her son a smile. "No, honey. I think both Grandma and Grandpa will be at the hospital."

"Are we soon there?"

Karen frowned at his grammar. "Just a little while longer, honey," she replied, striving to hang on to her control.

"I'm hungry," he whimpered.

"You're always hungry," his brother taunted from the back.

"As a matter of fact, I'm hungry, too," Karen said brightly, giving her oldest a quelling look via the rear-view mirror. "We can get something to eat in the hospital coffee shop as soon as we find out how your dad's doing. Okay?"

"Okay," Mark agreed.

"Now take a break," came the hard-voiced order from the back seat.

Karen's eyes shot to the mirror to catch his reflection with a "this is your mother speaking and I'm not kidding" look. Rand lowered his eyes.

For a few moments, relative peace and quiet prevailed—at least inside the car. Outside it was a different story. A motorist running a yellow light missed her car by a breath. As she attempted to push the brake pedal through the floor of the car with her foot, Karen flung her right arm out in front of Mark to back up his seat belt.

Mark decided that was the perfect time to begin wailing. "I hate this! I hate this whole day!" he sobbed. "We're all gonna die."

"Mark, please!" Karen eased the car back into the flow of traffic and her temper back into submission. "It was close," she said soothingly, silently cursing the ancestry of the other driver. "But we're fine, and no one is going to die." Brave words, she jeered at herself.

"Boy, are you really thirteen?" Rand asked sarcastically.

Karen prayed for enlightened motorists and spared another warning glare for her back-seat agitator.

Mark then made the mistake of wriggling in his seat. "I have to go to the bathroom."

"You always hafta go to the bathroom. All you ever do is eat and go to the bathroom," Rand gibed.

Karen's patience gave up the battle. "Rand, I've had enough of your snide remarks. What in the world is the matter with you?" Her eyes shifted back and forth between the street and the mirror; she saw her firstborn drop his head abjectly. Her heart clenched as she heard his whispered cry.

"Oh, Mom. I'm so scared."

Chapter Seven

Karen ached to bring the car to a dead stop right there in the middle of the nightmarish traffic and bawl with her two offspring, both of whom were sobbing now. Gritting her teeth and murmuring garbled words of comfort, she wove the car in and around the vehicular maze leading to the hospital.

After finally securing a place to park, she rushed the boys into the hospital, past the information desk and straight into the first visitors' lounge she came to. Breathing a sigh of relief at finding the room empty, Karen dropped her purse onto the nearest chair and swept Rand and Mark into her arms.

"Okay, now cry it out," she coaxed softly. "It'll help."

Neither of the boys held back. The dam of fear and anxiety burst, and Karen tightened her arms, absorbing her sons' shudders into her body. The moment was bittersweet for Karen. It had been some time since either of the boys had sought succor in her embrace, and an especially long time for Rand. At odd moments, catching herself gazing wistfully at an infant or toddler and consumed with a longing to cradle the child to her breast, she wondered if she was suffering the empty-nest syndrome. Usually the sensation of emptiness was fleeting and she went back to the reality of the present convinced that she was content with her life. Now, fiercely clasping their slim bodies to her heart, Karen wondered again.

Ignoring the tears stinging her eyes, she closed them and brushed one damp cheek over Rand's tangled hair and the other over Mark's tousled curls.

For this tiny, isolated moment, the boys were hers again, her beautiful babies. Soon, too soon, they would collect themselves, she knew. Very likely, Rand would be first. Then, together, they would go face the news about their father. But until then, Karen would savor the sweet feeling of being needed by her babies, even if the feeling was transient and contained equal amounts of pleasure and pain. As she had suspected, Rand was the first to withdraw.

"I forgot a hankie," he mumbled, avoiding her eyes by swiping at his nose with the back of his hand.

"There are tissues in my purse." She indicated the bag with a movement of her hand. "Give some to your brother, please." She was unable to keep her hand from creeping to the back of Mark's head, and her fingers stroked his fine curly hair. With a final snorting gulp, Mark stepped back.

"I didn't wanna act like a baby." Mark shot a fearful look at his brother, the infamous tormentor.

"Who did?" Rand muttered, absolving Mark of guilt, while shoving a wad of tissues into his hand.

"Neither one of you have..." Karen began.

"Only little kids cry," Mark sniffled.

"Sez who?" Rand demanded, mopping the moisture from his lean cheeks.

"Dad," Mark said, following his idol's example and applying damp tissue to his even damper face. "He said real men never cry."

Sounds exactly like something your dad would say, Karen thought, shaking her head. "Men are human, Mark, and all humans experience a need to relieve fear and pain at times," she said softly.

"Dad don't ever cry," Mark insisted.

"No," Rand agreed in a surprisingly adult tone. "Dad swears."

"Yeah, he does!" Mark blinked, startled. "He swears a lot!"

"Yeah." Rand's tone aged with a hint of cynicism. "Dad swears an awful lot."

In Karen's opinion, Charles's penchant for the more colorful expletives left a lot to be desired. She also thought that this particular vein of conversation had run out. "Well, given a choice," she observed, "I prefer tears to cursing as an outlet for easing stress." She ran an appraising glance over their faces as she picked up her purse. "You guys ready?"

Mark's face pinched. Karen noted the boy's frozen expression at the same instant Rand did. Rand moved faster. Stepping to his brother, Rand slung a thin arm around Mark's drooping shoulders.

"C'mon, punk," he said roughly. "Whaddaya wanna bet Dad's gonna be all right?"

"D'ya think?" The hopeful, trusting look on Mark's face was enough to break a mother's heart.

Somehow, from some hidden wellspring of maturing

strength, Rand found a grin. "Sure," he said with a confidence Karen was certain he didn't feel. "I'd put my allowance on it."

Strong words indeed. Karen smiled mistily, her chest expanding with pride for her boy, who was almost a man. Fighting back a resurgence of tears, she walked briskly to the door. "Come on, Mark," she said, extending her hand to him. "We'd better go, before your brother discovers he's wagered all of his junk-food money and goes into pizza withdrawal."

They found Judith Mitchell pacing the visitors' lounge outside the closed doors of the coronary unit. Tears flooded the slender, attractive woman's eyes at the sight of her grandsons.

"Oh, my poor darlings!" Judith rushed to embrace the boys.

Alarm flared inside Karen as Judith enfolded the boys protectively in her arms. "Is Charles worse?" she asked in a voice hoarse with strain.

"Worse?" Judith glanced up and blinked. "Oh! Oh, no." She shook her head distractedly and tightened her hold on the now-squirming boys. "In fact, he's much improved."

The boys made good their escape; Karen's relieved breath escaped. Suddenly she wanted to hug Judith—dear, sweet, *vague* Judith. Giving in to the urge, she stepped into the older woman's deserted arms.

"I'm so glad," she murmured, hugging the woman tightly before stepping back. "Tell us everything, please."

Judith's hand fluttered, the absent, helpless motion a clear reflection of the woman herself. Karen had always loved her former mother-in-law; it was impossible not to love the endearing woman. But Judith was just a trifle airy.

"Well, I don't know too much myself," Judith began, fortunately not noticing Rand's "tell us about it" expression.

Karen was back to shooting quelling glances at her not-yet-a-man son. "Then tell us what you do know," she said, gently prompting the frowning woman.

"When we arrived this morning," Judith replied at once, "the nurse told us simply that Charles was much improved." She glanced wistfully at the coronary unit's closed doors. "The specialist is in with Charles now, and so is Randolf." Her gaze drifted back to Karen. "They've been in there a long time, since right after lunchtime."

"I see." Karen gnawed on her lower lip, trying to decide whether the lengthy consultation boded good or bad. The fact that Charles's father, Randolf J. Mitchell, had been allowed to be present during the doctor's visit was unsurprising; Randolf was a member of the hospital's board of directors. She was beginning to get fidgety when she noticed Mark squirming in the chair he'd dropped into. Karen expelled a sigh and looked at Judith. "Are there public rest rooms nearby?" A maternal smile curved her lips. "Your youngest grandson is in dire need."

"Of course!" Judith literally leaped at the excuse to be doing something. "Come along, darling." She held her hand out to Mark as if to a toddler. "I'll take you."

For a flickering instant, sheer horror was reflected in the boy's eyes. Rand hid a burst of laughter behind a cough. Then, realizing his grandmother wouldn't dream of actually going into the room with him, Mark sprang from the chair. As the two exited the room, Karen heard her baby go to work on his doting grandparent.

"Is there someplace we could get something to eat in here?" Mark was heard to ask plaintively. "We didn't stop all the way down here, and I'm hungry, Grandma."

Though her reply was unintelligible, Judith's tone conveyed anxious concern for her darling. Karen smiled, and Rand shook his head.

"What a little con artist," he said, grinning his respect for his brother's talent. "Boy, he can always hook Grandma with one soulful look from his big brown eyes." His grin faded, and he was quiet for a moment. "I guess," he finally continued, a smile that was too wise and too full of acceptance curving his lips, "it's because he looks so much like Dad."

Karen wanted to deny his assertion, but in all honesty, she could not. Mark was a smaller image of his father. It was an unalterable fact. Karen could even understand why Judith had favored Mark from the instant she had looked into his face. Judith had seen her only child all over again in the infant. In all fairness, Karen acknowledged how very hard Judith had worked at being impartial. Staring into her son's eyes, Karen also acknowledged the near-impossibility of deceiving a bright child. An intelligent, sensitive child saw through the adult games with laser sharpness. At odd, weak moments, Karen had wondered exactly who was leading whom along the path labeled life—the adult or the child?

In possession of far more questions than answers, Karen merely stared at her son in aching despair.

Rand's smile forgave his grandmother, exonerated his brother and complimented Karen. "It's okay, Mom," he said, shrugging off her concern. "I don't mind looking more like you." His smile grew into a grin, revealing the man yet to come. His voice lowered dramatically. "You look like a sizzling sex poodle."

It was altogether improper. It was the wrong time and most assuredly the wrong place, but Karen couldn't help herself; she burst out laughing.

"A sizzling sex poodle?" She fought to compose herself. "Randolf Charles Mitchell, where in the world did you pick up that expression?"

"Around." Rand smirked.

Karen shook her head. Around. Around whom? She couldn't help but wonder, yet she wasn't sure she wanted to know. Nevertheless, she was on the verge of launching into the time-honored parental third degree when two men pushed through the heavy doors leading to the coronary unit. Their appearance wiped her mind of all but thoughts of Charles. Springing from the chair she'd perched on, Karen reached out to grasp Rand's hand. Her eyes darted from one man to the other before settling on Charles's father.

"Randolf?" Her voice held a strained mixture of hope and fear. "How is—"

"Better," Randolf answered before she could finish the question. "The attack wasn't as severe as originally feared." With a smile relieving the taut lines of worry on his face, he crossed the tiled floor to gather Karen and Rand into his arms.

"Grandpa?" The budding man had once again deserted the boy; Rand's tone pleaded for further reassurance. "He's not gonna—" he gulped audibly "—Dad's not gonna die, is he?"

"No, son, your father is not going to die." The authoritative answer came from the man beside Randolf. "I expressly told him I would not permit it." The doctor's compassionate smile contrasted with his stern tone. "It's bad for my image, you know."

Confusion flickered in Rand's brown eyes. The confusion gave way to understanding, which surrendered to appreciation. Rand's grin was back in place, accompanied by a suspicious brightness in his eyes. "Can we see him now?" he asked.

"Yes, you may—"

"Mom?" Mark's squeaked call interrupted the doctor. "Mom?" Sheer thirteen-year-old terror whispered through his lips.

"He's all right, honey." Stepping away from Randolf, Karen extended her hand, silently urging him to release his death grip on his grandmother's hand and join them. "The doctor has just told us your dad is better."

Mark's face crumpled, and he began to sob. Karen moved, but as he had earlier, Rand moved faster.

"Hey, Weepin' Willie, did ya hear that?" Much like his grandfather moments before, Rand gathered his brother into his arms. "Dad's gonna be okay." While stroking Mark's arm with one hand, Rand used his free hand to deliver a gentle punch to his brother's other arm. "Will you lighten up? Mom's nearly out of tissues."

"Besides which," Karen said, gently prying Mark from Rand's amazingly fierce embrace, "the doctor said we may go in to see your dad, and you don't want him to see you crying, do you?"

"No." Mark sniffed. "Can we go now?"

"In a moment," the doctor said. "But first let me brief you." As he'd expected, he received immediate attention. "Your mother is quite right, young man." He smiled at Mark. "You don't want your father to see you crying. It might upset him, and though his condition is much improved, he must not be stressed." His gaze shifted to Karen. "The preliminary test results are favorable. The attack was a warning, and though I won't go into detail at this time, I will tell you it was a warning that must not be treated lightly." Pausing, he stared steadily into Karen's eyes.

Karen experienced a shivery sensation of intuition or premonition; she wasn't sure which it was, but she didn't appreciate either. She wanted to shake her head in repudiation of whatever it was she felt. However, pinned by the doctor's intent regard, she nodded.

Satisfied, the doctor smiled. "Now then," he said briskly, returning his gaze to the boys. "I must urge you not to be frightened by your father's appearance. He is a very sick man, and it shows. Also," he continued, unperturbed when Mark blanched, "I don't want you to be alarmed by the assortment of machines and tubes attached to him. Though they are somewhat uncomfortable, they are necessary." He raised his heavy eyebrows. "Do you think you can handle it?"

"Yes, sir," Rand said at once.

"Yes, sir," Mark echoed, if waveringly.

The strength of his smile eased the strain on both boys' faces. "Good." He nodded sharply. "Now, regulations allow only two visitors at a time, but in this instance I will countermand the rules." He looked at Karen. "Ms. Mitchell, you may take your sons in to their father for ten minutes, no longer."

"Very well." Grasping one of each of the boy's hands, Karen moved to obey. She halted when he continued to speak.

"I will consult with you later, while Randolf and Judith are visiting Charles."

The chill of premonition shivered through Karen again. For one instant, rebellion sparked. Then the spark died, and she nodded once more. "Of course, Doctor." She managed to meet his eyes; she even managed a faint smile. He returned the smile, then escorted her and the boys into the coronary unit and to the door of Charles's room. As she crossed the threshold, Karen heard him give instructions to the nurse hovering near the door.

At the sight of his father, looking pasty and gray against the white pillow, Mark began to tremble; Karen could feel the tremors ripple the length of his arm and through the hand clasped in hers. Rand sucked in one sharp breath. A cry of denial rose to her own suddenly unsteady lips.

This could not be Charles Mitchell! The protest rang in her mind in a loud attempt to refute the evidence before her stricken eyes. This man who appeared so lifeless, so bloodless, in no way resembled the Charles Mitchell she knew and had once loved! Everything vital inside Karen rejected the validity of this man's identity. The man himself confirmed it.

"Karen?"

Having believed him asleep, Karen started. The voice was not—and yet strangely was—the voice she remembered. Her fingers tightening convulsively on her sons' hands, she walked to the side of the bed.

"Yes, Charles." With a tiny part of her mind, Karen recognized that her voice was not the same, either.

"Thank you for coming." Charles moved slightly, restlessly. The movement brought the boys into focus. "Rand, Mark?" A smile feathered his pale lips.

"Yes, Dad?" Rand's voice cracked just a little.

"Daddy?" Mark whimpered for a word of assurance.

Even ill, there was no way Charles could miss the abject fear his sons were feeling. For an instant, he appeared mildly annoyed, as if put-upon. Then a hint of compassion flicked in his eyes, and his lips twisted into a wry smile.

"Helluva way to get sprung from school, isn't it, guys?"

By the time she crawled into bed near midnight, Karen felt as if she'd been awake for a solid week. A variation on a tired joke ran persistently through her equally tired brain.

I spent a week one day sitting in a hospital with an ex-mate.

Ta da dum dum.

Muffling a sob, Karen buried her face in the unfamiliar pillow. Jokes. She longed to rant and rave and wail in frustration, and her weary mind was recounting jokes.

The midnight quiet was shattered by the trill of a giggle. Her eyes widening, Karen flopped onto her back and clapped her hand over her mouth. She was giggling! The thought contained an edge of hysteria. She was giggling, for God's sake! Grown-up women didn't giggle! Babies giggled; teenagers giggled! Mature adults did not giggle!

I don't want him in my home!

The silent protest screamed in Karen's head and defined the reason her mind was skipping along the edge of hysteria. She was tired—no, she was emotionally exhausted. Her response had been a delayed reaction to everything that had happened, beginning with Judith's phone call the previous morning and ending with her astonishing consultation with the heart specialist, Dr. Rayburn.

The good doctor had given her a concise description of Charles's present condition based on his examination of both patient and tests. In the doctor's opinion, the attack had been a definite warning. He had then concluded on a note of hesitant optimism for the future. Karen's tension had eased and she had been beginning to relax when the doctor had tossed a verbal bomb at her. Karen was still reeling from the explosive reverberations.

As clearly as if he were standing beside her bed, Karen could hear the even tone of Dr. Rayburn's voice, relaying to her Charles's suggestion that he could recuperate very well in her house in Maine. Now, as then, she cried out in protest.

"No!"

Karen's cry in the quiet room had as much effect as it had earlier in the small consulting room in the hospital. The doctor had offered her a chiding smile and a full measure of disapproval.

"Surely you would not deny your husband the ideal location in which to get well?"

The doctor's softly spoken charge echoed inside her head.

"Charles is not my husband," she had retorted immediately, reminded of the fact that Ben Rayburn was not only a physician but a close friend of the Mitchell family.

"But he is still the father of your children."

It was an irrefutable fact; there was no argument against his statement. "Yes, of course," Karen conceded. "But—"

Rayburn verbally closed in for the kill. "Don't you agree that the boys would feel relieved to know that their father is safely installed under your roof and under your care?"

"But what about Charles's parents?" Karen had demanded, recalling the comfort of the elder Mitchells' spacious suburban home and the guest room she now occupied. "Won't they want him close by?"

"Perhaps." The doctor's smile was too wise, and wry with understanding. "But Randolf is still very actively involved with his company, and Judith, though charming, is frankly quite helpless in a sickroom situation." He smiled again. "As I'm sure you know."

Having had firsthand experience, Karen did know how very useless Judith was in an emergency. Against her will, Karen had relived the time Rand had been thrown from his first two-wheeled bike. Karen had been at her shop, Charles had been out of town, Judith had been baby-sitting. Karen would never forget the sheer panic in Judith's voice when she'd called, begging Karen to tell her what to do. As calmly as possible, Karen had advised Judith to get Rand to the hospital, while assuring the older woman that she'd meet her there to take over. Karen had arrived at the hospital to find a pale but calm Rand and a devastated Judith.

Oh, yes. Karen knew exactly how useless Judith was in a sickroom situation. She had had little option but to nod her head, both in agreement with Dr. Rayburn and in defeat. Should she remain steadfast in her refusal to house Charles while he recuperated from the effects of the attack, and her sons learned of her refusal—which they most definitely would—they would never forgive her. Karen knew that she was well and truly trapped. She might, and did, rail silently against Charles for placing her in such an untenable position, but she had no choice but to offer him succor.

The deed was done; the plans were formulated. Upon release from the hospital, Charles would accompany Karen back to her home in Maine where, it was fervently agreed upon by all but Karen, he should fare well in the quiet atmosphere.

Now, hours later, Karen wanted to scream her frustration aloud. She was literally surrounded by people, yet she was very much alone. Unlike the night before, her bed was cold and empty.

Karen moved restlessly; she couldn't, wouldn't, think about the night before. Remembering Paul's fiercely tender possession would only undermine her dwindling store of strength, and she needed her strength for the days and weeks ahead. Yes, she wanted to scream her frustration, but she wouldn't. She was too tired, too susceptible, too close to tears. And she couldn't afford to give in to tears because she feared that if she allowed herself to start crying she might wail the house down.

But in the midnight quiet of the guest room in her former in-laws' home, with her children asleep in the room next to hers, Karen silently cried out in protest and desperation.

Paul.

Oh, fool! she chastened herself mutely. *Why did you refuse his plea to come to you in Boston?*

"Dammit!"

The edgy sound of his own voice echoing back at him, Paul tossed the tangled covers aside and sprang from the unfamiliar motel-room bed that had afforded him precious little relaxation or rest. The bed was not at fault. Indeed, the bed was firm and comfortable—but Paul wasn't. He was not firm in his conviction that he was doing the right thing by leaving Karen, nor was he comfortable with the miles now separating them.

Paul was hurting, in his mind and in his body. With wry self-understanding, he acknowledged that, were

Karen there to share the bed with him, the unfamiliar mattress would offer sweet surcease to his active imagination and too long denied, and now starving, flesh.

Into his tired mind danced a vision of her the night before, passionate, laughing, as hungry for him as he was for her. His body throbbing with a demand that could not be appeased, Paul muttered a curse.

Paul needed Karen, not merely in the physical sense but in every way there was. He needed her laughter as well as her impassioned murmurs. He needed her levelheadedness as well as her physical abandon. He needed her spiritually as well as physically. And the need had been growing with each successive mile as more distance came between them.

Pulling a robe over his chilled, naked body, Paul paced the inhibiting confines of the room and wished for a drink—a double. By itself, his thirst was sure sign of his mental condition. Paul rarely drank hard liquor, and then only in moderation. His tastes ran more to cool white wine and coolheadedness. Paul had not been handed his reputation as a shrewd banker and businessman; he had gained it by intelligent hard work. In his opinion, intelligence and indulgence did not coexist profitably. Nevertheless, at midnight in a lonely motel room in Connecticut, Paul wished he had a large measure of something potent and mind-divorcing.

In keen anticipation, he picked up the room-service menu. He sighed, acceptance replacing anticipation as he noted that room service was available only until eleven at night. Flipping the menu onto the desk-dresser, Paul resumed pacing.

How had it happened? he mused, cursing softly when his shinbone made painful contact with a corner of the bed. Ignoring the scrape, he concentrated on the question he'd asked himself.

How had it happened, this uncomfortable, unnerving state he now found himself in? Paul shook his head. He had exchanged a few innocuous remarks with a stranger on the beach. And from that most innocent of beginnings, he now found himself needing that stranger as a scholar needed books, as an addict needed a fix—merely to exist. But why?

Paul frowned. Why, indeed, this one particular woman? What was so special about Karen that made her different, at least to him, from countless others? And Paul had met countless other women, both socially and professionally. Yet not one of those other women had been able to catch his personal interest, although, modesty aside, he had been aware of how very hard a number of them had tried to capture his attention.

What made Karen special? Coming to an abrupt stop in the center of the room, Paul gazed blankly at the rumpled bed while he peered inward, seeking answers.

There had been an instantaneous attraction between them, he recalled, feeling a tiny thrill at the memory of her smiling up at him from her seated position in the sand. But Paul was well aware that there was more to the way he was feeling than could be explained as simple physical or chemical attraction.

Perhaps it was Karen's levelheadedness and stability that appealed to him. Paul conceded the possibility; after the years he'd spent attempting to deal with a rather unstable woman, that quality would appeal to him. But, he reasoned, there was much more involved here than mere levelheadedness and stability.

Perhaps it was Karen's warmth and generous spirit that charmed him. A faint smile tipped up the corners of Paul's lips. Yes, he had been most decidedly charmed by her warmth and spirit, especially since both attributes had been sorely lacking in his wife. But warmth and spirit didn't quite encompass all he was feeling, either.

Perhaps it was simply that Karen was, without question, a natural, down-to-earth, real person, meeting life on her own terms, with her own methods.

Into Paul's mind crept a vision of her large, outdated house, standing foursquare before the winds raking the land and the storms flung from the sea.

Paul smiled and sighed.

Karen Mitchell was like the house she had chosen to retreat to after the failure of her marriage. With a smile on her lips and a defiant toss of her head, she had deserted the excitement of the city to stand foursquare on ancestral earth. With her principles intact, Karen lived the only way she knew how to live, embracing the moralistic doctrine that Paul knew was tormenting her conscience because of her abandon in his arms.

A spasm of pain and sadness flickered over Paul's face. He knew there was no way Karen could rationalize a contradiction. He was also certain that, to her way of thinking, giving herself to him had been a contradiction of every one of her beliefs, regardless of the pleasure and satisfaction derived from her act of giving. Karen's self-recrimination had been her reason for rejecting his suggestion that he follow her to Boston.

Her rejection was the reason for the way he was hurting at that moment. Karen Mitchell, with her laughter and passion, her spirit and inhibiting fears, was the one person in the world that Paul Vanzant needed and ached for.

He needed her. His chest heaving with a deeply indrawn breath, Paul tossed off his robe and slid into the empty bed.

He needed her, not only in his bed but in his life, as well. And whether or not she acknowledged it, Paul instinctively knew that Karen needed him, too. All he had to do was convince her of her need.

"Dammit!"

Chapter Eight

I need him!

The cry stabbed into Karen's tired mind with increasingly depressing regularity. With each passing mile that brought them closer to the large house on the coast of Maine, Karen's thoughts persisted in conjuring up visions of the one person she didn't want to think about.

Where was he? Was he at home with his son and daughter-in-law in Philadelphia, or was he wandering again in search of whatever or whomever? It hurt Karen to think about it—to think about him. Still, weary after two weeks' vigilance at Charles's bedside, at the hospital and then in his parents' home, she could not stem the flow of conjecture.

Paul.

Forming his name, even silently, relieved a bit of the tension coiling along her nerves. The commitment to have Charles in her home to recuperate had been made.

Karen would abide by it, even if she was secretly resentful of the imposition. For while she might have held out against Dr. Rayburn and the elder Mitchells, she had caved in to the pleas of her children. She would play nursemaid to Charles, but her thoughts were her own. And Karen's thoughts were all on Paul Vanzant and her need to see him, talk to him, simply be with him.

Deep in thought, Karen was only marginally aware of her passenger, surrounded by luggage on the back seat of her car. Alert to her wandering attention, Charles made his presence known with a soft but audible groan. His ploy worked beautifully; Karen snapped to attention.

"Charles, are you all right?" Her gaze sought his in the rearview mirror.

"Yes, I guess so." Charles met her probing stare for an instant. "I'm just getting a little tired." His eyelids drooped. "It's been a long day."

Karen felt contrite immediately. Charles's mild complaint was valid; it had been a long day, and it wasn't over yet.

"Would you like me to stop somewhere?" she asked anxiously, chancing another quick glance at the mirror. "You could have a warm drink and stretch your legs."

"Yes...if you don't mind." His voice was little more than a weary whisper.

Alarm raced through Karen, chilling her body, momentarily freezing her mind. What would she do if he became ill? The road was virtually deserted, with few roadside stops. If Charles became ill, or had another attack...! Karen caught her thoughts up short. She was beginning to panic, and there was no reason for it. Hadn't Dr. Rayburn approved the trip? Surely if the doctor had thought there was any danger to Charles, he wouldn't have hesitated to state his objections. But the doctor hadn't objected. In fact, Dr. Rayburn had heartily approved.

Bolstered by the memory of the specialist's endorsement of Charles's plea to be allowed to leave Boston sooner than originally planned, Karen brought her fears under control. It would be all right, she assured herself. Charles would be all right. He was tired, understandably so, and that was all. But the arduous trip would be over before too long—thank heaven!

Karen drew a deep, calming breath. "I don't mind at all," she said, smiling into the mirror. "I could use a drink and a stretch myself." Her gaze drifted back to the road. "I'll stop at the next restaurant or diner."

They drove in silence for some fifteen minutes, and Karen was beginning to wonder if he had fallen asleep when Charles drew her attention to the golden arches rising above the highway in the distance. Nodding her acceptance of the fast-food restaurant, Karen slowed the car to make the turn into the spacious parking lot.

Though the late-fall air was cool, the sun had an Indian-summer warmth. After stepping from the car, Charles stood still, inhaling deep, reviving breaths of the autumn air.

"I missed the foliage," he said, strolling beside her toward the restaurant. "I was involved in a project, too busy to notice the change of seasons."

Karen didn't respond; she couldn't think of a thing to say to his remark. For as long as she could remember, Charles had always been too involved with some project or other—or, as she had later learned, with some woman or other—to take much notice of the seasonal changes.

While Karen went to the counter to purchase regular coffee for herself and decaffeinated coffee for him, Charles chose a table on the outdoor patio. He was standing in the sunlight by the brick enclosure, his profile to her, as Karen carried the steaming cups out to the open-air section of the restaurant. Her gaze remote, detached, Karen studied the man she had at one time loved above all others.

Charles hadn't changed much in the five years since their divorce. Except for a slightly drawn look and a grayish pallor in his cheeks, evidence of the heart attack he'd suffered, his appearance was the same. He was still an extremely attractive, dynamic-looking man. Above average in height, his body scrupulously toned by rigorous workouts, Charles was undeniably a handsome man. In addition to his exceptional looks, Charles's personality, and his masculine approach, had always set female hearts fluttering. And at age twenty, Karen had been no exception.

But Karen was no longer twenty and no longer quite as naive as she'd been when meeting Charles for the first time. Then she had been literally swept off her feet by him. Now, older, wiser and much more discerning, Karen, though moved to compassion by his recent ordeal, was completely unmoved by the attractive picture he presented bathed by sparkling fall sunshine.

"Careful, it's hot," she advised, handing him the foam cup. Tentatively sipping her own coffee, Karen gazed out over the waist-high patio enclosure. A faint smile tugged at her lips as her glance came to rest on a small play area, provided by the management for children restless from traveling.

It seemed to Karen that it had been a long time since her own boys had derived entertainment from the simple pleasure of a short ride down a slide or balancing on a teeter-totter. A soft sigh eased through her lips as, in her mind's eye, she saw her sons' bright faces as they laughed and begged her to push their swings higher and higher.

Suddenly Karen missed Rand and Mark, more acutely than at any other time since the divorce, and she ached to see them, touch them, hold them in her arms as she had the day of their arrival at the hospital. That unforgettable day was now two-week-old history. Randolf had escorted the boys back to school the day after the assortment of tubes and monitoring machines had been removed from their father and Charles had been moved from the coronary unit to a regular hospital room. On that day, in the midst of the relief displayed by Charles and his family, Karen had felt deserted by her sons, and she still felt deserted. Staring at the children's brightly colored playthings, Karen blinked against a rush of tears.

Apparently the play area also brought thoughts of the boys to Charles's mind. "Did I tell you I spoke to Rand and Mark on the phone before we left Boston this morning?" he asked in a murmur.

His question dried the gathering tears and drew her frowning gaze to his watchful eyes. "No." Karen shook her head. "Why did you call them?"

Charles moved his shoulders in a half shrug. "They were both so reluctant to return to school—" he shrugged again "—I thought I'd reassure them about the state of my health."

"And were they reassured?"

"Seemed to be." Charles paused to smile. "But it's difficult to tell with kids, isn't it?"

"Yes." Karen returned his smile, sharing with him, if nothing else, concern for the well-being of the children they had created together. "Children have a tendency to talk tough when they're frightened. And your attack frightened them very badly."

"And what about you? Were you frightened, too?" Charles gave her his most intense, melting look.

Immune to his charm, Karen didn't melt; she merely smiled. "Yes, Charles," she admitted, deliberately pandering to his need for an ego boost. "I was frightened." Her smile grew wry. "I have no wish for your demise."

"I'm glad to hear it. Knowing you were frightened gives me hope for the weeks ahead."

For an instant, Karen went absolutely still, barely breathing, afraid to think. But she had to know, had to ask. "What do you mean?" She had to force her fingers to ease their grip on the cup. "What are you getting at?"

His expression was one of superiority; Karen had always detested that particular expression. Now she discovered she resented it as well. "Don't smirk at me, Charles," she snapped. "Just explain what you meant by your remark."

Annoyance flickered across his face, revealing his dissatisfaction with her response. Karen could read his expression as easily as a first-grade primer. Always before, when she had been young and fathoms-deep in love, she had quailed at his mildest expression of reproof, quailed and hastened to appease him. Karen was no longer young or fathoms-deep in love with Charles. She no longer quailed at much of anything, and she couldn't have cared less if he was appeased or not. His expression made it evident that he was not thrilled with the mature Karen.

"You do realize that the boys are hoping for a reconciliation between us while I'm recuperating in your home," he finally replied in an infuriatingly condescending tone. "Don't you?"

"A reconciliation!" Karen exclaimed, stunned. "But it's been five years! Why would either one of them think—'' Her voice lost substance, and she shook her head as if trying to clear her mind. ''That's absolutely ridiculous!''

''Why is it?'' Charles retorted, his features betraying annoyance and anger.

''Why?'' In her shock, Karen failed to notice the renewed strength underlying his tone. ''Charles, we have been divorced over five years. Of course the idea of a reconciliation between us is ridiculous.''

''And I say it isn't,'' he insisted mulishly. ''We're both older, mature, more inclined to accept responsibility,'' he went on doggedly.

Karen couldn't believe what she was hearing. She was forced to stifle the temptation to demand: ''What's this 'we' bit? I accepted the responsibility of marriage from day one.'' Instead, she attacked from a different direction. ''And what about your latest, er, friend?'' she asked sweetly, recalling the svelte, ambitious blonde he'd introduced her to the last time Karen had taken the boys to visit their grandparents in Boston. ''Don't you think she—ah, what was her name again?—oh, yes, Claudia, wasn't it?'' His lips had tightened in growing anger, but Karen went on ruthlessly. ''Whatever. Don't you think *she* might object?''

''Yes, her name is Claudia,'' Charles said in a tight voice. ''And whether she objects or not doesn't matter. She doesn't matter. The important thing here is—''

''To get home before nightfall,'' Karen interrupted to finish for him. ''This subject is irrelevant,'' she continued impatiently, tossing her empty cup into a trash can, ''and closed.'' She spun away from him.

''The subject is not irrelevant,'' Charles argued, following her at a leisurely pace to the car. ''And will be reopened again when you're in a more receptive frame of mind."

Don't hold your breath, Karen thought, sliding behind the wheel and slamming the car door forcefully.

Throughout the remainder of the trip, the only voice to break the silence came from the car radio, which Karen had switched on before driving out of the restaurant's parking area. But inside her head, her thoughts seethed and popped like an untended stew coming to a boil.

How dare he? she railed silently. How dare Charles Mitchell assume that he had but to smile and snap his fingers to bring her to heel like a trained pet? And how dare he as casually dismiss his current paramour as not mattering? What had Claudia ever done to deserve his disdainful dismissal? Karen asked herself furiously. Come to that, what had Karen Mitchell ever done to earn his dubious favor?

Anger and tension gnawing at her, Karen arrived home exhausted and in a chancy temper. Tipped off to her mood by either her expression or her defiantly angled jaw, Charles prudently offered no resistance when she suggested they have a light supper, then retire for the night.

"I'll take the room across the hall from yours," he said between sips of the canned vegetable soup she had heated for their meal.

A protest sprang immediately to Karen's lips; the room across the hall from her belonged to Paul! Biting her lip, she caught back the declaration before it spilled from her tongue. A sense of despair filled her at the realization that the room did not belong to Paul and that it was doubtful he would ever occupy it again. Still, it grated on her to know that Charles would be sleeping in the bed that had supported Paul's body. As she opened her mouth to suggest he choose another room, Charles effectively silenced her.

"I want to be as close to you as possible," he said in a tone that held a hint of fear and uncertainty. His hand moved in an absent way to lightly brush his chest. "I need to know you'll hear me if I call for you during the night."

What could she say? Karen thought bleakly. How could she possibly deny him the assurance of having her within calling distance in the night in the event he suffered another— She cut off the unthinkable consideration with a sharp, brief shake of her head. She had no choice, she told herself, forcing a smile to her lips for him. And anyway, it was really only a room, an empty room. Paul was long gone from it.

"Of course, you may have any room you like." Karen's smile faltered as she glanced up, catching the gleam of speculation Charles quickly banished from his watchful eyes. "It'll only take me a minute to put fresh sheets on the bed." As she moved to get up, his hand shot across the table to capture hers. His action was too similar to Paul's motion of a few weeks earlier to be comfortable. Yet the action produced a different reaction in Karen. With Paul, her urge had been to turn her hand and entwine her fingers in his, but with Charles, she had to fight an impulse to snatch her hand away.

"There's no need to rush," he said, smiling at her as he gently squeezed her hand. "You've been driving all day. Relax and enjoy the rest of your soup. Join me in a cup of coffee."

"It's decaffeinated." Karen made a face.

Charles laughed. "It's really not that bad once you get used to it."

The way having him in her home wouldn't be that bad once she got used to it? Karen wondered, carefully sliding her hand from beneath his. In connection with that thought, an oft-repeated saying of her grandfather's sprang into Karen's mind.

A body can get used to most anything, even hanging if'n it hangs long enough.

Was that to be her life-style for who knew how many weeks or months—getting used to having Charles in her home, being constantly at his beck and call? The prospect was more than a little daunting. Deciding it just might be easier to get used to hanging, Karen got up to get the coffee.

When finally, after keeping Charles company for over an hour, then briskly changing the sheets on the guest room bed, Karen was free to seek the privacy of her own room, she did so with mounting trepidation. In truth, her room was not at all private. It was occupied by the unsubstantial, yet very real, presence of Paul Vanzant.

Long-denied memories crowding in on her, Karen quickly showered, pulled on a nightgown and slipped beneath the covers on her bed. She was cold and shivering, but her physical condition had little to do with the plunging temperature outside and everything to do with the sense of Paul permeating her mind. Paul was there, in her room with her, whether she wanted him there or not.

Karen fiercely fought against the sensation of being completely taken over by the lingering essence that was Paul, but she was swiftly immersed in thoughts of the last night they had spent together in that room, in her bed.

Seeing him clearly, feeling as if she had but to reach out to touch him, Karen saw Paul as he'd looked that last night as he'd silently stalked across the room to her, his eyes dark with intent, his firm jaw set in a determined thrust, his finely sculpted lips curved seductively.

A thrill of anticipation crept the length of her spine, and Karen felt again the breathless excitement she'd experienced at being swept into his arms before being tossed onto the bed. Karen's breathing grew shallow, and her eyes slowly drifted shut in surrender. The gates of memory flew open, releasing a heady rush of sweet remembrance. Paul was with her, beside her on the bed, within her—masterful, demanding, forceful and gentle with her by turns. And she was his, a wanton flame burning solely to illuminate his world. Their fire had burned through the night, leaping higher and higher until, near dawn, they had burned each other into emotionally charred exhaustion. Karen's soul still felt the sting of Paul's searing possession.

A stab of pain shattered the illusion of her wakeful dream. Moaning a protest against encroaching reality, Karen opened her eyes and concentrated on the source of her discomfort. The pain shot along her rigid fingers, cramped from gripping the bedding. With a sigh, Karen consciously relaxed her fingers and her body and her mind.

Paul was gone.

She was alone.

In her sorrow, Karen completely forgot the man sleeping in the room directly across from her own.

Paul was gone.

Was she back in Maine?

The thought came out of nowhere to break Paul's concentration. Exhaling a harsh sigh, he straightened his cramped back and pulled the oversize silver-rimmed glasses off to massage the bridge of his nose. Paul was tired. He was working too hard and sleeping too little. He knew it. He didn't particularly care.

It was November. It was cold. It was past midnight. The Thanksgiving holiday was three days away. Paul didn't particularly care about any of those facts, either.

Upon returning to Philadelphia in October, Paul had thrown himself into his work. Not the business of banking—he had retired from that and intended to remain retired from it. The business Paul had immersed himself in was a small company he'd acquired before his wife's sudden, unexpected death. At the time, the small company had been in financial trouble and floundering badly under inept management. Paul had taken over the company with the sole intent of dismantling it and selling it off piecemeal, thereby deriving a profit. After the shock of his wife's death, Paul had put off the order to begin the process of tearing down the failing company, thus allowing the business to continue on its stumbling course.

During the months following his wife's death, Paul had brushed aside his son's advice to either drop the ax on the company or take it on himself and whip it into shape, as Peter himself had done so successfully with his own wife's struggling company.

Paul had been back in Philadelphia less than a week, drifting through life like a soul in search of a body, when Peter had again made the suggestion that his father take an active hand in the small company. Peter's cool, offhand suggestion had been a godsend.

Seeking purpose, any purpose other than eating his foolish, middle-aged heart out over a woman, Paul acted on Peter's suggestion by investigating the company's possibilities. Very little time was required for Paul to reach the conclusion that, with applied intelligence and a lot of hard work, the company could not only be salvaged but made to show a profit. Paul had been applying both intelligence and hard work since then.

His efforts were beginning to show results, Paul acknowledged, both on the company's books and in his own thin, drawn face. The thought of his appearance brought a grimace to his lips. It would be some time before the small company was humming along and returning a creditable profit, but Paul, with little else to occupy himself with, was in no particular hurry. He had all the time in the world to steer the company into becoming viable—if he lived through the self-punishment of forgetfulness through work.

Forgetfulness. Paul's fingers curled into a fist. There wasn't enough work in the world to give him forgetfulness. How he longed to be able to close his eyes, just once, without seeing Karen, hearing Karen, needing Karen. Her face teased his memory. Her laughter haunted him. The thrill of her passion tormented his body.

Having allowed the thought of her into his conscious mind, Paul envisioned Karen back in the house on the Maine coast, back in the house and back in the bed they had shared that last night. His body tightened painfully as he relived the sweetness of Karen's surrender, felt again the thrill of possessing her, being possessed by her.

The very intensity of his feelings made Paul uneasy, and with grim determination he banished the memories from his mind.

What in the world was the matter with him? The question was almost like an old friend, so familiar was it to him.

He had been confused and angry most of the time

since he'd returned home, and he still was. That condition was another old friend.

Could he possibly be experiencing a delayed midlife crisis? Paul frowned. This consideration was completely new and unexpected. He voiced his opinion of midlife crises, delayed or otherwise, with a muttered, pithy curse.

Well, then, what the hell was the matter with him? Paul's smile was extremely wry. He was pining for a woman, that was what was the matter with him. And he didn't know quite how to handle his jumbled emotions.

Lord! Paul thought, raking a hand through his hair. How could he possibly know how to handle these unfamiliar emotions; he had never felt this way before. The realization stilled his fingers. Paul's hand fell to the desk unnoticed.

He had never felt this way before! Not even with his wife, the beautiful Carolyn, had he experienced quite this intensity of emotional upheaval, this need, this want, this consuming desire to simply *be* with another person!

Was Karen back in Maine?

Probably.

Then why was he in Pennsylvania?

Because she rejected your offer to be with her.

A sharp burst of humorless laughter broke the silence in the dimly lighted study. Suddenly impatient with the work he'd been straining his eyes over, with himself, with questions that hurt and answers that hurt even more, Paul shoved back his chair and rose to prowl around the solid oak desk.

Restless, dissatisfied, he paced to the bookshelves, only to pivot around again without glancing at a single title on the leather spines. He directed his course to a short black-leather-padded wet bar at the opposite end of the room. He was tipping a bottle over a wide squat glass when his hand was arrested by a drawling voice.

"If you're playing bartender, you can splash some of that Scotch into a glass for me."

Tilting his head, Paul peered at his son over the rims of his glasses. His impeccable business suit enhancing the muscular slenderness of his tall body, Peter stood in the study doorway, one shoulder propped indolently against the frame.

"On the rocks or straight up?" Paul asked dryly.

"I'm driving." Shrugging, Peter pushed himself away from the frame and strolled to the bar to grin at his father. "I'll have two ice cubes and a large dash of seltzer."

Paul's lips twisted with distaste. "A helluva thing to do to aged Scotch," he muttered, dropping two ice cubes into the glass, then drowning both whiskey and ice with seltzer. After handing the glass to his son, Paul raised his in a salute. "What shall we drink to?"

Peter's darkly handsome face took on a speculative expression, and his dark eyes began to glitter behind narrowed lids. "Let's see," he said, drawing his brows together in a frown. "We could drink to the future success of your new toy, but I think that's assured now, considering the killing amount of work you've put into it."

"Peter." A hint of warning sounded in Paul's voice as he recognized the edge in his son's voice; Peter was about to go for his father's throat—figuratively speaking.

"Or we could drink to your health," Peter went on, ignoring his father's warning tone. "But that's in some doubt, considering the amount of work you've put into that company."

"Peter." The note in Paul's tone was no longer a hint; it was a full-fledged warning to back off and shut up.

"Then again," Peter continued, unperturbed by the parental censure, "we could drink to the woman—whoever she is." Raising his glass to his lips, Peter took a sip of the Scotch while closely watching his father's face for a reaction.

Though he tried his damnedest, Paul didn't disappoint his son; a muscle jerked along his clenched jaw.

"Is she pretty, Dad?" Peter asked softly. "Are you in love with her?"

Chapter Nine

"Karen, where are my gray slacks?"

With a flicker of annoyance moving over her set lips, Karen sighed and shut her eyes. Gray slacks. Where were they? She had pressed them earlier that morning—and then she'd hung them in his closet.

"Have you looked in your closet?"

"Yes, of course, but... Oh, here they are. Sorry."

Yes, so am I. Karen didn't allow herself to think any further about how very sorry she was about many things, starting with her concession to the request to have Charles recuperate in her home and ending with Charles recuperating in her home. She didn't have time to think about it. There was simply too much to do. She glanced at the kitchen clock and smothered a groan. The boys would be home for the holiday weekend soon—picked up at school and delivered to her by their grandparents.

A second groan escaped her. Impatience danced along her nerves.

Why had she allowed Charles to talk her into inviting his parents to visit for the weekend? Karen grimaced. She knew precisely why she'd given in to his request; Charles had simply worn her down with pleas and promises of how wonderful it would be to have an old-fashioned family gathering for Thanksgiving. And, as his health had so very obviously improved during his stay with her, Karen hesitated to remind him that they had never gathered as a family for *any* holiday, even in the days when she had still believed they *were* a family. So in the end she had given in, ignoring his smug smile of satisfaction. But now, running behind schedule and distracted by yet another reminder of his ineptitude concerning anything vaguely domestic, even to the point of being unable to find his own slacks in his own closet, Karen was beginning to wonder if all her marbles were rolling around in the proper slots.

Get busy, Karen, she chided herself. Time waits for no man or woman, and there's precious little time to ruminate. Besides, if she did allow herself to think about it, she'd probably start wailing or tearing her hair out of her head. And either way, she'd be a shocking sight for Rand and Mark when they arrived for the Thanksgiving holiday—not to mention Judith and Randolf.

Making a face at her own whimsical thoughts, Karen opened her eyes and glared down at the pie she'd been working on when Charles had distracted her. A sour expression pinched her lips. She hated pumpkin pie. But, as Charles had so gently reminded her, both his parents loved pumpkin pie, and really, what was Thanksgiving without pumpkin pie?

Enjoyable? Karen had not offered the comment at the

time of the discussion. She had still been in shock after being informed that she would be entertaining her former in-laws for the holiday.

Now, crimping the edges of the piecrust with more vigor than necessary, Karen fumed in silent frustration. Until Charles had dropped his informational bombshell on her, she had been looking forward to the holiday simply because the boys would be home. She had even considered going out to a restaurant for the traditional meal instead of cooking it herself. Charles's news had ended her pipe dream of being waited on.

The combined scents of pumpkin, ginger and cinnamon tickled Karen's nose as she poured the mixture into the pie shell. A soft smile curved her lips. Too bad the finished product didn't taste as good as it smelled, she mused, sliding the pie onto the center rack in the oven. She was setting the oven timer when Charles sauntered into the kitchen.

"How do I look?" he asked, striking a pose for her.

Experiencing an eerie sense of déjà vu, Karen turned to face him. His pose was much the same as Paul's had been weeks before when he'd breezed into the kitchen after repairing the shutters. Swamped with a longing so intense she felt light-headed for an instant, Karen couldn't speak or even breathe. There before her, in Charles's stead, stood the one person she yearned to see. His aristocratic head was tilted at a quizzical angle, and his beautiful mouth curved teasingly. He was smiling at her, for her, only for her. Karen was forced to grasp the edge of the stove to steady herself, so great was the shaft of pain that sliced into her chest. In despair, she felt every minute of every aching hour she had lived through since driving away from Paul in that restaurant parking lot increasing her loneliness a hundred times over. Her heart, her mind, her body wept with need of him.

Paul.

"Karen?" Charles took a step toward her. "You look so strange. Are you all right?"

Karen blinked and began breathing again. "Yes, of course." She managed a shaky smile to reassure him. "The heat from the oven," she said, improvising. "It made me a little dizzy."

Unconvinced, Charles arched a skeptical brow. "You're pale. Are you sure you're okay?"

"I said I was." Stepping around him, she walked to the sink to rinse the flour off her hands and run cold water over her thundering pulse. Frowning, she stared at the vein throbbing in her wrist. This was ridiculous! Rattled, she flinched when Charles laid a hand on her shoulder.

"I think you'd better sit down." There was a hint of a command in his tone that abraded her nerves.

"I'm all right!"

Karen was suddenly impatient. She was a thirty-seven-year-old mother of two, mooning like a teenager over a man she'd known exactly three days! It had to stop. She could deal with her feelings of guilt over her moral lapse; she couldn't handle a bad case of lovesickness.

Lovesickness? Everything inside Karen went still. Love? A tremor ran down her legs, leaving them weak. Love! Unsteady, quaking inside, she stumbled to a chair, unconsciously obeying Charles's order. Her head whirling, she stared at the homey, domestic-looking clutter of sprinkled flour and baking utensils on the table.

She couldn't be in love!

"Here, sip this."

Karen started and frowned at the small glass Charles shoved into her hand. The pungent aroma of expensive bourbon filled her senses. Frowning, she glanced up at him.

"What's this for?"

"You." Charles's expression was grim. "It'll clear your head."

It'll take more than bourbon. Karen smiled at the thought. Charles thought she was smiling at him, and he smiled back at her.

"Go on," he urged. "Drink it."

Why not? Raising the glass, she sipped and choked on the potent whiskey. Charles laughed. Karen tossed him a wry look.

"Better?"

"Much better," she lied, taking another tiny sip. "My head's clear now." That much was true; Karen felt extremely clearheaded. She wasn't particularly happy with the condition. Mental lucidity brought the truth crashing home.

She was in love with Paul Vanzant!

But acknowledging her emotional condition and living with it were two entirely different matters. She didn't want to be in love with Paul; she didn't want to be in love with anyone.

Standing, Karen began to clear the baking debris from the table. She didn't have time to think about Paul or about love. She had too much to do. It was the day before Thanksgiving. Her boys were due within the hour. Karen's lips compressed. Her boys *and* her former in-laws were due within the hour, she corrected herself.

Damn! Why did life have to be so complicated?

"You never did answer my question."

Charles's aggrieved tone drew Karen from her fruitless contemplation. Pausing in the act of wiping the flour from the tabletop, she angled her head to frown at him.

"What question was that?"

Standing, he again struck his male-model pose. "How do I look?"

Karen couldn't decide whether to laugh or cry. Charles's self-absorption was beyond belief. She chose to laugh.

"You look like you just stepped off the cover of *GQ*," she said, controlling an urge to roll her eyes. "Very chic," she added, sighing inwardly as he preened visibly, not unlike a strutting peacock. "Very man-about-townish."

In all honesty, Karen had to admit that Charles did, in fact, present an elegant picture of the man on the go relaxing at home for the holiday. His choice of a blue-on-blue silk shirt complemented the hand-tailored gray slacks. His cheeks gleamed with a freshly shaved sheen. His shampooed hair looked squeaky clean. His perfect teeth glistened white in contrast to his sunlamp-tanned skin. All in all, he made Karen feel unkempt and grubby by comparison.

"I think I'll take a shower." Tossing the dishcloth into the sink, Karen headed for the hallway.

"What about dinner?"

"What about it?" Karen paused in the doorway to slant a challenging look at him.

Charles glanced around the untidy kitchen. "You haven't started it." His frown said more than words. "You do realize that my parents and the boys will be here any time now?"

How could she not realize it? Karen wondered when he persisted in reminding her of it. She hesitated, amazed at her unusual willingness to desert a messy kitchen.

Then she shrugged. Realizing that it would keep, she dashed into the hallway.

"I'll get everything together after I've had my shower," she called to him as she started up the stairs. "Meanwhile, you can load the dishwasher and start a fresh pot of coffee."

"Me?"

Karen paused at the top of the stairs, arrested by the note of shock in Charles's tone. His obvious amazement should not have surprised her. Charles had been spoiled all his life, first by his doting mother and then by his equally doting wife. Karen felt positive that every one of his girlfriends, past and present, had continued the tradition of catering to his every murmured whim. No wonder the man had been shocked at being told to load the dishwasher and prepare coffee.

"Never mind, Charles," she called to him. "I'll take care of it when I get back down." Shoulders drooping, she headed for her bedroom, deciding the chances of the relaxed, happy holiday she had envisioned were slim to none.

What kind of holiday celebration would Paul be having?

The thought crept into Karen's unguarded mind, stilling her fingers on her shirt button. A sigh of longing ruffled the quiet of her room.

Paul.

A rush of hot moisture drew a film over Karen's eyes. Then she blinked rapidly and shook her head. She had to stop this! It was not only ridiculous, it was impossible. For a moment out of time, she had stepped beyond the norm to engage in a blazing, thoroughly satisfying love affair. An affair, moreover, that had had precious little to do with love. Now her life was back to its normal, dull routine. The affair was over; her lover was gone. That was that.

Her lecture to herself over, Karen finished undressing and stepped into the shower. The gush of water from the shower drowned out the sound of her whispered plea.

Dear God! I can't be in love with him!

"I had no idea you were such an excellent cook, Patricia." Paul raised his glass in a salute to his daughter-in-law. "My compliments. I'm grateful to you and Peter for insisting I share your Thanksgiving Day meal."

"Thank you, Paul." A delighted smile enhancing her beautiful, aristocratic face, Patricia inclined her head in acceptance of his praise. Then she shattered the elegant illusion by aiming an impish grin at her husband. "Dare we tell your father that you assisted in preparing the meal, darling?"

Peter Vanzant's thin lips eased into a smile of supreme male satisfaction. "We may," he murmured, raising his glass to his mouth to acknowledge his father's toast to Patricia. "But please don't expect a gasp of surprise from Dad." Peter's smile slashed into a grin. "He wields a mean hand at the stove, himself."

"Really!" Patricia actually gaped at her father-in-law.

"I manage." Comfortable in the company of the two younger people, Paul relaxed in the dining room chair.

Peter laughed softly. "He manages very well," he observed in a dry tone. "But I agree, love." His tone had softened to a caress. "The meal was an artistic achievement."

"Give yourself a pat on the back, as well, love." Patricia tilted her glass in a toast to her husband.

Love. Paul controlled an urge to close his eyes—and his ears. He had heard the endearment countless times since his arrival at his son's home several hours earlier. Sipping his wine, Paul gazed at his son and daughter-in-law over the rim of the glass. Peter and Patricia were so obviously in love, and they didn't hesitate to voice the affection they felt for one another. The result of that love was the tiny, beautiful child napping in a cradle in the corner of the dining room.

Concealing a sigh, Paul gazed down at the table and saw another, smaller one set in a windowed alcove off a large, old-fashioned kitchen. Unbidden, his inner gaze skimmed off the edge of the imaginary tabletop to the carpeted floor beneath. His heartbeat accelerating inside his chest, Paul could *see* Karen, her eyes cloudy with passion, her moist lips parted, her arms held out in invitation to him...to *him*!

"...Dad?"

The sound of Peter's voice shattered the illusion. Swallowing a groan, Paul glanced up, a faint, self-mocking smile on his lips. "I'm sorry, I was preoccupied. What did you say?"

A tiny frown line drew Peter's dark brows together. "I asked if you'd care for dessert."

"No." Paul offered Patricia an apologetic smile. "I couldn't possibly eat another bite."

Patricia's nod was gracious. "Perhaps later."

"I—" Paul paused. In that instant, the decision was made. It was not his usual way. Paul rarely made a decision without careful consideration of all the possibilities involved. But this particular decision felt exactly right for him; he would go with it. "I'm afraid I won't be here later. I have something I must do."

"Surely you're not going home to work, Dad?" Peter exclaimed, scowling at the very idea of his father working on a holiday, forgetting that he had done so himself many times in his pre-Patricia days.

Paul raised a hand, palm out in the age-old sign asking for peace. "No, Peter, I am not going home to work." His lips twitched in amused anticipation of Peter's reaction to his next statement. "I'm going home to pack." Peter didn't disappoint him.

"Pack!" Peter's voice was rough with astonishment.

"Pack?" Patricia merely sounded confused.

"As in clothes into suitcases," Peter explained dryly.

"But where are you going?" The question came simultaneously from Paul's host and hostess. Peter answered his own query before his father had a chance to respond. "Are you flying to Texas to see Nicole?"

"No." Paul smiled and shook his head. "I spoke to both Nicole and J.B. this morning, and they are fine." He hesitated only a moment before asking quietly, "Peter, do you remember our conversation the other evening?"

"How could I forget?" Peter grimaced. "As I recall, the conversation was pretty much one-sided—mine. You refused to respond in any way."

"Yes, well—" Paul shrugged "—you must admit, your line of questioning was rather personal."

"What is this all about?" Patricia glanced from her husband to her father-in-law. "What conversation? When?"

Paul was content to stare at Peter until the younger man answered his wife. "I stopped by the house to see Dad after my meeting the other night," he explained tersely. "We had a discussion."

Patricia gave a long-suffering sigh but asked patiently, "A discussion about what?"

Paul continued to stare at Peter; Peter's angular features tightened.

"I'm waiting."

Paul nearly lost control and smiled. Peter sighed in exasperation and defeat.

"I asked Dad if his lady friend was pretty and, er, if he was in love with her."

"Peter, you didn't!" Patricia was visibly appalled at her mate's lack of both manners and tact. "Your father's personal affairs are none of your business!" Her cheeks bloomed with color, and she cast a stricken glance at Paul. "No pun intended!"

Vastly amused by this rare glimpse of his son being chastised by his wife, Paul chuckled. Peter winced. Patricia narrowed her eyes and gave her father-in-law a glittering look.

"Are you in love with some lucky lady?"

"Patricia!" Peter barked.

Giving up, Paul threw back his head and roared with laughter, unable to remember when he'd enjoyed the company of his family quite so thoroughly. If only Nicole and her husband were here, the day would be just about perfect, he thought as his laughter subsided. Just about, he corrected himself, envisioning the face that haunted his every waking hour.

"I'm sorry, Paul." Patricia's contrite tone drew Paul from his own thoughts. "I have no right—"

He cut her off gently. "Yes, you do. You have the right granted by affection and concern." Paul gazed at the son of his body and the daughter of his heart. Then he smiled. "I don't know if I'm in love. That's the reason I'm going home to pack. I must see her, talk to her." His mouth twisted into a wry smile. "She probably regards me as something of an old fool."

"You are not old!" Patricia protested indignantly.

"And far from a fool," Peter observed dryly. He studied Paul intently for a moment. Then an understanding, blatantly male grin revealed his hard white teeth. "Age hasn't a damn thing to do with it, Dad. *If* you love her."

Feeling oddly rejuvenated by their approval and support, Paul slid his chair back and stood up.

"That's what I intend to find out."

The traditional turkey-with-all-the-trimmings dinner was a smashing success. The disputed pumpkin pie was a smashing success. Karen was exhausted.

"Boy, I'm stuffed."

"That was the general idea." Karen smiled fondly at her youngest son. "First you stuff the bird, then you stuff yourself. It's the American way."

"Yeah." Mark's eyes glowed with happiness and contentment. "Thanksgiving's pretty neat."

"Yeah." Rand grinned. "It's almost as good as Christmas."

"Christmas!" Mark whooped. "Yeah! Will you still be here, Dad?"

"Yeah," Charles echoed enthusiastically.

"Yeah?" Karen chided, frowning.

"Aw, Mom, everybody says yeah," Rand grumbled.

"Yeah, they do." Mark nodded vigorously.

"And if everybody leaps off a cliff, will you follow?" Karen asked reasonably, her frown darkening as she noticed Charles's grinning encouragement of his sons. Annoyed, frustrated because it had always been this way, she shifted her frown to him. From the beginning Charles had opted to join forces with his sons, be one of the guys, while she'd been left with the role of disciplinarian.

"And you?" she charged. "Would you follow also?"

"Aw, Mom," Charles mimicked, earning laughter from his sons and indulgent smiles from his parents.

Karen couldn't win, and she knew it; besides, she was simply too darned tired to fight. Surrounded and outnumbered, Karen gave up the battle as gracefully as possible. Erasing her frown with a bright smile, she glanced at Judith and Randolf.

"Would you like coffee or tea or an after-dinner drink?"

"Coffee would be lovely." Judith smiled in appreciation of Karen's surrender. But then, as Karen knew well, Judith had always chosen to take the path of least resistance, which partially explained her son's lack of discipline.

"Coffee sounds good," Charles agreed.

"I think I'll have a brandy," Randolf said, sliding his chair away from the table.

"Why don't we have it in the living room?" Judith suggested, rising also. "It's so much more comfortable in there, and the fire's so cheery."

"Excellent idea, my dear." Randolf placed his hand at his wife's waist to escort her from the dining room. "Come along, Charles, we're in Karen's way here."

"Right." As Charles pushed back his chair, he arched his brows at Rand and Mark. "Why don't you guys go out into the fresh air. Go sink some baskets." He flicked his hand in the direction of the garage, indicating the rusting hoop with its tattered netting mounted on the side wall.

"Okay with me," Rand replied. He grinned challengingly at his brother. "ll play you a game of one-on-one."

Mark scrambled off his chair. "You're on!"

Within a matter of seconds, Karen found herself

standing alone in the dining room. A weary smile of acceptance twisted her lips as she gazed down at the remains of the holiday meal littering the two-hundred-year-old oval table.

What you need, Karen advised herself wryly, is a fairy godmother who isn't afraid of dipping her hands into hot dishwater. Or Judith's housekeeper, she revised as she began to stack her best china. If memory served, the housekeeper had been given the entire holiday weekend off.

Sighing softly, Karen turned to carry the first load of dishes into the kitchen, but paused at the sound of the front door slamming, followed by the aggrieved sound of Rand's voice.

"Hey, Dad! That basketball hoop's so loose it's about ready to fall off the wall. Can you fix it?"

"It's a holiday, Rand," Charles replied. "Make do today. I'll have your mother give the man who does the repairs a call tomorrow morning. Okay?"

"Yeah, I guess so." The door slammed again.

It's a holiday, Karen silently repeated, somewhat sarcastically. Damn, you could have fooled me! Telling herself to knock off the private pity party, she continued on into the kitchen. She didn't have time to wallow in self-pity; she had a table to clear, dishes, pots and a grease-spattered roast pan to clean, and coffee and brandy to serve. Boy! Aren't holidays fun!

By ten that night, Karen decided that there was a lot to be said for wallowing in self-pity; Charles was having tremendous success with the ploy. All he had to do was look dissatisfied and every member of the family leaped to make him comfortable.

She groaned with sheer bliss as she slipped into bed.

Closing her eyes, Karen soaked in the blessed quiet. Maybe, just maybe, she thought as she began to drift toward sleep, tomorrow will be less hectic.

It wasn't.

Karen was awakened early the following morning by two disgustingly wide-awake boys and their grinning father, all demanding to be fed. She was up and running from the moment her feet hit the floor.

The day was fine, crisp and cold. After breakfast, Randolf suggested an invigorating stroll on the beach. His suggestion was agreed to with enthusiasm. En masse, Judith, Randolf, Charles, Rand and Mark bundled up in warm jackets, gloves and assorted caps and scarves, then trooped merrily out the door.

Standing beside yet another cluttered table, Karen waved them on their way, grateful for the lull that enabled her to clean up the kitchen, make the beds and dump the first load of laundry into the washer in peace. It also afforded her a quiet minute in which to make the call to Gil Rawlins about fastening the basketball hoop; Gil was out of town for the weekend. Positive the boys, and Rand in particular, would be disappointed, Karen considered tackling the job herself, then rejected the idea. Who would get the meals and clean up afterward if she fell off the ladder and broke a bone?

No sooner had Karen finished in the kitchen than the red-cheeked, bright-eyed beach strollers trooped back into the house, requesting lunch. As she had surmised, the first words out of Rand's mouth were about the basketball hoop. To Karen's relief, though, he accepted her negative report with a philosophical shrug. At that moment, he was obviously more concerned with filling the emptiness inside his body than with exercise.

"Can I have a club sandwich made with the leftover turkey?" he asked.

"Oh, but—" Karen began, meaning to tell Rand that she was planning to use the leftover meat in a turkey pie for dinner. She never got the words out of her mouth.

"My, that does sound lovely," Judith agreed with her grandson. "I'll have the same."

Inwardly concluding that just about *everything* sounded lovely to Judith, Karen shrugged and decided broiled steaks would do as well for dinner. Lean steak was more in line with Charles's diet anyway.

Lunch was a pleasantly congenial meal. Karen thoroughly enjoyed the lively conversation once all the triple-decker sandwiches had been prepared and served. Between voracious bites of food, the boys regaled her with an in-depth account of all the shells they'd found on the beach and how much fun it had been having their grandparents as well as their father help collect them.

Though Karen found it nearly impossible to imagine the designer-attired Judith, Randolf and Charles grubbing in the sand for seashells, she smiled and took the boys' word for it, pleased the outing had been a success. There had been moments, too many in number, when Karen had suffered twinges of conscience and regret about denying her sons the fullness of a cohesive family experience. Gazing into the boys' animated faces, she decided the weekend was worth all the extra work and occasional irritation.

They were lingering over coffee and dessert when the front doorbell rang. Rand was already standing, since he had just asked to be excused from the table.

"I'll get it," he called, loping out of the dining room and down the hall.

"Now who could that be?" Judith wondered aloud.

"I haven't the vaguest idea." Karen shrugged.

"You weren't expecting more company, were you?" Charles asked, looking both suspicious and annoyed.

"No," Karen said, bristling at his proprietary attitude.

"Can I help you, sir?" they heard Rand ask in his best prep school manner.

Everyone grew quiet as they listened for a response. It came in a deep, attractive male voice that froze Karen's mind and shot adrenaline through her system.

"Yes. My name is Paul Vanzant. Is Ms. Mitchell in?"

Chapter Ten

The teenager had to be Rand.

Staring into the tall, skinny boy's brown eyes, Paul could see a masculine teenage image of Karen. He decided he liked the kid on sight.

"Hey, Mom, there's a man here who wants to see you."

Rand's voice broke in midsentence. Paul suppressed the urge to smile, recalling how embarrassed Peter had been at the same age when his voice had been changing. Then the urge to smile vanished, to be replaced by a humming tension as Karen, her face pale, her posture rigid, walked out of the dining alcove and along the hall toward him.

"You should have invited Mr. Vanzant inside, Rand, instead of keeping him standing outside in the cold."

Outside in the cold. Paul felt a bone-deep chill. He could sense her withdrawal. She was closing him out, had closed him out. Despair coiling in his mind, Paul stepped inside. After closing the door, Rand stood, his gaze moving from Paul to his mother. Karen didn't say a word; she didn't have to. The pointed look she leveled at her son said it all.

Rand shuffled his feet and cleared his throat. "Ah, I guess I'll, um, go talk to Dad," he stuttered, lowering his eyes.

"I think that's a good idea." Karen kept her gaze steady on Rand until he loped along the hall to the alcove.

Throughout the exchange, Paul felt the chill inside him intensify. A tremor of shock ripped through him when Rand mentioned his father. Charles was at the house! For the holiday or—? Ruthlessly cutting off the thought, Paul narrowed his eyes. Questions crowded his mind, but he held them at bay, waiting for Karen to make the first move. When she did, her voice was so strained that Paul was afraid he already knew the answers.

"Paul, what are you doing here. Why have you—"

"Here?" he interrupted her, sweeping the hallway with a glance. His remote tone and arched brows silenced her. She looked helpless for an instant. Then she sighed. Paul's own chest heaved in response.

"Come into the living room, please." Avoiding his stare, she turned to lead the way into the room Paul felt he knew more intimately than his bedroom at home. And yet her attitude made him feel like a stranger, an unwelcome stranger. The feeling induced a mixture of emotions in Paul, the strongest of which was anger.

"Won't you sit down?"

So polite, Paul thought, she's so damn polite. Suppressing an urge to grab her by the shoulders and shake her while demanding to know why she was shutting him out, Paul curled his fingers into his palms and decided he'd be damned if he'd play polite word games with her.

"Charles is here for the holiday?" he asked bluntly.

Karen flinched at his harsh tone but met his stare directly. "No." Her tone was even, inflectionless. "Charles has been here for over a month. I brought him back with me a week after he was released from the hospital." She drew a quick breath before continuing with her explanation. "Rand and Mark are home for the holiday, and Charles's parents are visiting. They picked the boys up at school and drove them home."

"I see." Paul smiled; it was either smile or curse. "Just one big happy family, hmm?"

Karen winced as though she'd been struck. "Paul, please—" She broke off and bit her lip.

"I'm sorry." Paul gave in to the need to swear softly under his breath. Self-disgust underlined each muttered syllable. He had lashed out in reaction to the fear creeping through him, and he had hurt her, insulted her. It was not like him, not at all like him, and yet...

Moving abruptly, he walked to the fireplace. He stared into the low, flickering flames, seeing in the blazing depths scenes of other, more satisfying moments spent in the room with her. His body tightening in response to memories as hot and vivid as the crackling fire, Paul raised his head and turned to gaze at her through eyes shielded by lowered eyelids. "I never even considered the possibility that I might be interrupting your holiday." His voice was low, reflecting the tightness gripping his body. "I never even considered the probability of your boys being home." A self-mocking smile briefly moved his lips. "All I thought about was my need to see you, to talk to you." He paused to examine her expression and eyes. Her eyes were shadowed by a wounded look; her features were pinched with lines of weariness.

Anger flared in Paul. When they had parted five weeks ago, Karen's face had revealed both her inner battle concerning her passionate, if brief, relationship with him and consternation over the possible effects of Charles's heart attack. Now, a mere five weeks later, her eyes still betrayed inner conflict, but she appeared on the point of exhaustion.

What in the hell is he doing to her? The question seared Paul's mind and strengthened his resolve. Drawing a deep breath, he said, "I had planned on staying awhile, to give us time to get to know each other." He smiled faintly. "And to give myself time to find out if what I suspect is true."

"What you suspect?" Karen repeated, shaking her head. "Paul, I don't understand. What do you suspect?"

"That I'm falling in love with you."

For one perfect, brilliant instant, undiluted joy shimmered through Karen. Paul was here, near enough to touch. Her fingers itched with the need to reach out and seek proof of his reality. Her lips burned with a fire only his mouth could quench. Her empty body ached for a completion he alone could give. Within that perfect instant, Karen could envision an end to endless nights of longing. Paul was here. She was whole. Life was radiant.

And then the instant ended.

Reality waited in the dining alcove. And reality was unchanged by a man who suspected that he was falling in love.

The death of the perfect instant left the agony of an imperfect reality. How many times since the day she had driven away, leaving him calling after her, had she secretly, silently cried out for him? How many times in all the long nights since then had she awakened, her body quivering with the need to be a part of his? Karen shivered in response to the answers that washed through her mind.

And now Paul was here, offering her the possibility of a different, brighter reality. But she could not let him stay. Karen had not sought love, had not wanted to love ever again. But she did love, was in love. She didn't suspect it; she was certain of it. And she could not let him stay.

The realization that she must deny herself and send Paul away struck Karen like a blow. She swayed with the shattering backlash.

"Karen!" His tone sharp with alarm, Paul stepped toward her.

Karen stepped back. Drawing in deep, controlling breaths, she held up a hand as if to ward him off.

"I'm all right." Her reedy voice belied her assurances. Straightening her spine, tightening her body and her nerves, Karen steeled herself to say what had to be said. The words of rejection and dismissal never made it from her mind to her lips.

"Aren't you going to introduce us to your guest, Karen?"

Karen jolted at the sound of speculation woven through the pleasant tone of Charles's voice. Reality was here and now, in the form of Charles and his parents sauntering into the room and the infinitely more important forms of the two wary-eyed boys hovering in the doorway.

Acceptance was not unlike the feel of living death.

For a millisecond, rebellion flared inside Karen; then, just as quickly, it was extinguished.

"Yes, of course." Karen was amazed at the even, casual sound of her voice. She was more amazed at her ability to smile as she turned to face them. "Charles, Judith, Randolf, this is Mr. Vanzant." She shifted to look at Paul without looking at him at all. "Mr. Vanzant, I'd like you to meet Charles Mitchell." She indicated the man who had come to stand beside her. "And his parents, Judith and Randolf Mitchell." Her smile grew easier as she glanced at the doorway. "And the boys are Rand and Mark."

Paul responded to the disruptive interruption like the gentleman and aristocrat he was. His expression cool but polite, he extended his hand as he moved forward. "Charles." Paul gripped Charles's hand briefly, then released it and turned to his parents. "Mr. Mitchell. Mrs. Mitchell."

"Mr. Vanzant." The three Mitchells responded in unison.

"Paul, please," he murmured vaguely, gazing at the two boys in the doorway. A faint smile relieved the coolness of his expression and lit his dark eyes from within. "Rand?" Paul stared at the older boy. At Rand's nod, he shifted his gaze. "Mark." With three long strides, Paul was across the room, extending his hand with the same respect he had afforded the adults. "I'm pleased to meet you both."

Wide-eyed and obviously surprised at receiving the same consideration as their elders, Rand and Mark hesitantly extended their own, smaller hands. The grip was completed, establishing contact on various levels of awareness. Both youngsters revealed pleasurable confusion.

A bittersweet ache filled Karen as she watched the man she loved touch her sons, physically and emotionally. The ache expanded as she watched each boy's reluctant response. The thought of what might have been teased the edges of her mind. With ruthless determination, Karen shoved the thought aside. The situation was growing more impossible by the minute. The glint of speculation in Charles's eyes was solidifying into... what?

"Vanzant." Randolf murmured the name in bemused contemplation.

Karen blinked and glanced at Randolf. As she looked at him, he frowned and murmured the name again.

"Vanzant?" This time his murmur held a questioning note.

Mentally shrugging off Randolf's odd behavior, Karen switched her gaze to the man turning to face her. Paul's stare was compelling; she couldn't maintain it and speak the words of dismissal. Her gaze shifted to Charles. "Mr. Vanzant was just—"

"Speaking to that colorful character who runs the store in town," Paul finished for her. "He told me that even though the bed-and-breakfast was closed for the season, Ms. Mitchell might be willing to accommodate me."

Karen was consumed by equal measures of elation and despair. She knew he couldn't stay but, but... Hope leaped higher than the flames in the fireplace.

"You want to rent a room?" Charles exclaimed. "Here?"

"Yes."

"But—"

"Paul Vanzant." No longer a murmur, Randolf's contemplative tone cut through his son's protest and drew a varied response from his audience.

Both Karen and Judith frowned in confusion.

Charles scowled impatiently.

Paul arched his brows in mild inquiry.

"The Philadelphia banker Vanzant?" Randolf asked, ignoring his family as he centered his attention on Paul.

"Yes." Smiling wryly, Paul inclined his head. And unbeknownst to Karen, with his quiet confirmation, choice and decision were plucked from her hands.

Randolf took command of the situation. Smiling broadly, he again extended his hand to grasp Paul's. "I've wanted to meet you for years but somehow kept missing the opportunity. It really is a pleasure to meet you, sir." The term of respect from the older man said reams more than his actual words. "And I'm positive Karen will be delighted to accommodate you." He beamed at Karen. "Won't you, my dear?"

What could she say? Karen hesitated as her options skipped through her mind. Then she granted Randolf's request—simply because she wanted to. "Yes, if you insist." She was careful not to look at Paul or Charles.

"Well, of course I insist." A flicker of a frown crossed his face as he noted his son's scowl. "Charles, Judith." Reaching out, he drew his wife to his side. "Surely you both remember all the times I've mentioned Mr. Vanzant's name?" Randolf glanced from one to the other. Impatience flashed in his eyes as he encountered a blank stare from Charles and a vague smile from Judith. "Good heavens!" he exploded. "How could either one of you forget the name of the banker who saved our company from financial ruin?" he demanded, conveniently forgetting that he himself had spent several minutes capturing the memory.

"It was a long time ago, Mr. Mitchell," Paul inserted in an attempt to ease the tension.

"Randolf, please," he murmured in an echo of Paul's earlier request. "But you're correct, of course. It was a long time ago." Randolf smiled at his son. "Charles was still in college." He looked pensive. "He very probably wouldn't have graduated if it hadn't been for you, Paul," he admitted with simple honesty.

Judith gasped in surprise. Charles bristled visibly.

"Dad, really, I'm sure it wasn't as bad as all that!"

"Are you indeed?" Randolf's head snapped up, revealing the shrewd businessman he'd become in the years between his son's college days and Charles's current position as vice president of the firm under discussion. "Then you'd better reorganize your thinking. I was within a hairsbreadth of losing everything." His features grew taut with remembrance. "And I mean literally everything. I had unwisely extended myself. I had been refused help by every banker in Boston and several other cities." His expression eased as he glanced at Paul. "Paul was the only one with the guts to back me. And he did it sight unseen, through my representative." A flush of color tinged his cheeks. "I never thanked you personally."

Paul's smile was easy and meltingly attractive. "You thanked me many times over by confirming the faith I had in your ideas for company expansion and your ability to make them work."

Fascinated by the conversation and the insight it gave her into a previously unsuspected facet of Paul's character, Karen was unconscious of the fact that Paul was still wearing his jacket, that they were all standing in the center of the living room and that the boys had disappeared at some point or other during the discussion.

Paul, on the other hand, was obviously aware of everything that went on around him.

"I wonder if I might remove my jacket?" Though his expression and tone were scrupulously polite, the eyes he directed to Karen had a familiar devilish gleam. "It's quite warm in here."

"Oh!" Karen flushed with embarrassment.

"Good grief!" Randolf muttered.

"How terribly rude of us all!" Judith fluttered.

Charles remained silent, staring resentfully at the cause of the sudden confusion and the reason for a revelation he obviously hadn't enjoyed. But then, he didn't need to say anything; his disapproval of Paul was a palpable force in the atmosphere.

Sparing a frown for Charles, Karen walked to Paul, hand outstretched. "I am sorry, Mr. Vanzant. Please do take off your jacket."

"Paul, I insist." The devilish gleam brightened in his eyes as Paul shrugged out of the garment. Ignoring Charles and his flustered parents for an instant, he smiled for Karen alone. "Thank you." His murmured response encompassed much more than appreciation of being relieved of the heavy outdoor coat.

"You're welcome." Karen's reply encompassed much more than an automatic social response. For the length of a sighing breath, their gazes tangled, meshed, blended.

"Have you had lunch, Paul?" Randolf's inquiring tone revealed his lack of awareness of the dreamlike spell cocooning Karen and Paul. At the same time, his voice shattered the moment.

Paul's lips twisted as he reluctantly glanced away from the soft glow in Karen's eyes. "As a matter of fact,

I completely forgot about lunch." His shoulders lifted in a half shrug. "I quite often do."

"Well, we'll take care of that," Randolf returned heartily. "Won't we, Karen?" But before she could respond, he added, "Karen makes the most fantastic turkey club sandwiches."

On her way to the closet in the hallway, Karen paused in the doorway, her fingers digging into the down-filled jacket. Randolf's reference to sandwiches reminded her of the lunch debris waiting for her on the alcove table. Resigning herself to kitchen duty, she was about to offer Paul something when Randolf spoke again.

"Was there any meat left, Karen?"

As she turned, Karen worked her lips into a smile. "Yes, plenty. Would you like a sandwich and a cup of coffee, Paul?"

"No sandwich, really." Paul smiled at her. "But I would appreciate the coffee."

"And we'll all have a cup with you, keep you company," Randolf said expansively. "How about a piece of pumpkin pie with it? Karen made it, and it's delicious."

"I'm sure it is, but no thank you." Paul glanced at Karen and smiled apologetically. "I'm sorry, but I never really liked pumpkin pie."

It was ridiculous, Karen chided herself. It was childish and silly. And yet she couldn't control the rush of pleasure his admission gave her or the satisfying sense of sharing a link with him, even such a ridiculous, tenuous link.

"That's all right, I—" She started to tell him she also never really liked the dessert, but once again, Randolf hastened to enlighten the other man.

"No need to apologize, Paul. It seems you and Karen

have something in common." He chuckled as Paul sliced a glance at him and arched a questioning eyebrow. "She doesn't like it, either."

"Really?" His tone inflectionless, his expression bland, Paul returned his gaze to Karen; she alone saw the warmth flickering in his dark eyes.

"There were croissants left over at breakfast," she said in her best hostess tones, thrilling to the light that flared in the dark depths of his eyes. "I'd be happy to warm some in the microwave for you if you'd like."

"Yes, thank you." His heated gaze caressed her. "I'd like that very much."

Another link had been forged between them; Karen knew it, but more importantly, she was suddenly aware that Paul realized it, too. Energy flowed through her, sweeping her weariness away. Her step light, she walked from the room, calling over her shoulder, "Make yourselves comfortable. I'll only be a minute."

As had happened after all the previous meals they'd shared, not one of the Mitchells offered assistance. Karen didn't care. Paul was there, back in her house, back in her living room, back in her life. Humming to herself, she made child's play out of the cleaning-up routine and had completed most of it before the coffee was finished.

After serving the coffee and croissants, Karen sat quietly, offering little to the conversation, content to simply be close to Paul once again.

He looked wonderful, she decided, studying him as she sipped the coffee she really didn't want. But there was a subtle change in Paul's appearance that puzzled her. Observing him, listening to him speak, Karen pondered the change, and then the answer struck her. The difference in Paul was not only in appearance but in attitude, as well. For all his aristocratic look, the man she'd first met on the beach had had an uncentered, rudderless look about him. The Paul now seated a few feet from her appeared purposeful and confident, the image of a man in control of his own life.

On reflection, it was obvious to Karen that something had occurred to transform Paul during the weeks they'd been separated. And with the memory of his near-confession of love for her singing in her mind, Karen's pulse leaped with the thought that she was in part responsible for the change in him.

Karen was almost giddy with the possibilities that sprang from her speculative thought and was oblivious to the watchful, scowling expression on Charles's face. Paul, on the other hand, was very much aware of her former husband's discontent.

He's suspicious as hell and jealous because of it.

Even as the thought formed in his mind, Paul silently responded to it. The response was as hard as it was swift.

The hell with Mitchell.

His attention divided between the elder and the younger Mitchell men, Paul was nevertheless aware of Karen's soft gaze and her thorough scrutiny of him. More than anything else in the world, he wanted to be alone with her. While engaging in genial conversation with Randolf, his body tingled with anticipation. While he took Charles's measure, his nerves twanged with impatience. In fact, Paul required every ounce of willpower he possessed to keep himself from insulting the Mitchells by grabbing Karen and rudely walking from the room.

A silent sigh of relief shuddered through him when, at Randolf's suggestion, Karen rose to show Paul to his room. Keeping a respectful distance between them, he followed her from the room and up the stairs. A frown drew his eyebrows together when, at the landing at the top of the staircase, she turned toward the front of the house.

"You're giving me a different room?"

"Yes."

Paul's frown deepened at the evidence of strain in her voice. Assuming she was putting him in a room farther away from hers for appearance' sake, he chided gently, "But I liked the room I had before." He felt a premonitory flash of anger at the way her lips tightened before she replied.

"I can't give you that room, Paul. Charles is using it."

And is Charles using you, too? Paul clenched his teeth to keep from snarling the thought aloud. "I see," he murmured tightly, his anger mingling with fear as he stepped into the unfamiliar bedroom. Charles had been alone with Karen in the house for several weeks. Had he used those weeks to— Paul ruthlessly cut off the thought, actually afraid to follow it to its natural conclusion. The feeling he had experienced earlier of again being outside in the cold returned. Suddenly Paul had to know exactly where he stood with her. Moving decisively, he shut the door, enclosing them in privacy. Denying himself the right to touch her, he held her still by locking his gaze with hers.

"Has there been a reconciliation between you and Charles?"

"No!" Karen denied with a swiftness that was sweetly satisfying to Paul. "Charles is here to recuperate, and that is absolutely all he is here for."

"Then you don't want me to leave?" Paul asked, and held his breath.

"Leave!" Karen's anxious expression sent a shiver of relief through him. "No, Paul, I don't want you to leave."

"I'm delighted to hear you say that—" Paul flashed a rakish grin "—since I had no intentions of leaving anyway."

Randolf monopolized practically every one of Paul's waking minutes throughout what was left of the weekend, so Karen saw very little of her unexpected tenant. And as Judith was forever at Randolf's side, Karen saw too much of Charles for her own peace of mind. Charles had taken to acting very strangely—at least whenever his parents weren't around.

Then, in addition to her resentment at being denied Paul's company and her annoyed concern over Charles's suddenly blatant show of affection for her—usually at mealtimes, when everybody was in attendance—Karen was puzzled by several seemingly unrelated incidents.

The first was not unexpected and occurred at the breakfast table the morning after Paul's arrival. Looking bored, Rand wolfed down his meal and asked to be excused from the table. He then prowled noisily from one room to another until Judith, frowning with concern, asked him what was troubling him, thereby giving him the opening he had obviously been waiting for.

"There's nothing to do," Rand complained in the grating tone of voice only children can achieve.

Charles dismissed Rand with a flick of his hand. "Go look for shells on the beach."

Karen shot a narrowed look at Charles. She had wondered how long his role of "buddy-father" would last.

Karen had never doubted Charles's love for his sons, but she never overestimated his patience with them, either. It had always been thus; Charles could only take children in small doses, even his own children.

"We did that yesterday," Mark whined, jumping in to support his brother.

"For God's sake!" Charles threw his napkin on the table. "There's got to be something that you kids can do to amuse yourselves. Go shoot some baskets."

"Charles, you must not get upset!" Judith cautioned him in a soothing tone.

"How can I not get upset with all the aggravation in this place lately?" he demanded, sweeping his gaze from Rand to Mark and then to Paul.

Staring at his father, Rand's expression betrayed conflicting emotions of remorse and rebellion. Mark began to cry.

"We can't shoot baskets," he sniffled. "The hoop's ready to fall down."

"Well, find something to do," Charles ordered. "And I want you both to stop your damn complaining."

"Charles!" Judith exclaimed.

"Really, son," Randolf chastised.

"Don't swear at the boys." Karen's voice was low but contained a warning edge of steel, and her eyes were cold with purpose. "I mean it, Charles. As long as you're in my house, you will not curse at the boys. I won't tolerate it."

An angry, embarrassed flush climbed from Charles's neck to his cheeks.

"Oh, Karen, I'm sure he didn't mean it the way it sounded!" Judith protested her son's innocence.

"Of course he didn't!" Randolf insisted. "It was common language usage; a slip of the tongue."

"Yes. Common." As she turned to look at the elder Mitchells, Karen's gaze was snagged by watchful dark eyes. Paul hadn't said a word; words were unnecessary. The approval shining from his eyes championed her position. Feeling the strength of two, she faced her former in-laws. "The term is common, and I will not permit it to be used on my sons. Not even by their father." Without a blink, she swung her gaze to Rand and Mark. "If you are bored, you could always occupy yourselves by cleaning up your rooms."

"Aw, Mom!" Making a sour face, Rand stomped from the room. Looking at Karen as if he suspected she'd slipped a cog, Mark trailed after his brother.

"You're not letting them grow up," Charles sniped peevishly, slumping in his chair. "I'd bet they hear a lot worse than 'damn' from the other kids at school."

"I'm sure you're right." Pushing her chair back, Karen rose and began clearing the table. "But they are not going to hear it at home." Juggling the stacked dishes, she walked from the alcove.

As if her action had been a signal, the room emptied quickly. His expression much the same as Mark's when he was pouting, Charles picked up the morning paper and disappeared into the living room. After a murmured discussion, Judith and Randolf announced they were driving into town, then beat a hasty retreat. A smile curving his lips, Paul finished clearing the table.

"You don't have to do that." Not looking at him, afraid to trust herself to even glance at him, Karen methodically stacked the dishes in the dishwasher.

"I know." Just as methodically Paul rinsed the dishcloth and returned to the alcove to wipe the table.

Completing the loading quickly, Karen switched on the machine. "All done," she called to him, escaping into the laundry room. Even over the sound of water running into the kitchen sink as Paul again rinsed the cloth, Karen could hear his soft laughter.

The second incident occurred late in the morning and was really not so much an incident as a set of circumstances that induced an odd sense of confusion in Karen.

She was dusting the living room. The house had been unusually quiet for some time except for Charles, who had been underfoot all morning, making a supreme effort to be ingratiating and charming and getting very little response from Karen.

She was busy, and long since immune to his practiced lines. She was also distracted, which Charles didn't appreciate at all.

Where was everybody?

The question had been nagging at Karen intermittently for over an hour. Paul had vanished from the house before she'd emerged from the laundry room. She hadn't seen hide or hair of either of the boys since they'd stormed from the dining alcove. And, though Judith and Randolf had returned to the house after spending less than an hour in town, they had immediately gone out again, informing Karen that they were going to take a stroll on the beach.

Frowning at her own contrariness for fretting over the quiet after longing for quiet, Karen impatiently pulled her arm free when Charles caught her by the wrist.

"Why don't you leave that till later and sit down and talk to me?" he demanded, every bit as petulant as his thirteen-year-old son when he was down with a cold.

"It has to be done, Charles." Karen repeated the phrase she'd uttered countless times during the weeks he'd been there, wondering, as usual, how he thought the work got done if she didn't do it.

"Can't it wait?"

"For whom?"

Charles subsided with a disgruntled sigh. Smiling wryly, Karen continued dusting. She was arranging a copper potpourri pot on a gleaming, newly dusted table when all the missing persons appeared at once, shattering the quiet.

Judith and Randolf were in fine spirits and ready for lunch, which didn't surprise or confuse Karen.

Paul was quiet but not exceptionally so, which didn't surprise or confuse her, either.

It was Rand's and Mark's attitude that gave her an odd sense of confusion. Their eyes were bright, their cheeks glowed with healthy color from the sting of the cold sea breeze, and not a trace of their earlier pouty moodiness remained in either young face. Saying little, they both consumed their lunch at their usual starving-animal speed. The instant they had drained the last drop of milk from their glasses, Rand and Mark politely asked to be excused from the table. Seconds later, the front door banged shut.

Were they coming down with something? Karen asked herself. They had behaved too well, been too quiet. They hadn't even exchanged one insult, let alone their regulation number!

The third incident was comprised entirely of a familiar sound that registered on Karen later that afternoon.

The house had grown quiet again after lunch, but this time Karen knew, or at least had an idea, where everyone was. The boys had not returned after leaving the lunch table; Karen assumed they were scavenging for shells on the beach. Judith was ensconced in a chair in the living room, lost to the world in a murder mystery she'd picked up in town. Randolf had taken Paul off somewhere to talk business. Charles, irritated and frustrated by Karen's refusal to take anything he said seriously, had gone to his room for a nap. And Karen, realizing she had caught up with the daily chores, had decided to wallow in a long, hot bath.

Her skin rosy from the hot water and softened from the oil beads she'd tossed into it, Karen took her time dressing. Telling herself it had absolutely nothing to do with a desire to appear attractive to Paul, she very carefully applied just a tad more makeup than usual.

Thinking of Paul, remembering him in her room, in her bed, sent icy chills down her spine and warmth to her face. Light-headed with memories and a rush of emotions too numerous to sort out before starting dinner, Karen was already in a pleasant state of confusion as she drifted out of her room.

She heard the sound vaguely as she entered the kitchen but, caught up in an echoing memory of a man telling her he thought he was falling in love, Karen took no notice of it. It was after she had gently come back to earth to face the necessity of preparing a meal for seven hungry people that the sound intruded on her consciousness.

It was the steady thump-thump of a basketball being bounced on a macadam surface and then the solid twang of the ball striking a firmly attached hoop before dropping through a basket.

Chapter Eleven

By itself, the solid sound of a basketball striking the rim of a well-anchored hoop would not have been cause for in-depth consideration for Karen, had it not been for the fact that the looseness of that very hoop had precipitated the scene at breakfast.

Obviously someone had tightened the hoop—but who? Karen frowned in consternation.

Paul. His name leaped into her mind as if it belonged there.

Ridiculous! Karen shook her head, negating the very idea. Aside from the fact that Paul had made the repairs necessary to prepare the house for the coming winter, he had been walking and talking very softly since his arrival the day before, and she couldn't think of a single reason why Paul would feel inclined to accommodate two fractious teenage boys.

Since Karen was equally certain Charles hadn't attempted the job or even thought of doing so, that left Randolf. Yet she found it nearly impossible to imagine her very proper sixty-four-year-old former father-in-law dragging out the necessary tools, then teetering precariously on a ladder, even for his grandsons.

Of course, there was always the possibility that, impatient with the situation, Rand and Mark had decided to take matters into their own hands and fasten the hoop themselves. Possible but improbable. Karen knew her sons. Rand and Mark were both quick and agile when it came to participation in almost any sport. But the other side of their personality coin revealed an almost total lack of coordination in any and all activities that were domestic in origin. In other words, both boys were all thumbs around the house.

Karen readily accepted the responsibility for Rand's and Mark's ineptitude, and she found it hard to believe they had attacked the chore of fixing the hoop, no matter how restless and bored they were. But if not the boys, then who had accomplished the task?

Feeling as though her mind had completed a fruitless circle, Karen shrugged her shoulders. Speculation was getting her nowhere, and she had a meal to prepare. Besides, all she had to do to solve the mystery was raise the question at the dinner table.

Karen broached the subject the minute they were all seated and served. "Did I hear you guys shooting baskets a little while ago?" she asked casually.

"Uh-huh," Rand murmured around the food in his mouth.

"But I thought you couldn't shoot because the hoop was too lose."

Mark grinned happily. "It's fixed now.

"That's nice." Karen held on to her patience, reminding herself that children were only forthcoming when you didn't want them to be. "Who fixed it?"

"Mr. Vanzant." Rand supplied the answer between swallowing and shoveling another forkful of mashed potatoes into his mouth.

"Yeah," Mark concurred. "Mr. Vanzant fixed it right after we got back from our walk on the beach."

Concerned with filling the emptiness in their respective stomachs, neither boy noticed as four pairs of adult eyes homed in on Paul Vanzant. Nor did they note the adult facial expressions displayed, ranging from resentment in their father's face to amazement on the faces of their mother and grandparents to wry amusement on the face of the man the others were staring at.

"You tightened the hoop, Paul?" Randolf asked, sliding a glance over Paul's hand-tailored slacks and cashmere sweater, then to his well-cared-for hands.

"Guilty as charged," Paul confessed.

"Why?" Charles's voice was grating.

Paul slowly turned to give Charles his undivided attention. "Why not?" he countered reasonably.

"It wasn't necessary." Charles glared at Paul. "The handyman would have fixed it Monday."

"To what purpose?" Paul asked reasonably. "The boys won't be here on Monday."

Nonplussed and obviously frustrated, Charles pushed his chair away from the table and stood up. "This discussion is ridiculous!" His lips twisting unpleasantly, he stared at Karen. "All this fuss because two kids can't amuse themselves for one afternoon." Though he didn't add, "And it's all your fault," the accusation was implicit in his tone.

"Charles, please, calm yourself." Judith moved to get up. "This upheaval isn't good for you!"

"I know." He sighed heavily. "I don't feel too well. I think I'll lie down for a while." Without waiting for a reaction, he strode from the room.

Murmuring "Oh, dear!" Judith rushed after him. Jumping up, Randolf was right behind her.

For long seconds, silence weighted the room. Paul broke it gently. "I'm sorry. I certainly didn't mean—"

Karen interrupted him. "It's not your fault."

"No, it's my fault." Rand's cheeks were pale.

Karen's tone became brisk. "No, Rand, it isn't. There was no reason for your father to get worked up over this." Her shoulders moved in a helpless shrug. "I don't know why he was so upset, but then, I never did understand his sudden mood swings."

"Is Daddy okay, Mom?" Mark asked, blinking to stem the tears filling his eyes.

Furious with Charles and silently condemning him for frightening his sons, Karen got up and circled the table. Standing between Rand and Mark, she hugged their trembling bodies close to her own. "I'm sure your dad is fine," she murmured soothingly.

"But, what if—" Rand's voice failed, and he stared up at her fearfully. Before Karen could form words of reassurance, Paul responded to the question Rand could not force himself to ask.

"If your father isn't okay, we'll drive him into Portland to see a doctor."

Rand turned to Paul. His hopeful yet fearful expression caused a wrenching pain in Karen's chest. "You will, Mr. Vanzant? I mean, you will be here with Mom, drive Dad to see a doctor?"

Paul's serious expression was eased by a gentle, understanding smile. "Yes, Rand. I promise you I will be here."

Karen was caught between the urge to smile and the need to sigh. She also understood exactly what kind of reassurance Rand was seeking. Hovering on the edge of manhood, Rand needed to know that there would be another man in the house to take control if Charles suffered another attack.

And she had actually believed she'd instilled in her sons the concept of equality between the sexes. Karen gave in to the sigh.

With one child seeming satisfied, the other had to be heard from. His lower lip trembling, Mark gazed pleadingly at Karen. "Do we have to go back to school tomorrow, Mom?"

"Yes." Karen's tone was clear, with a no-arguments firmness.

"But what if...something happens?" A fresh surge of tears spilled onto Mark's cheeks.

"Then I'll come and get you and bring you home." Paul again answered for Karen. Then he made a suggestion that normally would have elicited surprised protests from Rand and Mark. "But for right now, if you want to feel useful, you could help your mother by clearing the table."

Karen was amazed, not only by his suggestion but by her admittedly pampered sons' reaction to it. They nearly knocked her over in their haste to do his bidding.

Telling herself she should feel angry or at least impatient with Paul for arrogantly taking control from her, Karen could not deny the feeling of relief that swept through her. In his steady, dependable tone of voice, Paul had relieved Rand's and Mark's anxiety and, to a great extent, her own. Karen felt weak with gratitude. At the same time, she felt a sharp twinge of curiosity. It was obvious from their acceptance of his words that both boys believed Paul and trusted him to make good on his promises. How, she wondered, had Paul managed to gain their trust in such a short period of time?

Pondering the question, Karen moved to help with the cleaning up but went still as she remembered Mark telling them that Paul had fixed the basketball hoop after their walk on the beach. But was one walk on the beach enough to instill trust? she asked herself. An answer sprang into her mind immediately. Hadn't she reacted with the same feeling of trust in Paul after a brief meeting on the beach? A frown tugging her eyebrows together, Karen raised her head to stare at him.

"Something wrong?" Paul asked, his eyes darkening with concern.

"No, not wrong." Karen shook her head. "I'm just curious about what you and the kids talked about during your stroll on the beach."

A light of understanding and amusement relieved the darkness shadowing his eyes; a smile eased the tense lines around his mouth. "Heavy stuff," he murmured, slanting a quick glance toward the kitchen to make sure the boys were beyond the reach of his low-pitched voice. "Life and sex and the difficulty of making the big step between the security of adolescence and the responsibility of manhood."

The traditional father-son discussion! Karen was struck speechless at the very idea. How many times had she asked Charles to initiate such a discussion with his sons? Karen didn't have to search for an answer; she had first made the request of Charles when Rand had celebrated his thirteenth birthday more than two years ago. In his familiar, unconcerned way, Charles had laughed, called her old-fashioned and insisted the boys could very probably instruct him on the subject. Of course, it had been a cop-out for Charles. Karen hadn't been in the least surprised; Charles had been copping out on everything serious all his adult life. But Paul was very obviously cut from much stronger cloth, Karen concluded—and not for the first time.

"You don't approve?"

Realizing that she was probably scowling, Karen smiled at him. "It isn't that I don't approve." She lifted her shoulders in a slight shrug. "I'm just surprised that you'd bother, that's all."

"Bother?" Paul repeated, giving her an odd look. "It wasn't a bother. I enjoyed our conversation." His smile was soft with reminiscence. "It's been a long time since I engaged in that type of basic discussion." He laughed. "Besides, it exercised my mind. Those kids of yours are very bright. They tossed some tough questions at me."

Parental pride flowed through Karen, warming her and easing the tension left over from the scene Charles had created. "They have their difficult moments but—" she smiled hesitantly as she raised her eyes to his "—they're pretty good kids, aren't they?" Karen wasn't quite sure why his opinion was so important to her; she only knew it was.

Paul's answering smile glowed in his eyes before it reached his lips. "They are very good kids, Karen. You have every right to be proud of them." His lips curved with heart-touching tenderness as he lifted his hand to her face.

"Mom?" Rand's call halted Paul's fingers an inch from her cheek, and with a philosophical smile, he drew his hand away.

"Yes?" Karen responded, strangely breathless.

"The dishwasher's loaded and running and everything's cleaned up. Can me and Mark watch TV now?"

Karen corrected his grammar automatically. "Can Mark and I."

"Aw, Mom!" Rand's groan blended with Paul's low chuckle. "Can we?"

Without conscious thought, Karen looked at Paul with a silent plea for his opinion of the request. A flicker of surprise moved across his face and briefly widened his eyes, quickly followed by an expression of deep pleasure. Holding her gaze with his, he slowly nodded his head. Again without thought, Karen acted on his judgment.

"Yes, you may," she called, laughing as the boys took off like a shot, as if afraid she'd change her mind if they didn't disappear from her sight immediately.

Paul went still, his expression expectant; then he grinned. "Isn't the silence wonderful?" he asked in a stage whisper.

"Beautiful," Karen breathed on a sigh.

"Let's escape." Paul's eyes gleamed with playfulness, and his grin broadened.

He looked so much like a little boy up to mischief that Karen burst out laughing. "Escape!" she gasped. "To where?"

"The beach?" One dark eyebrow arched rakishly.

"But it's freezing outside!"

The slanting glance he gave her had more the look of the devil than any little boy Karen had ever known. "Yes, but consider the fun we could have keeping each other warm."

Fun! Try as she might, Karen couldn't remember the last time she'd done something just for the fun of it. And if she was honest with herself, she had to admit that his suggestion had appeal, a lot of appeal. Yet she hesitated, telling herself she really shouldn't leave the house. The boys might need her for something. She had guests. Charles was obviously not feeling well. No, she really shouldn't leave the house. But...Karen looked into Paul's eyes and was lost.

"I'd love a breath of fresh air."

The words were barely out of her mouth before Paul grasped her hand and took off down the hall to the closet. Cautioning her to be quiet by placing one finger across his lips, he carefully removed their jackets. After helping her with hers, he urged her toward the back door, pulling his jacket on as he walked. A loud sigh of relief whooshed through his lips as he shut the door behind them.

"Ah, alone at last," he said teasingly, reaching for her hand. "I was beginning to think I'd have to kidnap you to have a private conversation."

Laughing spontaneously, Karen slid her hand into his and felt a thrill as he entwined her fingers in his. "Where would you kidnap me to?" she asked, feeling suddenly lighthearted and young again. "I hope someplace decadent and exotic," she added before he could respond.

"Decadent and exotic, hmm?" Paul murmured. He drew her with him as he stepped off the veranda. "I'll have to think about that." His expression somber, contemplative, he strolled onto the beach.

Though cold, the night was still. Instead of their more usual thundering rush to crash into the beach, the ocean waves swelled gently before caressing the shore with a murmured swish. "Take your time," Karen said, tilting her head back to gaze up at the brilliance of millions of stars and one incredibly beautiful pale yellow moon. "What a gorgeous night!" she whispered in an awed tone. "Just look at that sky."

Lifting his head, Paul stared at the heavens a moment

before transferring his gaze to her face. "I'd rather look at you." Untwining their fingers, he released her hand to bring his arm up and around her shoulders, drawing her body close to the warmth of his. Lowering his head, Paul brushed his lips over her ear. "You're beautiful, Karen," he murmured. "And much more inspiring to me than the light of trillions of stars."

Excitement charged through Karen, stealing her breath, clouding her senses. Need nipped at the heels of excitement, the need to hold him, touch him, taste him. Her lips parted with eager anticipation as he drew his mouth in a tantalizing line to hers.

"Oh, Paul." Her voice was a whisper that misted his lips.

"Say it again." With maddening slowness, he brushed his lips back and forth over hers. "I want to hear you say my name again."

"Paul."

"Lord, Karen, I missed you unbearably." Raising his other arm, he crushed her willing body to his. "I thought I'd go crazy with wanting you while we were apart," he groaned, taking her mouth fiercely.

His kiss was hard, impatient, fiery and wonderful. Curling her arms around his neck, Karen clung to him, taking everything from him, giving everything to him. Had she actually convinced herself she could continue to exist without ever again experiencing the spiraling heat and excitement only Paul could generate inside her? she asked herself muzzily, stroking his teasing tongue with her own. The mere thought of never again knowing the safety of his embrace, feeling the power of his kiss, sent a wave of cold fear through her, and her mouth became desperate with hunger.

Paul's hands moved restlessly over Karen's bulky

jacket, searching for the soft woman beneath the heavy material. He muttered a curse as he drew his lips from hers to explore her face. "I want to undress you," he murmured, skimming his lips over her closed eyelids. "I need to feel you, all of you, against me."

"Yes," Karen sighed. Then reality intruded. "Paul, we can't!" she cried.

"I know." His breath shuddered from his body as he rested his forehead against hers. "I know."

They stood clasping one another, silently comforting each other until the cold penetrated their jackets to chill their bodies. Paul dropped his arms and stepped back when Karen shivered involuntarily.

"You're freezing," he said, moving away from her. "I must take you inside."

Although Karen knew he was right, she held out against reason. "But we didn't have our conversation."

"No?" Paul asked with wry amusement. "I thought we said a great deal." Taking her hand in his, he started for the house. They were almost to the veranda steps before he spoke again. "Randolf tells me that he and Judith are driving the kids back to school tomorrow."

"Yes. Then they'll go on to Boston." Karen glanced at him. "Why?"

Paul answered with a question. "Charles will be staying here?"

Karen lowered her gaze to the veranda steps. "Yes. At least until after the Christmas holidays."

"Then so will I." Paul's voice was soft, but steely with determination.

"You knew him before, didn't you?"

Monday mornings had never been Karen's best times and being interrogated by a moody ex-husband on a

Monday morning following a tiring holiday was the absolute pits. Gritting her teeth, Karen slowly turned away from the coffee maker to face Charles.

His expression stormy, his lips flattened into a thin line of disapproval, Charles glared at her from the doorway.

"Him?" Karen asked, being deliberately obtuse.

"Vanzant." Not unlike a toddler in a fit of temper, Charles stomped to the table and dropped onto a chair. "You knew him before he arrived here Friday afternoon, didn't you?"

Karen considered denial or evasion for a moment but decided it wasn't worth the effort. "Yes, I met Paul over a month ago," she replied quietly.

"How did you meet him?" he asked with sharp suspicion.

Karen arched her eyebrows at his persistence but again answered honestly. "He was looking for a room. Calvin Muthard sent him here."

"But hadn't you closed the bed-and-breakfast by then?" Charles didn't attempt to hide his annoyance; he had never approved of her opening the house to paying guests.

"Yes." A hint of her thinning patience tightened her tone; Charles chose to ignore.

"You let him stay here even though you had closed the house for the season?"

"That's right."

Anger flushing his cheeks, Charles studied her narrowly. When he spoke again, his voice was low and not at all pleasant. "You were lovers, weren't you?"

Karen's patience snapped, and so did she. "That's none of your business."

"Which means you were," Charles snapped back. "Weren't you?"

"Yes, we were." The cool, controlled response came not from Karen but from the man standing in the doorway to the veranda. "So what?" Paul added, sauntering into the room.

The color deepened in Charles's cheeks, indicating his mounting anger. "You're intruding on a private conversation, Vanzant," Charles said nastily.

"Rude of me, I know," Paul drawled, crossing the room to stand beside Karen. "But since I'm directly involved, I think I'll continue to intrude."

As irritated as Karen was by Charles's audacity in presuming to question her about her private life, Karen felt a jolt of alarm as his breathing increased and his color became mottled. She took a hesitant step toward him. "Charles, are you feeling all right?"

Charles glared at her. "No, I'm not all right." His chest heaved as he inhaled swiftly. "I'd hoped the weekend would be good for me, but I guess it was too much too soon." A thoughtful, almost crafty expression flickered over his face. His voice dwindled to a sigh. "I'm tired."

Really alarmed, Karen rushed to his side. "Do you have any pain?" Her voice was strained by a concern that was obvious to both men. Karen was too busy taking Charles's pulse to notice the smirk of satisfaction he aimed at Paul

"No—" he sighed heavily "—well, just a twinge."

Karen's throat closed. What in the world would she do if Charles suffered another attack right in her kitchen? In an unconsciously revealing move, she turned to Paul. "Will you drive us to the hospital in Portland?"

"Certainly," Paul replied promptly.

"I don't think it's necessary." Charles's voice overlapped Paul's. "At least not yet," he added when he noticed the mildly skeptical look on Paul's face. "It's gone now. I think I just need some peace and quiet for a few days."

"Are you positive?" Karen asked anxiously.

"Yes," he insisted weakly. "I just need some rest."

The tightness in Karen's throat eased as she saw the color recede from his cheeks. She exhaled a sigh of relief. "Can I get you something?"

"I could drink a cup of decaffeinated coffee," he said tiredly. "If you don't mind?"

"Of course not!" Karen whirled around to get the coffee, and missed the smug look Charles leveled at Paul.

That morning set the pattern for the two weeks that followed, for Charles literally kept Karen on the run. He seldom complained, but then he didn't have to complain. All Charles had to do to get Karen's undivided attention was grimace faintly and moan softly. Karen rarely found more than a few moments to be alone with Paul, and so she didn't notice his expression growing harder and more stern with each passing day.

To Karen's relief, Charles refrained from mentioning her relationship with Paul. In fact, except for the occasional periods when he displayed discomfort, Charles couldn't have been more charming or easier to get along with. His good mood ended with a burst of childish temper at the beginning of the second week of December.

Before they had left Boston, Dr. Rayburn had made arrangements for Charles to consult with a specialist in Portland. Karen had driven Charles into Portland for his first appointment the second week of November. At that time, the doctor had been satisfied with Charles's progress and had said he would like to see him in a month. Karen set the fuse to Charles's temper by suggesting Paul drive them into Portland so that Charles could keep his appointment.

"Isn't it enough that I have to bear sharing this house with your lover?" Charles shouted at her. "I will be damned if I'll let you coop me up in a car with him!"

Karen backed down. Paul's expression became grim.

"He's using you," Paul said harshly, capturing Karen alone in the hallway as she was putting on her coat the morning of Charles's appointment.

Karen shrugged helplessly. "I know. But he's not well, and I—" Her voice failed when she saw the anger that flashed in Paul's eyes.

"Isn't he?" Paul's eyes glittered behind his narrowed lids. "I'm beginning to have strong doubts about the seriousness of Charles's condition."

Since Karen had doubts of her own, she could hardly argue. Her shoulders rose, then dropped tiredly. "Perhaps the specialist will allow Charles to go back to work and resume more normal activities."

Paul arched one eyebrow. "Will you be present during the examination?"

"Well, no, but—"

Paul cut her off abruptly. "That's what I thought. Which means you'll have no way of knowing what the doctor says to him, will you?" Karen conceded his point by shaking her head slowly. Paul's expression gentled. "Karen, I think it would be to your advantage to have your own consultation with the specialist. For all you know, the doctor may have told him he could return to Boston after the last visit."

Though Karen didn't want to accept the possibility that Charles was deliberately extending his recuperative period, she knew that he was capable of doing so should it suit his purposes. She simply couldn't comprehend what his purpose could be in this instance. She frowned at Paul. "But Charles has always said that this is the dullest place on the East Coast. What reason could he have for wanting to remain here?"

"You haven't figured that out yet?" Paul's lips slanted wryly. "Charles wants to stay because he wants you."

Karen blinked in amazement. "Oh, Paul, that's ridiculous! Charles and I have been divorced for over five years. Why would he suddenly decide he wants me?"

Paul ran a cool but very flattering glance over her gently curved body. "I can think of many reasons," he said dryly, "because I share them."

"But he had me and let me go!" Karen protested.

"Did he really let you go?" Paul countered. "Or did you walk away from him?"

"I didn't walk, I ran!" Karen exclaimed.

"Did he try to stop you or talk you into staying with him?"

Karen lifted her head. "I didn't give him the opportunity."

"Precisely."

Karen still couldn't accept the idea. "But it's been over five years, Paul," she said doggedly.

"Five years of self-indulgence," he retorted. "Five years of who knows how many different women. Five years of instability. And now a heart attack has made him face his own mortality." Paul paused, then shot another question at her. "Has he ever mentioned a current, er...relationship?"

Karen sighed as acceptance finally shuddered through her. "Yes. While he was in the hospital, Charles told me he had recently ended a relationship." She moistened her lips, then went on in a whisper, "He admitted to me that none of the relationships he'd engaged in had been as satisfying for him as our marriage had been."

"There you go."

Karen stared at Paul for long seconds. Then she nodded once, sharply. "I'll talk to the doctor."

Chapter Twelve

As it turned out, Karen didn't need to consult with the specialist. Charles himself made the meeting unnecessary with the first words out of his mouth on leaving the doctor's office.

"Good news," he said jauntily, clasping her arm to draw her with him toward the door. "The doctor said that if I continue to improve at the same rate I can go back to work after the holidays."

Since she had decided to consult with the specialist, Karen was tugging against the hold he had on her arm, resisting his efforts to get her out of the office. His announcement took all resistance out of her, and she allowed him to lead her from the building to the car.

"Well, isn't that good news?" Charles asked impatiently when she didn't respond immediately.

"Yes, very good news." Karen carefully pried his

hand from her arm. "I'm glad he's satisfied with the progress you're making.

"I thought you would be."

Suspicion rose in Karen's mind at his smug tone and expression. It appeared more than a little odd to her that immediately after Paul's suggestion to her about having a talk with the doctor, Charles had suddenly been given good news. Had Charles overheard the discussion between her and Paul earlier? she wondered, frowning as she unlocked the car. He had supposedly been in his room, getting ready to leave for the drive into Portland, but... Karen slanted a glance at Charles as she slid behind the wheel. Could he have been standing in the upstairs hall, eavesdropping? Though Karen didn't like to believe that Charles would listen in on a private conversation, she knew Charles was capable of listening at keyholes if he thought it to his own advantage.

"Is something wrong?"

Karen blinked. "What?"

"You've been scowling at the steering wheel for several minutes," Charles said. "Is something wrong with it?"

"Oh! No." Smiling faintly, Karen thrust the key into the ignition and started the car. "I was, ah, thinking." And getting nowhere with my thoughts, she added silently. Backing out of the parking space, Karen decided that speculation was pointless regarding her suspicions both about whether Charles had indulged in a little eavesdropping and whether the specialist had in fact given Charles his good news during his previous visit in November.

As she drove out of the lot and into the stream of traffic, Karen mentally shrugged. What Charles was up to, for whatever reason, didn't really matter. In less than a month he'd be returning to Boston. She'd be free, with the time and the opportunity to explore the possibility of a lasting relationship with Paul.

Paul. Karen silently repeated his name, thrilling to the image of him that filled her mind, and nearly missed a streetlight that was turning red. Waiting for the light to change, Karen got lost in a dream of a tall, aristocratic-looking banker. Charles's voice shattered her pleasant musings.

"I want to celebrate. Let's have dinner in the most expensive restaurant in town."

Karen frowned and eased her foot from the brake as the light turned green. She didn't want to have dinner in any restaurant in town, expensive or otherwise. She wanted to go home to Paul. Searching for an excuse to reject his suggestion, she scanned the sky.

"I think I'd just as soon go straight home, Charles," she said reasonably. "I really don't like the look of that sky."

"Oh, come on, Karen. Your boyfriend will be all right on his own for one day." Charles snickered and added, "And I use the term *boy* loosely."

Karen's fingers tightened around the steering wheel. "That's not very funny, Charles." Her voice was as tight as her grip.

"You're damned right it's not funny!" Charles twisted in the seat to glare at her. "The man's almost as old as my father, old enough to be your father. I never realized that you had a father fixation, Karen." He paused for breath. Karen opened her mouth to protest, but he didn't let her get a word out. "Is that why you left me? Was I too young, too modern for you?"

His attack was unwarranted, unfair and grossly incorrect. Karen was suddenly angrier than she'd ever been in her life, so angry she couldn't speak for a moment. Twisting the wheel, she drove onto the access ramp to Interstate 95. She was going too fast, and the car swayed.

"For crying out loud!" Charles exclaimed. "Are you trying to land us in a heap by the side of the road?"

Karen eased her foot from the accelerator, then carefully merged with the stream of traffic. She didn't trust herself to speak until the car was moving along smoothly at a legal fifty-five miles per hour.

"Any more remarks like that and I'll happily dump you by the side of the road." Karen's voice was harsh; her fingers trembled as they gripped the wheel.

"I could've had another heart attack," Charles whined. "You scared the hell out of me."

Karen counted to ten, and as she did she counted the number of times Charles had verbally hit her with the heart-attack shtick since she'd brought him to Maine. Memories flashed rapidly across her mind, memories of all the times Charles had frightened her with complaints of shortness of breath, twinges of pain and excessive weariness. The last time had been the night before, while she and Paul had laughed together as they cleaned up the kitchen after dinner. Suddenly Karen felt like the world's most gullible fool.

Damn him! she thought, but corrected herself immediately. No, she should be damning herself! For while it was true that Charles had effortlessly manipulated her for weeks with the threat of another impending attack, she had allowed him to manipulate her, just as she'd allowed him to manipulate her with sweet talk and promises during the years of their marriage.

Hadn't she learned anything in the years since their divorce? Karen asked herself with sharp impatience. She had believed herself mature, adult, independent, but...

Karen's lips tightened with self-disdain. Due to her own immature, self-imposed mental state of guilt and remorse because of her relationship with Paul, she had been the perfect patsy for Charles. And as Charles had always been an opportunist by nature, he had immediately identified and capitalized on her weakness. In truth, Karen knew she had earned every second of worry and torment Charles had given her.

"Aren't we going to stop for dinner?" Charles's voice sounded much the same as Mark's when he was pouting and also betrayed the uneasiness he was feeling because of her lengthy silence.

"No, I told you I want to go right home." Karen's tone was vaguely disinterested. She was much too angry to care if Charles was discontent or disappointed. Her eyes narrowed on the road, and the first fat snowflakes plopped onto the windshield. Karen could have used the snow as an excuse but couldn't be bothered.

Obviously aware that her desire to get home had little to do with the weather, Charles didn't mention it, either. In his frustration he took a verbal stab at her, striking her most vulnerable spot.

"He's a grandfather," he sniped nastily.

"So what?" Karen said, unconsciously echoing Paul's bland tone of a few weeks earlier.

"He's too old for you."

Karen shrugged, and that was when Charles struck.

"I'd bet Rand immediately figured it out that you and Grandpa were getting it on." He sneered. "And I'd also bet that by now Rand has painted a pretty lurid picture for Mark." Patently satisfied with the shocked gasp he'd wrenched from her, Charles smiled smugly and settled into his seat.

"Shut up!" Karen's demand lacked strength, for as

appalled as she was by his crudity, she was more appalled by the content in his deliberate choice of words.

"Why?" Charles shot back, digging at her vulnerability. "Don't tell me you didn't realize that Rand had to get wise to what was going on? The kid's not stupid, you know." His lips twisted. "Paul betrays himself and you every time he gives you one of those hot, hungry looks." He raked her body with a jealous, thwarted glare. "And you're no better when you look at him. It's obvious to anyone with eyes to see that you and he are lovers. And it's pretty disgusting."

Karen knew that Charles was pulling strings, playing his game of manipulation, and yet she felt sick at the image that rose in her mind. The image was of Rand, his expression cold with disgust...disgust with her.

No, oh, please, no! The cry of despair rang in her mind. She was in love with Paul, so deeply and irrevocably in love with him that she no longer felt ashamed of the physical relationship they'd shared. In fact, she longed to repeat it. She felt empty and incomplete without Paul beside her at night, making her a part of him by becoming a part of her. She believed Charles's assertion that her feelings were revealed when she looked at Paul; Karen had seen those feelings reflected back to her in Paul's expression. But had Rand noticed, misinterpreted and been disgusted by the proof of what she and Paul were feeling for one another? Karen shuddered at the thought.

"Not a pleasant consideration, is it?"

Oddly, it was the complacent purr of Charles's tone that reactivated Karen's common sense. Another image filled her mind, the image of Rand as he'd looked the day he'd left to go back to school. Rand had hugged Karen and thrust his hand out for Paul's handshake.

Rand's expression had revealed love for her and respect for Paul. The memory was clear and revealed Charles's willingness to use any means, even his own son, to attain his desires.

Suddenly sheer fury swept through Karen, dispersing weeks of accumulated doubts and uncertainty. And, just as suddenly, she knew what she had to do. She'd had enough of Charles Mitchell and his machinations.

Her decision made, Karen turned off the interstate at the next exit, circled around and drove onto it again, heading back to Portland.

Alert, his eyes gleaming with victory, Charles favored her with his most dazzling smile. "I knew if you thought about the situation you'd see things my way." His voice was as smooth as glass, his tone all gracious condescension. "I'll have a talk with Rand sometime during the Christmas holidays and explain the circumstances to him."

"Circumstances?" Karen asked, deliberately nudging him into talking himself into a sealed box. "What circumstances?"

"Why concerning you and Vanzant, of course." Charles flicked his hand as if to dismiss the older man. "I'll explain to Rand that this kind of thing is natural for a woman your age, one who has been on her own for too long. Rand's old enough to understand how a lonely woman could be seduced by an older, experienced man." His smile nearly earned him a smack in the face. "But enough of that. I'll take care of that problem at Christmas. Right now, I want to know what restaurant you have in mind for dinner."

Karen was hard-pressed not to laugh out loud. The man's conceit was outweighed only by his gift for self-deception. A woman her age, indeed! She didn't even waste time looking at him.

"I haven't any restaurant in mind, Charles," she said blandly. "I'm driving you to the airport." Though several inches separated them, Karen could actually feel him stiffen.

"Airport?" he repeated starkly. "What for?"

"Why the obvious, Charles." Karen flashed a brilliant smile in his direction. "I'm going to toss you on the first available plane to Boston."

"But the doctor said I was to have two more weeks of recuperation!"

"But he didn't stipulate where, did he?" she countered.

"But my heart!"

"My foot!" Karen spared a glance from the wet, snowy highway to sear him with a disdainful look. Merely returning her gaze to the road was a dismissal. "You have used your health against me for the last time, Charles." Her voice was devoid of compassion. "I'm not responsible for your life or your physical condition—you are." A wry smile curved her lips. "But I'll stop by the doctor's office and ask him if it's safe for you to fly if it will calm your fears."

"I'm not afraid!" Charles said heatedly, sounding exactly like his thirteen-year-old son. "And you don't have to stop by the doctor's office. I wouldn't stay with you now if a dozen specialists advised me not to travel." He hunched down in the bucket seat and thrust his jaw out belligerently. "I can't imagine why I ever considered starting over again with you," he muttered.

"I can't, either," Karen said in amazement. "Because to tell you the truth, Charles, you didn't stand an ice cube's chance in hell...Paul Vanzant or not."

* * *

Several hours later, Karen was again driving on Interstate 95, and though the snowfall was growing steadily heavier, her spirits were as light as a spring breeze. Most of those hours had been spent anxiously waiting at the airport, as they had learned on arrival that the Boston flight was fully booked. For a few moments, Charles had reverted to his attitude of superiority, but after one close look at Karen's implacable expression he'd agreed to wait on standby. To her relief, when the Boston flight was called, there were three no-shows, probably due to the weather. When the plane took off, Charles was on it.

Peering at the highway through the curtain of lacy white flakes, Karen smiled and decided she loved the cold, wet stuff. Her fingers were icy and her toes were cold, but Karen didn't mind; she was eagerly looking forward to a warm bed and an even warmer Paul Vanzant. Karen laughed aloud at the prospect.

''Where the hell are they?'' Unaware of growling the question aloud, Paul followed it up with a muttered string of curses that would have curled a maiden lady's eyelashes.

Prowling through the house like a wild thing, he strode to the long, narrow windows facing the road. Pulling the drapes aside, Paul frowned at the unbroken ground cover of white obscuring the lines between the driveway and the front lawn.

Speculations and fears, each more chilling than the rising wind, tumbled through his mind, freezing Paul in place. Had Karen had car trouble? Had there been an accident on the slick road? Had she been injured? Had Charles prevailed and talked Karen into spending the night in Portland—with him?

"I'll ruin the son of a—" Paul clamped his lips together. He knew that driving on the thin layer of snow had to be a nightmare. Part of him was hoping she'd decided not to attempt the trip until the storm was over and road crews had cleared the highway. Yet another more possessive part of Paul rebelled at the idea of Karen being snowbound with Charles.

Paul knew, had known after being in the house one day, that Charles was determined to win Karen back again. And Paul was equally determined to prevent Charles from succeeding.

"Karen's mine." This time Paul was fully aware of speaking out loud and of the harsh sound of his voice in the too-quiet room. Why hasn't she called? he asked himself for the dozenth time. His narrowed gaze scanned the white landscape. His patience thinned. "Dammit! If she doesn't call or get home soon, I'm going after her!" The vow was no sooner out of Paul's mouth than the eerie glow of a car's headlights pierced the hazy swirl of white. Paul was across the room and to the door before the car made the turn into the driveway.

"Where the hell have you been?"

Paul's rough voice was like a crooning caress to Karen. Swinging the car door shut, Karen trudged through the snow, unconcerned with the cold wet soaking her shoes. A pang speared through her chest at the sight of Paul moving toward her, his tall frame outlined by the blaze of light from the house. He looked so natural coming from her house, so perfectly right.

"I've been tying up a few loose ends," she replied, a carefree smile curving her lips.

"What?" Paul started to return her smile, but before she could say another word he frowned and glanced around sharply. "Where's Charles?" Draping a sweater-clad arm around her damp shoulders, he turned and hurried her into the welcoming warmth of the house.

Karen didn't answer until the solid thunk of the closing door shut out the keening wail of the wind. "Charles is on a plane headed for Boston."

Paul had placed his hands on her shoulders to help her remove her coat. At her response, his fingers flexed, digging into the material. "On a plane," he repeated with soft incredulity. "But how? Why?"

Slipping out of her coat, Karen whirled to face him. "How? Very simply. I drove him to the airport and waited until the plane took off." Her head lifted with an unconscious regality. "Why? Because I was thoroughly fed up with his manipulative, disruptive influence. In short, I tossed him out."

The garment he was clutching forgotten, Paul stared at her in disbelief for a moment, his lips twitching against a smile. "But was that safe?" he asked somberly, winning the battle with his mouth.

"I hope so." Karen drew in a deep breath as she turned to the hall phone table. "And I intend to find out right now."

Gazing down at the jacket still clasped in his hands, Paul absently hung it in the closet. "You're calling his doctor?" he asked as she punched in the Portland number.

"Yes. I didn't get the opportunity to talk to him earlier...." She broke off, then said, "Oh, yes, this is Karen Mitchell. I'd like to speak to Dr. Jennaue, please. Yes, it is important." While she was waiting, Karen tapped her fingernails on the smooth tabletop and glanced at Paul. "I'll tell you all about it after I've spoken to the doctor."

Paul inclined his head. "All right."

"There's a problem, Ms. Mitchell?" Dr. Jennaue asked with direct briskness.

"I'm not sure, Doctor." Karen's hand tightened reflexively on the telephone receiver. "I, er, put Charles on a plane for Boston a while ago, and I wanted your professional opinion on whether that was a safe thing to do," she said quickly, then immediately held her breath.

"Safe? Why shouldn't it be safe? I told Mr. Mitchell last month that he could resume normal activities—within reason, of course. Surely he told you?" Impatience could be heard in the doctor's tone.

Karen's eyes narrowed on hearing confirmation of her suspicions. Charles had been lying to her for weeks—forever! Gathering her thoughts, she answered, "Ah, yes, but I wasn't positive if flying came under the heading of reasonable activities. Thank you, Doctor, and I'm sorry I bothered you."

"No bother at all," the doctor said, then contradicted himself by hanging up without the courtesy of a farewell.

As her finger depressed the disconnect button, Karen gazed at Paul. "Charles was lying. The doctor told him to resume normal activities during his visit last month." As she relayed the information to Paul, she punched in another number, long-distance this time.

"You're calling the school?" Paul correctly guessed.

"Yes."

It required a few moments, but finally Rand's anxious voice traveled across miles of telephone wire.

"Mom, is something wrong?"

"No!" Karen said at once. "No, Rand," she went on in a calm voice. "I just thought you should know that, with the doctor's permission, I took your father to the airport to catch the late-afternoon plane to Boston."

There was dead silence for several seconds. During

those agonizing moments, Karen fought against the urge to launch into defensive speech, explaining to her son that she couldn't tolerate his father's presence a minute longer. The inner battle was hard-fought, but she won.

"You kicked him out, didn't you?" Rand demanded.

Karen thought about evasion and immediately rejected the thought; that was Charles's method, not hers. "Yes, Rand, I kicked him out." She held her breath and waited for condemnation.

"About time, too." Rand's voice didn't crack at all; his tone had the depth of growing maturity. "I was wonderin' how long it would take before you got fed up with his bellyachin'."

Tears rushed to Karen's eyes, and she blinked against the sting. A long, muscular arm circled her waist, and a warm male body pressed reassuringly against hers, giving her the strength to whisper her son's name. "Oh, Rand."

"I—I love Dad, Mom, but that doesn't mean I can't see him for what he is, you know."

"I know." Karen made no attempt to stem the flow of tears running down her face. Obviously misreading the situation, Paul tightened his arm protectively and pressed the strength of his body closer to hers. Literally surrounded by understanding and protection, Karen suddenly laughed. "I'm so proud of you, Rand. You're going to be a fantastic man."

"Yeah, I know." Like most young people uncomfortable with praise, Rand reverted to wisecracks. "Ain't you the lucky one?"

"Yes, darling, I really am," Karen responded softly, seriously. Rand was quiet for a moment, and she heard him swallow. When he spoke again, his voice was husky.

"Is Mr. Vanzant still there?"

Karen's feeling of well-being wavered, and she stiffened. Again she considered and rejected evasion. "Yes, he is."

"Good deal," Rand said briskly. "I worry about you being all alone up there...and, ah...I like Mr. Vanzant, Mom. I kinda think he's good for you. Will you tell him I said hello?"

Karen didn't attempt to conceal the relief she felt at receiving her son's words of approval. "Yes, of course I will," she choked out. "I'd better let you get back to whatever you were doing. I'll see you in two weeks."

"Yeah, Christmas! I can't wait." Rand laughed. Then he said softly, "And Mom? Don't worry about Mark. I'll explain everything to him."

Wondering if the day would ever come when her son ceased to amaze her, Karen cleared her throat. "Thank you, Rand. I love you very much."

"Yeah, I know." Rand's voice was husky again. "I love you back. Bye, Mom."

Karen's voice trembled as she said goodbye, her hand trembled as she cradled the receiver, and her eyelashes trembled as she blinked against a fresh surge of tears.

"Problems?" Paul murmured, tightening his arm around her waist even more.

Snuggling closer to his warmth, Karen shook her head. "Just the opposite." She sniffled and laughed. "My boy's growing up, Paul. Not only does he understand his father and accept him for what he is, but Rand understands the situation between you and me."

"Indeed?" Paul moved his hips slightly, making her aware of the fullness of his arousal.

"Yes!" Karen gasped, shivering in response. "He—Rand said he's glad you are here with me." Her breathing grew erratic as he slowly moved his hips. "Um, he said he likes you and thinks you're good for me. Oh!" She gasped again as his free hand sought her breast.

"Rand's a bright, savvy kid and I like him, too." Relaxing his arm, Paul turned her, drawing her body into intimate contact with his. "And I like Mark." Lowering his head, he lightly touched his mouth to her slightly parted lips. "And I like you best of all," he whispered, wrenching a moan from her by piercing her mouth with the tip of his tongue.

"Oh, Paul." Despite her wet, cold toes, Karen was suddenly burning up, on fire for him. Curling her arms around his waist, she arched her body into the heat of his. A sound of hunger murmured deep in her throat when he stroked his tongue along her lower lip. "Oh, Paul, I ache for you!" she admitted in a whispery cry, past the point of sensuous game-playing.

"And you can obviously feel how much I need you," he muttered, nipping gently at her lip. "So," he murmured, laughter edging his tone, "what are we doing standing here in the hallway?"

"Good question." Stepping back, Karen smiled and slid her hand into his. "It's been a long, eventful day."

Paul didn't have to be coaxed. Spinning around, he strode to the stairs, tugging her with him. As they mounted the stairs, he slanted a look at her. His dark eyes glittered with promise. "The way I'm feeling now, I think I can guarantee that it will be an even longer, much more eventful night."

Weeks of separation followed by weeks of being together without the opportunity to actually be together had created a voracious mutual hunger approaching starvation. In a replay of their first time together, they left the bedroom door standing wide open in their haste to touch, taste, caress and tear the clothes from one another's body. The bed was a haven eagerly sought.

Paul's mouth was hot and hungry on Karen's as his body joined with hers in a joyous rush. It was wild and wonderful. It was electric and sweet. It was homecoming. Satisfaction was swiftly attained and just as swiftly forgotten in the renewing heat of desire.

Paul's stamina was startling, and Karen found the strength to match his. Paul was dominant, Karen submissive. In turn, Karen became the aggressor, Paul the supplicant. Their reward was exhausted repletion.

While the snowstorm raged outside, whipping the roiling waves into a white-crested fury, rattling windows and blanketing the land in a coat of pristine white, Karen and Paul slept deeply, wrapped in the warmth of one another's arms.

Sprawled luxuriously across Paul's silver-flecked, dark-haired chest, Karen woke to the lulling sound of a calm sea and the whitish light of a snow-covered world. Feeling tired but contented, she snuggled closer to Paul's warmth and rubbed her cheek against the springy curls of his silky chest hair.

"Good morning." Paul's gently expelled breath ruffled the hair on top of her head.

Karen's lips curved into a satisfied smile as she tilted her head to the side to gaze up at him. "Good morning. Did you sleep well?"

"Hmm." Paul's eyes gleamed as he dipped his lightly bristled chin in a nod. "I feel terrific. How about you?"

Karen's smile deepened. "I feel wonderful." She paused for effect. "And utterly exhausted."

Paul's lips curved into a smile of supreme male satisfaction. "I did promise you an eventful night."

"You kept your promise." She was quiet a moment as memory stirred. Then she laughed with delight.

Paul's smile widened. "What's so amusing?"

"I just remembered something Charles said."

A frown banished Paul's smile. "What did he say?" he asked, his arms tightening around her possessively.

Karen's laughter bubbled. "He said you were too old for me."

Instead of joining in her laughter as she'd expected him to, Paul grew somber. Her laughter fading, Karen gazed up at him.

"What is it?" she asked, beginning to frown.

"Charles was right, Karen." Paul sighed. "I am too old for you."

Chapter Thirteen

"Paul!" Rearing back, Karen attempted to free herself from his embrace. Her expression and her tone revealed sheer incredulity. "How can you say that after the night we just spent together!"

Refusing to release her completely, Paul eased her from his chest to the mattress beside him. "I can say that because it's true." Leaning over her, he raised a hand to rake long fingers through her hair, tangling them in the disheveled mass. "Look at you," he murmured, searing a dark-eyed gaze the length of her nude body. "Do you know what I see when I look at you?"

Karen's throat was too tight to allow the passage of words. A sinking sensation invaded her stomach. With her mind's eye she could see herself as she imagined Paul saw her. And what she saw was a woman who looked every one of her thirty-seven years. She loved good food, and the results were firmly packed around her hips. She had borne two children, and her body bore the marks. Her breasts, though still firm, no longer retained the high thrust of youth. Her hands revealed her willingness to work and showed none of the soft silkiness of idle pampering.

Never before had Karen been dissatisfied with her appearance. She had never been beautiful. But she had always been attractive, and that had been enough until now. Now Karen longed to be beautiful...for Paul. Beginning to hurt deep inside, Karen shook her head. "No, what do you see when you look at me?"

"I see a woman in the full bloom of life—lovely, vibrant, gloriously alive. And you deserve a man like yourself to build a future with." Paul's sigh and smile hurt her heart. "Karen, I am well into middle age. I haven't all that much future to offer."

With his hand buried in her hair, it was difficult for Karen to move without causing a sharp tug of pain in her scalp. But she did, ignoring the tears in her eyes as she struggled to sit up. "Paul, that's ridiculous!" she cried indignantly. "You literally wore me out last night!" she admitted, blushing.

"Thank you for that." Paul's voice was husky with emotion. Raising his hand, he traced her features with his fingertips as if imprinting the feel of her on his skin. "But there was a reason for my prowess last night. After weeks of missing you, then being near you but denied the right to touch you, I was starving for you."

"No, no," Karen protested, shaking her head vigorously. "That might explain last night, but what about that first time? You were every bit as...as aggressive the first time we made love."

Jolting up, Paul grasped her by the shoulders. "Of course I was aggressive!" he said in a gritty voice. "I had not been with a woman in over six years!" The instant the words were out of his mouth, Paul bit down hard on his lip as if he wished he could bite back the confession. "Oh, damn!" he groaned, wincing at the sight of her baffled expression. His fingers flexed convulsively in the soft flesh of her shoulders. "Karen, listen to me. Until the day I met you, I honestly believed that I was impotent."

Impotent! Karen blinked. Paul? Karen laughed; she couldn't help it. He had to be kidding! But he wasn't, and she knew it. Her laughter held a note of hysteria. "I'm sorry," she gasped, fighting against the natural succession of tears after the laughter. "But, Paul, I can't believe..." Karen's voice faded.

Paul sighed and loosened his grip on her shoulders. "Believe it, Karen. I was celibate for over six years, not by choice but because I felt no stirrings of desire for any woman—until I met you." Leaning toward her, he kissed her with a reverence that brought tears to her eyes. "And I've been thanking God for our meeting, and for you, ever since."

Sitting naked on the bed, tears trickling down her face, Karen felt weak with compassion for him and grateful for being the woman who had been there at his reawakening. Sniffing, she brushed impatiently at her wet cheeks. "I'd like you to know that, although it was by choice, I had been celibate for over five years before I met you."

His fingers tightened again on her tender skin, making a lie of his protest. "You shouldn't have been! You're too young to deny yourself the pleasure of love." His lips twisted into a wry smile. "And that's what I've been trying to tell you. I am past the age of giving you the pleasure you deserve."

Suddenly impatient with him, Karen shook off his hands. "You are not old!" She shouted the denial, yet at that moment, with his somber expression revealing every scoring line of experience, Paul did indeed look his age.

"But, my love," he murmured in an aching tone, "I am too old for you. Do you realize that I have a son older than you are?"

Her eyes widening with disbelief, Karen skimmed her gaze down his body, admiring the trim, well-toned look of him. Impossible, she decided. Even though he had told her he'd never see fifty again, Paul simply could not be old enough to have fathered a child who was now forty or near enough to it to make little difference. "Paul, really..." she began, only to break off at the sound of his introspective murmur.

"I was seventeen."

"What?"

Paul shuddered and glanced away from her. "Nothing." With startling suddenness, he sprang from the bed. "I'm hungry."

Karen's eyes narrowed. "Paul, you simply can't let it go at that! What happened when you were seventeen?"

Paul had started for the bathroom; he didn't stop. His only response was an impatient shrug that rippled over his muscular shoulders and down his attractively tapered back.

"Paul!" Karen's tone was laced with the same note of command she occasionally had to use on her children. And she derived the same result; Paul stopped in his tracks.

"Over breakfast, Karen. Okay?"

Karen resigned herself to the delay with a sighed "Yes, Paul."

The bowed windows in the dining alcove framed a Christmas-card scene of sparkling white snow blanketing the landscape and mantling bushes and tree branches. After her delighted cry on her first sight of it, Karen didn't notice. She was too busy studying Paul.

Pondering his intriguing murmur, she barely touched the food he'd helped her prepare. Sipping her coffee, Karen bided her time until he'd finished chewing the last bite of his breakfast. She pounced the instant he placed his napkin on the table.

"You were seventeen?" she prompted softly.

Paul's smile contained genuine, if wry, amusement. "I should have added tenaciousness to your list of attributes."

Karen stared at him stoically.

"Right." Paul nodded sharply. "I was seventeen when my son Peter was born." He smiled as her eyes grew wide with surprise. "He was legitimate. His mother and I were man and wife."

Karen glared at him. "I assumed you were! But you were so young. How in the world—" Karen stopped speaking simply because the question was stupid—she knew how!

"Karen, are you sure you want to hear the story of my life?" Paul grimaced. "I assure you it is very dull fare."

Karen indicated the snowy world beyond the windows. "I'm not going anywhere. And I don't believe you could be dull if you worked at it."

"I fell in love with Carolyn the first time I saw her, the day her family moved into the house on the small estate next to ours." Though Paul began his recitation in a droning voice, his tone gradually changed, becoming soft and pensive. "I was hiding behind the line of yews that separated the properties, curious about the new neighbors.'' His lips curved in a tender smile of remembrance. ''I was six years old. Carolyn was five. She had long, shining hair and she was the most beautiful creature my young eyes had ever seen. I immediately fell into a state of adoration and stayed there.''

Karen experienced a stab of emotion too similar to jealousy to be examined. Carefully controlling her expression, she merely arched her eyebrows questioningly.

Paul laughed. ''Incredible, isn't it?'' Since he didn't expect a response, he didn't wait for one. ''I loved her. No—'' He shook his head. ''I worshiped the air she breathed.'' Paul shut his eyes, and his expression sent a shaft of pain into Karen's heart. ''She was slender and delicate and unpredictable and so stunningly beautiful.''

A mirror image of herself flashed into Karen's mind, and she had to bite her lip to keep from crying out for him to stop. She didn't want to hear anymore; she wanted to run away and hide. But even as she berated herself for having insisted he tell her his story, she urged him to continue. ''Go on.''

Paul complied like an automaton. ''Carolyn discovered me peering at her from behind the yews, and from that day on we were practically inseparable. We were best friends until the year I was sixteen and she was fifteen.'' He smiled sadly. ''Then we became lovers.''

''Oh, Paul.'' Karen's voice was soft with understanding and compassion.

Paul didn't seem to hear. ''We were so very young and so very dumb.'' He shrugged. ''We knew nothing about birth control, of course, and, unprotected, Carolyn conceived almost immediately.'' His smile held the wisdom gained during the forty-year interval. ''I'm sure you can imagine how the news was received by our parents.''

"Oh, yes," Karen murmured, thinking of Rand.

"Her mother went directly into a decline, her father threatened to, er, dismember me." Paul winced at the mere idea. "My mother cried off and on for a week, my father retired to his study, refusing to look at me. But in the end, Carolyn and I were married—with their blessing. I was in my senior year of high school when Peter was born six months later." A soft glow entered Paul's eyes at the mention of his son's name. "As had happened with his mother, I adored my son from the instant the nurse unwrapped his blanket to present him to me minutes after he made his appearance in the world." He chuckled. "I still adore him, and that devil knows it."

Karen had to swallow before she could articulate. "And your daughter?"

"Ahhh, Nicole," Paul responded in a loving murmur. Then he gave a short, helpless laugh. "As luck would have it, Carolyn didn't conceive again until after Peter's ninth birthday. I had thought it would be nice to have a daughter, but I couldn't imagine..." Paul's voice faded on a note of wonder, then came back with a note of awe. "Though I wouldn't have believed it possible, my daughter was exquisite from birth, even more beautiful than her mother." He exhaled a heartfelt sigh. "Nicole was in a car accident several years ago and was left with a scar on her right cheek, but she's still exquisitely beautiful." He smiled into Karen's eyes. "Her husband, J.B., would die for her without a second thought, he loves her that much."

"As you loved her mother?" Karen's voice revealed a longing ache. She breathed a sigh of relief when he appeared not to have noticed.

"Yes, until—" Paul broke off abruptly to change the subject. "Is there any coffee left?"

Alert to his evasive ploy yet cautioning herself to be patient, Karen slid her chair away from the table. "There's a fresh pot. I'll get it." Grasping the carafe, she stood up, frowning when he pushed his chair back.

"We may as well clear the table," he said in answer to her silent, frowning query.

"You were saying you loved Carolyn until..." Karen prompted some ten minutes later when they were again seated at the neatly cleared table.

Avoiding her direct gaze, Paul sipped his steaming coffee, then shifted to glance at the carpet. A sensuous smile curved his lips. "This dining area holds some very pleasant memories for me," he murmured.

Karen had a fleeting vision of herself, naked and eager, wantonly stretched out on the spot where his dark-eyed gaze rested, and choked on a swallow of coffee. "Yes, well, ah—" She cleared her throat. "Are you digressing?"

"No, I'm stalling," Paul admitted wryly.

With the sudden realization that she really had no right to probe into his past, Karen reached across the table to clasp his hand. "Paul, I'm sorry. We'll discuss something else. The snow, the coming holidays, the—"

"Karen, shut up." Paul's voice was low, rich with his appreciation of her understanding. "I loved Carolyn until the day I found out that she was unfaithful to me, had been unfaithful to me for over ten years. That was over six years ago." His eyes narrowed and he watched her closely, waiting for her reaction. He didn't wait very long.

Karen's eyes widened as she absorbed the enormity of what he'd said. "You mean," she breathed, "that it was on learning of her infidelity that you became—"

"Yes." Paul spoke quickly, interrupting her before she could say the hated word.

"Did you consult a doctor?"

Paul's spine grew rigid, and he lifted his head. "No."

Karen was appalled at his unequivocal reply. "But Paul—" she began in protest, but again he cut her off.

"I didn't need a doctor, Karen," he said harshly. "Very likely because, for a long time, the last thing I wanted was intimate contact with a woman—any woman."

Karen didn't respond; she couldn't. She had to concentrate on merely breathing. She hurt all over, for herself but more intensely for Paul. What she would finally have said in the event she found both breath and voice Karen was never to know, for at that moment, in an eerie repeat of another time they'd been alone in the alcove, the phone rang.

"I'll get it!" Grateful for the diversion, Karen scrambled to her feet and fled to the kitchen wall phone. Without ever having heard the voice before, Karen knew at once that it belonged to Paul's son, Peter.

"Ms. Mitchell?" His voice was deep and dark and incredibly sexy. "This is Peter Vanzant. May I speak to my father, please?"

"Yes, of course," Karen said, picturing him in her mind as a younger version of Paul. She decided she liked him, sight unseen. "Just a moment, please." She turned to find Paul watching her, his expression tense, revealing. Karen knew his fear was that the call concerned Charles. Her smile reassuring, she held out the receiver. "For you," she murmured. "It's your son."

Karen started to move away after handing Paul the phone, but he slid an arm around her waist and drew her tightly against him. As he held the receiver loosely, she couldn't help but overhear the conversation.

"Yes, Peter?"

"Dad, J.B. called a few moments ago. Nicole's in labor."

Paul's only reaction was the compulsive tightening of the arm encircling Karen's waist and the terseness of his tone. "Is there a problem?"

"No. It's early, but only by two weeks. J.B. just wanted to let us know."

"All right, Peter. Thanks for calling."

"You flying to Fort Worth, Dad?"

The inflection in Peter's voice reached Karen with revealing clarity; Peter knew his father very well. Paul's smile was wry. "Yes, Peter, I'll be flying to Fort Worth."

"That's what I thought. Give Nicole and J.B. our love and tell them Patricia and I will be bringing little Paul out to meet his cousin the day after Christmas. And, Dad, call us the minute the baby arrives."

"Of course, Peter."

There was more. Paul asked after Peter's wife and son, but Karen was tuned out, her mind numbed by the realization that Paul was leaving. And although she understood his desire to be with his youngest child at the birth of her first baby, Karen felt frozen by the possibility that once he left Paul might not return.

Her fear grew during the next few hours as Paul swiftly and efficiently booked airline reservations for his flight to Fort Worth and prepared to leave. His remote withdrawal reinforced the possibility, changing it to a probability.

In her determination not to emulate Charles by attempting to force the issue or be manipulative, Karen promised herself she would not pressure Paul by asking if he was planning to come back to her. And she maintained her resolve until he was ready to walk out the door; then she broke her promise to herself with a gush of blurted words.

"Will you be coming back?"

"I don't think that would be wise, Karen." Though Paul's eyes were tender, his tone was adamant. As she stared at him, a thousand arguments rushed through Karen's mind. One word found its way to her lips.

"Why?"

Paul's chest moved as he exhaled deeply. "It wouldn't be fair to you." He held up a hand to silence her when she would have protested. "I have a memory, an image of you in my mind that torments me. The memory is of the first day we met, when you sat across the table from me while in the kitchen. You said, 'I love babies' when I told you I have one grandchild and another on the way. The image in my mind is of the expression of longing on your face." As he had earlier that morning, Paul reached out to trace her features with his fingertips. "I'm past the age of starting another family, Karen, even if I were certain I could, which I'm not."

"Oh, Paul, I don't—" Karen began.

"I am fifty-six years old, Karen!" Paul said harshly. "And, as I told you before, that doesn't leave much of a future to offer you."

"Dammit, Paul!" Karen exploded, forgetting her determination not to apply pressure in her fear of losing him. "When you arrived here the day after Thanksgiving, you told me you thought you were falling in love with me," she said, grasping his hand to hold it to her cheek. "Well, I don't think I'm falling in love with you—I know I'm in love with you." She paused for breath, taking courage from the light of emotion her confession of love ignited in his eyes, but hurried on before he could respond. "And as to the future, no one ever knows how much or how little we have of that. When I married Charles, the future seemed as never-ending as youth. Well, I'm now past the age of believing in forever spring, and though I know I can be content without ever having another baby, I'm not as certain I can ever again be content without having you." Falling silent, Karen clutched his hand and waited breathlessly for his reaction.

Paul closed his eyes as if he were in pain. When he opened them again, they were suspiciously bright. Moving her hand, he slid his palm to the back of her head; then, tangling his fingers in her hair, he drew her mouth to his. His kiss was hard and hungry and desperate. Karen barely had time to respond before he released her abruptly and turned to pull the door open.

"I must go now or I'll miss my plane." His voice was husky with emotion. He stepped outside, then turned to look at her, absorb her, with intense dark eyes. "I'm still not sure, but I'll think about everything you said." Paul hesitated, took another step into the glistening snow, then turned to stare at her once more. "But there is one thing that I'm now absolutely sure of," he said softly. "I do love you, Karen—deeply, maturely, in a way I never loved Carolyn." Leaving her that one precious gift, Paul turned and strode to his car.

Why doesn't he call me? Please, God, make him call me. Karen was getting used to the litany. It had run through her mind continuously for three excruciatingly long days, ever since Paul's departure four days before.

Throughout those four days, Karen had made a production out of busy work. She had laundered literally everything in the house that would fit into the clothes washer. Every room in the large house was spotless and gleaming with a fresh coat of polish. She had even tackled the detested job of cleaning the kitchen cabinets. She had been anxious to do anything and everything to keep her mind as well as her hands occupied. But after four days of industrious labor, though her house was in order, Karen's mind was in a muddle of uncertainty and fear.

And in a strange way, even in her fear of losing Paul, Karen understood and sympathized with the position he had taken. Karen also knew that there was more, much more involved in his decision than the span of years separating them.

Though proud, Karen knew Paul was a man of deep loyalties. Because he had loved, he had persevered with his marriage even after learning of his wife's infidelity. Because he was proud, Paul had borne the fear of impotence in stoic, if misguided, silence. Because he was loyal, he had endured alone while keeping his family together.

Karen acknowledged sadly that she loved Paul because of all his fine qualities, even though they might prove the reason she would lose him. The paradox was nearly unbearable.

Unabashed tears glistening in his dark eyes, Paul stood at the nursery window, staring in awe at the tiny form of his new granddaughter. Like her mother before her, the infant was exquisite in her perfection. But the cost of her entrance into the world had been high—almost too high, for while fighting to give life to her daughter, Nicole had come perilously close to losing her own.

As to the future, no one knows how much or how little we have of that.

Paul heard Karen's voice as clearly as if she stood beside him in the hospital corridor. *I love you.* Paul wasn't sure if his silent message was meant for the tiny bundle in the small nursery basket or the woman who commanded his every thought and emotion. But then, it really didn't matter. The message applied to both.

By late afternoon of the fourth day, for want of something to do, Karen was reduced to checking her food staples and writing a grocery list. She was bent over a piece of paper on the kitchen counter, about to add baking powder to the list, when she heard the unmistakable sound of a car pulling into the driveway. For an instant, she froze. Then the pencil went sailing into the air as Karen spun to make a mad dash to the door. Hoping, yet afraid to hope, she swung the door open.

"Paul." Every hope, every dream, every aching ounce of love Karen felt for him was wrapped within the whisper of his name.

Looking far less urbane, sophisticated and intimidating but infinitely more relaxed, freer and younger than Karen had ever seen him, Paul smiled, strode into the house and swept her into his arms. His kiss was deep and hungry and spoke eloquently of his need of her. Karen reveled in being crushed beneath his demanding mouth and moaned a soft protest when he raised his head and stepped back. As he moved, he caught her hand with his, as if not wanting to lose contact entirely. Gazing at him, Karen felt her heart flutter at the emotion burning in his dark eyes. Her pulses leaped with his first words to her.

"I want to try to make a baby with you." Paul's voice was low but firm with certainty.

"Is this a proposal of marriage?" Karen asked in a dry, crackling whisper.

Paul's smile held the promise of heaven and the glitter of devilry. "I guess it must be, because I feel positive that Rand would never forgive me if I suggested anything less than marriage."

Wanting to cry, wanting to laugh, and in the end doing both, Karen managed to ask, "And Rand's opinion is important to you?"

Paul replied at once. "Of course, as is the opinion of Mark and Peter and Patricia and Nicole and J.B., and little Paul and my darling new granddaughter." His smile and tone deepened. "Their opinions are very important—for the future."

"Catch it, Paul!" Mark called excitedly, jumping up and down in the sand near the water's edge.

"You'll never make it!" Rand whooped, proud of the toss he'd made.

The bright orange Frisbee arced high against a brilliant blue spring sky before diving to earth inches from the blanket Karen was sitting on. Scrambling to her feet, she swooped down and plucked it from the sand an instant before Paul came to a panting halt in front of her.

"They're trying to kill me," he gasped, indicating her laughing sons with a backward toss of his head. "Me, the father of their unborn brother or sister!" His teasing eyes lowered to the barely discernible bulge in Karen's jeans.

Controlling her own bubbling laughter, Karen managed a concerned "tsk-tsk" and a frown. "Correct me if I'm wrong, Mr. Vanzant," she said, biting her lip, "but weren't you the one who suggested the game in the first place?"

Paul flicked his hand dismissively. "That's beside the point, Mrs. Vanzant. I hardly expected—"

"Hey, when do we eat?" Rand shouted, drowning out his stepfather's complaint.

"Soon," Karen called, releasing her pent-up laughter. The happy sound wafted along on the warm, balmy air, drawing an exchange of contented grins from Rand and Mark.

Paul groaned, very loudly. "I suppose you now expect me to grill the hot dogs and hamburgers for dinner?" He arched one dark brow at her arrogantly.

Karen tapped the Frisbee against her thigh as she contemplated his question. Then she smiled nicely and fluttered her eyelashes. "Surely you don't expect me, in my delicate condition, to stand over a hot, smoky charcoal grill?" she asked sweetly.

Paul made a very unsophisticated face at her. "If the delicate lady will remember, I did offer to take the family out for dinner," he reminded her smoothly.

"Go out to eat on Memorial Day?" Karen widened her eyes in feigned shock. "Why—why, that's positively un-American!"

"Yeah, right." Paul said, imitating Rand's tone perfectly.

Karen's joyous laughter rang out again. "God, I love you, Paul!" she gasped.

Catching her by the waist, Paul swung her into the air, then pulled her into his arms when he set her down again. "You know what? I love you, too."

"Are you two gonna spend the whole holiday making mush or are we gonna eat sometime soon?" Rand groused as he stomped through the sand toward them.

"Yeah, anyway, I'm hungry," Mark seconded, trailing his idol.

"Yeah, anyway," Paul mimicked, bending to drop a swift kiss on Karen's mouth. "Okay, you win. I'll cook." He stole another kiss before glancing at the boys. "But you kids can haul the food and assorted necessities out to the grill. Hop to it!"

With cries of "Yes, sir" and "You got it," the boys sprinted toward the house.

Returning his undivided attention to Karen, Paul smiled in satisfaction. A shiver tiptoed down her spine at the gleam that sprang into his eyes.

"Paul," she laughed, "are you thinking what I think you're thinking?"

"What else?" He laughed with her. "And if we were alone..." His voice trailed off suggestively.

"But we're not," she reminded him, surging up to give him a quick kiss.

Paul's hand snaked up to grasp her hair, holding her still for a soul-stirring kiss. "I can wait," he murmured against her lips, laughing softly as she shivered in response. He kissed her again, deeply this time. When he lifted his head, his expression was somber, almost reverent. "As long as I know you're here, mine, only mine, I can wait." Working his free hand between them, he placed his palm on her gently rounded belly. "We have our entire future before us. Anticipation will sweeten our private moments together."

* * * * *

Dear Reader,

Some books are a lot like babies. Once they're actually born, you quickly forget all the weeks of backache, heartburn and swollen ankles. You forget the pain involved in giving birth the first time you hold in your arms—or in this case, your hands—a precious individual unlike any ever conceived and born before. You can only hope the world will be good to your baby.

I love *Hazards of the Heart.* I appreciate your inviting Jake and Libby and little David into your home for a visit. If it's a good visit, please share with me. Send pictures. A mother likes to know who her children's friends are.

Love,

Dixie Browning

HAZARDS OF THE HEART

Dixie Browning

Prologue

Jake had been watching the blonde with the big front deck for some time now. He didn't know why, exactly. She wasn't the most beautiful woman in the room by any stretch of the imagination. Maybe it was the fact that a guy didn't see too many pregnant women at these bashes. Not all *that* pregnant, at least. She looked about twelve months gone.

His gaze moved around her table. He had recognized two of the four people there. Charles Alderholt had run for governor in the past two elections. Old Charlie ought to know better than to wrap a fifty-inch belly in a tartan cummerbund. Hell, he looked even more pregnant than the blonde.

Sitting at the same table, with some bleary-eyed bimbo practically jumping his bones, was Walt Porter. Old Raleigh family. Jake knew him in the way that men from the same general area and the same general tax bracket knew each other. He'd heard somewhere that Porter had got married awhile back. From the looks of the broad, he'd picked a real loser, but then, from the looks of them both, they probably deserved each other. Alderholt should have known better than to park his pregnant wife with a pair of booze hounds while he went table-hopping. Poor little mama was looking sicker by the minute.

Jake looked around at the large man in the plaid cummerbund, who had just risen and wandered over to another table, leaving his wife and his inebriated friends behind. Old Charlie must be at least sixty by now. Who'd have thought he'd wind up marrying again at his age, much less planting a brand new crop of little Alderholts.

Still staring absently at the Porter-Alderholt party, Jake turned his thoughts to his own family. He wondered what they were doing tonight. His wife had taken their five-year-old son and a baby-sitter to their beach place. Jake was to join them when and if he found time.

He should have gone with them. Johnny got tired on long trips. The baby-sitter was little more than a kid herself, and Cass wasn't noted for her patience in the best of circumstances. Civic duty be damned, he should never have allowed himself to be roped into this thing! Cass had bought the tickets and then changed her mind at the last minute, when it was too late for him to bow out. He should have just doubled the size of his annual check, mailed the damned thing in and gone to the beach to look after Johnny, but she'd insisted that one of them had to attend, and it had been easier to go along than to argue.

Of course, she was playing games again. He ought to be used to it by now, but he wasn't. Conquest was the name of the game, and he'd learned soon after they'd been married that while Cass thrived on the chase, she quickly grew bored with the catch. He'd hoped all that would change after Johnny was born, but evidently, it hadn't.

Jake's gaze strayed back to the pregnant blonde. Was she as miserable as she looked, or was she just laying a guilt trip on poor old Charlie because he wasn't dancing attention on her? Hell, she was here, wasn't she? Wearing a designer hatching jacket and about three carats of blue-white on her soft little hand?

Another bored socialite. Charlie should have known better than to marry a school kid and then ignore her. If there was one thing that drove Cass wild, it was to be ignored. By any male, regardless of age, financial bracket or marital status.

Jake belched discreetly. French cooking had never agreed with him. He shifted restlessly in his chair, waiting for the last speaker to run out of steam, for the band to start up, for people to start milling around so he could ease out the side door, his philanthropic duty done for another year.

He'd give a hundred bucks not to have eaten that damned yellow stuff with the blobs of black in the gravy! He'd give another hundred for a barbecue and beer.

Uh-oh. The blonde was in some kind of trouble, and Papa was nowhere in sight. Porter and his woman were too far gone to notice—either that or what she was doing to him under the table was about to render him *hors de combat*.

Jake snorted in disgust. It was no skin off his nose what they did, but little Mama looked as if she just might go into labor right here in the middle of the hotel ballroom.

His eyes narrowed as he watched for some sign. It was none of his business. God knows, he had enough trouble keeping his own marriage on track without borrowing from Charlie Alderholt, but somebody ought to do something.

Where the devil was Charlie, anyhow? Jake looked around, and then looked back at the blonde. Damned little fool had no business even being here. Charlie should've known better, even if she didn't.

Now she was leaning over toward Porter, tugging at his arm. Her eyes looked dark, almost panicky, in her pale face, and instinctively Jake began to ease his chair away from his table. He'd been seated with a couple he knew only slightly, both of whom had turned their chairs toward the front as soon as the speakers had begun.

Wake up, Porter, go haul your friend's ass back online and get him to take his wife home where she belongs!

But Porter, one arm around his own woman, only lifted the blonde's wrist from his sleeve as if it were something he'd found under a wet rock, and dropped it.

Stinking bastard, Jake thought dispassionately. Even if she wasn't his responsibility, no man had a right to treat any woman that way, especially one in her condition.

Jake stood and began making his way past the intervening tables with some notion of calling Porter's wife's attention to what was going on. Surely another woman wouldn't just brush her off that way. Just then a scattering of applause broke out and the restless audience began to break up.

A noisy party whom he vaguely remembered having

met once or twice at the Gap moved between him and the Alderholt-Porter party. A woman with the figure of a ballpoint pen cried his name, flung her glittering fists on his chest and held up her cheek to be kissed, and by the time Jake got free again, little Mama was nearly at the door of the ballroom. "Mrs. Alderholt," he called, elbowing his way through the milling throng. She wasn't hard to follow. The crowd parted like the Red Sea as soon as they caught sight of her prominent condition.

"Mrs. Alderholt!" he called again, lunging to catch her arm just as she reached the heavy glass front doors. Where the hell was the doorman, anyway? Where the hell was her husband? Was the little fool deaf?

"Mrs. Alderholt, if you need—"

"Were you speaking to me?"

Her eyes reminded him of wet oak leaves. Dark, opaque green—red-rimmed now, with a smudge of mascara just beginning to puddle underneath. Blinking, she looked pointedly down at the hand on her arm, and Jake snatched it away.

"It's raining," he said, feeling like a fool now that he'd finally caught up with her.

"Yes." She lifted her chin as if the small defiant gesture alone could stop the rain, summon her pumpkin—and maybe turn poor old Charlie into Prince Charming.

"Mrs. Alderholt, I couldn't help but notice you were looking sort of...uncomfortable?" Damn, where was his brain? This was none of his business! Still, if she was going into labor, she didn't need to hang around all night waiting for Alderholt to tear himself away.

"I'm sorry, my name's not Alderholt," she said very quietly. "But thank you for your concern."

There was a brittleness about her that made Jake uneasy.

"Ma'am, if you'll wait right here—no, maybe you'd better sit down. Look, I'll go find Charlie and— Did you say you're not Mrs. Alderholt?"

"No, I'm not, but if you wouldn't mind finding me a taxi, I'd appreciate it very much," she said with a calmness he knew damned well was all wrong. There was a dignity about her that didn't jibe with red eyes, a bloated belly and swollen ankles, but Jake knew better than to argue with a woman. Especially a stranger. Especially a pregnant stranger!

He left to round up a cab. Collaring a doorman, he slipped him a folded bill and murmured, "Taxi. Make it five minutes ago, right?"

And then he was back again, hovering helplessly over the gravid female he had somehow got himself involved with. Fortunately the cab pulled up before he could blurt out a promise to go with her to whatever hospital she chose, stay with her during her ordeal and help her kid with his math homework if the need ever arose.

While his own car was brought around, Jake watched the taillights waver off down the wet street. He swore softly under his breath. What the hell was he doing, playing Don Quixote for some other man's woman? He had enough problems of his own!

One

"Here she is, in all her glory, folks," Libby murmured softly to the woman in the mirror. Gray-streaked blond hair swept up for the occasion, a black silk designer dress, circa prepregnancy, black stockings with nary a runner in sight and a waistline that measured a full nine inches smaller than her 34 B cup. "Not bad," she whispered. "Not half-bad, all things considered."

So how come she kept seeing a plump frump in polyester and a ponytail, whose measurements didn't vary more than a couple of inches from one end of her torso to the other?

"Mama, can I have—"

"May I, David," Libby corrected automatically.

"May Billie and me have—"

Libby opened her mouth and closed it again.

"—some popcorn?"

"You and Billie may pop corn *after* supper, if Billie

thinks you deserve a treat." There, that struck a balance, didn't it? No demands to clean off a plate, no threats concerning bedtime hour. She was learning, but it wasn't easy. Motherhood had never been easy, but at least now she didn't have someone else undermining her every effort at guidance. Now, if she could learn to be an effective father as well as an effective mother, David just might have a chance of growing up to be a well-adjusted individual, instead of a clone of the father he resembled so much.

Libby kissed her son goodbye, offered the baby-sitter, who also happened to be her cousin, a few last-minute suggestions and tried to ignore David's fleeting look of panic. It had taken five weeks before he would board the school bus without a scene. After that, she had started leaving him one or two evenings a month with Billie.

"I'm off, then. See you later, crocodile!"

"Mom, it's *alligator,*" David said with a groan, and she slapped her forehead in mock chagrin.

The car started on the third try, which was encouraging. She checked the potholed driveway for balls, bats, bicycles and other natural hazards, and then she sniffed. Was her perfume too strong? Oh, heavens, she should have asked Billie.

The underwires of her black lace bra stabbed her in the armpit when she reached forward to release the emergency brake, and she wondered why in the world she hadn't worn something more comfortable. It wasn't as if anyone would know what color her underwear was, for pity sake!

Libby had no trouble finding the hotel after the twenty-five-minute drive into town. She'd scoped it out the week before when she'd taken David to the dentist.

But at two in the afternoon, it hadn't looked quite so...big. The parking lot hadn't been quite so full, and there hadn't been all those glittery pink lights.

A long dark car glided to a halt before the canopied entrance, and a uniformed man stepped out to open the door. The parking attendant palmed a tip, slipped into the car and drove it off, and Libby watched the couple enter, wondering if they were there for the reunion. Wondering if she knew them.

Wondering if the heel of her ten-year-old black *peau de soie* pump was really loose, or if it only felt that way. Were pointed toes still in, or were they out again?

Blast. She should have worn her sneakers driving in, only she'd probably have forgotten and worn the things inside. Oh, blast!

Libby purely hated being intimidated. After enduring twelve years of being put down by an expert, not to mention by the most expensive divorce lawyer money could buy, she had sworn *never again!*

And here she was, cowering. Spineless as a raw egg! Afraid to go inside, afraid no one would know her—afraid they *would*—afraid she'd turn into an adolescent pumpkin again, and everyone would laugh.

She'd better get out of here. But then it would all be wasted. Oh, blast, why had she spent all that grocery money on a bottle of French toilet water?

Scowling, she sat there in her five-year-old station wagon, between the white Mercedes and the big black Ford, and ran through the routine once more. "Listen, wimp, they're not even going to remember you!"

You hope.

"And even if they do, do you think they're all just dying to discover how fat-face Libby Dwiggins happened to wind up with a waistline, a designer dress and an overdose of *eau de toilette?* Ha!"

Tired of arguing with herself, Libby braced her shoulders and tilted her chin. She took a deep breath and reached for the door handle, then changed her mind and switched on the local news station, telling herself she might as well catch the weather report before she went inside. Living in the country, it paid to keep abreast of things like that.

Sighing, she had just begun to nibble off her lipstick when someone leaned down to breathe whiskey fumes in through her half-open window. "Well, hel-*lo* there, li'l darlin'. You been waitin' out here all by your lonesome? Ol' Pete would never keep a lady waitin'. Why'n'cha move over, hmmm?"

Libby hastily began to roll up the window, but the drunk shoved his elbow in where his fingers had been before. "C'mon, now, honey, don' be like that. Ol' Pete jus' wants to show you a good time. Ol' Pete likes li'l—"

Suddenly old Pete was lying flat on his back on the pavement, and a large man in a dark suit was dusting off his hands.

Libby gaped through the partially open window. She was still gaping when the stranger dragged the drunk across the parking lot, draped him decorously across one of the black marble planters that flanked the front entrance, and sauntered back to her station wagon.

Finally she gathered her wits enough to squeak out her thanks.

"Don't mention it," the man said dryly.

Jake had been sitting in his own car when the blonde had pulled in beside him. He'd given her an automatic once-over, his mind on other matters, and then done a slow double take. Did he know her? Was she someone he ought to remember? If so, he was going to be embarrassed when he couldn't come up with her name.

Ah, hell, this had been a lousy idea from the beginning. He'd trashed the letter of invitation as soon as he'd got it, but then, after thinking about it all day, he'd gone back, unlocked his office and retrieved the damned thing before the cleaning crew came by. He seemed to recall entertaining some pseudo-philosophic notion that if he couldn't face the past, he didn't stand a snowball's chance of building any kind of a future.

Which was sheer bilge. He'd already *built* his future. At least, he was a damn sight closer to it than he would ever have believed possible a few years ago.

His gaze strayed back to the blonde. *Did* he know her? The hotel was full of people, not all here for the same reason, but she was about the right age. Jake was forty. She looked a few years younger, but then, he was older than the rest of his graduating class, thanks to a fool stunt that had gotten his neck broken and cost him a couple of years.

With more interest than he'd shown any woman in a long time, John Hatcher Healy, alias Jake Hatcher, leaned against his car and studied the woman in the pink neon glow. She ought to know by now that her kind of hair was too heavy to wear in that style. It was the slick, straight kind of hair that always lost out to the law of gravity. Nice style while it lasted, though. Her neck was long, slender, unusually elegant. Jake had never been a neck man, but he had enough of a classical education to recognize the beauty of hers.

Did he know her? Probably not. He would have remembered.

He saw her lift that well-defined jaw another degree,

as if she were aware of his scrutiny. Somewhere in the back of his mind, a bell began to clang softly.

Yeah, there was something familiar about that attitude, all right. He might not remember her name or her face—it had been twenty years, after all, and a lot had happened in the meantime. A lot that he had sworn to put behind him.

But he remembered that chin. He'd been wondering about it when he'd seen the drunk stagger up to her car and try to put the moves on her. He'd lay odds it wasn't the first time she'd reacted to danger by leading with her chin. As a big-time loser doing his damnedest to make a comeback, Jake could have told her she was just asking for trouble.

The hotel doors opened and a small group spilled out, accompanied by the sounds of revelry from the ballroom across the lobby. The party was getting ripe. *Okay, Hatcher, decision time. You gonna go inside? Or you gonna hang around the parking lot all night?*

Jake levered his rangy, six-two frame away from his car, turned toward the entrance and then suddenly swung back toward the blonde in the station wagon. Leaning down to her window, he rasped, "Look, lady, I don't know what your problem is, but if you're going to sit out here in the dark looking for trouble, you just might find more than you bargained for."

"No, I—that is, I'm going inside. The reunion. That is, I'm..."

"Chicken," Jake said softly, and watched, amused, as she cranked that elegant little chin up another degree or two. It might work on some men. It hadn't on the drunk. It wouldn't on a man like Jake, either, he told himself. Which was why he couldn't figure what the devil he was doing, wrenching her door open a moment later to slide onto the passenger seat beside her.

"What are you— Get out of my car!"

"Lady, you've got the brains of a bedbug. What the hell do you mean, sitting out here in an unlocked car? Didn't your mama teach you anything?" Her mouth was hanging open, and he wondered why her parents had never bothered to put her in braces when she was a kid. Although the slight overlap probably added a certain distinction to her smile. If she ever smiled.

"I told you I'm going inside!"

"Sure you are," he drawled. "That's why you've been sitting here for the past twenty minutes, right? Trying to figure out which foot to put first."

"Do you make a habit of accosting strange women in parking lots?"

"Hell, honey, you're not all *that* strange. A little slow, maybe, but—"

Blindly Libby reached for her purse, which had fallen behind the console. With one hand on the door handle, she was ready to jump and run when his next words made her pause.

"I'm sorry. I don't usually butt in this way, but—"

"Oh, I expect you do. You're too good at it to be an amateur."

In spite of his irritation, Jake chuckled. "Yeah, maybe you're right."

"And I ought to thank you. I do thank you. For earlier. The drunk, I mean. I probably shouldn't have left the window open, but—" But her car smelled like wet sneakers, thanks to David.

"You shouldn't have left the window open or the door unlocked. In fact, you shouldn't be here at all."

"I reached the same conclusion not ten minutes ago.

About being here, I mean. People shouldn't try to turn back the clock. It never works."

"The reunion?"

"Uh-huh. It's my class, but..." From the corners of her eyes, Libby studied the stranger, who was lounging against the far door. He hadn't made a single threatening move, other than being there. On the other hand, if he hadn't been there a few minutes ago, she would have had to deal with the drunk herself. And while she didn't doubt that she could have handled it—she could have opened the door suddenly and knocked him down, then locked her doors and leaned on the horn—still, she hadn't, and he had, and she owed him for that.

"Yeah, me, too," the man said, and she turned to study him more openly.

"Do I know you?" Black hair, with more than a touch a gray. Eyes dark—maybe brown, maybe not. Mouth... The term *bitter* came to mind, and she wondered briefly at the description and then went on with her mental inventory. He looked as if he'd come up the hard way, but at least he had made it, if that suit he was wearing was anything to go by.

Libby knew about men's clothing. Walt, her ex-husband, had spent more on his own back in a month than she and David together spent in a year. For a man whose family had been rolling in money for generations, Walt was surprisingly miserly where his wife and son were concerned. But then, that was just one more of his little cruelties. Making her beg for every penny and then criticizing her for the way she dressed.

"Figured it out yet?"

Startled, Libby shook her head, and then reached up to shove in the pins that slipped from her upswept hair. "Sorry. It's been a long time and my eyes aren't what they used to be.'' Which was why she was wearing her contacts.

''Right. You'll probably hear that excuse more than once tonight, that is if you're planning on going inside.''

''Are you?'' Libby asked tentatively. Maybe it wouldn't be so scary if she had someone to hide behind the first few minutes.

''Are you?'' he countered.

''What's the matter, don't tell me you're afraid to go in there.''

''As you said, it's been a long time, and I doubt that I'll remember many faces. I haven't kept up with anyone from the past.''

''Then why'd you come?''

Jake shrugged. He'd asked himself that same question more than once since he'd left home tonight. He still didn't know. Some kind of symbolism, he supposed, but damned if he intended to try to explain that to some middle-aged housewife dressed up in her Sunday best. ''Look, if you want to, we could go in together, look the old gang over, pay our respects and then get the hell out, duty done for the next twenty years.'' The offer surprised Jake as much as it surprised the woman.

''I'm game if you are,'' Libby replied. ''To tell the truth, I hate like the devil to have gone to all this trouble and expense for nothing.''

The tickets hadn't been that much. Just enough to cover the costs, Jake figured. As if reading his mind, she said, ''Not just the ticket, but my new scent. I think I overdid it.''

Leaning over, he dutifully sniffed the air near her right cheek. ''Just right. Je Reviens?'' he asked, and even in the semidarkness, he could see her eyes widen. They were large, possibly green, and either her lashes were naturally dark or she had a deft hand with mascara. For some reason, he was pretty sure it was nature's quirky gift. Pale blond hair, much too glossy to have come from a bottle, and dark brows and lashes. Cassie would've killed for a combination like that.

"You're good," Libby said admiringly as she let herself out. Either that or he'd known a lot of women.

Jake met her halfway around the car. "Jake Hatcher," he said. "I figure if we start out knowing even one other person at this bash, we'll be ahead of the game."

Libby grinned, and Jake decided he'd been right about the tooth. It definitely added something. "Libby Porter," she said. "I used to be Libby Dwiggins."

He'd been right about that, too. The name didn't ring any bells. "Nice to know you, Libby Porter. Shall we?" He extended an elbow, and she tucked her hand in the crook.

The band was loud, but surprisingly good. Libby winced, and Jake leaned down and murmured against her ear, "Maybe they supply earplugs. I could ask." Evidently she wasn't a regular patron of nightclubs. The decibel level was about average.

"I'm pretty good at reading lips. I'll manage."

"Bombs away, then. Uh-oh. Name tags at two o'clock. Want to take evasive action?"

"If that's who I think it is, evasive action isn't going to do us any good. Hall monitor, secretary of everything, worst snitch in school."

"I thought she looked familiar. She collared me once for posting a vacancy sign on old Harry's hat." Old Harry being the principal. Jake smiled at the approaching woman and reached out to scoop up two tags from among the few left, ignoring her look of avid curiosity.

"We'll take these, thanks," he told her, and turning

away, he frowned down at Libby's V-necked dress with the modest shoulder pads and narrow belted waist. "Uh...where shall I put it?"

"How about that waste can over there behind the bar?"

"Right." Jake disposed of the tags and after a brief conference with the bartender, returned with two drinks. "White wine all right?" His own was seltzer in a wineglass. With an olive. It had been a long, dry spell, but some lessons a man didn't have to learn twice.

After half an hour of mingling, peering at name tags and explaining that their own had gotten mixed up and were in the process of being replaced, Jake steered Libby toward a bank of potted jungle. "Look, I don't want to cramp your style, Libby. If you want to wing it, feel free. Now that I've got my bearings, I'll be okay."

Libby tried not to let her disappointment show. It was hardly the first brush-off she'd experienced, and this one at least had the advantage of being polite.

"Sure. I'm okay now, too," she said, smiling as if she weren't tempted to dive under the nearest palm tree. "And Jake, thanks for everything. Out there, I mean—and this." She waved a hand vaguely toward the gyrating couples on the dance floor.

"Look, if you want to dance or anything—" he began, but she shook her head quickly.

"Oh, no! That is, thanks, but no thanks. I don't."

"Don't, or won't?"

"Can't. Don't know how. Not very well, at least."

Shrugging, Jake reached up and captured one of her hairpins just before it fell, shoved it in and then stepped back. "That I can't believe," he countered gently.

"Believe it. I was born with two left feet."

Jake glanced down at her trim feet in the fragile silk

shoes. He said nothing, simply lifting his thick black brows.

"But look, don't let me stop you. See that woman over there in the green sequins, with the long red hair? She's a terrific dancer. I've been watching her. I think her name's Candy or something or other. Why not go over and renew an old friendship?"

Jake followed her gaze, sized up the woman in question and shrugged again. If she wanted to get rid of him, no problem. He hadn't planned on adopting her. "I can't quite place her."

"Don't worry, I expect she'll place you," Libby said softly. Jake shrugged, and a moment later she was watching him weave his way across the crowded floor. She didn't know Jake Hatcher from Adam's off ox, but one thing she was sure of. He wasn't the sort of man any woman could forget, not if she'd ever experienced that sexy, masculine appeal of his at close range. Libby had known arrogant men before. Walt, for instance. But unlike her ex-husband, Jake's arrogance had nothing to do with what he owned and everything to do with who he was.

As she watched the green-sequined redhead react to Jake like kudzu on a pine tree, Libby reminded herself that she had room in her life for only one male, and that male was her son, David. This whole reunion thing had been a mistake. It wasn't as if she had any real friends from her high school days. She'd been the quintessential nerdess, the butt of everyone's favorite jokes.

"I thought I recognized that blond mop of yours. Libby Dwiggins?"

Libby spun around at the sound of a friendly voice. Her gaze went up and up and up, and her eyes widened. "Kenny? Kenny Smith?"

"Hey, you remembered me!"

"As if I could ever forget the only member of the senior class who was nice to me when being nice to Libby Dwiggins wasn't cool! Oh, Kenny, how in the world *are* you?"

He hugged her and held her away, silently pursing his lips as his gaze roved over her with brief, if flattering, attention. "Hey, look at you! I knew I should've put in my bid before the rush started." He reached for her left hand and touched the ring on her third finger. It was an inexpensive one she'd bought herself—her freedom ring, she called it. She had put away Walt's gaudy diamond set for David, but she hadn't felt quite right without something on the third finger of her left hand.

They talked about Kenny's job as a social worker in New Jersey, and Libby told him about moving back into her old home, and they laughed and tried to pick out familiar faces. The sweet-faced butterball in pink was the head cheerleader. Oh, and wasn't that the star quarterback? The one with the beer belly? He still wore the sideburns that had been popular back then, and Libby felt a sudden, quite unexpected kinship with him.

"That's Ted Smith, the football star, isn't it?"

"Yeah—I think he owns his own garage now."

"I used to have the most awful crush on him," she confessed.

"Mine was on Cheryl." The cheerleader. "Remember that last game, when I tripped and spilled a hot dog loaded with chili in her lap?"

Libby laughed, and Kenny led her out onto the floor before she quite realized what he was doing. Having reached the lofty altitude of six feet eight in junior high school, he'd been something of a misfit, too, although basketball had saved him from complete social ostracism.

But he'd always been kind, and as Libby bumped knees and toes in an attempt to follow his lead, she told herself she might have known he would end up helping others the same way he had helped her through a miserable adolescence.

Jake, leaning against the wall, sipped at his third seltzer and watched the two laughing people galloping gracelessly across the floor. She'd been right. She wasn't very good. But then, with that tall drink of water for a partner, it was small wonder.

She really came alive when she laughed. Her hair was nearly undone by now, the shaggy coil brushing her shoulders. Her cheeks were flushed and her eyes—they were green, just as he'd thought—sparkled like wet oak leaves. Good or not, she wouldn't have any trouble finding partners.

Handing his glass to a passing waiter, Jake left. Coming here had been a waste of time. He'd run into several guys he used to know, but then, when he'd introduced himself as Jake Hatcher, they'd looked puzzled. Not wanting to get into explanations of why he'd dropped his last name when he'd started the long climb out of the gutter, he'd moved on.

Of course, the redhead was another matter. Candy Travers. Twice divorced, and game to try her luck again. She'd remembered him, remembered his name, and made it pretty obvious that she was more than willing to pick up where they'd left off before. Which, if he remembered correctly, had been at a house party in Blowing Rock, in an indoor Olympic-size pool...sans suits.

Two

With Billie asleep in the guest room and David, his mouth showing vestiges of a toothpaste mustache, sleeping soundly in his bunk bed, Libby hung up her black dress, changed into her pajamas and dragged out one of several boxes she had yet to unpack since moving back home after her divorce.

Oops! Maternity clothes. She *definitely* wouldn't be needing those again. Oh, and here was her great-grandmother's blue bowl. It was one of the few things from her family that Walt had coveted, and she'd delighted in reminding him that under the terms of their agreement, it was not marital property. After so much humiliation, she had savored the small triumph.

Another box held her old stamp collection, an unused photograph album and a bundle of twenty-year-old letters from a pen pal in Holland. Ancient history.

Naturally it was in the last box she searched in. Libby

remembered telling someone who had made the same remark once that it would be silly to go on looking after finding what they were searching for in the first place they looked. For her troubles she had earned a dirty look and a snide remark.

Dusting her hand on the seat of her pajamas, she pulled out the high school annual and leaned her back against the washing machine as she began leafing through it. There were hardly any autographs. No one had offered and she hadn't had the nerve to ask. Except for Kenny Smith, who had scrawled some illegible sentiment, wishing her either gut cheese and jag, or good cheer and joy.

Funny how pinched all the faces looked. And how very young. Dwiggins, Libby. No clubs, no superlatives. Her grades had made her eligible for Honor Society, but she'd never been invited to join, and she'd lacked the courage to ask. Poor, pudgy little dumpling, her earnest, nearsighted glare hidden behind owlish plastic-rimmed glasses. No wonder she hadn't attracted many friends!

Libby flipped the pages. It wasn't her own picture she'd been searching for. F, G, H...Hall, Haltzer, Hawthorn. No Hatcher. She closed the book and dropped it back inside the carton, along with her old college textbooks and several *Man From U.N.C.L.E.* comic books.

Dammit, she *did* remember him! He looked different after twenty years, but she was almost certain she remembered him...only the name Hatcher wasn't in the book, and neither was his picture.

The rest of the week passed uneventfully, and by the middle of the following week Libby had all but forgotten Jake Hatcher and the class reunion. She called Aunt Lula over in Davie County to tell her how much she appreciated being able to count on Billie to baby-sit occasionally, and listened to a compendium of advice in the event she should ever find herself stricken with lower-back pain.

After seeing David off on the school bus, Libby started the wash, smeared on a film of lip gloss and grabbed her purse. She had a dozen errands to do, including depositing Walt's child-support check, which had been late, as usual. She suspected he deliberately delayed it, hoping she would call and beg. One of his favorite games had been keeping her short of money so she would have to ask for whatever she needed. It gave him a sense of power.

According to one of their mutual friends, Sara Dwyer, Walt had always been a control freak, even in kindergarten. Sara had grown up with Walt, attending the same exclusive schools, their families summering at the same exclusive resorts. Surprisingly Sara and Libby had become good friends, but when the split came, Sara had sided with Walt. Like to like. It wasn't enough that Walt got to keep the house they had built together, the cottage at Roaring Gap and the two newest cars—the wretch even got to keep their friends!

But in the end, Libby kept the only thing she truly valued. For months, ever since it became obvious that her marriage was disintegrating, the question of custody had terrified her. Walt's family owned half the county, including the best law firm within three hundred miles. By the time the divorce papers were signed, she had lost all the weight she'd gained back after David was born, and all of the self-confidence, too.

Walt had used the threat of taking David from her to cut even the minimal settlement allowed her in the prenuptial agreement, and she had been too frightened to realise that it was an empty threat. Besides, Walt didn't really want a child underfoot. He had told her more than once that he'd played the husband-father bit long enough to know that it really wasn't his thing. At forty he was eager to cut his losses and try something new.

By that time, Libby had been only too glad to be cut, but David was another matter. The first time she had come upon her son crying and asking why Daddy didn't like him anymore, the dregs of a long-dead love had been flushed away for good. If it wasn't for David, Libby would have taken great pleasure in throwing his tiny settlement back in his face, but pride wouldn't put food on the table or a roof over David's head, and with David needing her more than ever, she couldn't very well go out and find a job that would support them both, even if jobs were plentiful for middle-aged, inexperienced women. The prenuptial agreement hadn't left much room for negotiation, but at least she'd been able to get a reasonable amount of child support.

Ten years earlier, in the throes of her first and only love affair, Libby would have signed away her right arm if Walt had asked her to. He'd been handsome, charming and extremely wealthy, although she hadn't known it at the time. When she had finally realized just which family of Porters he belonged to, and what they stood for in that area, she couldn't believe he had wanted her.

Of course by that time, she had lost her puppy fat, and as the uniform of the day had been blue jeans, she had been right in style. Country was in, and Libby was nothing if not country. The genuine article, as her New York City roommate had proclaimed.

Then, too, she had still been a virgin. That had evidently been something of a novelty in Walt's circle of friends.

When the time came, she had signed the agreement. She would have signed her own death warrant if he'd asked her to, but he had assured her that it was only a formality. "See, the thing is, my family owns this law firm, and they think they have to do these things to earn their keep. It doesn't mean a thing, sweetheart, it's just a formality."

And blindly, blithely in love, she had signed away her rights. The next time she had given it a thought it had been when Walt had told her that in light of that same agreement, she should consider herself damned lucky. As it was, he was being more than generous in the amount of child support he was willing to pay.

"Generous, my sweet fanny," Libby muttered now as she whipped into the bank's parking lot. At least she'd had sense enough to get away from Raleigh. Her parents had moved to Florida, and her old home had been between tenants, most of the farmland having long since been sold off to finance her parents' retirement. The house was old, but it was comfortably familiar, with plenty of room for a large garden and maybe even a few chickens. Libby had rented it from her parents, who hadn't wanted to take her money, but she'd told them that Walt insisted.

Ha!

Naturally there was a line at the bank. Lunch-hour traffic. Libby fidgeted. She wanted to get back in time to hang the clothes out, because if she used the dryer, the little dials on the electric service meter spun around like a souped-up top.

"Libby?"

This time it was Libby who spun around, her heart slamming up against her faded Zoological Society T-shirt. "Jake! What are you doing here?"

"Nothing illegal, I assure you." Grinning, Jake thought this was more like it. T-shirt and jeans, sneakers and ponytail. A touch of gray, but it blended with the gold into a damned attractive amalgam. He hadn't planned on following up their first meeting, but on the other hand, he'd never been one to sneer at fate. "How about you?"

"Last in a long list of errands. The monthly deposit."

Alimony, probably. He'd wondered if she was divorced when he'd noticed the ring on her third finger, left hand. It wasn't a wedding band, but as it was the only ring she wore, he figured it must have some significance. Besides, her name hadn't been Porter back in high school.

"Have you had lunch?" he asked.

"I seldom bother." Libby's mind shifted automatically into a defensive position. He was going to invite her to lunch. She would have to insist on paying her own way, and she couldn't afford it, having blown far too much on that blasted reunion thing.

"Seldom bother to *eat?*"

Taking her place before a free teller, Libby handed over her deposit, already made out, and turned back to Jake. "To eat lunch. I always eat a good breakfast and a good dinner, so that—but why am I telling you this?"

Jake's eyes twinkled. Under the bank's bright lights, he looked even more attractive than she'd remembered. There were deep grooves bracketing the mouth she had first thought of as bitter—and saw no reason now to change her mind. He had the kind of cheekbones that made his skin stretch leather-tight down over a solid jaw. Altogether a formidable face, she decided—except for the eyes. Why was it that underneath the twinkle, she sensed so much sadness? So much pain? She sensed it, wondered at it briefly and then mentally began to back away.

"Look, I'd better dash," she told him with a blinding, lap-toothed smile. "I still have to—but it was nice seeing you again, and—oh, goodness, would you look at the time!"

With the delicate precision of a forty-ton bulldozer, Jake plowed through her polite excuses. "You don't eat lunch, but you do eat dinner, right?"

Libby snatched at her deposit slip and took a step backward. Moving up to the counter, Jake slid over a thick envelope without ever releasing her from those dark, compelling eyes. "Okay, so we'll have dinner."

Panic struck, and she began to back out the exit lane. "Oh, no, I couldn't. I have to—that is, I promised—"

"No problem. We don't have to make it tonight. I've got a meeting tomorrow night, but how about Thursday? About seven?"

"Jake, I—"

"What are you afraid of?"

"Afraid?" Libby nibbled at her lower lip. Was she afraid?

Damned right she was afraid! And it wasn't just because of the way that David might react. Since the separation he had reacted with either embarrassing hostility or equally embarrassing adulation to every adult male she had spoken with even casually. After years of Walt's neglect, he was so starved for masculine attention that she hadn't dared think about dating, even if she'd had the opportunity.

"What's your address?"

"I don't have an address. That is, I do, but it's a rural route number." Why am I even considering this? she asked herself frantically. This man has danger written all over him! Caution: Jake Hatcher may be hazardous to your heart!

"Okay then, tell me how to find you. Oh, and what kind of food do you like? Ethnic? Steak? Seafood?"

Libby dropped her deposit slip, bent over to pick it up and collided with Jake halfway down. He kissed his fingertip, placed it on her forehead the way she'd done to David a hundred times, and her defenses crumbled like a paper fortress. "Tell you what, we'll wait and decide which restaurant later. Now, how about those directions?"

It might have been sunspot activity. It might be the holes in the ozone layer. Whatever the cause, Libby's mature, well-insulated brain suddenly shorted out. Fizzle, sizzle, zap! She heard herself saying, "Look, why don't I just meet you somewhere? There's this Mexican place—"

"Casa Gallardo, Tijuana Fats, Casa Azul, Casa—"

"That one. Azul whatever." She'd heard Billie mention it last week as having good, affordable food.

"You're the boss," he conceded. "So it's Thursday night, seven, in the lobby. I'll see you there."

Libby drove home in a daze. What on earth had come over her? She had neither the time nor the emotional energy to waste on getting involved with a man, and she was very much afraid that any dealings at all with a man like Jake Hatcher would constitute involvement. On her part, at least.

It was that sneaky shot about her being the boss. If the man had deliberately aimed for her biggest weakness, he couldn't have scored higher!

On Thursday night Libby changed her dress four times and finally settled for her gray-black-and-gold paisley slacks with the dark gray knit top. Walt had hated the outfit from the moment she'd told him that she'd bought it on sale at a discount store.

Billie had been recruited once more, and Libby explained to David that she was only going out to dinner with an old school mate.

"Can I imbite Jeff to dinner at our house?"

"May I, David. And of course you may in*vite* Jeff," Libby said as she hugged her son good-night. It was the first time he had asked to have any of his new friends over. She took it as a good sign.

Libby had never been comfortable in social situations, although for a while after her marriage to a wealthy, extremely social Raleigh man, she had learned to play the part with some success. Once her marriage had started coming apart, however, she had concentrated all her energies on being there for David. Since moving back to her home town, she had gone alone to a few movies, a few lectures and one high school reunion, using them as an excuse to ask her cousin Billie to come baby-sit.

She had done it far more for David's sake than for her own, needing to prove to him that even though she left him for a few hours, he could trust her to return. Each time, he seemed a little more secure, but Libby knew he was still struggling with his anger for what his parents had done to him. At this stage, his moods seemed to swing between fierce dependence and equally fierce independence.

Casa Azul was easy enough to find, and Libby pulled in only three cars away from where Jake sat waiting. He was there to help her out almost before she had set the parking brake. She looked up, blinked and took a deep breath, bracing herself to accept the hand he held out to her.

Oh, mercy. Did all men look so incredibly sexy under night lighting? Was it the setting, or was it just Jake?

Or was she getting weird in her old age?

"What are you sighing about?" he murmured, the sound of his voice as deep and raspy as a lion's purr.

"You wouldn't believe me if I told you."

"Try me."

She thought quickly and came up with the most plausible excuse she could think of. "That wasn't a sigh, it was my stomach growling. I'm starving," she said, and Jake threw back his head and laughed.

"Yeah. Me, too," he said, still chuckling as he ushered her inside. It occurred to Jake that he had laughed more in the short time he had known her than in all the past seven years.

He offered her wine, but because she had to drive home later, Libby declined. So did Jake. She considered it a mark in his favor. Walt had never let a little thing like driving afterward keep him from enjoying a party to the fullest. Which meant that Libby had never been able to enjoy them at all, for he wouldn't hear of her driving his high-priced European sports car.

It had been one more reason for her to stop going to parties, not that Walt had protested her staying home. He'd already made it painfully obvious that he would never lack female companionship.

Stop thinking like a wife and begin thinking like a woman, Libby reminded herself. But not *too* much like a woman, she amended cautiously.

As if by mutual consent, they stuck to safe topics, such as politics and religion. Libby didn't ask what Jake did for a living, or what he'd been doing these past twenty years. In return, Jake respected Libby's privacy enough not to ask about the ring on her finger, about the shadows behind those sudden, almost-too-bright smiles, or the calluses on her small, beautifully shaped hands. They were both careful to avoid touching on the personal, yet by the end of the evening, each felt they knew the other considerably better than before.

Jake found himself enjoying her quirky sense of humor and her independence. As a general rule he found fiercely independent women a bit abrasive for his taste, but there was a gentleness about Libby Porter, a vulnerability even, that struck a responsive chord deep inside him, and he admitted to himself that with any encouragement at all he might find himself sexually attracted to her. Still, as that encouragement didn't seem forthcoming, he saw no reason why they couldn't enjoy the occasional evening out. Convivial, congenial companionship. Nothing threatening on either side.

Libby was relaxed. She was also tired. She had breezed through her usual chores to leave herself time to clean the gutters, put up a new clothesline and repair a broken back step. Now she stifled a yawn. They were on their fourth cup of after-dinner coffee, having both declined dessert, when Jake said casually, "The band at the hotel the other night wasn't half-bad. I understand they play there every weekend, if you'd like to try your luck at dancing."

She grinned and shook her head. "Thanks anyway. I doubt if your insurance covers the hazard of dancing with Libby Porter."

"Ever hear of steel-toed shoes?" He stood and held her chair, and Libby glanced down at his size twelves. Jake was a large man, in all respects.

"I've never heard of steel-toed dancing slippers."

"Didn't you ever take ballet lessons?"

"You saw me with Kenny Smith at the reunion. Did it look to you as if I'd studied ballet?" She laughed, and Jake decided braces just might be overrated. There was something to be said for a less-than-perfect smile. A lot to be said for hers, in fact.

A week later Jake called and asked Libby to go dancing with him at the hotel where they had first met. Hearing her start to refuse and then hesitate, he wondered if maybe, like him, she occasionally got tired of staring at one more in a long line of empty evenings alone.

"Of course, if you've got other plans," he said. Hell, what made him think he was the only man she knew?

"Jake, I told you I'm not much of a dancer."

"We don't have to dance if you don't want to. We can listen to the music, watch other couples, have dinner and unwind. I need it, even if you don't, and if I don't go out, I'll just end up working."

"Oh, so you're one of those, hmm?"

"Afraid so."

"All right, but I'm warning you, if you insist on dancing, don't say I didn't warn you."

"I think you've managed to get your point across." He grinned. Wondering if she was smiling, too, he found himself picturing that lap-toothed grin of hers and smiling even more broadly.

At thirty-eight, Libby's skin was considerably thicker than it had been back in her more impressionable years. The fact that no boy had ever asked her to dance until she was too old to learn gracefully was pretty low on her list of things to worry herself sleepless over. All the same, she wished she had taken advantage of a few lessons back when she could have afforded it. Walt wasn't a dancer, either—at least not with his own wife.

The days dragged by, but finally the weekend rolled around. Jake was picking her up at home, and she debated inviting him in to meet David, but for David's sake, she decided against it. If he got his hopes up over the man who had come to pump out the septic tank, a man who spit and swore and had a naked woman tattooed on his right bicep, she didn't dare take the risk of exposing him to Jake Hatcher.

With a cheerful wave and a final word of advice to Billie, Libby let herself out as soon as she heard the crunch of tires on her graveled driveway. Jake was already halfway up the front walk. She met him there, and without comment other than to say that she was prompt, he took her arm and reversed directions.

They didn't talk much on the way into town. Libby toyed with the handle of her purse and cut frequent glances toward Jake's profile. It would have looked right at home on Mount Rushmore, she decided. Forcing her eyes deliberately to the front, she inhaled the subtle scent of leather upholstery and a masculine cologne—cedar, sandalwood, citrus?

Oh, Lord, something tells me this was a big mistake.

The doorman was suitably obsequious, the food excellent for all it tasted like wet cardboard to Libby, and the music didn't seem quite so loud as she remembered. Certainly no woman could have asked for a more attractive, more attentive dinner date. She told herself that maybe her luck was finally turning. She might not be any man's dream lover, but she was here, wasn't she? Jake was looking at her as if she were more interesting than the wallpaper, which was a novelty in itself. Walt had spent so much time staring over the top of her head whenever they went out to eat that she'd often been tempted to feel for a halo...or horns.

And if she needed any other evidence that where there was life there was hope, David had brought home a friend from school and they had played quietly for more than two hours without a fight. And the foot valve on the well pump had only been waterlogged, so she wasn't going to have to buy a new pump. And the weather had turned cool enough so that she could wear her favorite dress, one she'd splurged on back in the days before she'd lost her last illusion of a happy ever after.

"Penny for them," Jake murmured.

"Weather, illusions, fights and foot valves."

His eyes widened. They were dark, neither brown nor gray, but an oddly attractive blend of both. "What are you, a meteorologist, a magician or an engineer?"

She laughed. "You left out the fights. Actually, none of the above. Harried home owner. Mine's not exactly new, in case you didn't notice."

"You live with your parents?" He'd wondered about that. It wasn't too surprising that a woman, either divorced or temporarily unemployed, might move back home to care for aging parents.

"My parents retired to a one-bedroom house in a one-streetlight town in Florida. They think it's heaven. I still have family in the area, of course. Aunts, uncles, cousins..."

And a son. One very dear, very troubled, very wonderful son. "And a—" she started to say.

But Jake apparently didn't want to talk about family, hers or his. For an instant, his face tensed, all expression wiped away. It happened so quickly that Libby thought she must have imagined it, especially when he stood and reached for her hand. "Steel toes," he said with that lazy, familiar grin. "Shin guards, too, just in case you're a high stepper. So do your worst, lady, I'm ready for you."

With a demureness that would have shocked her had she even been aware of it, Libby accepted his hand, stood and moved into his arms. "How can I refuse such a gracious invitation?"

Later she would blame it on the slow, seductive melody, an old love song from the forties she vaguely remembered hearing her mother sing while working in the kitchen. On the other hand, Jake's cologne, as subtle as it was, was not entirely innocent of blame.

The last thing on earth she wanted to blame was those arms that held her as if she were infinitely fragile, infinitely precious, and the hard chest that somehow drew her cheek to rest against it as they slowly swayed to the music.

Jake didn't actually dance. What he did do was hold her so that every square inch of her body was electrically alive, inside and out, to every square inch of his. Libby forgot to breathe, and when she remembered, she had to concentrate on the process so intently that she forgot she couldn't dance.

"See?" Jake murmured against her ear. He had to lower his head, because even with her three-inch heels, her ear barely came up to his shoulder. "I told you you could dance."

"Is that what we're doing?" she blurted out before she could control her tongue. "I didn't say what you just heard. I didn't say a thing."

He chuckled. Resting his cheek against the top of her head, he swayed gently from side to side, and after a while it occurred to Libby that neither of them had moved their feet in some time.

"Smart man. You knew I wouldn't be such a hazard as long as I didn't move my feet while we were dancing."

His arms tightened until she could feel his rib cage, feel the shape of his masculine hips. "Honey, that's where you're dead wrong. As hazards go, I'd rank you right up there with live volcanoes and acid rain."

As soon as she regained control of her tongue, Libby reminded him that it was getting late. Jake didn't argue. They were silent on the way home, and this time Libby knew better than to look at him. Halfway out of town, Jake switched on a classical music station, which reduced some of the tension that had sprung up between them.

Merciful heavens, what had she been thinking of? Had she honestly thought she was immune? Just because she had never slept with any man but Walt, and that had ended years ago, did she think her sexual nature had been permanently laid to rest?

Maybe it had. These days the one-man, one-woman system was about the only safe course, and even that was not without hazards. Besides, she wasn't anywhere near ready to even think about...that sort of thing.

"Look, um...I'm going to be out of town for a couple of weeks," Jake said as they neared her turnoff.

"Yes, well, I've just remembered that I promised to visit my aunt and uncle, and I can't put it off much longer." She twisted her purse handle again. The gold-chain handle hadn't been designed for such service. It broke, and she retrieved her purse from the floor.

"So I guess we'll both be tied up for a while," Jake said, and numbly, Libby nodded.

Nothing had changed, she told herself as she let herself inside after a brusque and rather hurried good-night.

Nothing at all. She was following the same familiar pattern. Like a hungry, homeless mutt, falling all over her own clumsy feet to lavish affection on someone who neither needed it nor wanted it.

Three

Jake sprawled in the oversize leather chair and stared at the bottle of Scotch whiskey, feeling only the faintest wisp of regret. It had been years since he had given in to the temptation. Of alcohol, at least.

One demon at a time, Jake, old man—one demon at a time.

Weaknesses of the flesh came in a multitude of forms. The one he was currently wrestling didn't happen to come in a bottle. Instead it had slipped past his guard in the guise of a stubborn-jawed female with a glossy crop of gray-blond hair, eyes the color of oak leaves and hips that flared sweetly from a waist he could almost span with his two hands.

Libby Porter. Libby—what had she said she'd been before? Wiggins? Priggins?

Whatever. She'd been married at least once. Which meant that she was now widowed or divorced or separated. Regardless of all he *didn't* know about her, Jake was pretty sure she wasn't the type to run around on a current husband. Some women, maybe. Some women surely! But not Libby Porter.

So...did he want her enough to risk getting involved, or didn't he?

For the first year or so after Johnny—after Cassie—Jake had been in freefall. It had been in a one-cell jail in a one-horse town in southwest Virginia, where he'd woken up with two black eyes, a broken nose and a right hand the size of a Smithfield ham, that he had finally been forced to face up to what he'd become.

Moose Capehart had been a year behind him in high school. The kid had been shooting for a football scholarship until he'd got messed up with drugs and dropped out. Some fifteen or so years later, as a deputy sheriff, he had recognized the bruised and bloody boozer who'd been thrown into his neat, ruffle-curtained jail on a D and D.

"Man, you are *dumb,* you know what I mean? I mean you are *real dumb!* I used to think you was a real butthead on account o' being one o' them country-club types from over'n Buena Vista, but I didn't push it, man. I mean, hell, you couldn't help it if your old man was loaded any more'n I could help it if my old man come home knee-walking drunk ever' payday of his life. That's the breaks, I figgered."

"Yeah, well—good seein' you again, too, Moose. How much you charge for a drink in this place?"

Jake had been lucky the guy hadn't dismantled him on the spot. Instead he'd done worse. He'd had his wife, a corn-fed, gingham-upholstered type, bring him over a breakfast tray that had made him sick just to smell—sausage, ham, eggs, pancakes and coffee. After Jake had finished off the pot of black coffee and covered the obscene feast with a napkin, Moose had started talking. About responsibility. About religion. About setting an example for those less fortunate.

Jake had let it roll over his head. It had been all he could do to keep from puking his guts out.

"Now you take me," the creased and spit-polished deputy had said self-righteously. "I got in trouble, and it was my own dumb fault. But I straightened up, man. I got my GED and went to Forsyth Tech, and then I met Nancy Louise and started going to church."

Jake had made some snide remark that he had regretted a thousand times since. He hadn't listened to Moose's sermon, but some of it must have sunk in. A week later he had signed himself into purgatory.

Once he'd dried out and started on the long, slippery climb back, women had been the least of Jake's worries. After winding things up in Virginia, he had moved down to Raleigh and enrolled at State, and eventually moved back to Winston. With both his parents gone by then, there had been no real reason to stay away.

Somewhere along the line it had occurred to him that he wasn't yet quite dead below the belt. He had taken a look around him, considering the odds, but as he'd never particularly cared for the game of Russian roulette, he had simply dug in his heels and worked harder. Worked until he could sleep without dreaming. Or at least dream without weeping.

How many years had it been now? Four? Closer to five. Five years without a drink, nearly that long without a woman.

And then he'd had to run afoul of that damned reunion thing and a woman named Libby Porter! He was beginning to harbor the unwelcome notion that sex just might no longer be all he needed, or even all he wanted, from a woman.

Absentmindedly massaging his temples, he muttered, "Keep it simple, Hatcher. Stick to the basics. You want a woman? Okay. Nothing strange about that."

But a lot had changed over the past few years. It was a different game now.

On the other hand, Libby Porter didn't strike him as the kind of woman who played around. She wasn't some round-heeled bimbo out for a good time. They'd been classmates, after all. She had mentioned having grown up in the house where she was currently living. It had once been part of a small dairy farm. You couldn't get much more wholesome than a dairy farmer's daughter, could you?

Jake's family was vintage Stratford Road. When he'd opted out of returning to prep school for his junior year, his family had grudgingly agreed to allow him to finish at Reynolds High. Society Hill, as it had been called in his parents' day...probably still was.

Jake had had other ideas. He hadn't been about to attend any school where he'd be a year and a half behind everyone else, where most of his classmates would be the younger brothers and sisters of the kids he'd grown up with. At least out in the county he could start fresh, without dragging a whole lot of personal baggage along with him. He'd chosen West Forsyth. His father had pulled a few strings, and Jake had commuted those last two years on his 750 Norton street bike. His family hadn't been too happy about it, but as in most things, they had let him have his way.

The Healy name had stood for something in those days, even in a town built on tobacco money, underwear money and just plain old-fashioned money. A few generations ago a local chemist named Urias Jacob Healy had mixed up a little something for a neighbor in the back room of his Fourth Street pharmacy that cleared up poison ivy practically overnight. Thus was a dynasty born, a fortune made that each succeeding generation of Healys had multiplied.

To old Urias Jacob's simple five-percent aqueous solution of a common chemical was added color, odor and a clever advertising campaign, and the next generations had prospered exponentially.

It had been Jake's father who had branched out into cosmetics. Using the family's pharmaceutical skills and the very best advertising firm money could buy, he had started out with Healy's Essence of Lotus Cosmetiques. Later, sniffing the wind, he had shifted gears and thrown everything behind a new line. Ms. T. Pharmaceuticals, named for Jake's mother, Tansey, had catered to a new breed of women who were cleverly conned into believing that the foundation of power dressing was a line of toiletries with a new name and a crisp, almost masculine new scent.

At Tansey's death, the old man had lost heart. He had followed her in less than two years, but before he had died, he had broken with tradition enough to sell the firm to a Japanese consortium, give each of his three children a million dollars seed money with no strings attached, and then he had donated the rest to various charities.

Jake's older brother had invested in a jet plane. He had died when he and his new toy had crashed somewhere over the Pacific. His sister, Eleanor, was living in Colorado with husband number three, their combined nest eggs having built a popular ski resort.

Jake, the youngest, had chosen to build his empire in Virginia, away from the influence of the Healy name.

He had married a Richmond debutante, and with the ink barely dry on his degree in chemical engineering, he'd gone into plastics, elaborating on a technique of injection molding and adding certain innovations along the way. Between the toy manufacturers, optical-frame makers and a few choice government contracts, he had multiplied his seed money a dozen times over by the time his own son had been five years old.

Jake closed his eyes. A soft groan emerged from the hard line of his lips. *Johnny, Johnny...*

The shrill purr of the phone pulled him out before he got in too deep, and he lunged for it. "Yeah, yeah, whaddya want!"

He could practically feel the throb of reaction on the other end. Briefly he regretted his loss of control. "Sorry. This is Hatcher," he said in a growl that was only marginally less rude.

He heard a sigh, and then a quiet hum. Whoever the poor devil was, he'd lost his nerve. Jake couldn't much blame him. It was...what the hell, it was five minutes past midnight! Whoever the bastard was, he deserved being chewed out! And if it happened to be one of his old drinking buddies from Virginia who had tracked him down and wanted to resurrect the good old days, so much the better.

That had happened a couple of times. People he'd known in the past. Not the good past, but the past after they had lost Johnny. After Cass had left him. After Jake had seen the bottom of too many bottles and too many bars, not to mention a few select jail cells.

The phone rang again, and before he could speak, a breathless voice blurted, "Jake, I'm sorry, but I think I must have left my glasses in your car tonight. Would you please look in the morning, and if you find them, could you please leave them somewhere for me?"

"Libby? You don't even wear glasses. What's this really about?"

"I do so. That is, I wear contacts, but I always carry my glasses in case I have to take them out. I—my purse must have come open when I was—at any rate, they must have fallen out. I hope they're in your car, because if they're not, I don't know what I'll do."

"Hang on, I'll check and call you right back."

"You don't have to—yes, would you, please? I need to know whether or not to lie awake all night worrying."

Jake heard the small catch in her voice, part laughter, part sob. Damn her, anyway, for getting to him this way! He hung up after promising to call her back in five minutes. Within four he was back inside, the needlepoint case in his hand. Curiously he slipped out the contents and examined them. Old habits die hard. One of the first products his plastics company had turned out in that other life of his had been frames. Top-of-the-line plastic frames, wood-grained, leather-grained, designer styles and colors.

These were rimless, wired across the top, lightly tinted and thicker on one lens than the other. The lady had herself one hell of an astigmatism, he mused as he held them up before his own eyes.

He dialed the number she had given him. "Libby? Got 'em. No, you didn't step on them, they're fine. Shall I drop them off on my way out of town in the morning?"

"I don't want you to go out of your way. Are you taking I-40 out of town?"

He was taking 421. "Yeah, sure."

"East or west?"

"West. Shall I bring them on by?" It would mean a slight detour, but what the hell.

"Um...well, there's this grocery store near the Clemmons exit where I do most of my shopping, so if you could just leave them there with the manager, I can pick them up."

Clemmons was almost as convenient to 421 as it was to I-40. Libby named the store, and Jake said he'd drop them off first thing. He pressed the disconnect button in the middle of her slightly incoherent thanks and then continued to stare down at the receiver, cursing her in a halfhearted way for doing it to him again.

Damn! When the sound of a woman's voice over the phone could turn him on this way, he was in pretty bad shape. A woman with an astigmatism! A woman whose hair was grayer than his own. A woman whose right central incisor lapped ever so slightly over the left one, making him want to feel it with his tongue.

Making him want to feel *her* with his tongue...

Oh, geez, if this was what too much celibacy did to a man at forty, he wasn't sure he'd ever make it to forty-one!

As the crow flew, Libby's supermarket was about halfway between a job Jake's firm had recently bid on, and his office north of town. Her house wasn't that much farther out. If they landed the Davie County job, he'd probably be out in her neck of the woods pretty often.

Jake was a big-iron man. Having hit bottom after losing first his son, then his wife and then his business, he'd started the long climb back by getting another degree, this one in mechanical engineering. A few years ago he had sold a tract of land he owned in the mountains, moved back home and bought into a heavy-construction firm. His partner, Bostic Clodfelter, was a sixty-one-year-old widower with a daughter living down in Mobile, Alabama. The two men had spent two weeks together in a fishing shack on a deserted island off the coast, where primitive didn't begin to describe the lifestyle. Once back in civilization, they had both been ready to sign the partnership papers with no further discussion.

Since then they had been expanding slowly but steadily. When the federal highway bill had been signed, they had added half a million dollars' worth of equipment to their fleet of heavy metal in readiness.

Jake dropped off Libby's glasses on Monday. A few hours later he was on the site of the first of three jobs they were considering bidding on. After only a brief inspection of the terrain, he turned thumbs down. He didn't like blasting, not on these grades. With a minimum of 800,000 cubic yards of dirt to be moved, most of it granite or shale, the wear and tear on the equipment would cut too deeply for comfort into their modest profit margin. Four percent they could live with. Even three. On a job like this, with the additional equipment they would have to rent, it would be closer to two.

On Tuesday afternoon he checked out the next project. Short span bridge, closer to home. They could probably handle it without having to transport the big screed by using preformed components and bringing in the small crane. This one was worth sending Mac's crew in for a tighter estimate.

There were two more possibilities, one of which Jake judged worth the time and expense of working up a bid, the other he considered too hazardous for any crew that wasn't half mountain goat. Their crews were used to working the Piedmont and points east, not west in more mountainous terrain.

By the end of the week, Jake had finished up the preliminaries. He'd figured six days, told Libby two weeks, and done the job in less than one. He stayed over another day in an effort to convince himself that he wasn't rushing back on her account.

He wanted to call her the minute he hit town, but because he was so damned hungry for the sound of her voice, he didn't. Not the first night, nor the second one. Monday, he figured. Or even Wednesday. He'd give himself a decent cooling-off period, and maybe on Wednesday night he would call her and see if she wanted to go out somewhere and eat.

But after laying out his plans with the cool precision of an experienced engineer, Jake found himself going out of his way to shop at her grocery store. It was downright disgusting! He never shopped for groceries more than a couple of times a week. He wasn't that particular what he ate. Most of the time he ate out, anyway.

On Saturday he picked up milk. He drank a lot of milk. On Sunday afternoon, he realized that he was practically out of bread. He might want to make himself a sandwich at home instead of going out every night. On Monday, when he was supposed to be working up a set of figures on the Hopkins Hill job, he was tilted back in his office chair, twisting a pencil between his thumb and forefinger as he stared at the intricate shadow cast by a chart rack and the corner of a filing cabinet.

What the devil, she wasn't all that special, he told himself. He could take her or leave her, so why not just take her and be done with it? What did he have to prove, anyway?

Okay, so he happened to have an addictive personality. He'd kicked booze, hadn't he? He'd kicked cigarettes, and if he had to, he could damned well kick Libby. Figuratively speaking, of course. There was no way he'd ever get hooked on her. That part of his life was over. That part of him was stone cold dead.

So where was the danger? All he had to do was keep it light. Keep it on the surface. Hell, she probably wasn't looking to get involved again any more than he was!

Wednesday, he figured. He'd wait until Wednesday and give her a call. Her place or his, wherever she was more comfortable. He shouldn't have to spell it out for her.

At five-thirty he was halfway home when the craving for Moon Pies hit him out of the blue. A staple commodity, they could be bought in most every convenience store in the southeast portion of the United States, but Jake had a hunger on him for a Moon Pie from a certain supermarket near Clemmons. Before he could begin to question the urge, he was headed into the sunset along with the usual clog of going-home traffic.

Her station wagon was the first thing he saw when he pulled into the parking lot, and he nearly creamed a Honda. Deliberately he made himself circle the lot twice before he eased into a vacant slot and switched off the engine.

Now, what was it he was out of? he asked himself as he clicked the ring full of brass keys as if they were worry beads.

Oh, yeah. Milk.

She was browsing the produce, a battery of fluorescent lights glinting on the familiar crop of silver-gold hair. She did the cookie aisle, and Jake grabbed a bag at random. He followed a discreet two rows away while she finished loading her basket and took her place in the checkout line, and then he eased in behind her, feeling unaccountably vulnerable. His basket held a bag of cookies, a can of succotash, a pouch of Red Man tobacco and a box of pink tissues.

While Libby shuffled through a thick wad of coupons, Jake admired her hair. Thick and glossy, it fell straight as rain to her shoulders. Cassie used to go every two months for what she'd referred to as a body perm. He'd eventually discovered that it was something she did to her hair, not her body.

He glared at the back of Libby's head. Dammit, didn't she even know he was here? He was close enough to see the mole on the back of her neck, and she didn't even know he was here!

"Libby? I thought I recognized you."

Coupons scattered like a covey of quail. Jake retrieved a handful from the floor and handed them over.

"Jake, what on earth are you doing here?" she cried when she'd fished the rest out of her basket. "I thought you were out of town!"

"Nah, I got back a few days ago."

Why didn't you call me? The words hung between them like smoke from a skywriter's tailpipe.

"I, uh...hey, this is a nice store. I, uh...needed some milk."

She laughed, sounding as if she'd just run all the way up a down escalator. Breathless. "Me, too. That is, milk and everything else. Why do I keep hearing that inflation's so low? I know this was cheaper last week." She held up a bottle of dishwashing detergent.

"It's cumulative. Why not use paper plates?"

"The ecology."

"You could always eat out. The restaurant industry would appreciate the patronage."

"My budget wouldn't."

"You know what they say."

"What who says?" The woman in front moved out and the clerk began unloading Libby's basket. Jake realized that he'd forgotten to get the milk he'd come for.

"I don't know who said it, come to think of it, but I know I've heard it."

"Heard *what?*" she demanded with a soft little chuckle that trailed cool fingers up and down his spine.

"That two can eat as cheaply as one."

"I wouldn't be too sure of that."

Before he lost his nerve, Jake dived into the opening he'd created. "Okay, so why don't I grab us a couple of steaks, steal a couple of potatoes out of your basket, and we'll go to my place and test the theory?"

He watched while her crooked incisor sampled the soft pink flesh of her lower lip, watched a pair of lines form between her eyebrows and made himself resist the temptation to smooth them away.

"I've got all these perishables," she said, gesturing, and obediently, he glanced at the groceries the clerk was unloading onto the scarred conveyor belt. Ice cream. Ground beef. Milk. Chockie Bears. Cap'n Crunch.

Chockie Bears? Cap'n Crunch? A six-pack of apple juice?

But it was the Flintstone vitamins that did it. Warning bells began clamoring inside his head. Jake felt the very beginning of panic. He stepped back, bumped into a cart with a kid in the basket and mumbled apologies, staring at the childish treats as if they had suddenly sprouted horns. "On second thought," he mumbled, "I, uh—my—that is, I think my sink's clogged up."

"I've got a knack with clogged pipes."

"Yeah, well—the super—that is, I'd better get back. Maybe another time."

"You could come home with me. My sink's not clogged. I'd planned spaghetti tonight, but I always make enough for a platoon."

"Thanks, but no thanks. Oh, gee, would you look at that! I forgot the milk. Excuse me, Libby—lady—" Like a cornered rat, he deserted the checkout line, leaving his cart blocking traffic, leaving Libby and the strange woman staring after him. Ducking around a pyramid of canned pineapple, he hurried to the far end of the store and leaned over the meat display. His eyes were closed, but he saw with painful clarity a blue plastic bowl with yellow rabbits around the rim and a pool of milk and soggy cereal spreading out around it. His face twisted as he heard the childish voice asking, "Daddy, why is milk always blue when it spills?"

"Jake? Jake, are you all right?"

Drawing a deep breath, he opened his eyes and stared down at the small, callused hand on his sleeve. "Yeah. Yeah, I'm fine, Libby. I just forgot to pick up..."

No. No more lies! When a man reached the point of lying about his grocery list, it was time to pull out.

"Jake, why don't you come home with me? You can watch the news while I make the sauce—I cheat and use bottled, but I add stuff. It's good."

"Honey, I'm sure it is, and you're kind to ask, but I'd better pass it up. It's been a long day and I've got a lot of catching up to do. You understand."

Her eyes said she did. Said she understood all too well. Jake watched her turn away, her chin—that stubborn, elegant, angular jawline of hers—saying what she was too proud to say in words.

Oh, hell, he'd hurt her feelings. That had been the last thing he'd meant to do. Whatever he'd meant—whatever he'd intended, he had never wanted her to be hurt by anything he said or did.

Crossing his arms, he leaned against the cold metal rim of the meat counter, blocking the pork chops until the woman reaching around him for two center-cuts muttered a rude remark.

By the time Jake got outside, Libby was already gone. He pulled out into traffic and found himself turning southwest instead of northeast. The least he owed her was an apology, he told himself.

Four

Jake didn't take time to consider what he was about to do. There was something between him and Libby. Whether he wanted it or not, it was there. Once he'd had a steel splinter lodged in the thumb of his heavy work gloves. The thing had been impossible to find, even with a magnet, but it had irritated the very devil out of his thumb. He'd finally ended up throwing away a brand-new pair of horsehide gloves to put an end to the constant irritation.

He should have ended it right there at the supermarket. There was no reason on God's green earth for him to go after her. The trouble was, he was no longer running on reason. He was running on libido. He was running on sheer gut instinct.

A short time later, Jake pulled up behind her wagon just as she was unloading her sacks. She turned and waited, not smiling—looking almost wary. Then, reaching past the tailgate, she hauled out a bag and settled it on her hip. It was the one with the kids cereal on top. Jake told himself he could handle it.

Yeah, right. The way he'd handled it in the supermarket. He'd taken one good look at her groceries and hit the panic button.

"Hello again. Change your mind?" she asked, and briefly Jake considered making some excuse about noticing that she had a low tire or needed a valve job. It still wasn't too late.

It was too late. It had probably been too late the first time he'd ever laid eyes on her.

And then it hit him. The first time. It hadn't been the reunion, it had been... "Raleigh, wasn't it? About seven or eight years ago? Some fund-raiser or another?" He lifted the sack of groceries from her arm. Through the wreckage of his past, a memory came back to him. "You wore a black velvet tent with a big white organdy bow on the shoulders, and you were sitting at a table with Charlie Alderholt and the Porters."

Porter. Her name was Libby Porter!

Jake winced at his own stupidity. Two engineering degrees, and he was about as sharp as a Ping-Pong ball.

"Jake, are you feeling all right? Why don't you come in the kitchen and sit down while I unload this junk, and then I'll make us a pot of coffee." She leaned inside the station wagon again, and watching the way she moved, the way she looked, Jake wondered why he hadn't tumbled before. Wondered why he didn't get the hell out while there was still time. Wondered what there was about this one woman that kept drawing him back like a five-dollar yo-yo.

Hell, she wasn't even all that outstanding. Strictly speaking, her hips were too wide for her waist, her jaw too firm for that swan's neck of hers, and as for her smile...

Okay, so she had a great smile, but other than that, what was so special about Libby Porter? He could take or leave a dozen Libby Porters, any day of the week.

She emerged with the last sack of groceries and nodded toward the house. "You looked so awful in the store I hated to leave you there alone. Are you feeling better now?"

He held open the screen while she fumbled for her key. "Migraine," he mumbled, wondering just when he had turned into a chronic liar. "Used to have 'em a lot. Haven't had one in over a year." That much, at least, was the truth.

Jake still wasn't quite sure why he was here. Okay, so he'd been mildly attracted to her. She was a spur in his glove, an itch he'd considered scratching. But that was before he knew she had a kid. Before he'd remembered where he'd seen her before, pregnant as a pea pod. That particular kind of involvement he didn't need.

There was a coloring book under the kitchen table, a couple of toy trucks over near the refrigerator, and half a dozen of those bright colored plastic cubes with the holes and pegs on them. Johnny had had a bushel of the things. Jake used to step on them barefoot and threaten to hide them unless Johnny picked them up after he finished playing with them.

"Jake, why don't you—" she began, when he turned on her.

"You've got a kid," he said flatly.

Carefully removing a box of vermicelli from one of the sacks, she nodded slowly. "Yes. His name's David."

"Why didn't you admit it right up front?"

Libby's eyes glinted green fire. Up went the chin.

"Admit it? Is having a child some sort of crime in your book?"

"It might've kept me from wasting my time, that's all."

He watched her pressure gauge shoot up into the red. "Well, now you know, so please don't feel like you have to linger."

"Dammit, Libby, listen to me! If I'd known—"

"No, you listen to me, Jake Hatcher!" She slammed the box down on the counter with no regard for the contents, and Jake winced, his nerves feeling every bit as fragile as the shattered vermicelli. "I didn't ask you to come barging into my life like a blasted steamroller! Not the first time, not the second time, not *any* time! That was your idea!"

"Yeah, well, it was a lousy one!"

"Then why don't you leave? I certainly don't need you. I didn't need you that night of the reunion, when that drunk made a pest of himself. I could've handled him easily enough."

Jake leaned against her refrigerator, crossed his arms over his chest and closed his eyes, waiting for her to finish blowing off.

"And I certainly don't need your permission to have a son!"

"You remember that night, too, don't you?"

"Remember what night?" she snapped.

"The first time we met."

"I don't remember anything! At least I didn't until you mentioned it. Oh, maybe I did, sort of, but I thought it was from school," she admitted grudgingly. "Your picture's not even in the annual, though," she accused. With a bunch of carrots in one hand and a bag of green beans in the other, she was leading with her chin again. Some people never learned, Jake thought.

He felt tired. He felt drained. But oddly enough, he no longer felt quite so defensive. "I remembered you, Libby, but not from twenty years ago." His eyes searched her face as if looking for all the changes the years had brought...and finding them. "From the fund-raiser. I remember one extremely pregnant woman wading through the crowd. It was raining that night, and I followed you out to the lobby, thinking you belonged to Charlie Alderholt, remember?"

Her eyes met his and glanced off. "You found me a cab. I—I had a headache and decided to leave early. If I forgot to thank you then, thanks, Jake. Now I think you'd better leave."

Caught up in remembering the rainy March night, remembering the touching mixture of fragility and determination that had caught and held his attention, Jake didn't move. He had wondered at the time why her husband wasn't looking after her.

Now he knew. No wonder she had looked so sick.

They were both still caught up in the same seven-year-old memory when somewhere in the house a door slammed. A childish voice called out, "Mom! Can Jeffie and me—"

"Jeffie and I," Libby corrected automatically, her gaze still on Jake's face. She saw—thought she saw—a stricken look in his eyes just before a familiar stoniness sealed off all expression.

The boy was small for his age. Dark. Wary. He looked like Porter, but he had a lot of his mother in him, too. The attitude, for one thing. That damn-your-soul tilt to his chin. At the moment, he was scowling up at Jake, and Jake realized that he was scowling right back. He fought down a surge of resentment.

David sidled closer to Libby and grabbed an armful of thigh, his eyes never once leaving Jake's face. Libby's fingers combed through her son's hair, and it occurred to Jake in that instant that he couldn't recall ever having seen Cassie touch Johnny in a simple spontaneous gesture of affection.

He was hurting. Still, he made an effort to smile. It wasn't the boy's problem, it was his own, and it was time he learned to handle it. "So this is your son," he said.

Great. He sounded about as friendly as a No Trespassing sign.

"This is David. David, say hello to Mr. Hatcher."

"I don't like him, Mama," the boy muttered.

Libby flushed a dull shade of magenta. She knelt and gripped the tiny shoulders, and David ducked his head, peering resentfully out of the corner of his eyes at Jake. "David, I want you to apologize to Mr. Hatcher right now. He's a guest in our house."

"Don't want him here." His eyes were dark green, like his mother's. They were rapidly filling with tears, and Jake felt something tearing apart inside him, leaving jagged, painful edges.

"Jake, I'm sorry," Libby said quietly. She stood, with the boy leaning on her. "David usually has better manners than this. Go to your room now, David, I'll speak with you later."

The small face crumpled and burrowed into Libby's belly. Jake felt like two cents' worth of dirt. The kid spun away with one furious last look at Jake, and slammed the door behind him, and Libby's shoulders drooped. She sighed. "I'm sorry. You can see now why I don't invite men home with me."

Jake's eyes frosted over as he followed the familiar course of allowing anger to replace old feelings of guilt and grief. "I guess I can't. Why don't you tell me?" he said, deliberately stoking the anger. Anger he could handle. Anger was easy.

Libby was running water over a sink full of vegetables. "David still misses his father," she said. "Walt—that's my ex-husband—"

"I know who Walt is, remember? He's a self-centered, amoral jerk."

Libby's head came up, a look of surprise on her face. "You know him?"

It was a telling remark, and Jake felt his trumped-up anger begin to dissipate. It wasn't Libby's fault that he had a thing about kids. About the kind of ties that could choke the life out of a man. But just in case she'd misunderstood what he'd been offering her, it was time he set her straight.

No, dammit, he didn't have to set her straight, because he'd never offered her anything! "Look, I'd better be running along, Libby. It was nice seeing you. Maybe we'll do it again one of these days."

"I doubt it."

Jake was in no mood to deal with either the proud tilt of her head or that vulnerable look in her mossy-green eyes. He shrugged and took out the keys to his truck, fingering them restlessly. "Hey, look, you know how it is," he said, covering guilt with a handful of empty words. "Some men, once they hit forty—"

"Yes, I know. You don't have to explain."

No, he didn't, Jake told himself as he strode out to his truck. She probably knew better than most women what damned fools men could make of themselves, at forty and any other age.

A week later, Jake found himself back on Idol's Dam Road. He'd been in the vicinity, and with no conscious decision, he turned off toward Libby's place with nothing in mind other than seeing that she was all right. He had no intention of getting involved. Still, she was alone out there. Sometimes a woman alone needed a helping hand.

Yeah, right. Saint Jake to the rescue!

He hadn't deliberately chosen the middle of a school day, but he was just as glad the kid wouldn't be there. Jake had done some heavy thinking over the past few days. He had reached several conclusions, conclusion number one being that the world was full of kids. They were everywhere you looked, and there wasn't one damned thing he could do about it.

Conclusion number two was that he wouldn't have wanted it otherwise. If something had happened to him, and Cass and Johnny had been left behind, he wouldn't have wanted them to give up on life, to live without men in their lives. Johnny would have needed anther father, someone to help him grow up.

As for Cass…

Not in a long time had Jake allowed himself to think about his ex-wife. It was painful, guilt and anger being no small part of that pain. It wasn't until after Johnny's death that he had learned the full extent of her infidelities. Learned that she'd been in the habit of meeting her lovers at the beach—had, in fact, planned to meet one there that last time, which was why she'd locked Jake into attending the fund-raiser so he wasn't able to go with them.

Cass had planned to leave Johnny at home with the live-in nanny, but the woman had come down with the flu at the last minute, and she had hired a neighborhood teenager to look after him at the beach while she met her current lover.

Jake should never have permitted her to take the boy without Mrs. Raye, who was more of a mother to him than Cass had ever been. Jake's only excuse was that he had been busy. He had deliberately stayed busy, throwing himself into his work, trying desperately to keep from facing the fact that his marriage was falling apart.

But the thing that hurt worst of all, even after seven years, was knowing that it had been his own phone call that had caused his son's death. Jake had wanted to speak to Johnny, to assure him that Daddy would be there the minute he could get away. They'd been out on the beach, Johnny and the sitter, and hearing the phone, the girl had dashed inside to answer it, cautioning Johnny to stay right where she left him.

By the time she'd gone back outside, it had been too late. From the tiny footsteps, they figured he'd been following a sandpiper, or maybe a ghost crab, had strayed too close to the surf, and a wave had caught him, washing him out to sea.

One brief moment, and Jake's world had come to an end. Bright blue eyes, yellow curls that Cass had wanted to cut, and he had wanted to keep—that inquisitive, delightful child's mind, gone. Forever extinguished.

"Daddy, why is milk blue when you spill it and white when you drink it?"

"It has to do with the breakdown of light, son—with small particles that filter out certain frequencies—uh, colors—"

"What are par'cles?"

* * *

Jake was sitting in the company truck, parked in her driveway when Libby saw him. If she hadn't recognized those brawny shoulders in the leather jacket, the shape of his head, the way he sat with one muscular forearm draped across the top of the steering wheel, she might have taken him for a meter reader or some other utility worker in the neighborhood.

"Jake? What are you doing sitting out here by yourself?"

"Nothing, I—hello, Libby." He heard the warming of his own voice and began mentally buckling on armor plate. "I just happened to be working in the area, and I thought I'd stop by and see if you were okay."

"That's nice," she said, still sounding puzzled. "Won't you come in for a cup of coffee? I made some soup—it's nearly noon, if you're hungry."

"No thanks. I guess I'd better run along, but thanks all the same."

So why was it that a few minutes later Jake found himself seated at Libby's kitchen table, hands freshly washed, sleeves turned up to hide the grease stain on his right cuff from where he'd been checking a balky fitting on the Dynapac?

The first time he had ever laid eyes on her—a pregnant, miserable stranger across a crowded room—she had made an impression on him. The next time he'd seen her had been seven years later, in another city, another setting. He hadn't remembered her, not really, yet there'd been something about her that, rational or not, had reached out to him.

But Libby in her own kitchen was something else again. And it was that something else that was making Jake more uneasy by the minute.

It wasn't the kitchen. That was about as ordinary as

they came. Brick-pattern vinyl floor, yellow enameled cabinets, circa 1930s, mason jars of sprouted vegetables in the windowsill—carrot tops, turnip tops, a sweet potato vine.

No, it wasn't just the kitchen, and it wasn't just Libby, either. It was the combination of the two that made him feel as if he were juggling sticks of dynamite on a short fuse.

She was wearing a pink cotton jumpsuit and a pair of grubby sneakers. Hardly seductress equipment. She smelled like soap and spice, and her hair, as usual, was obligingly obeying the laws of gravity by sliding out from under the red bandanna she had used to tie up her ponytail.

Jake told himself he was being foolish. No man could be this turned on by Betty Crocker in pink coveralls. How could anything so sweet and wholesome be so damned sexy? Who'd have guessed that the smell of soap and gingerbread and chicken soup could act as an aphrodisiac? That was hitting below the belt. Literally!

Jake had been raised in a twelve-bedroom house by a staff of five and a couple of absentee parents who believed children should be relegated to third-floor playrooms, club nurseries and boarding schools. All he remembered of the kitchen was black-and-white tile floors and a dragon in a white uniform.

As for the kitchen in his efficiency, it was white and stainless steel and it smelled of pine-scented disinfectant, courtesy of the woman who came in for an hour or so three times a week. The kitchen in the Virginia house had been the best of the lot. Lots of copper stuff hanging around, blue pottery on the shelves. Cass had supervised the decoration and then turned it over to their housekeeper. Decorative, his ex-wife surely was. Domestic, she had never even pretended to be. It had been Jake who always woke up in the middle of the night to fetch a glass of milk and a cookie for Johnny whenever he had a bad dream. It was Jake who had shared his son's breakfast at the lime-washed pine kitchen table, who had baked him a chocolate birthday cake from a mix and gaudily decorated it with gumdrops after Cass had ignored his simple request and ordered a towering, spun-sugar monstrosity from her favorite bakery.

"It's my own recipe," Libby said now, bringing him back to the present. Her cheeks were flushed as she set two full bowls on the table and opened a tube of saltines. "You should see my ex-mother-in-law's cook's favorite chicken soup recipe. Gallons of cream, tons of butter and a flock of fat hens, and that's just for starters."

He hadn't come here to swap recipes. He didn't know exactly what he had come for, but it sure as hell wasn't chicken soup! But she was looking at him expectantly, and so dutifully, Jake picked up his spoon. "This is good," he murmured a moment later. "Tasty."

"Lots of backs, lots of onions and celery, a few thighs and a tiny squirt of lemon juice. David likes it with noodles."

"So he can suck 'em up."

She glanced up at him then, and he could have kicked himself. "How did you know that? Did you used to do it, too?"

"Don't all kids? Pass the crackers, please."

They ate in silence for a few minutes, and Jake found himself staring at the faint gleam of moisture on her lips...wondering if they would taste of Libby or of chicken soup.

Wondering just when he had taken complete leave of his senses.

Five

Jake left Libby's house a few minutes later in a thoroughly rotten mood. By the time he reached his office, his mood had deteriorated still further. He snarled at Alice, their quiet, efficient secretary, glared at Bostic when he stuck his bald head through the door a few minutes later, and swore when he smashed his right forefinger trying to force a balky filing cabinet slide.

"Trouble?" Bostic asked.

"The next time you buy office equipment, stay away from the secondhand places," Jake grumbled. "You ready to go over those figures for the Stokes County job?"

"Later. Alice says the copy machine's down. She's having a replacement sent over. You want to hold that finger under cold water for a few minutes, son. Take the fire right out of it."

Jake wished to hell he could cure a few other pertinent parts of his body so easily—one of them being his head.

At five past five, he placed a call to a woman he had dated occasionally since he'd been back in Winston. Gillie was an executive secretary at a philanthropic foundation, a folk music fan straight out of the sixties, a dyed-in-the-wool liberal and a nondrinker. If she'd had any idea that the foundation she worked for had been established by his great-aunt Minnie Senate Healy, Jake would have steered well clear of her, but she was a recent transplant from New York, and as far as she knew, he was simply a big-iron contractor, single, a nondrinker who could tolerate both her politics and her taste in music, in small doses.

Gillie Novatny was an extremely good-looking woman, beads and bangles notwithstanding. A product of the times, she was emancipated enough to have propositioned him on their second date, and secure enough not to be put off when he had diplomatically turned her down.

Tonight the outcome just might be different. Tonight Jake was needing something to take his mind off a certain green-eyed, gray-haired blonde with one too many barbs to her hook.

Quietly Libby cleared a space on the low table and laid the storybook down. Tired from helping her rebuild an old chicken pen out behind the house, David was sound asleep, his favorite stuffed toy in one arm. His eyes had closed by the time she'd got to the third page, and by the end of the chapter, he'd been breathing in that slow, even rate that signified sleep.

She sighed, wondering not for the first time if she had made a mistake when she'd opted to move back home.

Walt might have agreed to buy her an inexpensive house, if such a thing could be found, but his name, not hers, would have ended up on the deed. What kind of security was that?

If she had stayed on in Raleigh, David might have had a few years of private school—he'd been enrolled almost since birth. But it wouldn't have lasted. Sooner or later, Walt would have found an excuse to keep from paying the exorbitant rates, and then David would have suffered the loss of his school friends as well as the loss of his home and his father.

No, it was better this way. Begin as you mean to go on. One of her teachers, a hundred years ago, had told her that, apropos of something she had long since forgotten.

So she had begun with her own old home, which was a slightly shabby farmhouse on five acres at the end of a narrow country road. It wasn't perfect, but her parents had offered, and Libby had been only too glad to take them up on their offer. There was room for David to run wild, room for her to grow all their vegetables, and it was only twenty minutes or so from where her Aunt Lula and Uncle Calvin lived in Mocksville.

She had started David in public school, and once he'd grown used to the idea that she would still be there when he came home each day, he had gradually settled in. The trouble was Libby, herself. She was simply going to have to force herself to get involved. It had never been easy, but she'd done it once and she could do it again.

The trouble with living out in the country was that she had no close neighbors. There were times, in fact, when she was in danger of forgetting that she'd been christened Libby, and not Mama.

All of which might explain why she had latched on

to Jake Hatcher like a barnacle on an oyster shell, she told herself. It was an apt analogy, she decided as she tilted the shade of the night-light and pulled the door partially shut. Jake could be as tight-lipped and hard to reach as the crustiest oyster. She hadn't the least notion of what was inside that shell of his, but she'd be willing to bet it would be something special. Something succulent, nourishing and incredibly tender. It might be rewarding to try and pry open his shell. On the other hand, if he didn't like children, there was no point in it. Why tantalize herself with a taste of forbidden fruit?

Back in the kitchen, Libby set up the ironing board. Her mother had declared her own emancipation with the advent of no-iron clothes. Libby could still remember the day Dulcie Dwiggins had vowed to burn her ironing board as a sacrifice to Saint Polyester. Funny how the cycles repeated themselves, she thought, licking a finger to test the heat. Here she was ironing again.

Here she was, dreaming again.

Sooner or later a new generation of busy women might discover that ironing was a miserable waste of valuable time, but chances were, they would never learn the folly of dreaming.

Unfolding a small blue shirt, she smoothed it over the board, picturing a larger shirt, khaki or maybe white, and wrinkles that would release in a drift of steam hints of citrus and sandalwood. Instead of grippers designed for little fingers, there would be buttons and buttonholes. Buttons that could be unfastened, buttons that would remind her of—

"Of things best forgotten!" she muttered, slamming the iron down on its heel. Since when had she taken up fantasizing? Since when had ordinary household drudgery stirred up dreams of hard, masculine chests, narrow waists and lean flat abdomens?

Not to mention all the rest.

Jake saw Gillie to the door of her west-end apartment, declining an invitation to come in for decaf and cheesecake. He took the crooked cement steps two at a time, his thoughts already swinging back to the dessert Libby had offered him after he had polished off two bowls of her chicken soup.

Gingerbread arms and legs. There had been a foot, too, and a head with a frontal lobotomy where a misplaced raisin had come unstuck. "I save the perfect ones for David and eat the parts that get broken off," she'd explained. "You don't mind, do you? It all tastes the same, but since he helps me make them, I save the best ones for him. David knows how many are left in the tin. I'm teaching him subtraction that way."

Jake had got the message. Libby and son were a closed corporation. He had nibbled a few more appendages with his coffee and left soon after that, asking himself why the hell he cared, anyway.

He knew the answer. He just hadn't liked it. The more he thought about it, he told himself as he stripped down to his briefs and climbed into his bed, the less he liked it.

Dammit, the woman wasn't all that special! Gillie was prettier. Probably smarter, too. She knew her way around, knew what she wanted out of life and how to get it without being offensively aggressive. Whereas, Libby Porter...

Jake tossed restlessly for the better part of an hour before he fell asleep, his thoughts skipping over the past few hours with a tall, willowy creature with startlingly black hair, who wore layered silks and handmade jewelry and smelled of some exotic musky scent, to a gap-toothed woman in faded pink cotton coveralls who didn't bother to cover her gray, and who smelled of soap, chicken soup and gingerbread men.

A week passed. Jake was spending most of his time in Davie County on the Dutchman's Creek job. More than once he'd been forced to chase off kids who thought culverts and preformed concrete barriers were dandy playground equipment.

The job was running behind schedule, and Jake had been estimating how soon he'd be able to pull the graders off for another job. It was near quitting time. Unseasonably warm for November. Leaning against the truck, he took off his hard hat, mopped his forehead and glanced at the thickening sky. The last thing they needed now was rain! Absently he patted the pocket of his khaki shirt. He'd give twenty bucks for a smoke, but he'd quit smoking about the same time he'd quit drinking. At this point, he was beginning to think a man needed a few minor vices just to keep from going over the wall.

Suddenly he came away from the truck. "Hey, what the hell do you think you're doing?" he yelled at the small, dark-haired boy disappearing into the opening of a twenty-foot length of culvert.

Libby's kid? He was about the right size, the right coloring. But Libby's place was nowhere near here. "Don't you know you can get hurt that way, boy?" Jake muttered, his long, muscular legs eating up the distance. "Out!" he ordered, reaching in to grab a fistful of sneaker-clad foot.

He hauled the culprit out and held him up by the shoulders, checking for any sign of damage. Dammit, his men couldn't be expected to baby-sit every kid in the neighborhood! This was a construction site, which meant it was one gigantic hazard! Where the hell was this kid's mother? Who was supposed to be looking after him?

About that time an older boy came panting up. Evidently he'd been hiding behind one of the big Cats. "You two boys know better than to hang around here. Where do you live?"

Eyes as round as chinquapins, the older boy, who looked to be about twelve years old, jerked a thumb over his shoulder. "We didn't steal nothin', mister, honest."

"Yeah? How do I know that?" Jake growled. Scaring hell out of these two just might be the biggest favor anyone ever did for them.

"Y-you could search us."

Knowing all too well what had drawn them to the site—what would have drawn any normal kid, Jake continued to scowl, but his heart wasn't in it. "You guys wouldn't be planning to drive off one of my Tonka Toys now, would you?"

The two kids looked at each other, glassy-eyed, and then looked back at Jake. Behind them was every boy's dream playground—dozers, scrapers, backhoe, even a TR-500 they had brought on-site yesterday for the final grading. Hell, it was irresistible. An attractive nuisance in legal terms, which meant they had to carry a fortune in liability.

"Just don't get any bright ideas," Jake warned. "You touch a single bolt on any of this equipment, and your arm's gonna fall off, y'hear me, boy?"

"Yessir, I won't. Uh...sir? How old do you have to be to drive one o' them big yellow bucket things over there?"

Somehow, without Jake's knowing quite how it happened, the three of them spent the next half hour or so making the rounds. First Jake would point out the most obvious dangers, describe them in gory detail, and then he'd plop each boy in turn up into the high seat of each machine. With visions of a battery of OSHA inspectors bearing down on him, he took the time to explain the controls, how they worked, and why no one without sufficient strength and years of training was allowed anywhere near them. Then, after having them both practically swear a blood oath never to set foot on a construction site again until they were old enough to vote, he piled them into the crew truck and drove them home, where he had a word with a harried woman who'd been searching the neighborhood for her sons.

Ah, geez, he didn't need this, Jake told himself as he drove home. Yet, oddly enough, he felt more at peace than he'd felt in years, as if somehow he had laid a few old ghosts to rest.

Drinking had been only one part of the pattern of self-destruction Jake had followed after Johnny had drowned. Cass had been smart to leave him. Grief might have brought them closer; instead it had completed the job of driving them apart. Then, having lost the most important things in his life, Jake had thrown away the rest. His business. His self-respect. On the long climb back to respectability, he had insulated himself against feeling by the simple expedient of avoiding any woman he even suspected he might come to care for, and avoiding children altogether.

So when had the change taken place? When had he lost the rest of his mind? No man with half a brain would tempt fate by grabbing for the gold ring twice in a lifetime.

But then, a man didn't meet a woman like Libby Porter twice in a lifetime, either. The boy was a complication, but Jake was beginning to think he just might be able to handle it.

He didn't bother to call first. Taking a chance, Jake drove out to her house after he'd showered, shaved and dressed in clean khakis, a black turtleneck and a denim jacket. He took the truck instead of driving his car. Ten years ago he would have worn a suit and tie. Ten years ago he'd probably have been driving something a hell of a lot showier—a lot more expensive, at least—than either the small four-by-four pickup or the modest American-made sedan.

But then, ten years ago, he'd been John Jacob Hatcher Healy, not Jake Hatcher.

Libby opened the door wearing a peach-colored chenille bathrobe with a chain of safety pins dangling from the lapel. Her hair was hanging in damp clumps around her shoulders, and her feet were bare. Behind her, some guy on a PBS channel was demonstrating a method of root grafting, while the scent of popcorn and wood smoke eddied out to meet him.

Her eyes widened. If her jaw didn't quite drop, it gave that effect. "Jake, what are you—I mean, won't you come in?"

"Am I disturbing you? I just happened to be in the neighborhood." *Yeah. Sure you did.*

She stepped back and then closed the door behind him. The smell of some exotic blend of coffee was added to that of the popcorn and wood smoke.

"Actually, I drove out hoping you'd be here."

"That was a pretty safe bet," she said with a low,

thoroughly enchanting chuckle. "I still don't know why, though."

"I guess I just wanted to see you again."

Jake didn't remove his jacket right away, although the house was warm. The fire in a tiny brick-faced fireplace was smoking slightly. There was a half-empty bowl of popcorn on a footstool, an empty cup on the coffee table, and no one had bothered to pick up the assortment of jigsaw puzzle pieces, toy trucks and picture books scattered around the room.

Without apologizing for the clutter, Libby swept a book of pirate stories off the armchair and invited Jake to take off his coat. "I'll make some more popcorn. I bought this old wire popper from a yard sale last Saturday—we'd been looking for one forever. I had the fireplace opened up again after we moved in."

She was babbling, Libby told herself. No wonder he looked as if he might turn tail and run any minute now. "We used to pop corn in the fireplace when I was little. Did you do that when you were a boy?"

Jake merely looked at her. If he'd ever popped corn in his life, he didn't remember it. His mind was too busy thinking of what she would look like under that godawful peach-colored thing and the flannel gown that was hanging out the bottom.

"Take off your coat. It's hot. I forgot to turn down the furnace when we lighted the fire, and—do you take cream and sugar?"

"No cream, no sugar and no popcorn...thanks just the same."

She looked so crestfallen, he wished he had accepted the entire menu. Instead, while she hurried off into the kitchen, he wandered over to the fireplace and examined the draft lever. By the time she came back with a tray, a steaming cup of coffee and a plate of cheese and gingerbread parts, he had broken the lever loose from the stuck position and the chimney was drawing nicely. He sat down in the chair farthest from the heat and then shifted to remove a plastic rocket launcher from under his left buttock. Somehow, this wasn't the way he had pictured things when he'd decided to see her again.

"It was stuck," he murmured, watching a soft flush of color come and go on her freshly scrubbed face. "The damper." In the reflected light of the fire, her eyes looked dark as the inside of midnight. Jake found himself staring.

"I thought it was broken. Uh—do you mind having gingerbread body parts again?" Libby set the plate down hurriedly when the crisp cookies began to slide off the plate. Oh, blast! Just when she had resigned herself to forgetting all about him, he went and turned up again! How was a body supposed to settle down to the real world when temptation kept jumping out in front of her?

They sipped coffee, darting quick glances at each other. Now that he was here, Jake couldn't think of a single thing to say. He should have called first. No—what he should have done was stay the hell away!

What did he want with her? Libby wondered. The first time, which was really the second time if not the third, they had met purely by accident. She could have been a stranger and he would still have done the same thing, getting rid of that drunk for her.

And the next time? That, too, had been sheer accident. They'd run into each other at the bank, and one thing had led to another....

Oh, for heaven's sake, the man had never even made a pass at her!

So what else was new? a familiar inner voice whispered maliciously. She was hardly the kind of woman men made passes at. Walt had, but she'd been young then, with a brand-new figure and a brand-new self-image because of it. Living away from home for the first time in her life, she had felt like someone else and it had been reflected in her attitude. Several men had asked her out on dates before Walt, thinking she was something out of the ordinary. Which she certainly was not. Walt had lasted longer than the others for the simple reason that before he could discover that she was plain old Libby Dwiggins, he had asked her to marry him, and she had accepted.

But eventually the clock had struck midnight. The ball had ended, and now she was back at her own smoky hearth—older, sadder, but evidently not much wiser.

"So...have you seen any good movies lately?" she asked brightly. Then, closing her eyes, she groaned. "I can't believe I said that."

"No. And why not?"

"No which, and why not what?" she asked, confused.

"No, I haven't, and why can't you believe you asked that?" She was seated on the couch, her feet drawn up beside her. Jake pulled a domino out from underneath him, studied it a moment, and then joined her on the couch. "My chair seems to be booby-trapped."

"Sorry. David was feeling feverish and I put him to bed early. Usually he does a better job of picking up."

Jake had reason to doubt that, but he kept quiet. She was obviously not much of a disciplinarian. Or maybe she was just trying to make up to the kid for his not having a father—which might be okay for the short haul, but not for the long. Not that it was any of his business.

"Jake, do you realize I don't even know what you do for a living?"

"You never asked."

"I just did...in a manner of speaking."

"Heavy metal. Big iron. I'm a contractor."

She stared at him blankly, and without thinking, Jake reached for her naked foot and shook it gently. "Heavy equipment. We clear tracts of land for construction, we build roads, small bridges—that sort of thing. Raw earth and big yellow machines, that's us."

Jake talked for a while about some of the jobs they had done in the area, all the while absently stroking Libby's foot. Gradually, so gradually neither of them was aware of just when it happened, his words dwindled off. His fingers moved slowly over the sole of her small foot, lingering in the arch, cupping her heel, exploring the shape of each toe.

Libby's breath caught somewhere between her lungs and her throat. Her eyes were round, her mouth soft. Jake closed his own eyes, rested his head on the back of the couch, and expelled a deep, shuddering sigh.

Suddenly he was burning up, and it had nothing to do with the heating system in the drafty old farmhouse. He wanted her so much he could taste it! Wanted to fold back the lapels of that shabby old bathrobe, untie her sash and then begin on the buttons of her flowered flannel nightgown.

The foot slipped from his grasp, and Libby sat up straight, not quite looking at him. "Would you—um, like more coffee? It—it's decaf. Half hazelnut and half something I can't even pronounce."

But even as she spoke, they both knew coffee wasn't what he wanted. Nor was it what Libby wanted. Later, Jake didn't know whether she leaned toward him or he simply dragged her onto his lap. Whichever one of them instigated the move, the result was the same. Incendiary.

She was quivering all over. Seated on his lap, her mouth was too high for him to reach easily, and so he laid her over on the pillow and somehow managed to shift his body around until everything fit just right.

More than all right!

She tasted of coffee and gingerbread with just the faintest hint of butter on her lips. Her hair smelled of wood smoke and the same fragrance she'd been wearing the night of the reunion.

Jake's loins tightened. He parted her lips with his and dipped into the sweetness beyond while his hands slowly stroked her back, soft cotton flannel against soft satin skin. Warm, fragrant, womanly...

In the small part of his brain that still functioned, he realized that it had been years since he had kissed a woman just this way. Maybe he never had. Maybe kissing was different with each woman. He'd never thought much about it before.

Or maybe it was just different with Libby.

There was the wanting—the kind of aching, throbbing need that made a man hungry to get past the appetizer to the entrée. But there was more than that. Something he could never recall having experienced before. A need to give? A need to convey something just beyond the realm of words?

Jake lifted his lips to her eyelids, traced the curve of her cheekbone, her temple, and nibbled the downy lobe of her ear. When she gasped, he allowed his lips to trail down the rim of her jaw—that stubborn, elegant, maddening jaw—and then he took her mouth again.

You're getting in way over your head, man, a voice whispered.

Jake ignored it. He found her breasts, their sensitive peaks hardening in his palm, and he felt her tremble.

"Libby," he whispered hoarsely, "we won't go any farther than you want to go, I promise you."

"I want—" She sighed as he tasted the tender flesh in the curve between her neck and her shoulder. "I want..."

"Yeah, me, too," he murmured. Wanted until he was blind, drunk, wild with it. Wanted like he had never known he could want again. It didn't make sense, not at his age. Not with his record. Not with a woman like Libby.

A woman with a son.

Six

Libby ignored the warnings that were going off in her head like a fire alarm. Thus ignored, they gradually faded away until there was only the faintest whisper to remind her that she would be sorry, sorry....

"I never imagined anything so beautiful could come wrapped in flannel and chenille," Jake murmured. With her robe lying open, he had unfastened the buttons on her gown, leaving her all but naked from the waist up.

"I'm not—" she started to say, parroting phrases she had heard too many times ever to forget them. *Did you think you were beautiful?* Walt would jeer when he wanted to hurt her. *You think you're desirable? Sorry, babe—you're not even particularly interesting.*

Libby's hands clutched at his shoulders, her eyes clinging to his. She would have died if she could have known how expressive they were. This was Jake, she reminded herself, not Walt. And she was no longer a corn-fed farmer's daughter, overweight and insecure.

Dammit, she was an attractive, intelligent, independent woman! She deserved to be admired! What's more, she *was* interesting, too!

Jake fought his own inner demons. He hadn't meant to start a conflagration. Hell, he hadn't even meant to kiss her. But he had, and then one kiss hadn't been enough, so he'd thought he would just look, maybe touch, and then wrap her up in her cotton batting again and put her back on the shelf where he'd found her.

Who did he think he was kidding? "Honey, I'm too old to be making out on a parlor sofa."

"I know," she said breathlessly, her eyes glued to the reflection in the mirror over the fireplace. Jake's wide shoulders, his muscular back bent over her. His dark head above her blond one—her pale, naked breasts, their tips jutting like dark thimbles between the square-tipped fingers of Jake's tanned hands.

It was like watching two strangers, yet more intimate than anything she had ever experienced. Drowning in the quicksand of desire, she whispered, "Jake—I think this is probably a mistake."

"I think you're probably right," he murmured, his parted lips dragging softly across her own.

Twisting his mouth on hers, he deepened the kiss, scattering the last remnants of common sense—both his and hers—to the four winds. "Ahh, Libby," he groaned a long time later, "I thought I was past the dangerous age. Evidently I was wrong." Drawn inexorably by the taste, the texture, the sweet womanly scent of her, he kissed her again, each thrust of his tongue mirroring an act that was wholly carnal.

Libby moaned. Her arms tightened around his neck,

her fingers moving restlessly through his hair. Jake tried to spare her his full weight, but on the narrow cushions, it wasn't easy.

"Libby—honey, don't you have a bed?"

She shook her head, and when his kisses strayed over her chin to her throat and beyond, she protested, "Ah, Jake, no...please!"

Jake, no, please. Jake was going out of his mind with long-denied hunger. "No" wasn't what he wanted to hear, wasn't what he'd expected to hear.

But maybe it was what he needed to hear. Awkwardly he rolled off, one knee to the floor, and then righted himself to sit beside her, his breath rawly audible. When she turned onto her side to curl around his hips, he felt like shoving her away, but he didn't. Instead he reached behind him and clumsily patted her on the shoulder.

Okay, so it wasn't entirely her fault that he was tight as a drum, that his heart was going like a jackhammer. But dammit, he was too old for this! It had been more than twenty years since he'd started something he couldn't finish—something he couldn't turn off as easily as he had turned it on.

Libby lay on her side, her fists tucked up under her chin, and stared at the wilted bouquet of autumn leaves David had presented her with the day before. She felt as limp as a line full of wash on a rainy winter Monday. As a mature, experienced woman of thirty-eight, she'd have thought she would be able to handle rejection with a bit more grace.

But then, Jake hadn't rejected her, she reminded herself. She had rejected him. At least she'd been smart enough to do that much, knowing that the last thing in the world she needed at this point in her life was to fall in love again.

Suspecting that it might already be too late.

"You all right down there?" Jake asked.

Libby nodded, and then, realizing that he wasn't looking at her, told him yes, she was. And if you believe that, she added silently, you're an even bigger fool than I am.

Uncurling herself, she sat up and began buttoning her nightgown. Jake was leaning forward, elbows resting on his thighs, forehead in his hands. His breathing, if still a bit raw, was almost steady by now. She tried to ignore him, but it was like ignoring an avalanche. By the time you were aware of it, it was usually too late to escape.

Over the years, Libby had grown better at hiding her feelings. She smoothed back her hair, retied her robe, and wished she could think of something devastatingly clever to say.

Or even something halfway coherent. For some reason, she was reminded of her first kiss. It had happened during her junior year at West Forsyth, on a Tuesday just after lunch break. Mack Shaw, class clown, had caught up with her halfway down the hall. He hadn't spoken, hadn't even glanced at her, and Libby had pretended not to notice him. She'd known better than to speak first and let herself in for one of his cutting remarks.

Suddenly Mack had shoved her against the wall and smashed a dry, bruising kiss on her mouth. Before she could even react, he was racing off down the hallway, waving his hands over his head and shouting, "Touchdown! Hey, you guys owe me five bucks, so fork over!"

Memories were supposed to lose their power to hurt after so long, weren't they?

Dammit, what was the protocol for a situation like

this? She'd better start reading *Cosmo* again. "Would you care for another cup of coffee?"

"No thanks. Uh, Libby—I want you to know that I didn't come here with this in mind. Seduction, I mean."

"I didn't think you had," she replied gravely. It was true. He had never given her the impression that he was bowled over by her middle-aged charms. Mildly interested, perhaps, but certainly not bowled over.

On the other hand, he was here...again. If he wasn't after her body, what was he interested in, her scintillating conversation? Her gingerbread men? "Why did you come, Jake?"

He shrugged, and she fought the urge to lay her hand against the supple muscles of his back. He had the kind of long, wedge-shaped build that narrowed down to a taut, narrow behind. In other words, the kind of body any woman with a viable hormone in her body would find irresistible.

"Jake, I'm not very good at this kind of thing, so would you please help me out?"

"Help you out how? I did offer, you know." His smile almost broke her heart it was so beautiful. Unfortunately it never quite reached his eyes.

Once again Libby sensed a deep, lingering sadness and wondered at it. It wasn't the sort of thing she could ever ask him about. "Just play straight with me, Jake, that's all I ask. I mean, you show up, and then I don't see you for a while, and then you show up again, with no notice. I don't know what you want from me. Friendship? I'll gladly be your friend, but after what just happened—I mean, that kind of thing—" She sighed and lifted her hands, palm up.

"You want it on the level, right? No games?"

"No games, please, Jake. At our ages, we're past that stage, aren't we?"

Jake had the grace to look embarrassed. "I'm beginning to think some of us never get too old to play games."

"Not me. Before I'd even learned the rules, I'd already lost the game."

Thinking of the man she had married, Jake had to agree. But then, no one had twisted her arm. Shotgun weddings had long since gone out of style. In Porter's circle, which had also been his at one time, things seldom reached that stage, thanks to the best lawyers money could buy. "Were you in love with him?"

"With Walt?" Libby leaned forward just as Jake leaned back. She stared at the tips of her naked toes, wishing she'd had the good sense to wear her slippers. "I thought I was, at least. The first time he asked me out on a date, I thought I'd died and gone to heaven. I couldn't believe he had actually asked *me*."

"Because of who he was, you mean."

"No, because of who I was." She frowned. "Oh, you mean his money. I didn't even know about that. If I had, I'd have probably still been standing there with my mouth hanging open. Jake, I never even had a date until I was in college. Even then it was a rarity."

Somehow he found that a bit hard to believe, but he would reserve judgment. She could have been a late bloomer. "You didn't know he was loaded? That's a little hard to swallow."

Libby bristled. "Well, he didn't *act* rich! And he certainly didn't look rich. He wore jeans just like everyone else, and he drove a pickup truck. He said his folks had this farm in Wake County. How was I to know it was a tax shelter? The only farmers I knew were the kind who worked fourteen-hour days and seven-day weeks."

"So Cinderella kissed her frog and he turned into a prince before her very eyes, right?"

"Wrong. Cinderella married her prince and he turned into a frog. Warts and all."

"That's what I mean by games, honey. I expect Porter wanted to be wanted for himself, not just his bankroll. It's a common failing among the more solvent members of society. You must have been pretty naive."

"For naive, read dumb as a dipping gourd. We'd been dating for about six weeks when he gave me a Cartier watch for my birthday. I didn't even know enough to be impressed. I mean, I knew it wasn't a Timex, but it never occurred to me—I mean, it was the first time any man had ever given me a piece of jewelry. I'd probably have been almost as excited if it had come from a box of Cracker Jacks."

Jake was looking at her with one eyebrow halfway up, and she said defensively, "Well, I *did* let him know how much I appreciated it. Goodness, I must have thanked him a hundred times." She glanced up at him, a smile teasing the corners of her mouth. "Poor Walt. I'm afraid he didn't get his money's worth that time. If he'd only realized that I didn't have sense enough to be impressed, he could have saved himself a bundle."

Jake shook his head. He began to chuckle. "Honey, you were ripe for the plucking. How the devil did you manage to get past puberty without learning anything? Most girls wise up before they're even out of pigtails."

"Nobody ever offered to teach me. Is it too late for makeup classes?"

Taking her small hand into his large one, Jake traced the row of calluses at the base of her fingers. He tried to picture her as she'd been at fifteen, or twenty—or even thirty. "It's probably not worth the effort," he said. "I wouldn't lose too much sleep over it, though. In all the ways that matter, you strike me as a pretty savvy lady."

A pretty savvy lady. Libby liked the sound of that, even if she didn't quite believe it. "I just wish I'd struck Walt that way. Or his lawyers."

"Rough, huh?"

Wordlessly she nodded.

"How do you feel about him now? Is it all gone?"

"Not...entirely," she said somewhat regretfully. "In a way, I think I'll always love him, or at least, I'll love the little boy he must have been. He told me once he was raised by a dozen servants. I thought he was joking, but now I'm not so certain."

Jake fell silent. The same thing had happened to him, to a lesser degree. Aside from the usual social rounds, his father had enjoyed the salmon fishing in Scotland and the elk hunting in Montana. His mother did the Paris fashion-show route, and visited a couple of spas each year, one of which was in Switzerland. Jake had never been invited along with either parent. Maybe it went with the territory.

After a moment, Libby said thoughtfully, "I guess maybe it's more like pity I feel for him instead of love. I don't think Walt can help it, even if he's aware of it. I mean, no man would deliberately choose to be such a cold-blooded bastard, would he?"

Jake laughed. Wrapping one arm around her, he hugged her to him, and then he stood, feeling considerably better than he'd expected to be feeling a few minutes earlier. He could have debated the theory of deliberate choice, but he didn't.

A few minutes later he left, wondering if the non-players weren't the shrewdest gamesters of all. Maybe he should have leveled with her. For starters, he could have told her his name was Healy, not Hatcher. She had asked why he kept coming back. He could have told her that he wanted something from her—he just hadn't figured out what it was yet. Or how long he would go on wanting it. He probably should have told her he had no intention of getting in so deep he couldn't get out again when it was over.

How many brownie points did a man earn for honesty?

Five days later, Jake called and asked her out for Saturday night. "Dinner? Dancing? Maybe a movie? You call the shots."

"Oh, Jake, I can't. I promised to take David to a father-son thing over in Davie County this weekend. My uncle has invited half a dozen or so single parents with their children."

"Father-son?"

"Well, except for me. And Jeffie's mother. Most of the others are from Uncle Calvin's Young Men's Sunday school class, and since he and Aunt Lula have this place over near Smith Grove with a cabin and a pond, he thought it would be a good place to get together. David's been looking forward to it so much. We'll be sleeping over."

"What about Friday night? Or Sunday?" Jake asked after the briefest of pauses. The call had been purely impulse. He had decided not to see her again, so dammit, why couldn't he just take the reprieve she'd offered him and give thanks?

Because he couldn't, that was why.

"Jake, I'm sorry. But thank you for asking me."

He hung up. "Thank you for asking me," he mimicked, his expression anything but polite. Five minutes later, he had her on the line again. "A father-son thing, you say?"

"Jake? Well, yes...that is, mostly fathers and sons. I explained all that."

"Yeah, sure. There'll be one other woman and a bunch of men with their sons. You told me."

"Two more women, actually. Aunt Lula will be there. And one of the sons is a little girl. Her father's not kicking up a fuss, so I don't see why I should. What are you, a militant feminist, or a chauvinist?"

"I'm neither one. I just thought you might feel uncomfortable with all those men along, and...well, I thought maybe..."

"Jake, I practically grew up there. The pond used to be stocked with bass and bluegills, and Uncle Calvin used to take me fishing there. Now it's stocked with hybrid striped bass, but fishing is fishing, and I do know how. But thank you for your concern."

"Yeah, well...I just thought if you—look, just forget it, okay? Sorry I bothered you. I'll see you around."

Before Libby's smile had quite faded, he was back on the line. "Listen, why don't I just sort of tag along. For the day, I mean, not for the whole weekend. Just to sort of be there if you need a hand. I mean, David might get a backlash or something, and if all the other kids have dads there, he might—well, you know. I'm pretty good with machinery."

Libby, who could take apart a spinning reel, clean it and put it back together again as well as any man, found herself smiling again. Diplomatically she agreed that perhaps it would be a good idea to have another man along, just in case.

She hung up, telling herself it was an excellent idea. In a crowd, David might get along better with Jake—with all the other men there, that was. It was only on his own turf that David got territorial. If she was ever going to have any personal life at all outside being a mother, she was going to have to help him through this stage where he saw every man as either a threat or a potential new daddy.

Half a dozen times during the week Jake almost called up and uninvited himself. He didn't, telling himself it would be an excellent test. After that business with the kids at the Dutchman's Creek site last week, he'd been doing some thinking. It was the first time he had actually dealt one-on-one with any child since Johnny. And while he would never have deliberately sought out a kid for that purpose, he thought he had handled it pretty well. He hadn't cried. He hadn't hated them both for not being Johnny. Instead he had let each one of them sit on a machine while he answered their questions, and then driven them home, all without falling apart.

He was mending. He would never get over the loss of his own son, but that didn't mean he had to go through life avoiding any kid under the age of twelve, the way he had done for the first few years.

On Friday morning he called to get instructions on how to find the place. Hearing Libby's voice again, he felt himself begin to relax, felt a kind of warmth steal over him, almost as if he'd just downed a jigger of smooth, aged Scotch. They talked a few minutes about nothing in particular, and when he hung up after promising to drive out that evening, and again on Saturday,

Jake told himself the feeling was due solely to the fact that he was finally dealing with this business of kids. That it had nothing at all to do with Libby personally.

Yeah. Right. For a minute there, he almost had himself believing it, too!

Libby was struggling to pull a hooded sweatshirt down over the arms of her impatient son when Jake's silver pickup pulled up between her uncle's Buick and Bunny Binford's Camaro. She had been watching for his car for the past few hours, but of course she might have known he would drive the truck. More in keeping with the macho male-bonding purpose of the whole affair.

Everyone else had been there when she and David had arrived, and she had fully expected to feel uncomfortable, for outside of her aunt and uncle and Bunny Binford, who was David's friend Jeffie's mother, she didn't know a soul. However, one of the things she had learned during her nearly thirteen years of marriage was how to get along in a group of strangers without going into a full-blown panic attack.

"Hi," she greeted softly when Jake came within range. David took one look, glowered and dashed away, and she shrugged a silent apology. It was too soon to expect miracles.

"I brought soft drinks, hot dogs and a bunch of other junk. It's in the back of the truck." With that lean, lazy, hip-switching walk of his, he looked positively dangerous! Libby reconsidered the possibility of panic attack.

"Oh. Good," she said a little breathlessly. "I—we were supposed to catch our supper, but Uncle Calvin's helper slipped up and fed the fish this evening. Evidently they're too stuffed to rise to a lure."

Jake couldn't take his eyes off her. She was squatting

beside an open canvas bag from which protruded a pair of flannel pajamas and a rag doll that looked as if it had been rescued from a landfill. In that position, her jeans were stretched tightly across her generous posterior. With a pair of scuffed and stained yellow sneakers, she was wearing a purple turtleneck, a rust-colored headband and a faded red flannel shirt. The combination should have looked like hell, but somehow it didn't.

As he reached her, she glanced up and smiled that guileless, imperfect smile of hers, and he felt the definite beginnings of a core meltdown. *Danger, man! If you're smart, you'll get the hell out of here before it's too late!*

"Yeah, well...I brought along a spinning rod, too, just in case it's needed," he said almost apologetically.

He had brought along three rods, three reels, a stringer, a basket, a net and enough tackle to decorate half a dozen Christmas trees, having made a run on Sears's sporting-goods department the night before.

Swallowing her self-consciousness, Libby began the introductions, acutely aware of the speculative glances that followed their progress around the six-acre pond. Bunny Binford, for instance, was all but salivating before Libby had even got out the names.

"Haven't we met somewhere before? I knew some Hatchers over in the western part of the state."

"No, ma'am, I don't think so. I'm sure I'd have remembered."

Libby steered him away to meet his host and hostess, and they talked for a few minutes with the Dwigginses before Aunt Lula excused herself to carry the little girl, who was called Peanuts, into the one-room cabin where several sleeping bags had been arranged. "Poor little dumpling. Too much excitement," she murmured, openly enjoying the role of surrogate grandmother.

After Calvin had wandered away to supervise the lighting of the bonfire, Jake said, "A father-son thing, hmmm?"

"It started out that way, I think, but one thing led to another. I guess you could call it a parent-child thing." They had reached the truck, and Jake forked out a couple of cold drinks, having declined the offer of a beer from one of the other men. They carried two sacks of groceries over to the picnic table, where Bunny was presiding, and Libby noticed for the first time that the other woman's profile resembled a young Elizabeth Taylor, except that her eyelashes were even more spectacular. Nobody with lashes that long should be so darned likeable!

This time it was Jake who steered her away, mentioning something about sorting out fishing tackle. Libby hid her surprise better than Bunny did. The other woman obviously wasn't used to being neglected in favor of fishing tackle.

"So, David likes to fish, does he?" Talk about the kid, Jake told himself. Keep your eyes, your mind, and most definitely your hands, off his mama!

"He hasn't done all that much of it. Walt only liked deep-sea fishing, and we were never invited along."

"He seems to get along real well with his uncle."

Libby nodded. "That's one of the reasons I moved back home instead of staying on in Raleigh." Her eyes were on her son, but she was acutely aware of the man beside her. She was dangerously, recklessly attracted to him. Did he know it? Probably. She'd be an open book to a man like Jake Hatcher. He was more in Bunny's league.

Instead of stopping by the truck where his fishing tackle was, Jake steered her toward a fallen log some distance away from the leaping bonfire that had just been ignited, urging her to sit and then dropping down beside her. He dug the heels of his boots into the dirt, and for several minutes neither of them spoke.

And then he said, "Libby, there are a few things you don't know about me."

Libby's fingers tightened their grip on her bottle. She focused her eyes on the sliver of a moon that was rising against the amethyst glow of sunset. She might have known it was too good to be true. He was married. He was engaged. He was destined for the priesthood. The best ones were always out of reach.

Only why had he waited to tell her until it was too late? "Look, there's the moon," she said too brightly. Whatever he was going to tell her, she didn't want to hear it.

Jake hadn't intended to tell her anything. What difference did a name make? Okay, so the second time around he had wanted to make it on his own, without the help of family connections. Where was the crime in that?

But in light of what she'd told him about Porter's approach, it suddenly didn't seem quite so harmless. Was it a game? It hadn't been intended that way. It had been purely a business decision.

Okay, it had been *partly* a business decision.

But suddenly it was important that she know who he was.

Seven

"It's Healy," Jake told her. "Hatcher's my middle name. It was my mother's maiden name."

"I know," Libby said quietly as she connected the dots she had poked in the ground with a stick.

He was thunderstruck. "You know! How the hell could you know?"

"Something Aunt Lula said about old Mr. Healy's drugstore on Fourth Street. Her mother used to work there when she was a girl, and there used to be a Miss Ada Hatcher who would come in every Wednesday morning like clockwork to get 'A Little Something For Sister.' That was the way she always said it. Aunt Lula says she remembers her, but I expect she just remembers hearing about her."

"That would be my Great-aunt Ada. The 'little something for Sister' was probably paregoric. Poppy juice in various forms was perfectly legal back in those days."

Jake shook his head and asked, "But how the devil did you connect all that to me?"

"Hatcher. There aren't that many around here. Then, too, the first time I met you...remember? Not the reunion, but that fund-raiser? It wasn't the sort of bash I'd have expected a construction worker to attend, so I looked in my high school annual again for the list of those whose photos weren't included, and there was John J. Hatcher Healy. Something just clicked."

"How long have you known?"

Libby tossed down her stick and slanted him one of her shy smiles. "Only two or three days, and I wasn't really sure even then, but my instincts are usually pretty sound."

Damn her instincts! Having finally screwed up his nerve to bare his soul, Jake was feeling distinctly deflated. It wasn't a feeling he particularly enjoyed. "What happened to your fine instincts where Porter's concerned?" he asked, and then wished he hadn't.

"I guess maybe they developed late in life," she replied quietly, making him feel even worse.

Jake began to relent. Okay, so she'd guessed about the name. But whatever else he might have told her, he had changed his mind. Talk about your instincts; one in particular was clamoring for him to get the hell out of there before it was too late. It was called survival instinct, and his had been running well into the red zone ever since the second time he'd seen her.

"But Jake, why?"

"Why what?" he grumbled. He picked up the stick she had tossed down and drew a circle around three of her dots.

"You know—the name."

He shrugged. "Hell, I don't know. Call it a business

decision. It's a long jump from body lotions and after-bath splash to boom drills and padfoot rollers. No point in confusing the market."

"I'm surprised you got away with it. You must know a lot of people around here."

"Times change. Industries, like dynasties, rise and fall. Old families die out or move away and new ones move in. Nobody pays much attention."

"What about old friends?"

The bonfire flared, sending up a shower of sparks into the still evening air. Several yards away, men were telling fish stories. Bunny and Aunt Lula were laying out the supper makings. A few boys were listening to the stories, a couple were arguing the merits of crickets over worms, and one demanded to know why he couldn't just peepee behind a bush instead of going all the way to the outhouse.

"Friends scatter, too," Jake said quietly. "How many of our mutual classmates have you kept up with over the past twenty years?"

Libby wrapped her arms around her knees and stared at the figures silhouetted against the fire. David was one of them. "None, I guess, but then I never had any close friends in high school. You must've had hundreds. You were one of those mythical figures we nerds could only worship from afar."

Relenting in spite of himself, Jake took hold of her ponytail and gave it a gentle yank. "Did you worship me from afar, Libby?"

"If I thought your ego needed it, I might tell you I did, but the truth is, I sort of had a crush on the head of the science club. You remember...what's his name? He had red hair and glasses and he always wore striped shirts and a tie?"

Jake laughed aloud. "Thanks a lot!"

They both fell silent, thinking of friends past and present. In Libby's case, there weren't many. In Jake's, perhaps too many...once. Money had always had a certain drawing power. Sooner or later, however, someone with more of it came along. He had spent all of thirty seconds mourning the loss of his old schoolmates, and a bit more thinking of the friends he and Cass had made in Richmond. Once things had started falling apart, they had quickly drifted away. Jake hadn't blamed them, nor had he particularly missed them.

Maybe there'd always been this element of lone-wolfishness in his makeup, he didn't know. He did know it was safer. Lonesome was a hell of a lot more bearable than having your guts ripped out.

"Although there was this one guy," he said thoughtfully. "Moose Capeheart. Must've been a year or so behind us. You remember him."

"The name sounds familiar, but I can't place him."

"Big guy. Played football. Got caught smoking the wrong stuff once too often and was kicked out."

"My goodness, they actually did that back then, didn't they?"

"Age of innocence, relatively speaking. I almost wish we could go back. Anyhow, Moose did. Go back, that is. Took a GED, wound up working in a small town in Virginia as a deputy sheriff. Maybe one of these days I'll give him a call, let him know where I am."

If Libby considered a small-town sheriff an unlikely candidate for friendship with the scion of one of the town's wealthiest families, she had better sense than to say so. Jake had his own reasons. He was a very private man. As well as being drawn to his strength, she was drawn to the depths she sensed when he was in this pensive mood.

Supper was blackened wieners, smoky, sizzling with juices, and loaded with extras. The third time Jake declined a beer, he mentioned being allergic to alcohol. After that, there were no more offers.

A sticky-faced David came and pushed himself in between Jake and Libby, and while Libby mopped him off, Jake turned to talk to Calvin Dwiggins. One of the other men, a CPA with weekend custody of his eight-year-old son, joined in, and the talk became general as one by one the children fell asleep and were bedded down inside the cabin.

Libby left with her sleepy son and returned after half an hour. "Two more down for the count," she said, "if you count Ikky."

It was only a bit past nine, but it seemed much later. The days had shrunk until night seemed to fall with no warning in the middle of the afternoon. Jake dragged their log closer to the fire, and when she sat down, he took his place beside her, draping an arm loosely across her shoulders. While Bunny Binford watched from the other side of the fire, they talked about schools, about cold remedies and about the pros and cons of aquaculture in an area this far west. Sexy, stimulating stuff, Libby thought with rueful amusement. She wished it could go on forever.

"Saline content," her uncle declared. "That's what makes it so danged tricky. We're too far east here to do much good with mountain trout, and just about too far west for hybrid stripers."

"Always fall back on catfish and carp," someone else said, and they all laughed.

Libby leaned her head on Jake's shoulder and allowed

the peacefulness to seep into her bones. How long had it been since she had enjoyed such a gathering? Old friends, new ones, family—all ages from three to sixty-seven. No tensions, no axes to grind—nothing to prove to anyone. It took her back to her younger days, when she was just another little towheaded Dwiggins, one who could swim as well as any boy and fish better than most. The days before she realized that being overweight made her socially unacceptable, compounding the usual problems of adolescence a hundredfold.

"Having a good time?" Jake murmured after a while.

"Heavenly." She yawned and begged his pardon. "How on earth could I be sleepy at this hour?"

"Full stomach, long day. If you want to turn in, don't let me keep you. I've got to be getting back to town, anyhow. The mess on my desk is about two feet deep. Mostly EPA stuff. File it or face a firing squad."

Libby yawned again. "Sorry. I can't seem to stop. Wish I could just roll over right here by the fire, but I reckon my backside would freeze long before morning."

"Not if I kept it warm for you."

Her eyes flew to his and hung there. Her breath quickened, and Jake swallowed hard. Damn. So much for survival instinct.

Libby lifted her head from his shoulder and leaned forward, and Jake's arm fell away. "Did you see David watching the way you twisted that apple in half with your bare hands?" she asked quickly, her voice skittering over the words like a mayfly over the pond. "His eyes were big as saucers."

"I hope he was impressed," Jake said with a wry grin. "I was sure as hell showing off. Next time, though, remind me not to try it on one with wrinkled skin. That one must've been last year's crop."

She laughed, as she was supposed to, and Jake rose, stretched and said his good-nights around the fire. Libby watched Bunny Binford watching him, and felt a smug touch of possessiveness.

"Welcome to pull up a stump and stay over, son," Calvin invited. "I ain't offering to share my bedroll, nor the mattress in the back of my camper, but—"

"You'll share or sleep on the ground, old man," Lula shot back, and in the general laughter, Jake drew Libby toward the truck.

Away from the bonfire, the night was pitch dark except for the fingernail sliver of moon and a handful of stars. The air smelled of wood smoke, pond water and resinous pines. Nearby, a ripe persimmon plopped to the ground. Libby tried to soak up every detail to store in her memory.

"Will you come back out tomorrow?" she asked.

"Do you think it's a good idea?"

"I didn't mean—I meant, if you want to, you're welcome."

They were both fencing. Libby ached for him to come back tomorrow, ached even more for him to stay here now, but she was nothing if not a realist. Every minute spent in his company only made her hungrier for more, but she had David to think of. So far, Jake and David hadn't spoken more than a dozen words to each other, and none of those particularly friendly. Even if Jake was interested in a long-term relationship, that would be a problem.

On the other hand, if he was interested in something less than a long-term relationship, that would be even more of a problem, both for David and for Libby.

Not until they were standing beside the truck did Jake take her in his arms. Libby leaned her forehead against his chest, savoring the mingled scent of smoke, onions and Jake. It was a heady combination.

"Sure you're going to be warm enough tonight?" he growled against the top of her head.

"David's using my old sleeping bag, but I've got a quilt, a woolen blanket and a pair of insulated longhandles." How romantic can you get, she thought ruefully.

"My back-warming offer's still open."

She glanced up, laughter shining from her eyes, and Jake took advantage of the implicit invitation to lower his face to hers. Before either of them was quite prepared, what was intended as a simple, friendly goodnight kiss escalated to something considerably more.

With a low groan, Jake lifted his head to stare down at the pale blur of her face. He swore softly. Libby had time only for one deep, ragged breath before he was back again, taking her mouth with a sexual urgency that shook her to her very roots. She strained against him, wrapping her arms tightly around his waist. Jake held the back of her head in one large hand while his other hand moved restlessly over her back, dropping to curve over her hips. He turned her so that she was braced against the side of the truck and then he moved even closer, straddling one of her thighs with his own, shifting his pelvis so that she could be in no doubt of what he wanted from her.

And oh, she wanted it, too! Not since the early days of her marriage had she wanted a man this much! Not even then. At first she'd been too inexperienced, and Walt had not been a particularly patient lover. The novelty of her virginity hadn't lasted much beyond the honeymoon, and by the time she had gained even an inkling of her own sexual potential, he had all but lost interest in sex.

With her, at least. She hadn't known then about the other women in his life. That knowledge had come later. Too proud to beg, and too proud to let him know how she felt, Libby had thrown herself into all the worthy activities expected of the women in her new social set. After a while, she hadn't felt much of anything.

Until now. Until Jake.

"You know I want you, don't you, Libby?" he whispered against her throat.

She shuddered at the effect his mouth had on the sensitive nerves there. Oh, she knew! But how long would he go on wanting her? For a single night? A week? A year? How did a woman find out something like that? Did she dare ask?

"Libby? Sweetheart, did you hear me?"

"I heard you," she said in a soft rush of words. "I'm thinking, I'm thinking!"

Jake laughed, and some of the explosive tension seemed to evaporate. Bumping her forehead with his, he said, "Look, why don't we just give it a little more time, hmmm?"

He had nearly said: why don't we sleep on it? Under the circumstances, that might have been construed as a double entendre. Meanwhile a few hours of filling out EPA forms would probably solve his problem—at least temporarily.

But he had an idea it would rise again the next time they were together. And that was *definitely* a double entendre!

Jake knew he wasn't going to be able to stay away the next day, which was Saturday. But first he took the time to drop by the job site. Even with no crew there, he managed to kill a couple of hours checking the condition and the security of the machinery.

Dammit, there was no point in letting any woman think she was the most important thing in his life, because she wasn't. Jake had aligned his priorities a long time ago. About the same time he'd gone into partnership with Bostic Clodfelter, in fact. Eighty percent of him would be devoted to keeping the business in the black. Anything left over could be devoted to whatever the hell he felt like getting involved in, the catch being that twenty percent of a man's time was hardly enough to get him into any serious, long-term trouble.

At least, that had been the plan. Until lately it had worked out just fine. He had gone out with any number of women...once or twice. Gillie Novatny had lasted longer than any of the others simply because she didn't bore him to distraction after a few hours.

And maybe because he had known right from the beginning that she would never be a threat to him. Oh, she was attractive enough. Intelligent, she had a sense of humor, too. It was a bit too caustic for his taste, but they'd had a few good laughs together.

So why was it that he could see her once or twice a month and never give her a single thought between dates? Why was it that he could run into this short, hippy, gray-haired blonde in the bank or the supermarket and nearly bust the buttons off his jeans? Hell, the woman couldn't even dance! Her political savvy was no more than average. Her sense of humor was so off-the-wall she laughed in the wrong places at half his jokes—if she laughed at all.

So *why?*

Jake told himself that a man his age, a man with two engineering degrees, ought to be able to figure out a little thing like *why*. All it took was a coolheaded application of logic. An analysis of the various components.

The trouble was, where Libby was concerned, he was neither coolheaded nor analytical. All he wanted to apply was himself...to her! When a man could get turned on by simply sitting in a kitchen eating gingerbread parts, something was definitely out of kilter.

It was nearly three in the afternoon by the time he parked his pickup behind the assortment of vehicles at the Dwiggins place. Both boats were pulled up onto the bank, a trickle of smoke was coming from the chimney in the crude, one-room cabin, and half a dozen fishermen of assorted ages and genders were scattered around the banks of the pond.

Jake spotted her immediately. She was squatting down on the sloping dam, coaching her son, who seemed to have hooked into something pretty sizable. Watching the small drama unfold, he started around the pond. The boy, he was amused to note, had set his chin in a way that was purely Libby.

Jake felt a twinge of an old, familiar ache. David was nothing at all like Johnny. Neither as sweet nor as gentle. But then, Johnny had not lived to develop a seven-year-old's independence.

"Watch out for the holes in the bank," Libby called out as Jake started down the slope toward where the battle was in progress. "Between muskrats and erosion, they're all over."

"Erotic banks. Sounds interesting," he said with a grin.

"You won't think it's quite so interesting if you step in one and break a leg," she shot back. Turning her attention to her son, she said, "That's right, baby, don't give him any slack. Lift your tip, drop it, and then reel in fast! Lift, drop and reel—that's it!''

Baby? Hell, even a mother ought to know better than that. Jake's eyes met David's in an exclusively male look of commiseration as Jake paused halfway down the bank to watch. Maybe if the fish was big enough, the boy would forget what she'd called him. In public, yet!

She was doing a surprisingly good job of coaching, though. Jake watched as she reached behind her to pick up the net and move in for the kill. And then suddenly, she lurched and seemed to grow shorter before his very eyes.

Everything happened at once. David yelped and threw down his rod, Libby twisted, to tumble slowly in a graceful arc, landing flat on her back in the deepest part of the pond, while Jake skidded the remaining distance and dived in just as she surfaced again.

It was over almost as quickly as it had begun, at least as far as Jake and Libby were concerned. After several clumsy attempts, he managed to get them both back up on shore before the kid could dive in to rescue his mother. By that time, everyone was yelling something about the rod.

Jake cleared his sinuses, flung his dripping hair off his forehead and leaned forward, hands on his thighs, to catch his breath. Beside him, Libby was stretched out on the steep bank, facedown, her jeans liberally streaked with red mud and her sweatshirt plastered to her back. Her fingertips were already beginning to take on a purplish tint. It was only then that Jake noticed the cutting wind. He swore. Another few minutes and she'd be chilled to the bone, if she wasn't already.

''Mama, Mama, wake up!'' David tugged on his mother's shoulder.

"Honey, let's get you somewhere warm, fast," Jake muttered. To David he said, "Your mama's just fine, son. We'll dry her off and she'll be good as new."

Eyes still tightly shut, Libby whispered a rude word. "I told you to watch your step—I warned you! And then I had to be the one to step in a blasted muskrat hole! I'm so embarrassed."

"Mama, look at my fishing pole," David cried, and she rolled over and sat up, with Jake crouching behind her in an effort to block the piercing northwest wind.

Having satisfied himself that she was in no immediate danger, David dashed off to join the rest of the company in a race to recapture his spinning rod, which was streaking across the pond, tip first.

By the time Jake herded a complaining Libby into his truck, the game was in full swing, with Calvin and David headed out in one of the boats. Everyone else was casting from the bank, trying to hook the reel. Aunt Lula, with one eye on the race, assured Libby that she would look after David while Libby got herself a nice hot shower and some warm, dry clothes.

"You, too, Jake. Oh, and would you mind picking up a couple of cans of milk and some cocoa on your way back? I promised the boys to make a panful of cocoa the old-fashioned way tonight."

Jake turned up the heat full-blast. He wasn't all that cold now that he was out of the wind, but he was beginning to worry about Libby. She was huddled up in a small knot, staring down at her mud-streaked knees as if they were the most fascinating things in the world... which they well might be. He was in no position to judge, unfortunately.

"Hey, it's not all that bad," he said softly when they had driven several miles in silence.

"Yes it is."

"So you're wet. You're washable...aren't you? You're not going to melt and get my seat covers all sticky, are you?"

"I never felt so stupid in all my life," she said flatly.

"Then you're lucky." They were crossing the Yadkin River bridge. He reached over and covered her clenched fists with his right hand. "Honey, you stepped in a muskrat hole. You said yourself it was an erotic bank. It could have happened to anyone, even me, and I'm damn near perfect."

A small sound escaped her pale lips. It was a poor effort, but Jake figured it was better than nothing. "Thanks for the rescue, anyway," she said with a sigh.

"Anyway? What does that mean?"

"It doesn't mean anything. It just means thanks for the rescue."

"'Anyway,' you said. That's like a caveat after a compliment. What did you mean, thanks for dragging me through the mud? Thanks for not laughing when my shoe came off? What, Libby? I want to know what's the matter with my brand of heroics."

By then she was giggling. Jake suppressed an urge to pull over into the emergency lane and wrap her so tightly in his arms she'd never come unwound. "Hey, it's all over, honey, with no one the worse for wear," he said softly.

"I know, but I just can't help thinking that it could've been David. Jake, what if I hadn't been there and he'd stepped into that hole? What if he falls in while I'm gone? Oh, lordy, what if—"

"Quit it. No more 'what-if,' Libby. There are half a dozen people out there to keep an eye on him. He'll be all right."

Jake knew better than most people that "what-ifs" could drive a person crazy.

The moment they pulled up in her driveway, Libby jumped out of the truck. Jake followed her to the house, and she turned to tell him when to pick her up again, but when she unlocked the door, he followed her inside.

"You've got a washer and dryer, haven't you?" he asked.

She nodded. Shivering almost uncontrollably, she wanted only to immerse herself in hot water. After that, she might be able to function again.

"Okay, then I'll toss my things in with yours. You get the first bath, and I'll use whatever's left of the hot water. I'm easy to get along with."

"Wait a minute, what do you mean you'll toss your things in with mine?"

"Libby, be reasonable. It's at least half an hour to my place, without Saturday afternoon traffic. My laundry facilities consist of two communal machines in the basement, usually either busy or out of order. You want to get back out there before dark, don't you? If so, it seems only reasonable to me to double up here."

Double up. Libby didn't like the sound of that.

Yes, she did, too! That was the trouble; she liked it entirely too much. She had enough problems in her life just building a secure future for her son without complicating matters any further. And Jake was a complication of the first order.

Knowing full well she ought to send him on his way, she heard herself saying, "David's room's right through there. I guess you can use it to change in. Throw out your wet clothes, and I'll start the washer. They can wash on short cycle during my shower and dry during yours."

So much for a deep, hot soak. She had a thirty-gallon hot-water heater that took forever to recover.

"Of course, there is an alternative, in case you're into water conservation," Jake suggested, a wicked glint in his dark eyes.

Even soaked to the skin, with his hair looking as if it had been groomed with a hay rake, he was altogether too tempting. Libby crossed her arms over her chest.

"On the other hand," he said hastily, "there's no real shortage of water around these parts."

Eight

Any other man would have looked ludicrous wrapped in a quilt, with his bare, hairy legs hanging out. Not Jake. Any other man would have had the good sense to stay put, either in the living room, the kitchen where Libby had set coffee to dripping, or in David's room.

Not Jake. He prowled. Having confiscated the quilt off the foot of the bunk bed, he padded barefoot from room to room, examining windows that needed puttying, faucets that needed washering, even discovering the matchbooks someone had jammed under the front of the refrigerator to keep the door from hanging open.

Libby paused in the doorway long enough to tell him the wash was underway and should be done in about fifteen minutes.

"I'll wait," Jake muttered.

"I didn't think you were about to take off dressed like a Roman emperor." She grinned. When she'd picked out the dinosaur quilt for David's bed, she hadn't quite pictured it serving as a toga for a strapping, six-foot-two big-iron contractor.

Jake glowered at her, and she ducked into the bathroom and shut the door. Leaning against it for a moment, she clutched her robe and dry underwear to her chest and smiled. He was so… He was just so…

She didn't know what he was. All she knew was that being around him made her feel sort of itchy, sort of achy. As if she were about to break out all over with something that would mark her for life.

Falling into the pond and having to be hauled out over a muddy bank wasn't bad enough, she thought sadly. She'd had to compound the disaster by letting him drive her home and share her facilities. Now every time she stepped into her bathtub she'd be picturing him standing right where she was standing now, sluicing down, lathering up, tilting his head to wet his hair, lifting first one arm, then the other—stroking soapsuds down over his hard, flat belly….

"Oh, lordy," she moaned, shutting her eyes against the sting of shampoo.

With some vague notion of getting him out of her house before any further damage could be done, Libby knotted her bathrobe around her still-damp body a few minutes later and hurried down the hall to the utility room. Out of the washer, into the dryer. Thirty minutes, tops, she figured, and they could be on their way.

Efficiently she sorted the small load and tossed the heaviest things into the dryer. Her jeans and sweatshirt, Jake's jeans and khaki shirt. Their lighter things could go in at the last minute—her panties, bra and Orlon socks, his navy nylon briefs and—

"Jake! What about these wool socks?" she yelled without looking around.

"What about them?"

He was so close she jumped. "I didn't hear you come in," she accused.

"I'm barefoot. Next time I'll jingle the loose change in my pocket."

Her gaze dropped to the bunk-size quilt that was artfully draped around his loins, and bounced back up again. Face flaming, she set the switch and slammed the dryer door. "Maybe they'll dry if I lay them on top," she mumbled, practically throwing the socks down in her rush to escape the confines of the tiny utility room.

He didn't budge. "If you'll excuse me," she said pointedly.

"I won't."

"Jake—" Her eyes pleaded with him as he reached out and brushed her damp hair back over her shoulders. His hands settled there, and she felt the heat of him, felt as if she were bonded to him for life. "The—the coffee should be ready by now," she whispered in a desperate effort to distract him.

"Come here, Libby." Jake wasn't a man to be distracted. It was there in the dark gleam of his narrowed eyes, in the heightened flush of his lean and angular face.

Libby wrenched herself from under his hands, and then was sorry she had. It was as if a part of her own body had been ripped away. "I—that is, we could pick up marshmallows when we stop for cocoa." The words sounded like so much gibberish. They were.

"Marshmallows. Right. I'll make a note of it. Now come here, Libby."

What choice did she have? Could the tide resist the moon? In one last desperate attempt to hang on to her soul, she pleaded, "Jake, please don't start anything foolish. It's only going to complicate things, and neither of us needs—"

"I know what I need, Libby. I think I know what you need, too."

"No, you don't! That's the very last thing I need!"

He was so close she could see the crow's-feet at the corners of his eyes, see the random gleam of silver in his dark, thick hair. "What don't you need? You don't even know what I was going to say," he purred.

But she knew, and he knew she knew. Because it was what they both wanted, and suddenly Libby was too tired to resist any longer. Yes, she wanted him! She had dreamed of feeling the length of him pressing against her, dreamed of his arms holding her through the night. She wanted to bask in his quick, rare smiles, his even rarer laughter. Wanted to share the sadness that lay buried deep inside him, and if she couldn't share it, then at least comfort him for a little while.

It wasn't love, she told herself. Jake had never pretended to love her. But whatever it was he was offering, why shouldn't she accept it? It wasn't as if she was stealing something from someone else. No one would be hurt by it. Nothing would be changed. The sun would still rise tomorrow.

His gaze never leaving hers, Jake bent and swept her up into his arms. If eyes could be said to speak, his did. And what they were saying brought a rush of heat from the soles of her feet to the crown of her head. He shouldered the door to her room open and slowly lowered her to the crocheted rug beside the bed.

Libby came down to earth, literally and figuratively, as echoes from the past rose to haunt her, bringing with them the familiar feelings of inadequacy that she could never quite manage to erase, no matter how much weight she lost or how many pretty clothes she wore.

Her self-image had been formed early. Time had diminished its spell, but nothing could banish it completely. Walt had made excellent use of it once he had discovered her secret weakness. To this day, she was uncomfortable with her own nakedness. Her breasts were too small. Her hips were too wide. He had seen better legs on a piano. He had seen to it that she felt woefully inadequate in the bedroom, unsure of her ability to please a man even for the few minutes required for the sex act.

She closed her eyes, as if not seeing could somehow make her invisible.

Sensing a certain withdrawal, Jake didn't press her. Instead he moved around her bedroom, supremely unself-conscious in his ridiculous outfit, touching her silver-backed mirror, her hairbrush and the bottle of *eau de toilette* beside David's school picture. He couldn't remember a time when he had felt so protective and so damned horny at the same time.

Of course she was nervous. He was nervous, too. But it was going to happen, and waiting wasn't going to help either one of them. Besides, dammit, just being around her lately was keeping him in an almost constant state of arousal. At his age, that was ridiculous!

The whole thing was ridiculous. Look at them—she was standing over there, studying the bedpost, and here he was on the other side of the room, sneaking peeks at her, like some steamed-up fifteen-year-old!

Objectively speaking, she wasn't even particularly pretty. He couldn't for the life of him figure out what made her so damned special. The best he could come up with was a bunch of little things. Like the way she had of lifting her chin. Like the way her hair sprang thick and glossy from a cowlick at the very crown of her head. Like the way her eyes could soften one minute, grow serious the next, and then light up with little golden sparks of laughter.

Like the way he felt when he was around her. Warm, comfortable and comforted. Accepted with no explanations asked, none given.

Rounding the foot of the bed, he reached out and touched the chain of safety pins dangling from her lapel. "Nice jewelry. Understated."

"It's for emergencies. At least this way I always know where to find one."

"Speaking of emergencies, you don't have to worry. About me, that is. If I had the least doubt of that, things would never have gone this far."

"I know that, Jake. Me, too." After learning of Walt's indiscretions, she had made an appointment to be tested. That night she had moved into the guest room. "Jake, it's been a long time for me. You may as well know that I, uh—" She cleared her throat. "I've never been very good at it," she finished in a rush.

"That's what you said about dancing," he reminded her, a teasing smile playing at the corners of his eyes.

"Yes, and I was right, too, wasn't I?"

"I thought we managed pretty well," he said as he untied the sash of her robe. "Steel-toed slippers and all."

She swallowed hard and closed her eyes against what was happening. "I just don't want you to—to expect too much."

"Let me be the judge of that." His hands moved again and her robe slithered silently to the floor.

"That's what I'm afraid of. Being judged," she said

with a nervous laugh. Being judged and found wanting. Again.

The touch of his mouth in the hollow of her throat made her knees buckle. Jake caught her around the waist and lowered her onto the bed, following her down, and she lay there stiffly, afraid to move, almost afraid to breathe. Above her, Jake's face was suddenly the face of a stranger. A harsh, compelling mask that had been chiseled from stone.

Libby was too frightened by the intensity of what was happening to her to protest as he began touching her here, kissing her there—caressing her in ways that were both gentle and incendiary.

Oh, my glory, you can't do that! I'm coming apart!

But her only audible response was the catch of her breath, the occasional deep, shuddering gasp. And then, "Jake, what are you—Jake!"

"Hush, love—let me make you bloom."

Oh, oh, oh! She had never, ever *gone up in flames this way before!*

Desperate to hang on to a shred of sanity, Libby lifted her head and looked down at what he was doing to her.

And then wished she hadn't. If his kisses, his caresses, had set her on fire, the sight of those tanned and callused hands on her vulnerable flesh had the effect of throwing fuel on the flames.

"Help me," he ordered gruffly.

"Help you how? Jake, please—I don't know how. I'll do it all wrong."

"At least get this damned thing off me," he growled, and lifting her head again, Libby saw that the quilt was twisted around his waist like a misplaced, dinosaur-printed leash. Her lips began to tremble.

"Laugh and you'll regret it," he warned her, but

when a giggle escaped her and he sank his teeth tenderly into her throat, she found that she didn't regret it at all.

Eventually, working together with several rather interesting distractions, they managed to free him from bondage. By that time, Libby had gained a considerable store of confidence. She watched openly as he moved over her, the scent of her soap and her lavender sachets mingling erotically with a deeper, more sensual note.

Including two male cousins she had discovered skinny-dipping at the pond when she was nine, Libby had seen a total of three adult nude males. Until Jake. He was magnificent, his broad shoulders still tanned from summer, the dark hair patterning his chest, leading the eye downward to—

Oh, my.

"Touch me, Libby," Jake asked, and taking her hand, he guided her. Her gaze never left his. She was trembling, but she followed his lead, and then daringly took control until Jake had to lead her away for the sake of his own sanity.

Willing himself to patience, he gazed down at the woman who lay open and trembling beneath him. There was something incredibly touching about a woman's vulnerability. Jake had never thought about it before. At this stage of the game, he wasn't usually capable of thought. Yet in that very vulnerability, he acknowledged, lay a woman's greatest strength. What man in his right mind could ever hurt something so wonderful?

Carefully he traced the fragile line of her collarbone, slipping down into the valley between her breasts, and then trailing up one pale slope to circle the dusky tip. Her nipples were dark and generous, and he found himself wondering if she had nursed her baby.

Oh, God, not now! He didn't want to think of anything but this moment, this woman. That was all that mattered. To make it good for her, because he was pretty sure it hadn't been so good in the past.

Taut with his own urgent need, Jake forced himself to draw out the tension, as if by doing so he could make it last forever.

Nothing lasts forever, a voice inside him whispered.

His hand moved down over the slight dome of her belly, and he felt her muscles jerk in involuntary response. He soothed her with slow, circular caresses, and after a while, his fingertips moved down again, into the soft thatch of curls at the base of her belly. Libby gasped.

Jake groaned aloud. He couldn't hold off much longer. One thing to be said for being forty—theoretically, at least—was the increased staying power. With Libby, even that slight advantage was shot all to hell. He felt like a randy teenaged stud, all raging hormones and no finesse.

"Libby," he whispered urgently, "sweetheart, I don't want to rush you, but—"

"Rush me! Please," she begged, grabbing his shoulders to pull him down to her.

Libby was stunned by her own aggressiveness. She had been accused of many things in her life. Aggressiveness was not among them. But did it matter in the long run who took the lead in something as inevitable as this? Beyond rational thought, she dug her fingers into the slippery skin of his shoulders and drew him closer.

Molten gold. Pure, hot molten gold flowed through her body as he parted the portals and entered. Libby gasped. Her eyes widened, and Jake buried his face in the curve of her throat.

"Don't—move," he grated. "Don't even breathe!"

She thought she might have moaned his name. She didn't breathe.

"It's been awhile for me, too," he said when he had himself under some sort of control.

For Libby it had been forever. Never in this lifetime had she experienced anything so utterly compelling, so utterly mind-shattering. So utterly, bone-meltingly *right!*

Driven beyond her meager limits, she lifted her hips and wrapped her legs around his waist. Jake's powerful body began to tremble.

"I wanted—for you, precious, I wanted it to be perfect," he gasped.

But it was already too late. Perfection was already upon them. Driven heedless, headlong into the flames together, they reached for the burning sun...and found it.

"So sweet," Jake breathed a long time later. "So very sweet."

It was the sound of the old furnace rumbling on that aroused him. Judging from the angle of the sun outside the window, little more than an hour had passed, but that was enough. It was too much, Jake thought ruefully as he pulled a lavender-scented comforter up over Libby's naked shoulder.

Jake, old man, you've really done it this time, he told himself as he quietly closed the bedroom door behind him. You thought one fast tumble and you'd be able to get her out of your system?

Man, you've lost it. This time, you really screwed up!

Naked, he stood in the kitchen and poured himself a cup of coffee. He took it straight, but it didn't help. Staring thoughtfully at the bedroom door down the hall, he wondered if he had the guts to sell out, move away and start all over again. Maybe somewhere in the Ozarks. Maybe California.

Hell, why not the moon, for all the good it would do? There were some things that distance couldn't cure. Might help. Time would help even more, but there were no real cures. That was another lesson he'd learned the hard way.

Passing her room in search of his clothes a few minutes later, Jake heard her moving around. The sound of dresser drawers opening and closing. On the way back to the kitchen he heard the sound of running water.

At least she took the time to get dressed before she came out to join him. If she'd come out of there in that damned bathrobe of hers—or worse yet, in nothing—he wouldn't have been responsible for his actions.

Jake had dressed in the utility room. His jeans were damp along the seams, his socks wet. He couldn't have cared less. The thing now was to get out of here before he did something irretrievably stupid.

Something *else* irretrievably stupid.

"Remember, we have to stop at the grocer's on the way back out to the cabin," Libby said, not quite meeting his eyes.

Jake's face turned to stone. Having forgotten completely that he was going to have to drive her back out there, he'd been mentally composing a tactful disappearance speech.

"Yeah, well...you want a cup of coffee to go? It's still hot."

He had downed three cups of the stuff. Other than eating a hole in his gut, the coffee hadn't done much for him. He hadn't experienced any blinding flashes of wisdom...although it was a bit late for wisdom now. Next time he'd try coffee first. Better yet, *instead* of.

But there wouldn't be any next time, he reminded himself. Not for Libby and him. She wasn't the first woman he'd slept with since Cass, not that there'd been that many. And none at all in a long time. Promiscuity had never been his style. Still, he had a feeling this one was going to take a lot more forgetting than any of the others had done. He had instinctively known that, right from the first.

So what the devil had happened to make him forget it? "Let's go then," he growled, covering uneasiness with anger. He didn't like the way she was looking at him.

And then he didn't like the way she was *not* looking at him. "Libby, it happened, okay? It's a little late to be having second thoughts, so why don't we both just agree to forget it?"

Jake felt, rather than saw, the impact his words had on her. Up went the chin, back went the shoulders. He cursed himself for being an insensitive son of a bitch. He called himself a coward and knew it for the truth.

The drive back out to the cabin was conducted almost as silently as the drive in had been. Libby ran into the Food Lion for cocoa, canned milk and marshmallows. She grabbed a package of Oreos and then tossed a couple of chocolate bars into her basket. David deserved a treat for losing his fish, she told herself, ignoring the fact that David's weakness was gingerbread, not chocolate. She was the chronic chocoholic in the family. Just let trouble rear its ugly head, and she dived for the comfort of a Hershey bar. This was going to be a three-bar night.

On arrival, Jake turned the truck around so that it was headed out before he switched off the engine. The message was hardly subtle. "It's getting pretty late," he said. "Guess I'd better run along."

"Yes, I expect so," she said with exquisite politeness, just as if the marks of her fingernails weren't still embossed on the skin of his buttocks.

Jake studied the persimmon tree a few feet away while Libby stole a glance at his rigid profile. Drawing a deep breath, she turned to stare out across the pond just as Jake turned to look at her.

"Jake, if you—"

"Yeah, I'd better get along," he said hurriedly, and blindly she opened her door. Jake was out before her feet hit the ground. "Libby," he began just as David dashed up and yanked on his mother's hand.

"Mama, Mama!"

Absently Libby rumpled her son's hair while her eyes met Jake's over the hood of his truck. "Thank you for the ride, Jake."

Oh, God, I didn't say that! Face flaming, she blundered on. "If you'd like to come back—well, I suppose you won't, but if you did—to fish, I mean—well, you're welcome."

Anytime, day or night, for the rest of my life, you're welcome.

"Mama, listen," David cried, hopping from one foot to the other.

Libby told herself that this was what she'd been unconsciously bracing herself against from the first time she'd laid eyes on him. She must have known instinctively that he wouldn't stay around much longer than it took to break her heart. "Yes, David, I'm listening, darling," she murmured absently.

She told herself she wasn't stupid. A slow learner, maybe, but not really stupid. No woman was proof against a man like Jake Hatcher. He had made it perfectly clear right from the first that he wasn't geared for double harness. What had happened didn't change that. Pushing away the sadness that threatened to engulf her, Libby told herself that Jake had his own problems. The last thing she needed was another man with problems. She had enough of her own.

"I'm listening, honey," she said, shifting her attention to her son. "Tell me while we take these things to Aunt Lula. I bought marshmallows for toasting, what do you think of that?"

But Jake wasn't quite finished yet. He came around the truck and stopped, so close he could see the gray strands woven among the gold in Libby's hair. David glared up at him, his belligerent features a smaller replica of his mother's in spite of his darker coloring. Jake squatted on his haunches until his eyes were level with the boy's. Gravely he said, "You want to take real good care of your mama, David. She had a bad scare today."

"My mama can swim," the child retorted. "She wouldn'a drownded even if you hadn'a pulled her out. I was going to jump in and save her!"

"I know you were. I just happened to be closer, that's all. When a woman needs help, we men have to do what needs doing, right?" His voice dropped to a lower note and came out sounding oddly husky. "She's lucky she has you, son. You're both luckier than you know."

For a long time afterward, Jake thought about the expression on the boy's face. David had looked as if the concept were one he had never heard of before, much less experienced firsthand. What a hell of a marriage she must have had.

Libby stood in the clearing and watched Jake's truck drive off down the winding, graveled road that connected her uncle's property with highway 158. Through the thicket of ancient field pines, she watched the glimmer of silver until it passed through the far gate, some quarter of a mile up the road, and disappeared from sight.

"Mama!" David tugged on her shirttail, and reluctantly she turned away. "Mama, I caught a three pounder! Uncle Calvin and me caught my rod and the fish was still on it, and Uncle Calvin said that was 'cause I hooked him real good. Jeffie caught two little ones, but I want to eat mine for supper. Please?"

Jake took two aspirins with water and stared at the bottle of Scotch. Somewhat to his surprise, he found that he wasn't particularly tempted. He'd lost count of the times in the past when he'd crawled into the bottle to escape the inescapable. No thanks to his own strength of character, he had eventually managed to crawl out again. And stay out. It was either that or die.

But whiskey wasn't going to solve anything now, any more than it had in the past. Not that he was ready yet to admit that there was anything to be solved.

Abruptly he turned back to the specs he had been staring at for the past hour or so and tried to focus on the figures there. It would be a first—a big first—if they decided to go after a chunk of the new interstate. Small and relatively new in the field, they'd be bidding against some of the biggest contractors in the region.

But Jake knew for a fact that some of the big firms were top heavy. Bostic had worked for one of their competitors for years before he'd gone into business for himself. Now the two of them ran a lean, mean outfit. Small profit margin, overhead cut to the bone, with every penny saved put into first-rate men and equipment. They were good at anticipating trouble. Even so, there were always surprises. Breakdowns. Illness. Freak weather conditions. It all had to be figured in.

It would be a challenge, and right now, Jake could do with something to occupy about a hundred and ten percent of his brain.

Was she still out there? Had she managed to stay dry? If she caught cold, was she going to blame it on him?

A wintry smile broke through the hard set of his features as he balanced the pencil between his two forefingers and stared out at an ugly brick warehouse across the street. He'd worked through about six inches of backlog so far. Only half a dozen more inches to go. If he hadn't played hooky this weekend, he'd have been caught up by now.

No, dammit, playing hooky described some schoolboy prank that might have got him grounded for a week or so. What he'd done was so supremely stupid he couldn't believe he had actually done it. It wasn't as if he hadn't known better, either. Right from the first she had got to him. A stranger across a crowded room—only in this case, the stranger had been married and extremely pregnant, and he had just seen Cass and Johnny and the baby-sitter off to the beach, and was already wondering what the devil he was doing still in town when they were somewhere else.

Libby Porter. He might have seen her in high school, he didn't remember. But he sure as hell remembered seeing her at the fund-raiser. Even then there had been something about her that had got to him. The next time he had seen her, at that reunion thing, he hadn't recognized her, not right off, but he had suspected even then she was a hazard. Like a bad allergy. Knowing he was susceptible, a smart man would have stayed the hell away.

So what did he do? He took her to bed. He sat around a camp fire with her friends and family, all cozy and warm and comfortable, and then he took her to bed!

Staring unseeingly at the bottle amid the scattered papers on his desk, Jake continued to argue with himself. What the hell, she was an experienced woman. She understood the rules of the game, didn't she?

But that was just it. She didn't. For all she'd been married and had a child, she was as green as they came. God, she didn't even know how to hide her feelings! It had been right there in her eyes, plain as day. She thought she was in love with him. What was infinitely worse, she had probably managed to convince herself, in spite of a total lack of encouragement on his part, that he was in love with her.

He wasn't. Anything he'd had to offer along those lines had been used up a long time ago. There was nothing left. He could live with that. He had lived with it for more than seven years. But she needed to know the score before she got in any deeper, because a woman's mind didn't work the way a man's did. Hell, Libby's mind didn't even work the way most women's did!

So okay. Just to be sure, he'd better let her know, in the kindest sort of way, that while he liked her and respected her, and enjoyed her company, maybe it would be best if—

Abruptly Jake threw down his pencil and glanced at his watch. It was late, but not all that late. The kids had probably flaked out by now, and the rest of the gang was probably sitting around the camp fire singing old cowboy songs.

Or maybe comparing notes on the joys of marriage, divorce and single parenthood.

Nine

This time instead of driving down and waking the camp, in case they were all asleep, Jake left his truck by the outer gate and cut through the woods on foot. He'd be lucky not to break a leg, he thought as he picked his way carefully through pines, hardwoods, brambles and muscadine vines.

From the edge of the clearing, he counted five people seated around the fire, which by now had burned down to no more than a rosy bed of coals. Even with her back to him, he had no trouble picking her out. Arms wrapped around her knees and head tilted in that characteristic way, she was listening to something the high school coach with the eight-year-old was saying.

Damned redneck jock! Jake knew the breed. Gullins was the type who considered any unattached female fair game. Babes, he called them. Broads. Sweet li'l ol' things whose sole purpose on earth was to keep his beer cold and his bed warm.

Jake started across the clearing, his powerful stride flattening the clumps of wild grass and pine seedlings that sprouted between infrequent mowings. That jackass had a few things to learn about Libby Porter! What's more, he'd better be a damn quick study, or Jake was going to clean his clock for him!

A woman's clear laughter rang out in the cold night air, and he froze. Libby's laughter? No—he'd have recognized her husky chuckle anywhere. This was the other woman, Jeffie's mom, Bunny what's-her-name.

Jeffie's mom. David's mom. Mickey's dad, Kyle's dad, Peanut's dad...

Slowly Jake's anger drained away, to be replaced by a bitter dose of reality. He had about as much business being here as a cat did in a goldfish bowl. Obviously this little shindig had been cooked up by Libby's aunt and uncle as an opportunity for her to meet men with whom she had at least one thing in common: single parenthood.

Oh, sure, they'd invited another woman along as a smoke screen. Calvin and Lula added additional cover. But their motive was unmistakable. The whole affair had been planned to give their niece an opportunity to look over the field without all the pressure attendant on the usual singles scene.

So where did Jake fit in? The answer was obvious. He didn't.

Feeling more an outsider than ever, Jake turned his back on the warm glow of shared laughter and shared interests. Far be it from him to spoil things for Libby. If she found fulfillment in toasting marshmallows around a camp fire with a bunch of PTA leftovers, far be it from him to cramp her style. God knows, he didn't have anything to offer her.

Libby decided that if Mike Gullins asked her out, she would go. Their children got along well enough together, although Mickey was something of a bully. It would probably do David good to get a taste of the real world. Having attended a small, excellent private academy for preschool, kindergarten and the first grade, he'd been sheltered, she admitted it freely. Since moving back she had often wondered if she was being unfair to him. Walt had accused her more than once of coddling the boy, but then Walt had consistently undermined her authority whenever she'd tried to be firm. She might never have had the nerve to end her marriage if she hadn't seen all too clearly what their constant tug-of-war was doing to David.

Just since yesterday, though, he had begun to accept the company of men. Nor did he seem particularly intimidated by the older kids, possibly because it was his uncle's pond, which gave him a certain stature. Not only had he had an opportunity to make new friends, he had learned that his mother could enjoy male friends of her own without threatening his security in any way. Nor did he seem as inclined, with several men to chose from, to latch on to any one of them the way he had that septic tank pumper-outer.

Oh, yes, the weekend had been a rousing success, Libby thought bitterly as she pretended to listen to a rundown on the care and feeding of a future football star. So why did she feel as if all the color had suddenly leached out of her world, leaving it in stark, lonely shades of gray?

* * *

By the middle of Sunday morning, the excitement had proved too much for the younger children. Jeffie had a stomach ache, Mickey had jerked a fishhook into his thumb and had to be driven to Mocksville to have it cut out. He had delighted the company afterward by telling them how it had swelled up and turned green when the doctor had stuck a needle in it and shot it full of gunk so it wouldn't hurt.

The little girl, Peanut, had settled into the whine mode, and Bunny was making a concerted effort to find out everything she could about Jake Hatcher.

"Hey, look, if I'm poaching on your preserves, just tell me to go jump," she said with engaging frankness. "But if you two don't have anything in particular going for you, I'd sure like to try my luck. It's got to be better than fishing!"

They both laughed, and Libby gave herself full credit for not yanking out those gorgeous, inch-long eyelashes. "You're welcome to try, as far as I'm concerned," she forced herself to say.

"So tell me everything. Where'd you meet him? How does he like his women—scrambled, fried, easy over?"

Unavailable, Libby could have said, but didn't. In small, strictly limited doses. "We went to high school together, but I really don't know all that much about him. He's single. He owns half a construction outfit. Not buildings—roads, bridges, that kind of thing. He dances, he doesn't drink, and he has an apartment somewhere north of town. I don't know the address, but he's probably in the phone book."

"You left out the most important parts, like he's got the face of a fallen angel and a body that can turn a perfectly sane woman into a raving maniac, but if you don't have sense enough to knock him down, tie him up and drag him off to your cave, then I'm going to give it my best shot. Wish me luck!"

Libby wished she'd walk into a tree and break her precious little turned-up nose in three places, but was too polite to say it.

They arrived home just after four. The sky had already turned a nasty shade of puce. Libby was low on groceries, she had a car full of muddy, fishy clothes, and a splitting headache. When David began to whine, first about not being able to go home with Jeffie, and then about going out for a hamburger, her patience snapped.

"First we are going to unload the car. Then we're going to clean up the fishing tackle and put it away. Then we're going to start a load of wash, and then we're going to go to the grocery store. And then maybe—maybe—we'll get supper while we're out."

David's yell of triumph made her wince, and Libby asked herself, not for the first time, if she was being too hard on him or too lenient. Could a mother ever make up for the absence of a father? How?

And all that was before she hurried into her bedroom to dump her overnight bag and saw the rumpled bed, with David's favorite quilt hanging over the back of her bent-willow rocking chair.

As if the rain weren't dismal enough, they both came down with colds the next day. Meet new kids, she thought philosophically, meet new germs. David's cold, as usual, settled in his ear, and Libby spent a small fortune on doctor's bills and antibiotics, expenses she had once taken for granted.

With the resilience of childhood, David recovered in three days. He was bursting with energy, and Libby saw him off on the bus every morning, counting down the days before Walt was to pick him up for the following weekend. *If* he didn't beg off at the last minute.

Evidently this time it was a go. When Walt called to make arrangements to pick up David after school on Friday, he told her he had tickets to the State-Carolina game on Saturday.

Libby wondered if he had the slightest conception of how short a seven-year-old's attention span was. David would survive it. Walt just might not.

Her own cold had settled in her chest. She could barely talk. When Walt drove up and honked the horn on Friday afternoon, she was tempted to ignore him. Less than an hour before, Jeffie had called and asked David over for hot dogs, and he'd decided that would be more fun than spending the weekend with his father.

"Daddy'll just yell at me a lot. He always yells at me," he'd said, and Libby had had her work cut out for her changing his mind.

Not that she could blame him. Walt had never been much of a father, but if he got the feeling that she was trying to keep them apart, he could be extremely unpleasant.

"Hello, Walt. David's had a cold, and he's still on antibiotics. I've written instructions. Will you please see that he takes his medicine every morning with his juice?"

Walt's habitually arrogant expression turned petulant. "Oh, great. Just what I need, a sick kid."

"I'll be glad to let him stay home if you—"

"My mother's expecting him for dinner tonight." Which explained a lot, Libby thought wryly. "You're looking as beautiful as ever, Lib. Don't touch that, David. Are your hands clean? Libby, for God's sake, can't you even keep him clean?"

"He just got home from school, but his hands are perfectly clean." As for her looks, Libby knew she looked awful. Colds always treated her this way. Her skin turned transparent, there were shadows a mile wide under each eye, and she had an even lower tolerance than usual for her ex-husband. "I'd appreciate it if you wouldn't keep him up too late."

"Give me credit for half a brain, will you?"

"Oh, I do, I do. I've always given you credit for half a brain."

Walt muttered something under his breath, making Libby feel about two inches high. She hadn't always been that way—petty and vindictive. Mean as a snake. It was the cold, she told herself. By the fourth day, she would have snapped at an alligator.

At least she had no worries about David's safety on the two-hour drive to Raleigh. Walt cared too much for his precious car to risk speeding. Besides, he'd already had more tickets than the law allowed. One more and he'd be lucky to be able to call a cab!

She was still feeling miserable, lonely and unattractive an hour later when the phone rang. Thinking it was Billy or Aunt Lula calling to inquire about her health, she croaked a greeting, and then, on hearing Jake's voice, was torn between hanging up and hanging on. By the time she came to her senses, he was begging her pardon for bothering her.

"Jake, it's not a wrong number, it's me!" she rasped. "Jake? Don't hang up."

"Libby, what the hell happened to your voice?"

"Oh, that. Our church choir's holding auditions for the Christmas Cantata. The soprano parts are all filled, but there's still an opening for a baritone.'' That was another thing about her and colds—three days on antihistamines and she got downright silly.

''You're crazy, lady, you know that? Certifiable.''

''Tell me about it,'' she said morosely.

They were both silent for so long, Jake wondered if the connection had been broken. She couldn't regret what had happened any more than he did, but dammit, life went on. People made mistakes. The survivors picked up the pieces and went on from there.

Only Jake couldn't seem to move forward. ''Look, I've got to be over in your neck of the woods later on this evening. We had a slight accident late yesterday with one of the dozers—this damned rain! Anyhow, I've had a crew out there all day, and I need to check by, so if you're going to be home, I thought I'd stop in. And say hello. To, ah—to David.''

''Oh, well...''

''If you'd rather I didn't, all you have to do is say so.''

She couldn't. She opened her mouth to tell him it would be better if he stayed away, but no sound emerged.

''About five, then. What if I stop by that barbecue place and bring along enough for half a dozen sandwiches?''

''Jake, you don't have to do that. David won't even be here!'' As a protest, it was about as effective as an attack by a moth, her voice hitting on every third syllable. Jake ignored it. Now that he'd made up his mind to see her, he couldn't wait another minute.

He hung up the phone, stared down at his unsteady hand and wondered exactly when he had flipped out.

Libby didn't want him there. That's what she told herself as she raced through the house picking up toys, dishes, and straightening cushions and rugs. She repeated it while she showered, shampooed her hair and bent over from the waist to blow it dry with one hand while she polished her toenails with the other. Even half sick, she was efficient.

"Dammit, I didn't ask him to barge in here and mess up my life again," she muttered as she tried on one blouse after another, tossing them all onto the foot of the bed. "Just when I've got it together—just when—" She snatched off the peach flowered silk—for late November, yet!—and marched over to her dresser, where she dragged out her oldest sweatshirt. Once bright yellow, it had faded to the color of vanilla custard.

She sprayed a whiff of toilette water into the air and walked through it, then rushed to the bathroom and tried to scrub it off. He'd think she cared! He would probably think she had gone to great lengths to dress up for him.

Not if she could help it, he wouldn't, she told herself, and she had just started to strip off the custard-colored sweatshirt for a paint-spattered one when someone banged on the front door.

Muttering curses that came out as squeaks and wheezes, she strode to the door and flung it open. "Don't get close to me, I have a cold."

Her jaw was set on attack, and Jake resisted the urge to laugh. He resisted the urge to puncture her pitiful paper dragons, and he resisted, with far greater difficulty, the urge to drag her into his arms and kiss the living daylights out of her, cold germs, Olive Oyl voice and all.

"Here's this," he said instead, holding out a white paper sack.

"I told you David's not here."

His eyes gleamed briefly, and then he sauntered into the kitchen and placed the sack on the table. "I didn't want to take a chance on his coming home hungry. Besides, I can probably account for about three, myself."

"You ought to know better. Cholesterol."

Her arms were crossed over her breasts, her stance militant. Cheerfully Jake accepted the challenge. "I've never had a problem with the stuff. Good genes."

Before she could help herself, Libby's gaze dropped to the well-worn, close-fitting blue jeans. The way he was standing, with his legs crossed at the ankle and his hips braced against the kitchen table, he was blatantly, almost boastfully, male.

She had once heard an outspoken man described as an upfront kind of guy. Why the phrase should occur to her just now, she couldn't imagine.

Of course you can, you ninny, but it doesn't mean that!

"I've got all I need of the right kind, though," Jake went on. Libby closed her eyes as color swept up to her scalp. "HDL, LDL, LBJ—I never could keep up with these medical terms, but my doctor assures me that I've got the right mix of whatever's necessary. Blood pressure's fine, too, in case you were wondering."

Somehow, they got through the next few minutes. Libby explained about the custody agreement and the monthly visits, which as often as not ended up being canceled at the last minute, to no one's great disappointment. "Walt's taking him to a game tomorrow," she said with a slight frown. "I just hope it's not windy, because he has trouble with his ears."

"Does he have a hat?"

"Yes, but he won't wear it."

Somehow they got into a discussion of home remedies, and Libby soon forgot her concern over David's ears, which was probably what Jake had intended all along.

"Now, for a sore throat," he told her, "you can't beat a gargle of hot water, vinegar, black pepper and garlic. Works like a charm."

She shuddered. "No wonder you got out of pharmaceuticals."

Working together in surprising accord, they piled barbecue and slaw on buns, poured two glasses of milk and took the tray into the living room.

"Damper's still working all right, I see," Jake observed, testing the air for smoke.

"Thanks to you." Libby concentrated on not letting her sandwich fall apart in her hands. It looked wonderful. It tasted like rubber. At this rate, she might as well try his vinegar, pepper and garlic remedy. She wouldn't be able to taste it, and it might even help her voice. At least it didn't sound too fattening.

Sighing, she applied herself to her tasteless sandwich. That was another thing. Colds always made her feel fat.

Jake switched on her television set and tuned around to the news channel, giving them both something to stare at. Libby's eyes were too scratchy to wear contacts, but she refused to wear her glasses in front of Jake. On some women glasses were a fashion accessory. On Libby they were just glasses.

So she squinted. They sat side by side on the couch, not touching. Like two strangers in a bus station. The anchorman gloated over the bad news and cleverly put the usual negative spin on any good news that managed to squeeze in.

Libby gave up and concentrated on trying to decide whether or not the newscaster wore a hairpiece. He probably did. Shoulder pads, too. And didn't he used to have wattles?

Misery liked company. Feeling marginally better for having reduced a handsome, successful news anchor to a charlatan, Libby sighed and tucked her feet up beside her. Across the room in the ugly, old-fashioned fireplace, the logs burned hotly, sizzling occasionally as the flames found a hidden cache of sap.

Jake felt the tension that had ridden him all week begin to ebb, leaving him relaxed and oddly content. Had his parents ever spent an evening like this? If so, it was before his time. His grandparents, perhaps, at least in their early days, but by the time his parents had married, life for the Healys had already been complicated by too much money and too many commitments.

God knows, Cass would have thought he had lost his mind if he'd suggested a quiet evening at home together, sitting before the fire in companionable silence.

His gaze kept straying to the woman beside him. She looked tired. There were shadows under her eyes, and the tip of her nose was pink, which, oddly enough, only made her more attractive. It occurred to him that midlife crises in the male of the species could be a very dicey proposition.

Jake knew he had no business being here. Yet here he was. Not only that, it felt right. They didn't have much in common, considering that they'd been classmates. Different backgrounds. Different upbringing. She had a child. He didn't. He played his cards pretty close to his vest, and Libby was an open book.

Yet in spite of all their differences, there was one thing they had in common, and that was a constant, deep-seated loneliness.

"Was that more rain?" Libby murmured, glancing at the window. With the clouds, it was already quite dark.

"Sounded more like sleet. It's early for that kind of weather."

"We've had snow in November before."

"If you really want to talk about the weather, Libby, we will. I'll talk about the nightly news, the stock market—whatever. But that's not what I came out here for."

Her stricken gaze flew to his, and Jake reached over and covered her hands. They were icy cold. "Quit it, now. I didn't mean what you're thinking."

"What was I thinking?"

"That I'd come out here to take you to bed again?"

"You'd never do that!"

The bleakness left his face, and he almost smiled. Drawing her against his side, he tucked her head into the hollow of his shoulder. "Listen, I've been doing some thinking."

"I'm almost afraid to ask," she murmured. She was shockingly aware of his chest under her cheek, the steady rhythm of his heart, the powerful arm around her shoulder, and the clean, masculine scent that eddied up from his warm body.

"Libby, I think we have something pretty valuable to offer each other. The thing is, we need to have an understanding."

"And you've just discovered this—this valuable thing we have? You didn't know about it last weekend?"

It was the antihistamine talking. Libby would never have asked a leading question like that. Just because a man and a woman slept together once, that didn't mean anything. An understanding, he'd said. Suddenly she wasn't at all sure she wanted to understand.

Jake's hand found its way under her hair, and he began stroking her nape, his fingertips rough on her sensitive skin. "No, I didn't just discover it. It's been there all along—I guess I just wasn't ready to admit it."

"What changed your mind?" She wasn't going to be taken in so easily, not again.

"I'm not really sure. A lot of little things begin to stand out in my mind. Gingerbread parts. Grocery carts. A certain attitude that's rare these days. I know, I know, it sounds crazy, but suddenly, things started to add up."

"I don't have the least idea what you're talking about. Jake, if this is a game, I told you, I'm not a very good player."

"It's no game, Libby. I'm not quite sure what it is, but I do know it's not a game."

She buried her face in his shoulder, her hands clenched in her lap. "That's what I'm afraid of. I think maybe games might be safer, after all."

For a long time, neither of them spoke. Freezing rain struck the window. A log shifted in the fireplace, and Libby thought about Rosa, who had helped raise David. She wished she'd remembered to ask Walt if the housekeeper would be there.

But of course, Walt would never have taken him without help. Mrs. Porter was good for the occasional lunch, but children made her nervous.

"Libby," Jake said, interrupting her vague concerns, "I never told you, but..."

She waited. After a while, he began to speak, and Libby held her breath, knowing intuitively that what he was going to say would somehow change her life.

"Seven years ago I had everything a man strives for. A beautiful wife, a—a son. A nice home, a successful business. Friends."

It was almost as if she'd known. As if his pain were her own.

"What happened?" she whispered.

And then in a voice devoid of emotion, in terms that could not possibly be misunderstood, he began to tell her.

Ten

Sometime during the telling, the sleet had turned to rain. The fire had burned down to glowing coals, and for a while, neither of them spoke. Then, Libby covered Jake's hand with her own and she squeezed. Hard.

"Sorry for dumping on you that way," he said, his voice sounding uncomfortably raw.

"Jake, don't." Pressing her face into the hollow of his shoulder, she held him tightly around the waist. This, then, was the cause of that deep well of sadness she had sensed in him right from the first. To lose a child, a bright, beloved son—to have him one moment and lose him forever in the next, would be pain beyond bearing.

"There aren't any words," she whispered. "There just aren't." He hadn't said all that much about his wife, but he had to have loved her. Libby would have given all she possessed to be the woman Jake loved. To have the right to share his grief, to share his life. To give him another child, even though it could never take the place of the one lost.

Abruptly Jake leaned his head back. His eyes felt as if they were bleeding. He felt raw all over, yet oddly light, as if he'd shed a great weight.

In a sense, perhaps he had. The first few days after it had happened, he had sealed himself off. In shock, he had moved through whole blocks of time like a sleep-walker, making all the arrangements, saying all the right things to the right people. Dealing with Cass, who had been dealing with her own burden of guilt and pain. By convincing himself that he was handling it, he had managed to avoid facing up to reality. A month passed, and then a year. By the time the enormity of his loss finally caught up with him, he was completely alone.

He'd told Bostic a pared-down version of the truth. That he had lost a son and a wife, sold what was left of his business before he could lose that, too, tried to drown himself in booze, landed in jail on a D-and-D charge, and finally figured if he was going to kill himself, a bullet would be a hell of a lot simpler all around.

The old man hadn't asked for details. Jake hadn't offered any.

Now he thanked God for Libby's arms. She hadn't offered him sympathy—not in empty words. Nor had she asked any questions. After a while she shifted into a more comfortable position, and then was still so long he wondered if she'd fallen asleep.

"I was almost glad David was going to spend this weekend with Walt, even though he didn't want to go. He never does," she added apologetically. "But we've both been short-tempered this past week, and I thought it would do us both good to be apart for a weekend. Now I wish he hadn't gone."

"Don't. Honey, don't, for God's sake, feel guilty just because you're a human being. I've been down that road, and believe me, it doesn't go anywhere."

"I tried to tell myself it was because those two need each other, but that's not true. Walt was always buying him these expensive toys. You know, radio-operated model airplanes and an ATV when he wasn't even big enough to ride a bike. And then he'd get mad because David didn't know how to use them properly, and they'd get put away. David would cry and Walt would blame me for the whole debacle."

Jake pinched the space between his brows. "My father gave me his father's set of lead soldiers. That was just about the time they discovered that lead wasn't among the preferred food groups. My mother pitched a fit, and I never got to play with the things. I didn't bother to offer them to Johnny."

They talked, of all things, about favorite toys—Johnny's books and pirate hat. David's construction set and soldier doll. Jake's favorite had been a wooden logging truck. Libby's, a homemade stuffed monkey.

"A stuffed monkey? I thought all little girls liked dolls. Cass still had Ken and Barbie and trunks full of clothes when we were married."

"Oscar was so skinny—the stuffing in his tail was so lumpy, I had to adopt him because I knew no one else ever would. He was so ugly, I crocheted him this hideous sweater out of pink rug yarn, but that didn't help much, I'm afraid."

Jake nodded understandingly. They fell into a benign silence—a healing silence. When Libby offered to make coffee, he was glad for an excuse to escape the compelling ambience of the comfortably shabby parlor, with the comfortably worn furnishings. There was such a thing as being *too* comfortable.

"It's late," he said while the coffee was dripping. "I ought to be leaving pretty soon."

"Stay and have your coffee first. Maybe by then it'll have stopped raining."

Libby wasn't all that interested in coffee. She suspected Jake wasn't, either. She simply hated the thought of his being alone on a cold, rainy night. For all his outward strength, she had a feeling that deep down inside, he was even more vulnerable than she was.

Not that you would ever know it to look at him, leaning against the counter with his legs crossed at the ankles and thumbs hooked under his belt loops, with that padlocked look on his face.

Libby took a deep breath. Then, before she could lose her nerve, she said, "Jake, stay here tonight."

Jake's eyebrows plunged like a pair of diving hawks, and like a helpless rabbit, Libby waited for the feel of his talons in her back. She'd always been a social disaster, but this surpassed even her record. "I didn't mean—"

"Libby, you don't have to—"

"No, listen to me." Her mangled attempt at an explanation only made things worse. "I'm not asking for anything, Jake—not for myself. I just can't bear to think of your driving across town alone on a night like this, to an empty apartment. That is, it might not be empty. I mean, you probably have lots of—um..." Her unreliable voice wavered off, making her wish her vocal chords had given out before her brain had. "What I meant was that since David isn't here, you're welcome to use his room. Oh, lord, I'm sorry," she finished helplessly. It wasn't bad enough to make a fool of herself, she had to do it in a voice like a rusty hinge! "Oh, crud," she muttered, utterly defeated.

"Don't apologize. If you mean it, I'd like to stay, but Libby—if I stay, it won't be in David's room. You understand?"

She nodded. It was what she'd truly intended, after all, and not on account of the rain. At least not altogether.

Jake poured coffee into two mugs and Libby turned out the lights and locked up. He didn't have pajamas, and she didn't have anything that would come near fitting him.

"I have germs," she reminded him.

He placed the two mugs on the bedside table and began unbuttoning his shirt. "Nothing I can't handle."

"I hope you won't be sorry." And trying desperately for lightness, she added, "I can always heat you some pickle juice if your throat starts getting sore."

"And I'll massage your chest for you. It sounds pretty congested."

Her eyes, shadows notwithstanding, glinted with laughter. "You're too generous. Shall I mix up a mustard plaster?"

"Do and you'll sleep alone," Jake teased.

"So that's the secret of turning aside unwanted masculine attention. Not that I ever had all that much trouble."

"The men must have been blind."

Libby stepped into the bathroom. Through the thin paneled door she could hear Jake moving around in her bedroom. She still couldn't believe she had asked a man to spend the night with her.

Yet, how could she have let him go after what he had told her tonight? He needed her, she told herself. And she needed whatever she could have of him—whatever was left over from Johnny and Cass, even if it wasn't exactly love.

The sheets were cold; Libby usually wore socks to bed in the wintertime, but somehow, it didn't seem fitting under the circumstances.

"Aren't you freezing?" she asked as they sat and sipped their coffee, leaning against the headboard.

"No. Are you?"

"My feet are. My clock runs down when I have a cold."

"I could wind it for you." Jake's offer was accompanied by something resembling a tired leer.

But they both knew it was too soon. Here she was, Libby thought, in bed with the most beautiful man God had ever put together, and all she wanted to do was hold him. It had to be her cold. How could any woman feel sexy knowing she sounded like a bullfrog and probably looked even worse?

Beside her, Jake thought of all the places he could have been tonight. At that country-western bar with the cute little radiologist who'd called him just last week. He had dated her a few times last summer. Or with Gillie, drinking seltzer over near the School of the Arts, listening to some Irish dudes playing drums and pennywhistles.

The last place he had expected to find himself was here in Libby's bed, yet he could think of nowhere he'd rather be. And oddly enough, not for the usual reason—although he wasn't fool enough to believe that condition would last much longer.

Jake placed his cup on the table and switched out the light. Libby wiggled down under the covers and waited to see what came next. Whatever he needed from her tonight was his for the asking. Tonight and always.

With no conscious thought, they spooned together, Libby on her left side, Jake curved around her. She placed the soles of her feet on his shins, and his arm around her waist tightened convulsively. "You weren't kidding about cold feet, were you, honey?"

"I warned you."

"Next time, wear socks."

"I usually do, but I was afraid you'd laugh."

"Never," he vowed. She could feel him shaking, but he didn't utter a sound. His breath caressed her cheek and his hand spread over her stomach, sending a coil of warmth deep inside her, where she had been cold for too long. "I'm not laughing, honey, honest."

"Just wait until you come down with my cold, then we'll see who laughs last."

"Quit threatening me and go to sleep, will you?" He chuckled, and Libby closed her eyes and smiled into her pillow.

Libby never knew what had awakened her. A branch striking the side of the house? The wheezing old mantel clock in the living room that struck only when it took a notion to?

Jake had been awake for several minutes. He had woken up with his usual morning erection, and was trying to convince himself that a cold shower would be a hell of a lot safer, all things considered.

"Did you say something?" Libby murmured sleepily.

"Uh-uh. Go back to sleep, honey."

"Mmm, it's so nice and warm." She snuggled her plump backside into his pelvic region, and he groaned.

Warm. Right. Try hot as a firecracker. With a short fuse.

He knew the minute she felt him. She stiffened, trying to pretend she hadn't noticed anything out of the ordinary.

"Nothing personal," he said gruffly, and then wondered if she was fool enough to believe him. Hell yes, it was personal! As a largely celibate male, it was nothing he wasn't used to dealing with. Any other morning, he might have swung out of bed, done a few calisthenics, hit the shower and been right as rain by the time he had his eyes open good.

Only this wasn't any other morning. This was the morning after he'd spilled his guts for the first time since Johnny had died. This was the morning after he had shared a bed with a woman, asking nothing of her but the comfort of holding and being held.

This wasn't any other morning, and this wasn't any other woman. This was Libby. Jake turned her face toward him and kissed the corner of her mouth. It was going to take more than a few morning exercises and a long cold shower to cure what ailed him this time.

"Libby?" he asked tentatively, and when she rolled over and buried her face in his throat, he swallowed hard and crushed her against him. *Libby, Libby, what are you doing to me? What am I going to do about you?*

Libby had already given her heart, unconditionally. For all the good it had done to tell herself it wasn't wise, wasn't even wanted, she had done it anyway. Now she offered her body with the same reckless generosity.

Jake managed to regain control of his emotions, but his hands were none too steady as he lifted the cotton nightgown over her head. Not one word had she spoken, but it was there in her eyes, the same way it had been before. More than he was ready to see. More than he was ready to accept.

"Honey, if you don't want—"

She covered his mouth with her fingertips. "I want," she said simply, and it was all the encouragement he needed. Later on he might have regrets. Later on he might reconsider the wisdom of letting himself get this involved, but right now he was beyond the reach of reason.

Her body was deliciously warm. She smelled faintly of soap, faintly of woman, and Jake knelt above her and let his hands follow his gaze down her body, over her smooth shoulders, over the small, full breasts with their dusky rose nipples.

He lowered his face to her breasts, savoring the warmth, rubbing the hardened tips with his beard-roughened cheek before bathing them with his tongue. Libby whimpered, moving restlessly under his attentions. Gray morning light spilled in through the window, highlighting the pewter threads in his hair, and she pressed his head tightly against her breast.

But Jake was not a man to be held for long. He explored with equal thoroughness every soft inch of her trembling body, claiming with lingering kisses the dimples behind her knees, the hollows behind her ankles, the soft swell of her belly and more.

Ah, much, much more...

When neither of them could stand to wait a moment longer, he positioned himself and lifted her hips onto his own thighs. Then he drew her up until the pouting tips of her breasts brushed against his chest, lifted her again, and brought her down on him, slowly, slowly, drawing out the exquisite pleasure until they were both nearly out of their minds.

"My God, woman, what have you done to me?" he groaned.

Libby was beyond speech. She wrapped her arms around him and clung even as her body joined his in a dance as compelling as time itself.

Jake hung on to his own control until he felt her seizures commence. And then, as her tight, hot sheath began to convulse around him, hurtling him toward his own climax, he shouted aloud.

A long time later they lay together, still entwined, with covers tangled around them. Jake felt the cold air on his back, but his front was burning, melded as tightly as possible to the heat of Libby's body. He stared blindly at the pale, striped wallpaper, at the corner of a wicker-framed mirror.

What was happening to him? What was this thing that had taken root in him when he wasn't looking? Carnal needs he could understand, but this went far beyond anything he had ever experienced before. Was it because he had confided in her? Was it because she had a son?

But that was crazy! He and the kid didn't even like each other. If anything, David was a complication.

Carefully he put her away from him and rolled over onto his back, staring up at the stained ceiling. Her roof had a leak, he thought absently. He wondered if she'd had it patched yet. Hell, it was only good sex. All right, great sex. But that's all it was, all he was looking for. He wasn't in the market for anything else. He had let her know how he felt about that right up front.

Hadn't he?

Libby felt a draft of cold air where there was none to be felt. She drew the covers up under her chin and wished it was still dark, so she could make a dash for the bathroom. She needed to shower and dress so she could think straight.

Although it was a little late now for thinking. If she had been in any doubt as to her feelings before, she could no longer deny the truth. After last night she could no longer hope to get over it, no longer pretend that it was only a woman's normal reaction to an attractive, likable man. The plain truth was that what she felt for Jake Hatcher was deeper, wider, richer by far than anything she had ever felt before. She wanted to be his lover, his friend, the mother of his children. The keeper of his dreams.

In other words, she thought ruefully, the same old syndrome. She wanted to give far more than anyone wanted to receive.

"Do you want the bathroom first?" she made herself ask.

"You go first. I'd better make a few calls, see if everything's all right on the site."

"You work on weekends?" she asked, forcing a bright look of interest.

Jake reached for his watch and strapped it on, not meeting her eyes. "With a dozer in a ditch, you work the clock around and then some. Reckon there's any coffee left over from last night?"

But before either of them could get out of bed, the phone rang. Libby grabbed her nightgown and hauled it over her head, wrong side out, and raced out to the hall.

"You ought to have a jack installed in your—" The words cut off abruptly. After one look at her stricken face, Jake was out of bed like a shot, stark naked. Standing behind her, he rasped, "Libby, what is it? What's wrong?"

"It's David," she said slowly. "He's disappeared!"

* * *

Jake took over. While Libby showered and dressed, he checked the levels in his car, placed a few calls and then burned several slices of toast. While she forced down a single slice, he showered and dressed, not taking time to shave.

"We'll take my car," he said tersely, helping her into her raincoat.

"Jake, that's not necessary. It's a two-hour drive. I know Walt's doing everything that can possibly be done. David can't have gone far." She had to believe that, or she'd die!

Jake could tell how much her tenuous control was costing her. He didn't bother to reply, but herded her outside and into the passenger seat of his own car. "At least I have a phone. You won't have to wait for two hours to find out what's going on."

She looked as brittle as glass, her eyes too large, too wild. Dear God, he thought, in silent supplication, let it be all right. Don't let it happen again, not this time!

Libby gave him Walt's number, and once out of city traffic, Jake placed the call and handed Libby the phone. "Who are you?" she asked. And then, "Oh. Have you heard anything, anything at all? Has Walt called the police? What about the—yes, I know, but—"

There was more. Jake waited, his mind clicking over rapidly, and then he took the phone from her. "Libby? What's happened?" His second thought had been a ransom kidnapping. Porter would be a likely target.

His first thought he had forcefully put out of his mind. He'd give anything if he hadn't told Libby about Johnny. It would be fresh on her mind, a reminder she didn't need of a worst-case scenario. "Libby?" he prodded when she sat there, frozen, staring straight ahead.

"A friend of Walt's answered." Her voice was unnaturally calm. "She said her name was Denise. Walt's not there. She's taking messages."

"And?" Jake prompted when she fell silent again.

"And? Oh... They don't know anything else. The three of them went to the game yesterday, and David wasn't feeling good by the time they got home, so he went to bed. Rosa sat with him." Rosa. Jake figured her for a baby-sitter, and didn't interrupt. Libby needed to talk, not to seal herself off. "Denise said as far as she knew, he was just fine last night when she and Walt got home, but when he didn't come down to breakfast, Walt sent Rosa upstairs after him and he was..." She swallowed hard, her hands knotted tightly in her lap. Reaching over, Jake took her left one and spread it over his thigh, holding it there.

"What about his clothes?"

"His clothes?" She sounded dazed. "I don't know."

"You said he didn't feel good. Is there any chance he might have got up in the night to—you know—throw up or something—and wandered back into the wrong room by mistake?"

"He has his own bathroom right off his old room."

She lapsed into silence again, and Jake concentrated on getting through traffic. It was heavy, and the rain had started up again. He considered turning on the radio and decided against it. Music wouldn't help, much less the usual body count that passed for local news these days. Jake pulled in at the rest stop and made her get out and walk around for a few minutes, rain or no rain. She needed a break. No, dammit, she needed to bend *before* she broke!

While she was in the bathroom, he raided the machines. She needed fuel. One piece of burned toast wasn't going to get her through the next few hours.

He had never seen the Porter place, but the neighborhood was pretty much what he'd expected. Wooded lots, about ten acres and up. A few rock and glass, but mostly old brick or new brick whitewashed to look old. Pricy landscaping, glassed-in swimming pools, tennis courts—the usual. It was a far cry from this place to the house where Libby lived now.

He wondered why. He wondered a lot of things that were none of his business, but that could wait.

Porter was there when they drove up. There were half a dozen cars in the paved circular drive, most with the carefully anonymous look that screamed police. With Porter's clout, the FBI had probably already been called in if there was the slightest hint that the boy had been snatched.

A uniformed woman, stick-thin, with black eyes and gingery hair, started bawling the minute they stepped inside. She embraced Libby with a stranglehold, and then stepped back, wiped her red-rimmed eyes and offered them both coffee and homemade buns. "I'm just so sorry, I can't tell you! I sat with David myself last night. I read to him until he went off to sleep. I declare, I thought he was all right! He said his stomach was a-botherin' him early on, but he didn't have a fever."

"I know, I know. It's not your fault, Rosa. But didn't anyone hear anything?"

"Not that I know of. I sat in the kitchen and watched the TV until Mr. Porter and Miss Keith came in, and then I went to bed. First thing I knew was when Mr. Porter called me this morning. I'm so sorry, I just don't know what to do! That poor little baby!"

Jake stood apart, watching while Porter conferred with one group of men and then another. The bimbo in tights and a big gauzy tent shirt perched on the arm of a chair and tried to look concerned, but as she kept glancing at her reflection in the glass patio doors and rearranging her pose, Jake didn't find the act particularly convincing.

God help the boy if this was his stepmother.

When the housekeeper began crying on Libby's shoulder again, Jake moved in to the rescue. Drawing Libby off to one side, he said, "I'm sure the house has been turned upside down, but what about the grounds? What about any playmates he might have in the neighborhood?"

Libby pulled herself together. Disregarding her ex-husband, who seemed to be doing little more than throwing his weight around and generally making an ass of himself, she turned to a man in a glen plaid suit. He had a look of authority about him, as well as a look of distaste for Walter Bettinger Porter III.

"Would you please tell me everything? I'm David's mother."

The officer took her into another room, and Jake started after them, then stopped. He was an outsider. He had no rights at all. He was there only as Libby's friend—as something more than a friend, he admitted silently. Something a hell of a lot more.

But that would have to wait.

Eleven

From the elegant Danish leather chair, Jake watched her closely. They had been there less than an hour, and since the first few minutes after their arrival he had been battling a powerful urge to get her the hell out of there.

And take her where?

God knows. At least to someplace where he stood a chance of protecting her. This was Porter's territory. It might have been Libby's home once, but somehow Porter had ended up keeping it while his wife and son had been relegated to a dump in the country some hundred miles away. Prenuptial agreement? Old family property? Total lack of integrity?

Stroking his itchy jaw, Jake wondered what she had seen in the man. There must have been something between them, but for the life of him, Jake couldn't figure it. Libby had more class in her little finger than that pedigreed blowhard would ever have.

On the other hand, she had married him. They'd had a child together. And no matter how protective Jake was feeling, he'd better keep in mind the fact that he was here on sufferance.

With a feeling of impotence, he watched as she moved restlessly around the room, touching a chair here, a table there. He tried to picture her in that setting, and failed. When she paused to stare out through an expanse of glass at the carefully naturalized grounds, he ached to go stand behind her, beside her.

But sympathy wasn't what she needed now. She was going to have to find within herself whatever strength it took to sustain her, because regardless of the outcome, Jake had a feeling Porter was going to be no help at all. If the boy was—

He swore silently. Neither all the king's horses nor all the king's men would be able to help her if the worst happened. All he could do was bleed for her. And pray—not that he had much clout in that particular arena.

Come on, Libby love, hang in there. It's not going to happen this time. Not again, please God.

She seemed to grow taller. Backlit from the tall window, her hair gleaming like a silvery halo, she squared her shoulders and lifted her head in a familiar gesture, and Jake felt something deep inside him crumble and wash away in a warm, healing tide.

He just hoped to hell that attitude of hers would get her through the next few hours. After that...well, they'd just have to take it one step at a time. Whatever happened, he would be there for her.

Unobtrusively Jake continued to watch the shifting tableau from across the room. He knew he must look like hell, wearing yesterday's rumpled clothes. His unshaved jaw was itching for a razor, and he felt a fierce desire for a cigarette.

So far, no one had challenged his right to be here, although Porter had sent him several suspicious looks. Under the circumstances, he couldn't much blame the poor bastard.

Libby pulled herself together. She took a deep, steadying breath, not daring to look at Jake for fear she would hurl herself into his arms and start crying. Crying wasn't going to help. With her congestion, she would probably asphyxiate herself!

Instead she turned to where Rosa hovered in the dining-room door, wringing her hands. The housekeeper was blaming herself. Libby knew that Rosa couldn't have loved David more if he'd been her own child. She would have moved to Winston-Salem with them if Libby could have afforded to keep her.

"My poor baby," the older woman cried softly, and Libby slid an arm around her narrow waist.

"Rosa, he's probably just hiding somewhere. You know David—he's as independent as a hog on ice. Always has been." But not since the separation. Not since his whole life had been turned upside down.

With quiet authority, Libby instructed the woman to make sandwiches and another pot of coffee and set them out on the buffet. That done, she turned to Walt and the policeman, who was asking about David's state of mind when last seen.

Libby shuddered at the term "when last seen." It sounded horribly like something one might hear on the six o'clock news, and she refused to think about David that way.

"He was fine," Porter said with a shrug. "Like I said earlier, we went to the game—I always have seats on the fifty-yard line. After the game, we drove directly to the club. We usually have dinner there on weekends. He'd gotten sort of whiny during the last half—you know how kids are. Wanting this, wanting that, needing to go to the bathroom every five minutes."

From across the room, Jake listened, picturing the scene easily. The jerk should have known better than to drag a seven-year-old kid through that mob. Whatever happened to Saturday afternoons at the zoo, with ice-cream cones and peanuts?

"The real trouble started," Porter went on, "when he pitched a fit over that damned rag doll my esteemed ex-wife lets him drag around." He shot her a scathing glance that made Jake's fingers ache to throttle him.

"You say he pitched a fit. You wanna describe that? Did he cry? Did he complain? Did he lose the doll or something?"

"No, he didn't lose the doll or something," Walt sneered. "I wish to God he had! I didn't notice the thing when we left home because he sneaked it out in his coat. I made him leave it in the car during the game, and that started it. When we got to the club, I told him to leave the thing in the car—they have an excellent nursery there. There was no need to drag in a piece of garbage that came from God knows where! Anyway, David refused to get out of the car, and one thing led to another. You know how it goes."

"Miss Keith," the officer began, but Porter interrupted before she could speak.

"Denise can tell you. We had plans to meet friends for dinner and needless to say, we were nearly an hour late. Denise tried to reason with the little wretch, but we finally had to give in and bring him home."

"You stayed here after that, then?"

Walt shrugged his shoulders dismissively. "Rosa was here. I told you we had an engagement. We dropped David off and went back to salvage what we could of the evening."

The officer had taken out a notebook and was jotting something down. He looked up and said, "This—uh, tantrum? Could you describe it? About how long did it last? What was the boy's state of mind when it was over?"

"Kicking, screaming, crying—for God's sake, haven't you ever seen a child have a tantrum before? I assure you, David has it down to a fine art by now. We both tried to reason with him. Miss Keith went out of her way to be friendly, but it seems my son has developed a few discipline problems while living with his mother." He shot Libby a malicious look. "I had to force him to apologize to her more than once, I can tell you."

Eyes narrowed, Jake was watching Libby. Her back was ramrod straight, that jaw of hers so square it could have chipped flint. She was ready to blow, and Jake couldn't blame her. The bastard didn't even have sense enough to know what a bastard he was!

Quietly Jake moved closer, ready to pick up the pieces if need be. In the back of his mind, a picture was beginning to form. Certain elements were beginning to come together....

Curiously Jake studied Porter's girlfriend. He didn't think she was the same one who'd been crawling all over him that night seven years ago, when Libby had got sick of the whole rotten scene and left. Cast from the same mold, though. Pretty enough in a vapid sort of way. Probably good-natured, but not too bright. Although she was evidently bright enough to have earned herself a pair of diamond dangle earrings that weighed in at about three carats each.

Damn Porter, Jake cursed silently. He could at least have had the decency to get his playmate out of sight! Although Libby was taking it like a thoroughbred. Not so much as a raised eyebrow at the introduction. It must have galled the hell out of Porter to find himself outclassed by the daughter of a small-time farmer. Jake had an idea that Porter's ego was founded more on the proceeds from a long line of robber barons than on any real accomplishments of his own. It was a risk among the silver-spoon set. After a few generations, the stock had a tendency to run to seed.

Libby tugged at Porter's sleeve, and Jake's hands unconsciously knotted into fists. "Walt, did David say anything yesterday about visiting any of his old playmates? He might have wanted to go play with the Walser boys, or even Peggy Lee Boren. Do the Borens still live on the corner? Have you called?"

Porter sent her a withering look. "Why don't you just go somewhere and have a nice quiet breakdown? I'm handling this, Libby!"

"Yes, but—" She stammered, and he deliberately turned his back on her.

Jake took her arm. "Libby, come into the kitchen where we can talk," he said quietly.

Walt spun around again, his even features marred by a sullen cast. "Just who the hell are you, anyway?" he demanded. "This is a family matter, so why don't you just butt the hell out!"

At a superficial glance, the two men were somewhat alike. Both were tall, both were dark, both had that indefinable air that hinted at a certain type of background. A closer look revealed that Walt's polish was only a surface patina, covering weakness and a lack of self-discipline, whereas Jake's was bone-deep, undiminished by rumpled clothing or an unshaved jaw.

Libby took hold of Jake's arm and urged him toward the kitchen. It was like trying to drag a bulldog away from a spitting cat. "Jake, let's go."

"Yeah, why don't you do that?" Porter snarled. "Obviously my ex-wife's taste in boyfriends is having a lousy influence on my son. Maybe I'll have my lawyer look into the custody thing again."

Which was so patently unfair under the circumstances that even Porter had the grace to look embarrassed. As far as Jake was concerned, that was all that saved him. That and the fact that regardless of the satisfaction to be gained from driving the bastard's nose through the back of his skull, Libby would be the one to suffer for it.

Every eye in the room was focused on the two men. The policeman's gray eyes were cool and speculative, the housekeeper's brown ones worried, Denise Keith's, underneath layers of navy mascara and frosted blue eye-shadow, openly curious.

But it was Libby's green eyes, haunted and unnaturally calm, that really got to him. Wrapping his arm around her, Jake drew her across the room, leaving Porter staring after them.

"Breathe, honey," Jake murmured. "Take a deep breath...that's right. Now do it again. You know he's only rattling his sword. He's scared, too. Give him credit for that much."

"Only if I have to."

Jake's smile didn't quite reach his eyes. "Right. The poor jerk has to feel guilty as sin on account of David disappearing on his watch. I reckon he's dealing with it the only way he knows how."

Libby breathed deeply in and out a few more times, and Jake wondered briefly if he should warn her against hyperventilation. "I've been thinking," he said. "Let me run something by you, okay? You remember telling me how David reacted whenever he thought you might be getting interested in a man?"

Libby looked puzzled. Rosa hovered over them, forcing on them food that neither of them wanted while Jake outlined his theory. Ignoring the chicken salad sandwich set before her, Libby heard him out.

When he was finished, she gripped the edge of the table until her knuckles showed white. "Jake, if you're right, then he might just be hiding! But wouldn't the policeman have thought of that?"

"The guy's not married. He obviously hasn't the least idea about how a kid that age might react to the notion of a new stepmother. Or stepfather, for that matter. In a case like this, any cop would probably be inclined to think of a ransom kidnapping, if not a custody snatch." He covered her hand with his. "Libby, I don't want you to get your hopes up too high, but I'd say there's an outside chance that Miss Keith might've given David the impression, deliberately or otherwise, that she and Porter will be getting married. You'd know better than anyone else how he would react to that."

"But he already has me. He doesn't need another mother."

"I know. And neither Porter nor his girlfriend strikes me as the nurturing type. Still, you never know how a kid's mind works. I overheard a few of the boys at your uncle's place comparing notes. David's little friend Petey told some pretty bloodcurdling tales about his stepmother. Kid's got a great future as the next Stephen King."

"I'd never thought about... But it makes sense. Remember my telling you how he is with men? Either he hates them on sight or he wants me to marry them?"

"Somehow, I don't think he took to Miss Keith."

"He threatened to blow up the plumber, but there was this septic-tank man right after we moved back home—he had a new tank wagon, with dual wheels and lots of hoses and gears and things, and David decided he'd make a dandy new father."

"Remind me to show him our new John Deere 892," Jake muttered. And then, giving her hand a squeeze and releasing it, he said, "Okay, honey, you find a phone and start calling around. Everything you say will probably be taped, but that's no problem. Just call all the places you can think of, even those that aren't all that close. Neighbors, playmates—everyone. Describe what he was wearing and find out if anyone's seen him since yesterday."

The cops would have already done all that, but something—just an insignificant detail—might have slipped their minds the first time. More important, Libby needed something to focus on. There was a brittle look about her that worried him. "What was he wearing?"

"His green coat, yellow sneakers—jeans, of course. And Ikky."

"Ikky," Jake repeated. "I'm afraid to ask."

She smiled, and it was like the sun coming out after a forty-day rain. "You know. Ikky. David's best friend, but don't make the mistake of calling it a rag doll. Boys don't play with dolls."

"Right. The Gulf War hero."

"Church bazaar edition. Homemade camouflage fatigues and yellow yarn hair. You'll recognize him if you see him, because David will be physically attached to the thing.''

''Right.'' Shoving back his chair, Jake got to his feet. ''You go get started calling around while I scout the grounds. I know they've been thoroughly searched, but little boys can hide in surprisingly small spaces. Kinda like mice.'' He was trying for another smile, but he guessed that was too much to hope for. ''Meet you back here in—'' he glanced at his watch ''—an hour. Either way.''

And then, gently he reached up and cupped her chin, lifting it until her eyes met his. ''Attitude, honey,'' he said softly. ''We're going to win this one, I promise you.''

Somehow, someway, God, we've got to win this one!

Forty-five minutes later, Jake wasn't so sure. He'd given the place a cursory once-over on the way in. At first glance, it had seemed like a boy's paradise, full of trees, with a greenhouse, a stable, a three-car, two-story garage. Hundreds of potential hiding places.

The greenhouse had been easy. It was empty. Evidently Libby had been the horticulturist, not Porter. There was a handsome chestnut gelding in the stable. Jake was no expert, but he'd bet even money the horse had cost more than his own car had. He searched the empty stalls, the loft and the tack room and then headed for the garage.

On the way, he scanned the terrain. The underbrush had been carefully controlled, kept mainly to rhododendrons and ferns that looked wild, but probably weren't. There was an artfully arranged clump of rocks at one end of what appeared to be a dry creek bed.

On an impulse, Jake turned in that direction. There

was no water, thank God, not even a trickle, in spite of the recent rain. But evidently the thing flooded occasionally, because there was a culvert under the driveway, half-hidden now by dead leaves.

A culvert... Now why did that ring a bell?

It was midafternoon. The weather was cold and unsettled. It might not freeze tonight, but it would be too damned cold for a kid to be sleeping out.

Davie, come on, boy—where are are you?

A few leaves fluttered down from the gums, oaks and sycamores. Jake stood still, the damp wind cutting through his lightweight jacket, while he studied the lacy network of branches overhead. Where would a boy go to hide when the going got rough? Where would he hole up to keep the real world at bay? A playhouse?

No. Libby would have mentioned a playhouse.

Johnny, help me on this one, will you, son?

The creek bed drew his gaze again. Unbidden, he pictured a sudden rush of muddy brown water breaking through a dam of debris, following a timeworn course through the hilly country. He pictured a small boy kneeling in the dry bed, playing with his toy trucks.

Swallowing hard, Jake set his mind back on track. The creek bed was dry. If the glut of fallen leaves was anything to go by, it hadn't flooded in months.

There was still the garage to search, he reminded himself—easily a thousand square feet of hiding space.

Yet something held him where he was, as if his feet were rooted to the damp, leaf-strewn earth. Glancing at his watch, he saw that it was past time to check in with Libby. God knows, the last thing she needed was something else to worry about. Discouraged, he turned away.

And then turned slowly back again. That culvert... Something had snagged his attention, but what? Away from the fancy shrubbery and flawlessly manicured lawn immediately surrounding the house, the landscape was already winter bare. Raw red creek bank, thick, damp-barked tree trunks, squirrel-gnawed pine cones littering the carpet of leaves and pine straw, a scrap of yellow yarn…

Yellow yarn!

In three strides, Jake was on his knees, peering into the near end of the culvert. On the sunniest day it might not be hard to see inside, but on a gray afternoon in November, it was damn near impossible!

He called softly. "David? Are you in there, son?"

Nothing. Not a whisper. So why did he feel as if every cell in his body was on full alert?

Something was in there. Hiding. An animal, possibly. A stray dog, looking for a warm place to sleep?

No, a dog would have growled or run out the other end.

Jake figured he had two choices. He could go get Libby and let her try to talk him out, or he could go in after him. If it really was the boy. And with every passing moment, he was more certain that he'd run his quarry to earth.

"Listen, son, you remember what we talked about last weekend out at your uncle's place? Your mama needs you now. She's up at the house, calling all your friends to see if they know where you are. She's worried sick."

No response. Was it only his imagination, or had he heard leaves rustling? Those inside the culvert would probably still be dry enough to rustle.

"David, your mother's come to take you home. You and—uh, Ikky."

This was prime copperhead country. Jake could only

hope the recent cold snap had sent them all into hibernation.

"Ikky's losing his hair. Ever think about getting him a helmet?" Jake stretched out on his belly at one end of the culvert, hoping the kid wouldn't slip out the other end. It got dark so damned early these days.... "David? Your mama's pretty miserable, son. I think it might be a good idea now to go let her know you're all right."

Jake's pulses leaped. That had been a definite sniffle he'd heard. At the sounds of scuffling, he closed his eyes momentarily and then held out a hand to help the small, filthy figure crawl the last few feet.

It seemed like days, but it was hardly more than an hour before they were on their way west again. The policeman had turned out to be a pretty decent sort. What the hell could he have said after the boy had told him that he was only waiting until it was time to go home, that he had asked and asked his daddy to take him back home, but his daddy had yelled at him and pinched his neck, and David had decided to wait outside until it was time to go back home.

And then there had been Porter to deal with. Jake freely admitted that might have gone smoother if he hadn't been there. On the other hand, Libby had needed him. The jerk would have walked all over her if he hadn't stepped in.

Jake had sent Libby and David upstairs, with Rosa following along to pack his things. Denise hung over Porter's chair, and Jake figured she may as well hear what he had to say. All he wanted was to get it said and then to get Libby and her son out of there.

He opened his mouth to let fly a few home truths, when the bimbo interrupted. "Sweety, you didn't mean what you were saying about getting full custody, did you?''

''Keep out of this, Denise,'' Porter snapped.

''But Wally—''

Jake heard Libby coming downstairs. This could get real ugly, real fast, and dammit, she didn't need this! ''Porter, why do you keep throwing this custody business around? You know damned well you don't want full custody, even if you could bribe a judge to give it to you!'' Jake had already figured out that one. The grandmother was probably loaded, and Porter didn't want to take a chance on his son's portion going astray.

''Quite frankly, Hatcher, I don't see what business that is of yours. In fact, I don't see what you're doing here at all.''

''The name's Healy. John Hatcher Healy. And if it concerns Libby, then it's my business.''

Porter's pale eyes had narrowed. Denise made the mistake of popping her gum at that moment, and Porter slapped her on the fanny and told her to go play with her jewelry for a while.

Jake waited for the explosion. None came. Instead he watched in amazement as the lissome lady sauntered down the hall with every evidence of good humor. He heard her speak to Libby in the hallway, and he lowered his own voice. ''As to what I'm doing here, Libby wasn't in any shape to make a two-hour drive. I volunteered.''

''Oh, I see,'' Walt said, a sneer implicit in the comment.

The call had come in just after daybreak that morning. ''I expect you do,'' Jake said smoothly. ''To get back to this custody thing, if you and Miss Keith are getting married, I suppose you're figuring a court might consider a two-parent household more suitable than what Libby can provide, am I right?"

"I think that's between me and my ex-wife."

"Maybe. Or maybe it's between your son and your girlfriend, I don't know. I do know that it's not going to work. And I'm warning you, Porter, if you ever—*ever*—try to play your little mind games with Libby again, for any reason whatsoever, I'm going to drive you into the ground. And believe me," he added softly, "I'm looking forward to the pleasure."

Porter's face flushed a dark shade of red. His pale eyes moved over Jake's unshaved countenance, his wrinkled and now muddy clothing. He plucked an invisible thread off the sleeve of his pale blue cashmere sweater. "You're going to marry her yourself, Healy?"

"That's between Libby and me. You threw her away, Porter. She was the best thing that ever happened to you, but you were too stupid to know what you had. I almost feel sorry for you." Hearing the two women in the hallway part company, he added quietly, "If you're smart, you'll marry your lady friend. She's too good for you, but she just might feel sorry enough for you to overlook what you are."

And then, turning to where Libby and David waited with the housekeeper, he said, "If you're ready to ride, honey, let's go home."

David slept in the back seat, securely belted down, his head propped up against the coat Jake had rolled up in the corner. Ikky slept beside him, little worse for the day's adventure.

Jake wondered how David would like a puppy.

With one hand, he rummaged through his cassette holder and pulled out a Brahms from among the Haggard, Jones and Travis. He figured Libby needed some space right now, and a four-door sedan only offered so much of that.

By the time the tape ended, they were almost to Greensboro. Libby switched it off, drew in a deep breath, and turned to him for the first time since they'd pulled out of Porter's driveway. "Thank you, Jake. Not just for finding David, but for—for being there. I don't think I could have handled it if it hadn't been for you."

"You'd have handled it just fine," he told her. If it wasn't for the traffic, the child in the back seat, and the fact that once he made his move, he had no intention of being interrupted, Jake would have pulled over into the emergency lane right then and there and kissed her until neither of them had a rational thought in their heads.

But that, too, would have to wait.

Twelve

By nine-forty-five that night, Libby had broken three of her short fingernails by drumming them on the side table. She had washed every dish in sight, picked up everything that wasn't nailed down, and reread the front page of the *Journal* at least twice without taking in a single word.

And that was after seeing David bathed, fed and bedded down, and getting her own shower. She had put on a sage green velvet hostess gown that had languished forever in the back of her closet, added a dab of eye shadow, a wisp of peach-colored blusher and lip gloss, and then fought against the urge to scrub it all off and change into her oldest jeans.

Oh, heavens, he should have been here by now!

Should she have worn her suede flats instead of her slippers? Bedroom slippers were so…

Maybe he wasn't coming. Maybe he had changed his

mind and decided he didn't want to get in any deeper than he already was. She couldn't much blame him.

No, she refused to believe that. "See you later," he'd said. That could mean anything. Later next week. Later this year. Later after David had left for college.

"Oh, bosh," she muttered, and just as she turned away from the front window, a pair of low headlights swept across the front yard. There was a squeal of brakes, the slam of a car door, and Libby opened the front door, swallowing down a sickening surge of sheer panic. She hadn't felt like this since the day of her senior prom, when she'd been still hoping against hope that someone would invite her at the very last minute.

No one had, of course. And after it was all over and she had laid to rest her secret hopes, she had got over it. The same way she would get over this, if she had to.

Did a woman ever grow too old to hope?

Jake's eyes gleamed darkly as he stepped into the living room, his freshly shaved cheeks flushed from the cold. The fingers of his left hand worked over a set of keys, clicking brass against brass. "Sorry to be so late. If you'd rather I left..."

"Oh, no, you're not late! I was just getting ready to read the— That is, won't you—um, your coat?"

"Oh. Yeah, sure. Thanks." He shed his leather jacket, his gaze moving over her slender back as she made room for it in the closet.

Damn. Wearing that long velvety thing, she looked like the angel on top of a Christmas tree. He could at least have worn a tie instead of corduroys and a black flannel shirt. Nice going, man. You're really going to impress the hell out of her tonight, aren't you?

"I made fresh coffee. It's coconut-and-chocolate-flavored. I've been saving it for a special occasion."

A special occasion. Was that his cue? Jake felt his palms start to sweat. He hadn't exactly rehearsed it, but he'd gone over what he intended to say a few dozen times while he showered, shaved and dressed. It wasn't every day of the week that a man asked a woman to marry him. The first time had been relatively painless. He and Cass had been lovers for more than a year by then, and her family had been urging them for months to make it legal. Having just seen a new year in, neither of them had been entirely sober on the night he had finally got around to proposing.

Somehow Jake had a feeling coconut-chocolate-flavored coffee wasn't going to help much.

"Come on into the kitchen and I'll see what I can find to go with it. David ate the last of the gingerbread men, but I usually keep an assortment of cookies and crackers on hand for emergencies."

Jake figured this could easily be classed as an emergency. "Speaking of David, is he asleep yet?"

"He was pretty keyed up. I left him looking at treasure-hunting books. Usually he falls asleep with his light on and I go up and turn it off and cover him up."

Ignoring the two cups, the plate of crackers and cheese she had arranged on a tray, Jake said, "I'd like to go up and talk to him if he's still awake—that is, if you don't mind."

Wordlessly Libby shook her head. She couldn't imagine what he had to say to her son, but then, the two of them seemed to have some sort of unspoken understanding ever since they had showed up back at the house earlier that day. From an upstairs window, Libby had watched them walking back up the hill. Jake had looked grim, and David had looked tear-stained, even from that distance. He had been clinging to Ikky with one hand and to Jake with the other.

As Jake headed up the stairs, Libby stood in the middle of the kitchen staring blindly at a childish drawing pinned to the bulletin board. Dear Lord, if five minutes alone with a man affected her this way—drumming pulses, cold sweats, trembling hands—the last thing she needed was caffeine!

"Hello, David. Your mama thought you might be asleep by now," Jake said quietly. The boy was slumped back against the bedstead, arms crossed behind his head, a treasure-hunting magazine open over his chest. Ikky was beside him, carefully tucked under the covers.

"I stay up real late sometimes. Sometimes I stay up all night, longer even than Mama does."

"Yeah, me too. Kinda hard to sleep when a guy's got a lot on his mind."

David appeared to think it over. He shrugged. "Yeah. I guess."

"Sometimes talking things over with a friend helps," Jake suggested.

"Jeffie doesn't know very much about stuff like...you know. Divorce and all. His mama and daddy don't even fight much."

"Well, I'd say Jeffie's a pretty lucky boy, then."

"I guess." David plucked at the dinosaur quilt, and Jake cleared his throat. This wasn't turning out to be quite as easy as he'd thought.

"Are you going to marry my mama?"

Well, that was laying it on the line, all right. "I'll level with you, David. I'd like to marry your mama—I'd like that a whole lot, but not if you've got a problem with it."

Silence. If the kid was deliberately trying to make things tough for him, he was doing a damned fine job of it.

"See, the thing is, I really need your mama, David. Oh, I know—you do, too, but maybe we could sort of work out something."

"I don't know if there's room or not. There's lots of old boxes and stuff in the other bedroom."

"I guess your mama and I could come up with something if we tried hard enough. Maybe we could double up. Like you and Ikky do."

"Maybe. Do you like little boys?"

Jake winced. When he spoke again, his voice was rough, soft, like old burlap. "Yeah, son, I like little boys. I had one of my own once, but he—he died. And you want to know something? It hurts really bad. I guess that's why sometimes I can't get to sleep."

The small figure beside him was still for a long time. Jake wondered what the hell he was doing here, trying to explain to a kid who was too young to understand—hell, he didn't even understand himself. All he knew was that it was important that David understand right from the first that to most men, little boys were infinitely precious. Unique individuals to be loved, to be remembered. To be cherished.

"Maybe I'd let you play with Ikky sometimes," David said tentatively.

"I'd like that."

"I'm too big to play with dolls, but Ikky's still little. That's why I let him sleep with me."

"Yeah, I figured that."

"So if you want to live with Mama and me, I guess that's all right, too."

Jake reached out and then let his arms fall to his sides.

He wanted to—he felt like—but dammit, if he pushed too hard, the kid would spook. There'd be plenty of time later. All the time in the world. And this time, Jake would make the most of every rare and precious moment.

"I guess I'd better get back to your mama and ask her how soon I can move in with you guys. My place is pretty lonesome," he said, rising almost reluctantly.

"We have gingerbread a lot, but Mama gets cross sometimes, 'specially when she has a cold. Sometimes her eyes get real red."

"Then we'll just have to take care of her so she won't have so many colds," Jake said. He was almost out the door when David called his name.

"Jake?"

"Yeah, son?"

"Do you have a tank wagon?"

Jake's grin used muscles that hadn't been exercised in more than seven years. "No, but I've got something even better. Meet me here tomorrow after school, and I'll show you."

When Jake came down some quarter of an hour later, he found Libby in the living room on the sofa, the folds of her gown artfully arranged to cover the bare feet she had drawn up beside her. Two lamps had been left on, the harsh overhead light turned off. On the coffee table there was a tray containing a warming carafe, two cups and an assortment of crackers and cheeses.

"Did you eat supper?" he asked.

"I had a bowl of chicken soup with David," she murmured. But Libby wasn't thinking about food. She wanted to know what had passed between this man and her son. Jake looked somehow different, as if a spring that had been wound too tight for too long had finally been released.

He sat down beside her, leaned his head back against the cushion and closed his eyes for a moment, then he began to speak. "There's this old-fashioned custom, you know...something my grandfather mentioned when I was about twelve and just starting to get interested in girls." Opening his eyes, he turned to face her, and Libby's breath caught in her throat.

"A custom?" she repeated, her hand hovering over the carafe.

"Something about asking the man of the house for permission to pay court to one of his womenfolk."

Libby's eyes unexpectedly brimmed with tears as she stared at the ruggedly handsome man who had turned her life upside down in a few short weeks. Who *was* he? John J. Hatcher Healy, socialite, business magnate, rescuer of pregnant strangers at five-hundred-dollar-a-plate fund-raisers? Or Jake Hatcher, big-iron man, who drove a muddy pickup truck and ate gingerbread parts in her kitchen and dived into fish ponds after clumsy women?

How could any man who was powerful enough and tough enough to control thousands of tons of heavy metal, be gentle enough to earn the trust of a small, badly frightened child? How could a man who had survived the loss of a child and the breakup of his marriage ever find the strength and courage to start over and build a new life?

Libby was certain of only one thing where Jake Hatcher was concerned. Whoever he was—whatever he was—she loved him through and through—always would, and quite possibly always had.

"So," Jake said after a while, "I asked him."

"You asked—Jake, what are you trying to say?"

"Botching it, huh?"

"That's one way of putting it."

Reaching out, Jake drew her into his arms, arranging her so that she was leaning back against his chest. With his lips buried in the silken fragrance of her hair, he said, "Like I said, I asked him and he said he guessed it would be okay, and then he asked me if I had a tank wagon."

"You asked *who*—"

"I think that's *whom,*" he rumbled softly into her right ear.

"Asked whom *what?*"

Jake chuckled, and the sound resonated all the way to the soles of her feet. "Now you've gone and got me all mixed up. I asked David. As for the what, I asked him if he'd have any objections to my marrying his mama."

Libby swallowed a lungful of air and choked on it. By the time she had recovered, she was sprawled across Jake's lap, and he had somehow managed to get his hand inside her gown to thump her on the back.

"Honey, you're not a whole lot better at this business than I am. You want to cut it short?"

"No, I don't want to cut it short! Cut what short? I want to know what he said, and—and why you even asked, and... Jake, *do* you want to marry me?"

"Didn't I just say so?"

Burying her face in his warm throat, Libby let the tears that had been threatening all day spill out. Jake held her. He didn't attempt to talk. He didn't try to soothe her, didn't utter a single there-there. After a while, she sat up and knuckled her red-rimmed eyes. "I m-might as well not have bothered with eye shadow," she muttered. "Jake, I'm sorry. I don't usually cry, but it's been..."

"One of those days?" His smile might not have been calculated to render her totally helpless, but it had that effect.

"And nights. Last night, I mean—and then this morning." She dried her face on the hem of her gown. Straightening up, she tried for composure, giving it up as hopeless after the third residual sob. "But don't let me interrupt you. You were saying..."

Jake threw back his head and laughed. "Ah, Libby, how did I ever make it so long without you? You know what you are?"

Half-afraid to ask, she shook her head.

"You're real. You're more than skin-deep, you're Libby clean through. And sweetheart, you don't know how rare and wonderful that is." Slipping his arms around her, he toppled her so that she lay sprawled across him, and with his forehead resting against hers, he whispered, "Fortunately, I do."

* * * * *

Welcome to *Love Inspired*™

A brand-new series of contemporary inspirational love stories.

Join men and women as they learn valuable lessons about facing the challenges of today's world and about life, love and faith.

Look for the following March 1998 Love Inspired™ titles:

CHILD OF HER HEART
by Irene Brand

A FATHER'S LOVE
by Cheryl Wolverton

WITH BABY IN MIND
by Arlene James

Available in retail outlets in February 1998.

LIFT YOUR SPIRITS AND GLADDEN YOUR HEART with *Love Inspired!*™

LI398